STILL FALLING FOR YOU

USA TODAY & WSJ BESTSELLING AUTHOR

SIOBHAN DAVIS

Original Paperback edition of Only Ever You © March 2019

This paperback edition © November 2023

ISBN-13: 978-1-959194-93-4

Editor: Kelly Hartigan (XterraWeb) editing.xterraweb.com

Proofread by: Megan Smith, Bre Landers, Brenda Parsons, Elizabeth Clinton, Lauren Lascola-Lesczynski, Aundie Marie.

Sensitivity reader: Annette Gonzales

Cover design by Robin Harper www.wickedbydesigncovers.com

Cover imagery © depositphotos.com

Formatted by Ciara Turley using Vellum

Once there was a boy, with messy blond hair, vibrant blue eyes, and the most dazzling smile, who helped to mend all the dark, broken pieces inside me.

Ryder made a bad situation better. Falling for him wasn't just inevitable—it was the stars aligning and our souls connecting at the deepest level.

Plans were made, and for the first time ever, I had hope. I believed in the future we were going to build together.

Until he left, without even saying goodbye.

Years have passed, and though I have tried to move on, my heart still lingers on the boy who claimed it.

Now he's back, saying he wants another chance.

And I'm terrified I'm not finished falling.

NOTE FROM THE AUTHOR

This book is told in two parts and is written from dual POV. Part I focuses on juvie where Ryder and Zeta first meet because I felt it was important to show their backstory and illustrate the depth of the connection between them. They are seventeen/eighteen in this part, which takes up the first third of the book. Part II skips forward eight years when Ryder is now a famous rock star and Zeta is the girl he left behind with a broken heart.

This book deals with some heavy subject matter including mental health illness (depression, anxiety, PTSD) suicide, sexual assault, child abuse, loss of a child, violence, and addiction. If any of those are triggers for you, I suggest you don't read this book.

The prologue of this book is especially harrowing so please be warned. While I've tried to depict the scene in a way that's not too graphic, my beta readers have said it's "brutal but powerful." This scene is important because it helps us understand Ryder and it gives us an insight into the demons he battles within himself. However, if it upsets you too much you can skip it and move straight to Chapter 1. While the prologue is written in third person past tense, the rest of the book is written in first person present tense, as is my usual style of writing.

This book is emotional, raw, and angsty, but there are also lighter moments interspersed with humor and drama and there are plenty of romantic/sexy times too!

I hope you enjoy it.

STILL
FALLING
FOR YOU

PROLOGUE

The little boy cried for his mommy, his sobs growing more frantic when Ren shouted at him to stop. "Quit acting like a pussy," Ren snarled, landing another blow to the kid's gut with his booted foot.

"I want my mommy!"

The boy's anguished plea penetrated Jack's soul, and he couldn't stand idly by any longer. "Just let him go, Ren." Jack looked up at the older boy, their self-appointed leader, trying to mask the fear from his bruised and bloodied face.

Ren stopped his assault on the four-year-old long enough to stalk toward Jack, grabbing him roughly around the neck. "You dare to question me again?" he spit out, eyes shooting daggers into Jack's terrified gaze.

Jack should let it go, but he had to try one last time. "He's only a kid. He won't tell anyone. You don't have to do this. Please."

Ren shoved Jack into the hard, exposed stone wall at his back, tightening the grip on his neck as the partition rattled uneasily. Plumes of dust surrounded them as the wall ejected bits of loose stone. "That sniveling brat will run straight to his *mommy*"—he mocked the kid by using the same whiny tone

—"and tell her everything. You want to go to juvie? You know what they do to pretty boys like you in there?" His mouth curved into a sneer. "They'll ride your fucking ass so hard you'll forget you ever liked pussy."

"Stay the fuck down!" Vincent roared, lashing out at the crying boy as he tried climbing to his feet. The boy slammed to the floor on his back with his leg tilted at an awkward angle underneath him. Piercing screams soared to the rafters of the derelict warehouse at the abandoned airfield the gang used as their base. "There's no point crying, kid," Johnny taunted, pressing his foot down on the boy's broken leg, smiling maliciously as his screams grew more pronounced and the smell of urine trickled into the air.

Jack's lungs constricted along with his oxygen supply as Ren kept a tight grip on his neck. "This is going down. You're either with us or you're not." Ren drilled him with a dark look that sent chills tiptoeing up Jack's spine. He understood the threat, and he knew there was nothing more he could do.

Ren didn't misjudge people, but he wondered, in that moment, if he'd made a mistake bending his rules and letting the younger boy join the brotherhood.

Jack's soul splintered behind his ribcage as he nodded at Ren, making the only decision he could. Ren let him go, and Jack slumped to the ground, panting and rubbing his sore neck as he desperately sucked air into his needy lungs. Ren redirected his attention, turning around as the little nuisance screamed louder, but there was no one to hear him out here.

Crying was pointless.

There was no one coming to his aid.

Jack scrambled to his feet, locking eyes with Vincent. He too was standing back, watching as the other members of their pack surrounded the helpless little boy, attacking him with their fists and their feet, landing blow after blow, kick after kick, until the boy's strangled cries turned to whimpers and eventually died out.

The older teens kept kicking even as the little body at their feet stopped writhing.

Even as his tiny chest stopped moving.

Eventually they stopped, and silence descended as all eyes swiveled to Ren, awaiting instruction.

Pain lanced through Jack's chest, and Vincent averted his gaze in an attempt to hide his grief. When he lifted his chin up again, there was no trace of emotion on Vincent's face. There couldn't be. If Ren detected any weakness, he'd be as dead as that poor kid on the ground.

Talk about wrong place, wrong time.

Vincent kicked at debris on the filthy floor, and Jack swallowed the bile swimming up his throat while they both watched Ren prod the lifeless little boy with his foot.

"Fucking A." Johnny threw back his head, letting loose an animalistic howl as the rest of the gang joined in, howling and fist pumping the air like his death was something to celebrate. Jack, Vincent, and Ren were the only quiet ones.

Ren bent down, picked up the boy's limp wrist, and pressed his thumb to the place where his pulse should beat steadily. For a split second, he dropped his head and then he stood, grinning from ear to ear. "Take the body outside and bury it." He sent a pointed look at Johnny, his loyal number two. With a jerk of his head he motioned everyone else over to the other side of the warehouse.

Jack kept his head down as he trudged after the group of boys' he once hoped would become the family he never had, fighting tears the entire time. Vincent slanted a warning look in his direction, shoving his hands in his pockets and keeping step with him.

Ren stopped, and everyone waited for him to speak. His gaze traveled among his crew. "No one speaks of this. Ever. You take this to the grave." His eyes locked on Jack before switching to Vincent. Ren never missed anything, so it wasn't surprising that he'd picked up on Vincent's disquiet either. A shiver worked its way through Vincent's body, and he finally understood the meaning of real fear. "Understood?" Ren demanded.

The message was clear.

Talk and they'd be the last words you ever said.

PART I

JUVIE

A few years later

1

RYDER

"**F**resh pussy alert," Lopez hisses under his breath as we stand with our hands behind our backs, heads bowed, facing the whitewashed wall. It's the same drill every morning before school. I keep my eyes trained on the wall, ignoring the douche's bait. Wright and Kelly don't have the same smarts though. Idiots jerk their head around, instantly garnering the attention of Watson, the correctional officer on duty today. He's my least favorite of the bunch. Dude hates me with a passion unrivaled, and he never misses an opportunity to tell me.

And it's not because he knows about my past. As far as he's concerned, I'm Ryder Stone, and I'm guilty of the crimes recorded on the fake file that accompanied me when I arrived at the Orange County Juvenile Hall. If he knew my real identity, he'd probably kill me with his bare hands.

My records are officially sealed for a reason.

To protect me from retaliation.

And to close a door on one of the most shocking crimes the world has ever known.

Lots of people have a vested interest in forgetting what happened in the abandoned airfield that day.

I wish I could so easily wash my hands of it, but it stays with me constantly, lingering on my skin like a nasty rash that refuses to go away, worming its way into my consciousness like a terminal infection I'll never shake.

Not until it's claimed me.

Devoured me from the inside, destroying all evidence of the person I used to think I was.

Some days, I silently beg to forget. Pleading with a deity I no longer believe in, begging an imaginary God to take the pain away. Other days, I wish for a lobotomy or for someone to scrub my brain out with bleach so I don't remember.

But most days, I hope I *never* forget.

Because I deserve to live with this pain.

I allowed it to happen, and it's only right I should be punished every day for the rest of my life.

My stomach sours, and I squeeze my eyes shut as the memories, predictably, return to haunt me. His face flashes behind my retinas, and a painful lump wedges in my throat.

Watson barks at my fellow inmates, and it helps to drag me from the torturous slideshow playing in my mind. I forcibly toss those thoughts aside, tuning Watson out as he rips Wright and Kelly a new one for daring to look at the new girl being escorted inside.

While they have separate boys and girls units in the facility, female offenders convicted of more serious, violent crimes are housed with us in what is deemed to be a coed unit. Crazy stupid idea if you ask me. Although we don't sleep in the same pod as the four other girls presently locked up with us, we interact with them as normal during the day. They attend school with us, eat meals with us, and share the coed common areas with us.

Recipe for disaster.

Lopez is already banging Valeria, a hard-ass Latina girl, in here for gang-related crimes, so he has no business eyeing up the new girl, but that won't stop him. He thinks his shit doesn't stink and that he can do anything and get away with it. But he's a fucking asshole with a superiority complex and a brain the size of a peanut. He'll get what's coming to him. I've been locked up long enough to know there isn't much you can do without someone around here eventually finding out.

Watson, expectedly, pulls Wright and Kelly out of the line when his colleague Price appears, and we shuffle forward in single file behind the other officer while the guys are taken back inside to receive their punishment. That's probably earned them a couple hours in solitary. Not that those idiots will mind. Most of the guys in here put zero to no effort into their schoolwork. They don't give a fuck about getting their GED or educating themselves, but I do.

Having some kind of purpose and an expected daily routine is the only way I keep sane. The only way I avoid the drugs, sex, and fights that are far too commonplace in here.

Squinting up at the scorching hot sun as we walk toward the school wing, I relish the warmth beating down on my skin. Apart from the hour a day we are permitted outside for physical activity, traveling to and from the school building is the only other chance I get to feel the air on my face. For me, having spent a significant portion of my earlier life freely wandering around outside, that's one of the hardest things about being incarcerated. But I try not to complain.

At least I'm still alive.

I shut my train of thought down before it derails me again. It's bad enough that my nights are plagued with vicious memories and flashbacks. During the day, I try to focus on getting through my routine without thinking about that day. Without thinking about *him*.

Morning classes fly by, and I'm ravenous as we're led in single file to the cafeteria for lunch. "Fucking tuna cakes again," Young grumbles as we line up to be served.

"You say this every fucking week," I reply, shaking my

head. "You know the routine by now." I hate the shitty food as much as he does, but there's a certain comfort in familiarity.

"Would it fucking kill them to mix it up a little? I'll be having nightmares about tuna cakes for years after I get out of this hellhole."

"If that's all you're having nightmares about, you're good, trust me." I give the server a tight smile as she slaps two tuna cakes, a dollop of gray mashed potatoes, spoonful of carrots, and a serving of limp salad and dressing on a plate and hands it to me. I nod my thanks as I grab an apple and carton of milk from the next station before heading over to our table.

Lopez is already mouthing off about the new girl as I sit down. His voice seriously hurts my brain, but I put up with his shit because it's always better to keep the nutjobs close. Let him think I respect him if it keeps me on the right side. I've kept my nose relatively clean in here, and now that I'm on the home stretch, I intend to keep it that way.

Young is still complaining as he flops into the seat beside me, and my lips twitch, fighting a smile.

"Check out the rack on the new girl," Lopez tells Torres at the top of his voice, almost like he wants Valeria to hear him. I wouldn't put it past Lopez to deliberately wind his current fuck buddy up in the hope she starts something with the new girl. It's his usual M.O. Not that Valeria will need much encouragement I think as I look in the direction Lopez is pointing.

Damn. She's pretty.

Her long, dark hair tumbles over her shoulders as she leans forward, picking at her bland tuna cake with slim fingers. She pops a piece in her mouth, her face pulling into a grimace.

"See." Young nudges me in the ribs. "I'm not the only one who fucking hates fucking tuna."

"Everyone hates fucking tuna, but if you want to live, you eat what they give you. Simple. Get over it."

Young is my best buddy in here, but even he gets on my nerves sometimes. Hard not to when we spend so much time together. The two of us are the only ones in our crew with level four privileges, which means we have two and a half hours of free time each day and four hours of recreational time on weekends. That's a lot of time listening to my younger buddy complain about the food.

I haven't taken my eyes off the new girl. She's forcing the tuna down, grimacing the entire time, and I can't contain my grin. The food *is* fucking awful in here, but you need to just grin and bear it. It looks like she's already learned that lesson. "Even the new girl gets it, and she's only been here a couple hours." I push Young's plate at him. "Eat."

He flips me the bird, but he stops bitching and starts eating, and I'll take that as a win.

Young's like the little brother I never had, and I like looking out for him. Gives me something to do and helps me stop feeling like a worthless piece of shit, if only for short bursts of time.

The new girl is sitting at a table all by herself, but she doesn't seem phased by it. I watch her eyes subtly taking in her surroundings. She chews slowly as she discreetly scans the cafeteria. Valeria and her gang of bitches are sitting at the table in front of us, eyeing her warily. If she's aware, she's not letting on.

Officer Powell, the only female officer in the coed unit and one of the few to treat us with any shred of respect, steps up to the newbie, her mouth moving slowly as she speaks with her. The new girl stands, and I'm betting she feels every set of eyeballs glued to her banging body. Every person in this room is staring at her, and I want to stand up and scream at them all to leave her the fuck alone. It's the same every time a newbie arrives; although, looking at this girl, I have a feeling the spotlight will be on her for some time.

I was wrong before. She's not just pretty. She's fucking

beautiful. She's tall with legs that seem to stretch on forever, and she holds herself with a confidence that's sexy as hell. With her dark hair, big eyes, high cheekbones, and plump lips, she's the most stunning creature I've ever seen. I can't tell her age, because she most likely looks older than she is. All I know is she's under eighteen because otherwise she wouldn't be here.

Granted, I have minimal real-world experience with girls to be in any position to make such a sweeping statement, but she's hotter than those actresses I see on TV shows. The ones I usually imagine I'm fucking when I'm jerking off. Even in the shapeless white polo and too-big navy shorts uniform she's wearing, I can tell she's got a knockout figure. I hate to agree with anything Lopez says, but she's sporting an awesome rack that already has every male drooling.

I hope, for her sake, that she's got a pair of matching-sized lady balls.

Because she's going to need them if she wants to survive around here.

I HAVE my first close encounter with the new girl later that day. It's our obligatory outdoor activity time, and we're all outside, sweltering under the intense late afternoon heat.

"Fuck, even my balls are sweating," Torres exclaims, and Sofia rolls her eyes.

"Keep that fucking shit to yourself," Valeria spews, scowling as she scans the yard before rolling the end of her polo shirt up.

"Take it off, baby," Lopez encourages as his wingmen instantly reposition themselves so they're blocking his girl from view. Watson is too busy eyeing the new girl as she jogs around the yard to even glance in this direction anyway.

Valeria licks her lips, curling her finger at Lopez in a

come hither gesture. Lopez jumps on top of her, his hands pushing the polo up even farther until he's exposing her bra to the salivating male audience. She eyeballs me with a seductive smirk, but I stare impassively at her. It's not the first time she's indicated interest, and I'm tired of rejecting her advances. Although my body craves sex—I'm as horny as any seventeen-year-old guy—I won't lower myself to sleeping with her, and I don't want to start a fucking war with Lopez, so I do my best to ignore her outrageous attempts to grab my attention. When he starts fondling her tits, I look away, and my eyes instantly meet the new girl's. She's hunched over, with her hands on her knees, looking flushed.

My heart rate elevates as we lock gazes for the first time. Her chest is heaving ever so slightly, and damp tendrils of hair cling to her forehead. A light sheen of sweat glistens on her brow. It's not exactly ideal weather for running, but I admire her determination. Most kids in here are lazy as shit, uncaring about school, working out, or anything which would make the best of a bad situation. Most get sucked into the system, either banding with the gangs or falling prey to them.

I wonder which side she'll fall on.

As that thought pops in my mind, I vow to do what I can to keep her safe.

Her eyes bore into mine, almost like a challenge, and I get lost in the seductive depths of her gaze. Honestly, her eyes are the most startling brown. Like a warm burnt amber color, and the orange hues surrounding her pupils are like wild, flickering flames. I've never seen anything like them. She stares at me through these long, thick lashes and I fucking forget how to breathe. It's as if our surroundings have disappeared and it's only her and me.

Unspoken questions linger at the back of her eyes, and the way she's looking at me makes me feel like she's peeling back my layers, one at a time, until I'm exposed before her. I go to great lengths to hide who I am in here, and, ordinarily, I'd run a mile from someone inquisitive like her.

But the only urge I'm feeling in the moment is to run *toward* her.

The sentiment freaks me out.

But not enough to pull my gaze away.

Her tongue darts out, and she licks her lips before dragging her bottom lip between her teeth. I follow the movements greedily, and a wave of desire floods my body while my heart beats wildly in my chest.

I'm not sure how long we stare at one another for. Time has ceased to have any meaning. But she's the first to break away, hauling her gaze from me to look over at Lopez and Valeria who are now dry humping on the bench. Her bra is lowered to her waist, her tits bare for the horny audience. A few of the guys have their hands down the fronts of their shorts, rubbing one out as they watch them fuck around.

"What the fuck you looking at?" Valeria demands, glaring at the new girl with undisguised venom as Lopez stalls with his mouth around her nipple.

The new girl slowly drags her gaze up and down Valeria's body, and her mouth tugs up into a slight smirk. "I thought I'd left all the skanks behind at my old school. Guess I was mistaken."

Her voice is like molten chocolate, deep, sultry, and highly addictive. Thinking I might be drooling, I clamp my lips shut, smothering a smile as I watch her confidently challenge Valeria.

Valeria shoves Lopez off her, fixes her clothing, and then stalks toward the newbie. The guys trade excited looks. It's been ages since we've had any chick fights, and they're champing at the bit. I stand, ready to jump in and defend the new girl if necessary, when I spy Watson stomping this way. Valeria is too angry to notice, and Lopez is too turned on by the prospect of a girl fight to look anywhere else.

Leaning against the fence, I hang back, amused to see how this will play out.

"Say that to my face, bitch!" Valeria slams her palms into the new girl's chest, and she falls back a couple steps.

"Get your fucking hands off me." She doesn't raise her voice or attempt to physically retaliate, and that impresses me to no end.

"You're dead, ho. So. Fucking. Dead." A vein pops in Valeria's neck as she prods her finger into the new girl's chest.

"I won't tell you again." The new girl stares her down, and she has a considerable height advantage. Valeria may be fierce, but she's a tiny little thing. The new girl towers over her by at least a half foot, so it's almost comical watching this go down. But I'm not flippant about it either. Because what Valeria lacks in height and body mass, she makes up for in other ways. The new girl may not realize it, but she's just made a formidable enemy.

I can't decide if she's brave, naïve, or recklessly stupid.

"Valeria!" Watson barks, pushing his way forward. "Inside. Now!"

"What the actual fuck?" Valeria shoots a menacing look at Watson. Rumor is, she's fucking him for favors, and it appears those rumors are right if the entitled expression on her face is any judge.

"Now." Watson's tone brokers no argument. "Powell clearly saw you pushing Zeta." He gestures at his female colleague over his shoulder. "Don't make this any worse. Just come with me."

We have a name. *Zeta*. It's a fitting name for the beautiful, mysterious stranger.

Valeria deliberately shoves into Zeta's shoulder as she walks past, glaring at her with pure menace. "Watch it," Watson tells Zeta, his eyes lingering on her chest in a way that makes my blood boil. "Keep your nose clean around here if you want to stay in our good graces," he cautions, finally tearing his eyes away. My hands are clenched into balls at my sides, and a rush of aggression floods my system, begging to be unleashed. Right now, I could pummel Watson into a bloody mess. I take subtle deep breaths, in and out, in an attempt to cool my jets.

"Got it," Zeta says, showing no emotion. But the instant Watson turns away, she flips him the bird behind his back, and a few low chuckles ring out.

"Baby, you sure know how to make an entrance," Lopez says, eye-fucking her as he saunters toward her.

"I'm not your baby," Zeta says, folding her arms across her chest. Several groans ring out behind me, and my protective instincts kick up a notch. I take a step toward her, and her eyes dart to mine for a brief second.

"Not yet you're not," Lopez replies with a suggestive smirk.

"Not. Ever." Zeta holds up a palm to keep him at bay.

"Famous last words, baby." Lopez grins.

"I don't do sloppy seconds." She flicks a quick gaze over him. "And you're way too fucking short."

"Aw, now you're hurting my feelings," Lopez says, only half-joking. Guy's ego is floating somewhere around orbit, and he won't take too kindly to a remark like that.

"Do I look like I give a flying fuck about your feelings?" She arches a brow, and I'm struggling to contain the wide grin dying to rip free.

"Careful, sweetheart," Lopez mutters. "There's a fine line between flirting and insulting."

"And there's a distinct line between stupidity and intelligence." She wets her lips, and I can almost see the gears ticking in her skull. "Or maybe not so much in your case."

Lopez frowns. He can't work out whether she's just inferred he's stupid or intelligent.

Dumbass.

My smile breaks loose, and she notices, casting a surreptitious look in my direction as her own lips kick up slightly at the corners.

"Well," she says, preparing to leave. "It's been fun." Waggling her fingers in our general direction, she trots off, leaving a trail of infatuated hearts in her wake.

It seems my last few months in juvie just got a whole lot more interesting.

2

ZETA

I'm shaking all over as I jog away from the boys. Blood thrums in my ears, and my heart is racing scarily fast behind my ribcage. I can't believe I just did that. And I know exactly what I've done.

Drawn a target on my back.

But I knew coming in here that that would happen anyway, and it's better to take the opening shot than wait for the bullet to come at me. I suppose if there's anything I can thank my mother for, it's my ability to swim in a sea full of sharks.

I'm under no illusion about my future. If I can't navigate juvie, I'll never survive adult prison.

When I kept my mouth shut, I hadn't factored that into my planning. I thought juvie would be my ticket to freedom, but instead, it's my ticket to hell. It's all happened so fast that I haven't had time to come to terms with this new reality, let alone consider how I can extricate myself from the longer-term mess.

All that mattered was getting away from that asshole. In that moment, when it became evident that he was going to pin all the blame on me, that was the only thought playing on a loop in my mind. I couldn't stay there with him on my own. I would never have made it to eighteen alive.

So, I'm here, and I'll have to think up some way of avoiding the consequences.

But, for now, it's one day at a time. One step at a time. One minor victory at a time.

THE GORGEOUS ONE sends sly looks my way while I force-feed myself the sweet and sour pork the cafeteria is attempting to pass off as dinner. A few guys have tried to sit beside me, but I shooed them away with a glare, a snarl, and a few harsh words. The only other girls in this place are loyal to that skank. They shoot filthy looks my way, but I purposely ignore them, knowing it'll piss them off even more. As the only girls in the coed unit, it means I'll be sharing a pod with them, but at least I'll have my own cell. Until someone new arrives, if that happens.

I take a sneaky look at the gorgeous one while I sip my milk through a straw. He's talking to a younger boy at his side, smiling at something he says, and I can tell he cares about him.

One of the good things about being a loner is you learn to read people well. My people-watching used to drive Mom insane. She constantly chastised me, saying I preferred observing random strangers than engaging in conversation. What she didn't realize is that I never wanted to engage in conversation with *her*.

Why would I?

What the fuck did she ever do for me?

Besides bring me into this world, not a hell of a lot.

I'm gritting my teeth so hard I break through the straw, and little drops of milk splash my face. Out of the corner of my eye, I spot the table of girls laughing at me. *Are we back in kindergarten?* If that's how easily they're amused, maybe this won't be as bad as I fear. Ignoring the urge to roll my eyes, I pretend I don't notice, dabbing at my face with a paper towel.

I feel the gorgeous one's eyes on me again. There's just something about him that commands my attention. Something I can't put my finger on. It's embarrassing to admit, even to myself, how captivated I am with him. Nothing like this has ever happened to me before, but, I swear, the instant our eyes met, I felt something spark to life inside me.

A connection?

A bond?

A shared understanding?

A mutual dark side?

I don't know how to explain it or describe it, other than it confuses, scares, and excites me, all at the same time.

And I know what you're thinking. It's just because he's hot.

But it's not that. It really isn't. I mean, yes, he's fucking hot, undeniably so with that ripped body, messy dirty-blond hair, and those dazzling eyes. They're like a mix of yellow, orange, and brown with a faint green tint, and when he looked at me, I drowned in his gaze, zoning out as some weird vibe erupted between us.

And now I sound like one of those mushy romance books I love to read. Not the smutty ones. I've seen enough of that in real life to avoid reading anything similar. I prefer to read the overtly romantic ones where they're all subtle glances, shy touches, and sweet kisses. Inside, I laugh at myself, imagining I've wandered into my own love story.

As if those really exist.

As if that could ever happen in a place like this.

As if I could ever open myself up to another person in that way.

My back hurts the next morning, and I crick my head from side to side to try to loosen my stiff muscles. The mattress on the narrow bunk in my cell is hard and lumpy, the pillow flat as a pancake, offering no comfort or support, so it's no wonder I'm aching all over.

I'm yawning as I pull on the ill-fitting shorts and polo combo I was provided with upon arrival. A shudder works its way through me as I recall the humiliating intake process. Forced to strip completely naked, I then had to suffer the embarrassment of a full body search. At least it was Officer Powell. But having anyone search my vagina and the crack of my ass with gloved fingers is an ordeal I never again want to experience.

A loud yawn escapes my mouth again, and I feel dead on my feet. I only managed to get about three hours sleep, and I'm exhausted. The majority of the night was spent in a cold sweat, fighting heavy eyelids and doing my best to avoid sleep in order to ward off the nightmares.

The doors automatically unlock with a loud click at seven a.m., and I drag my weary body outside, waiting for the others to emerge from their cells. Without fail, each girl glares at me, but hostility from other females isn't anything new, so it doesn't bother me.

"Let's move out," Officer Powell says once we are in single file. I keep my head down and my hands clasped behind my back, like I was instructed yesterday. Powell walks alongside us, and every time she stares straight ahead, the girl behind me shoves me in the back, almost causing me to trip over my feet every few steps, but I manage to keep my balance, and I make it to the cafeteria in one piece. I'm tempted to launch my elbow back into her gut, but getting into a fight on day two would not set the best first impression. I might despise that perv Watson, but he had a point about keeping my nose clean.

Breakfast is sour grapefruit juice, burnt toast, and over-cooked boiled eggs, but at least it's more palatable than what I had to eat yesterday. Keeping my strength up is important in here if I'm going to defend myself, so I'll put up and shut up.

I've a forkful of eggs halfway to my mouth when the boy who was sitting with the gorgeous one yesterday arrives at my table. "Is anyone sitting here?" he asks, his voice trembling a little. His cheeks flush as he looks expectantly at me, and I don't have it in my heart to turn him down, even though that's my first instinct, especially after he asked so nicely. He's cute and a couple years younger than me, I'd guess, so I don't see the harm.

"Have at it." I gesture toward the empty chair with my hand, and his cheeks flare red. God, he's adorable.

The chair screeches along the tile floor as he sits down across from me. Brushing strands of dark hair out of his eyes, he clears his throat. "I'm Lucas. Lucas Young. But you can call me Luc."

"Nice to meet you Lucas Young a.k.a. Luc. I'm Zeta Williams." I almost stutter on my last name. But, in here, having people know what I supposedly did will be a help not a hindrance. Although, Luc doesn't react adversely to my admission, so he mustn't know.

"How did your first day go?" he asks, toying with the eggs on his plate.

I shrug, like it's no biggie. "About how I expected."

He smiles at me. "Ryder's right. You're brave."

My brows climb to my hairline. "Who's Ryder?" I ask although I can guess.

He laughs, absently looking over his shoulder. "Oh fuck. This is priceless. You mean to tell me you didn't notice him?" His chest rumbles with laughter, and I know I've called it right. He *is* referring to the gorgeous one. But I'm not about to let Luc know I *did* notice him. Would have to be blind not to. He's the hottest guy in this place, by a mile.

"What's so funny?" a deep male voice asks, sending shivers racing up and down my spine. I don't need to look up to know it's him. *Ryder.* I test his name out in my mind, and I like it. I like it a lot.

That weird buzz of electricity swirls around the table, and I wonder if he feels it too.

"Dude, I think I've finally found a girl immune to your charms," Luc jokes.

I almost pee my pants at the irony.

"Is that so?" Ryder's question is laced with amusement.

Slowly, I raise my eyes, roaming my gaze over his slim hips, washboard abs, broad chest, and wide shoulders and up to that delectable face. A face that belongs on a big screen where he can be adored by the masses. His lips kick up as my gaze wanders over his face, finally meeting his beautiful eyes. My heart goes crazy again, and my stomach lurches wildly as butterflies invade my chest. Hot damn. He's even more gorgeous up close. He is truly beautiful.

Ryder grins, pulling out a chair beside Luc. Sitting down, he leans back in his chair, casually crossing one leg over the other. "Yeah, I'm not buying that."

"Wow. Are you always this arrogant?" Heat spreads up my chest and onto my neck, and I will my stupid body to get with the program before he notices my crazy attraction to him.

"Do you always lie to yourself?" he coolly replies.

"Never," I snap. "I never lie to myself. Not when there are enough people in the world who do that for me."

I regret the words the instant they leave my mouth, but it's too late to reclaim them without drawing even more attention.

Ryder straightens up in his chair, all trace of humor gone from his face and his tone when he speaks. He stares at me for a minute, and I'm holding my breath in nervous anticipation. "I can relate to that. Respect that."

We continue to stare at one another, and something intangible passes between us. My heart rate kicks up, going a hundred miles an hour, as I struggle to decipher what the hell this thing is between us. He jerks back a little, a strange look on his face. Quickly composing himself, he extends his hand across the table. "I'm Ryder, by the way."

I eye his hand warily. Firstly, who does that? Secondly, I'm afraid I might spontaneously combust if we touch, skin to skin. Guess I won't know till I try. With more confidence than I feel, I clasp my hand in his, startled when a jolt of electricity whips up my arm. His palm is large, his fingers callused, but his grip is firm and warm, and I briefly wonder what it would feel like being held in his arms. I jerk my hand away the instant the thought lands in my wonky brain.

"Sorry." His face is flushed, and he looks a little … embarrassed?

"For what?" I inquire, my brow puckering in confusion. Is he apologizing for shaking my hand?

"For my, ah … for"—he scrubs a hand over the light layer of stubble on his face, his features twisting—"my hands are rough because of the guitar," he hastily adds. Luc bursts out laughing, almost choking on the food in his mouth. Ryder pins him with a "shut it" look.

"You play guitar?" I ask, instantly intrigued and also wanting to put this conversation back on some kind of normal footing.

He nods. "Since I was a kid."

"You any good?"

"He's fucking awesome," Luc confirms, grinning proudly.

I frown, not understanding. "Did you two know each other on the outside?"

Luc shakes his head. "Nah. Ryder was already here when I arrived."

I scratch the back of my head. "So how do you know he's an awesome guitar player?"

Luc shoots me a duh look, while Ryder answers my question. "Powell got approval to have my guitar brought here."

"I didn't think we were allowed to have anything from home."

"We're not, but Ryder's been here a while, he's got level four privileges, and I think Powell's got the hots for him." Luc winks, grinning.

Ryder's face contorts. "Knock that shit off. She's old enough to be my mother." A scowl mars his perfect features as a dark look briefly flits across his face, but it's gone so fast I'm not sure I didn't imagine it. "And I think I just puked in my mouth," he adds, smiling.

I can't help snickering, and Ryder's head swivels to me, a wide grin covering his mouth. "I'm not into older chicks." He leans across the table. "Unless you tell me you're older, and then I'm completely reassessing my stance."

Woah. Talk about direct. Is this the same guy who was stuttering and stammering a few minutes ago? He's a bit of a conundrum. Flirty one second and then shy the next. I can't get a good read on Ryder, which is unusual for me, and that only adds to his allure.

"I'm sixteen," I readily admit. "Almost seventeen."

"Then my statement, and my position, remains unchanged." He waggles his brows at me before diving into his breakfast.

"So, you're seventeen," I surmise.

"Yes," he confirms, "but I could be older. Not everyone is transferred to an adult facility when they turn eighteen."

I had heard that, but I wasn't sure how true it was. I make a mental note to ask my attorney about it at her next visit.

"Will you be?" I blurt, forgetting to engage my brain again. I don't usually flirt with guys, but Ryder is getting under my skin, making me say things I don't normally say.

He arches a brow. "Why, would you miss me?"

"I'd have to know you to miss you," I retort, sending him a smug look.

"Well, we can rectify that. You only have to say the word."

"Dude." Luc chuckles, nudging Ryder's shoulder. "You've got game."

Ryder rolls his eyes, messing up the younger boy's hair. "Watch and learn, my young apprentice," he teases, and now it's my turn to roll my eyes.

"How old are you, Luc, and how long have you been here?" I ask, deliberately changing the subject.

"I'm fourteen, and almost two years." His mouth turns down, and I hate that I've put that sad look on his face.

Ryder shoots me a look which I instantly interpret as don't pry. I subtly nod at him, and his gaze radiates gratitude.

"So, when do I get to hear you play?" I plant an overly cheery smile on my face while I divert the course of the conversation again.

"Are you free after school?" he teases with a playful smile.

"Hmm." I tap a finger off my chin, pretending to think about it. "Let me consider my busy schedule for a moment." Luc chuckles, and I'm glad he's broken free of his nostalgia. "Yep. I'm free."

"It's a date," Luc quips, jumping in before Ryder can respond.

And as my eyes are drawn to Ryder's once again, I can't help wishing that it was.

3

RYDER

I can't stop thinking about Zeta, and as the class enters the small school library, I find myself gravitating to her side. She stiffens, almost imperceptibly, as I walk up behind her. A second later, her shoulders relax, but she doesn't look around. I reach over her head, selecting the book I want to read. I watch her scanning the shelves, her eyes zooming in as her fingers skim over spines, while most of our classmates mindlessly grab any book before heading back to the classroom. "That one's good," I say when she pulls out the worn blue book I've read cover to cover at least five times. "If you don't mind depressive subject matter."

She glances over her shoulder at me, raising one brow, before returning to the book, reading the back cover. "I'm surprised they permit books like this," she says, a couple minutes later, turning to face me.

I shrug. "I think it helps that the material is relatable. Reading about a guy suffering from depression and suicidal tendencies might actually help put shit into perspective."

Her gorgeous eyes drill into mine, like she's hearing the things I'm not saying, and it makes me hugely uncomfortable. I shift on my feet, averting my gaze, pretending to read the back of the book in my hand, even though I've already read that one too. The library is small, and I've been here too long, so there isn't anything I haven't already read.

I was never a reader until I came to juvie, but I'll do just about anything to help pass the time and keep my mind occupied, and I've actually grown to enjoy it.

A couple of tense minutes pass before she clears her throat, and I whip my head up. "I don't usually read books like this, but maybe I'll give it a try."

"What kind of books do you normally read?" I lean against the bookshelf. We're alone in here now, and I want to take advantage of the quiet time.

Her cheeks flush a little, and now I'm even more curious. "Usually contemporary romance," she admits after a beat.

"Hey, nothing wrong with that. I liked *The Fault in Our Stars.*"

Her lips kick up at the corners. "You seriously read *The Fault in Our Stars?*"

"And *Everything Everything* and *We Were Liars*," I add, freely handing over my man card. A beautiful smile graces her mouth, and a strange fucking ache stabs me in the chest. I lean in closer to her because I'm inexplicably drawn to her and I can't stop myself. Lowering my voice, I whisper in her ear. "But you'll have to keep my secret. I have a rep to maintain." I wink at her without thinking, and she bursts out laughing.

"Oh my God. Did you seriously just wink at me?"

I straighten up, rubbing a hand along the back of my neck, slanting her a sheepish look. "Too lame?"

Her smile expands, and this girl could ask me to do anything in this moment, and I would be powerless to resist. "Pervy, more like."

I fake a wince. "Ouch."

"I bet you do that to all the girls," she teases.

"What, all five of you?"

Her smile drops off. "I'd kinda forgotten…" She clasps the book to her chest, looking off into space.

"It's natural. I can still remember how hard the adjustment was at the start." It's a tough environment to get used to in some ways; in others, not so much.

Tucking her hair behind one ear, she chews on the corner of her mouth as her brow creases. I watch a multitude of emotions wash over her face before she finds the courage to ask me. "How long have you been here?"

I wipe my suddenly clammy hands down the front of my shorts. "A while." My answer is purposely vague. I don't want to give anyone any reason to start connecting the dots.

"Oh." She peers intently into my eyes, sucking me deeper into her world. "I guess people don't really like to talk about it," she adds in a quieter tone. "How long and why they're here."

"It's not something we dwell on unless you're like Lopez or part of one of the crews. They like to brag about shit they've done."

"But not you." She astutely assesses me.

"No. Not me."

The teach pops his head in the doorway. "Williams, Stone, back to your desks now."

We walk toward the door, and at the last second, I tug on her elbow, holding her back. She flinches, jumping a little, and I instantly withdraw my hand. "Sorry. Didn't mean to startle you," I mumble, inwardly cursing myself. I'm such a fucking doofus around this girl. It's embarrassing.

"It's okay." She worries her lower lip between her teeth. "I just don't like people touching me." She looks away the minute she says it, and I can tell she had no intention of telling me that. It's nice to know I'm not the only one blurting stuff out. Perhaps she's as affected by me as I am by her.

"No touching. Got it." I hold my palms up, keeping my tone light.

"Thanks," she mumbles, stepping forward.

"You wanna have lunch with me?" I hurriedly ask before it's too late.

Her smile is coy as she looks back at me. "Sure. And you should ask Luc to sit with us too. I know you watch out for him."

My eyes pop wide. How can she tell that after one day in the place?

"I'm very observant," she says, answering my unspoken question, shocking me again.

Zeta is the type of person I should avoid like the plague, but she's far too interesting to ignore. She's the first girl I've ever felt a connection to, and even if it's risky, there's no way in hell I can stay away from her.

🎵

"So, how'd you end up with a name like Zeta?" I ask as we finish our dinner in the cafeteria later that day. Young is hanging off Zeta's every word, and I can tell he's majorly crushing on her. Not that I blame him or can even pretend like I'm not crushing hard either. Lopez has been sending me snide looks the entire day, and I know it's cause he's not happy I'm hanging out with the new girl. Well, screw him. He doesn't get to tell me who I can speak to or spend time with.

Her body turns rigid, and I figure I've hit a sore point, but I don't retract my question either.

She sighs a little, consciously dragging a hand through her hair. "My mom was a big fan of the actress Catherine Zeta Jones. She named me after her."

I remember watching *The Mask of Zorro* a few years ago in here, and that's how I know who she is. The facility's movie collection is completely outdated and all rated PG-13, but I've just found a reason to be happy about that fact.

She toys with the food on her plate before looking up with

a forced smile plastered on her face. "I guess I should count myself lucky that she didn't name me Catherine."

"Or Jones," Luc blurts, his cheeks reddening when he realizes how lame that sounds.

"Absolutely," Zeta agrees, easing his discomfort.

"Your mom chose well," I admit, shoving my empty plate aside. "You even look a little like her."

She blinks excessively before shaking her head. "Eh, yeah, no, I don't."

"What does Catherine Zeta Jones look like?" Luc asks me.

She's beautiful. I think it, but I don't say it because I don't want to embarrass Zeta. Or myself. "She's got long, dark hair, and she's really pretty," I say, hoping that doesn't sound too flirty.

"Don't insult my girl," Lopez says, sticking his ugly mug in my face. He winks at Zeta before dropping into the seat beside her, slinging his arm around her shoulder. "Zeta's smoking hot." He licks his lips as he checks her out, his gaze gravitating to her tits.

She pales, sitting up stiffly in her chair. Removing his arm, she glares at him. "Don't fucking touch me."

"I second that," Valeria sneers, standing with her hands on her hips and glaring at Lopez.

His gaze bounces between both girls, and a sly grin spreads across his mouth as he slouches in the chair, casually crossing his ankles. "If you came over here to tell me what to do, you can fuck the hell off, bitch." Lopez's grin turns menacing as he pins his fuck buddy with a withering stare.

She leans over him, her wavy black hair falling around her shoulders, gripping his chin and putting her face right up in his. "You can suck your own dick next time, asshole."

"Yeah?" Lopez knocks her hand away, grabs her ass, and yanks her down onto his lap. "I don't fucking think so. If I tell you to suck my cock, you'll suck my cock." He turns his head to Zeta. "Or I'll find a replacement." His intent is clear.

Valeria throws back her head, laughing, as she slides off Lopez's lap. I see her noticing Powell watching from the far corner of the room. "You think that bitch gives head like me?" Her hands are firmly back on her hips. "Puh-lease. She'd probably faint if you showed her your cock."

I know what Valeria's suggesting, but Lopez, given his giant-sized ego, interprets it differently. "That's more like it, baby," he purrs, thinking she's just complimented the size of his dick.

Zeta has remained quiet this whole time, but as she stands, I watch her preparing to say her piece. "I'm betting I've seen more cock than you've had hot dinners," she challenges, eyeballing Valeria like butter wouldn't melt in her mouth. Young is practically drooling as he hangs off every word Zeta says.

"And I'm betting you're full of shit," Valeria retorts with a smirk.

"I think there's an easy way to resolve this," Lopez butts in, rubbing his crotch as his gaze latches onto Zeta's chest. He's grinning like he's just won the lottery, and I want to smash his face into the wall. Rivulets of rage start trickling through me, and I grip the side of my chair, grinding my teeth hard.

"I wouldn't touch your cock if you paid me," Zeta supplies. "And I don't have to prove anything to any of you."

Powell moves from her position, heading this way. It's clear from the body language that something is going down, and she's ready to head it off at the pass.

"That's not the way things work around here." Valeria prods a bony finger in Zeta's chest. "And you can't disrespect my boy like that. Someone needs to teach you some manners."

Zeta snorts. "And you think that's you?"

I rise, hoping the movement will catch her attention. I'm trying to caution Zeta with my eyes, but she's solely focused on the girl in front of her. I'm not sure what Zeta hopes to achieve by antagonizing Valeria and Lopez, but she's treading on shaky ground.

"I will fucking gut you, girl," Valeria threatens.

"Not if I gut you first." Zeta's voice is like ice as she holds firm. Thrusting Valeria's finger away, she squares up to her, leaning right into her face as she says, "Just like I did with my momma."

4

ZETA

I hate myself for what I've just admitted, but I can't let that bitch gain the upper hand. Although I'm shaking inside, I hold my chin up, fixing her with a deadly stare. I can do this. I can act like nothing or no one affects me until she gets the message that I'm not about to be pushed around. Then, hopefully, she'll get bored and leave me alone.

"What's going on here?" Powell asks, materializing at our table.

"Your girl here says she's gonna gut me like she did her momma," Valeria confirms, with a look of disbelief splashed across her face. "Why is she here? She do that?"

"That's none of your concern," Powell calmly replies. "And I need you to come with me, Zeta. Your attorney is here to see you."

Without looking at any of them, I follow Powell out of the cafeteria. We walk side by side in silence, my stomach twisting sourly as my words repeat in a loop over and over in my head. When we reach the interview room, she stops with her hand on the door handle and turns to me. "I'm sure you have your reasons for saying what you said back there, but you don't want to mess with that girl."

I force back the bile traveling up my throat. "I don't have a choice. If I don't look like I can stand up for myself, she'll never leave me alone. I've met enough girls like her to know that."

"Watch your back. And stick with Ryder. He knows how to survive in here."

"Why are you being nice to me?"

"Keeping the peace is in my interests," she cryptically says before opening the door and ushering me inside.

"Zeta. How are you?" my court-appointed attorney asks as I take a seat across the table from her.

Peachy. Just peachy. I've just used my dead mom as a way to try to prove I'm a hard-ass. Made a mockery of her death like it doesn't upset me. But, of course, I don't articulate any of those thoughts. I shrug my shoulders, acting casual. "Fine." Resting my elbows on the table, I lean forward.

She pushes her glasses up the bridge of her nose before opening a file in front of her, thumbing through pages, muttering to herself and frowning as she flicks through the file for whatever she's looking for. After a few minutes, she slides a couple of sheets across the table to me along with a pen. "I need you to sign here and here." She points to certain sections on both pages.

"What is this?" I refuse to sign anything without understanding what I'm putting my name to.

"Official court documentation I need to log."

"Why?"

"Because it's procedure."

I take a few minutes to read over the documents before I sign, but it's a lot of convoluted legal jargon that I don't fully understand. Anyway, it doesn't seem like I'm signing my rights away to anything, so I scribble my signature and hand it back to her.

"I wanted to ask you what happens when I turn eighteen,"

I inquire. "Will I remain here or be moved to an adult prison?"

"That depends," she replies, returning the sheets to her file and closing it.

"On what?"

"On your behavior, how well you're responding to your treatment program, and what's in the best interests of your mental health once you come of age."

At the court hearing, it was determined I'm to meet weekly with a psychologist for individual counseling. It's due to start next week, and I'm nervous. Still trying to figure out how I should act and how real I should be.

My mouth turns dry as I wonder how best to phrase my next question. "Are there ever instances where a verdict is overturned? And if I wanted to, could we lodge an appeal before I turn eighteen?"

Her brow puckers, and she runs a thin hand through her frizzy, unkempt hair. "In your case, we could only lodge an appeal if we have grounds for an appeal. You confessed to voluntary manslaughter, and your punishment was decided. I don't see how we'd have any grounds for appeal unless there's something you're not telling me?"

I'm tempted to tell her the truth, but it's too early to admit I lied. If I tell the court how it really went down, there's a chance he won't go to jail and that I'll be sent back to him. Being locked up is preferable to that, so I shake my head and bottle the truth back up, deciding to wait until the timing is better, hoping by then it won't be too late.

"Did you manage to locate my aunt?" I ask, switching tack.

"Your aunt?" She frowns again, scratching the side of her head.

"Yes." I resist the urge to roll my eyes to the ceiling. "You asked me if there was any next of kin besides my *stepfather* ...

and I told you my mom had a younger sister. You said you'd try to find her."

"Oh." Her cheeks flush pink. "I haven't had time to investigate yet, but I'll get on that straightaway."

I have zero faith that she will, and it's probably a lost cause anyway. The only thing I know about my aunt is her name. I've never met her. Or, if I did, it must've been when I was too young to remember it. All I know is her and Mom were estranged, and they hadn't spoken in years. I overheard Mom on the phone one time, saying something about her working overseas. It's a stretch, but if she could be found, maybe, just maybe, the court would accept her as my guardian, and it'd give me the opportunity to come clean. Even if she doesn't want me, it's better than staying locked up for a crime I didn't commit.

Powell leads me to the common room after my meeting ends, and my heart jumps a little when I locate Ryder, tucked into a corner of the room, with a guitar slung around his shoulder. He's sitting cross-legged on the ground, lightly strumming the guitar with his eyes closed. I want to go to him, like we planned, but I don't know if he wants anything to do with me after my revelation. I'm rooted to the spot, drowning in indecision, wondering if I should just ask to go back to my cell and lick my wounds in private.

Almost like he can sense me, Ryder opens his eyes and lifts his head, his face lighting up when he spots me. Or at least, that's how it appears to be, but it's quite likely I'm delusional, wanting to read more into his friendship than there is.

He wiggles his fingers in the air, gesturing me forward, and I slowly place one foot in front of the other, moving in his direction. An anxious fluttering feeling descends on my chest, and I chew on the inside of my mouth as I get nearer. I watch him slide the guitar off, placing it gently on the floor beside him.

"You made it," he says, when I land in front of him.

"Yep." I sink to the floor, propping my back against the wall and pulling my knees up into my chest. I stare at my feet, unable to look him in the eye. He doesn't seem unhappy to see me, but how could he not hate me after the bomb I dropped.

"Hey." His voice is soft. "You okay?"

I bite down on my lower lip as I draw strength from somewhere and look up at him. All I see is compassion in his eyes, and that goes a long way toward settling my nerves. "Why don't you hate me?" I whisper.

Understanding washes over his face, but he's quiet for a couple moments before speaking. "You think I've changed my mind because of what you said?"

I nod. "Most people would."

He shakes his head. "Not around here." His eyes subconsciously scan the room. "Everyone in here has done something which justifies being locked up. You're not any different."

"But I … it was my *mother.* My mother is dead because of me." A genuine tear leaks out of the corner of my eye, because that part is true. "I mean, she wasn't going to win any mother of the year awards or anything, but she still brought me into this world."

He looks contemplative as he scrutinizes my face. "I'm guessing there's more to the story than meets the eye. But"— he hurriedly adds as I open my mouth to speak—"we don't need to talk about it. I can tell you're remorseful, and that's all I need to know. We don't have to discuss it. You're already upset enough." He lifts his arm, as if he's going to touch me, then he drops it back onto his lap, like he's thought better of it. Or maybe he remembers I said I don't like to be touched.

But I'd make an exception in his case. When it comes to him, I most definitely want to be touched.

I'm digressing, and daydreaming about guys should be the last thing on my mind. "I don't like having to use that to build a rep in here, but it doesn't look like I have much choice."

He nods in understanding. "I figured it was something like

that, and it might work. Or it might mean she comes at you a different way."

I lean my head back against the wall. "Please tell me she's almost eighteen and due to get transferred out?"

"Sorry to burst your bubble, but she's already eighteen, and there's no signs of her going anywhere."

"Great. Well, my other plan is to lie low, and hopefully, she'll get bored of coming at me."

"Yeah, I can't see that happening. There's no way the guys will leave you alone. You're new, and you're hot, and that's a winning combo in their minds."

"And what about your mind?" I tease, trying to look casual and not like I'm enormously pleased at his compliment.

He grins. "Oh, I'm no different than any other horny seventeen-year-old. You're prime spank bank material, babe. Best get used to it."

My mouth drops open. "You did *not* just say that to my face!"

"Would you rather I lied to you?"

"Absolutely not," I splutter, shocked at his bluntness but not in any way unhappy about it.

"Good, because a friendship built on lies is not worth having."

His good humor disappears, and a muscle clenches in his jaw as he looks away. I'm not sure what memories have returned to haunt him, but I know he's gone someplace else, and I make it my mission to pull him back. I take a proper look at the glossy black guitar resting on the floor at his side. "What kind of guitar is that?"

His gaze flits to his guitar, and the tense lines on his face relax. "It's a Fender CD-60S." He runs his hand lovingly over the body of the guitar. "It's about the only thing around here that brings me any joy, any peace." His face is an open book as he looks at me, and I see the truth shining in his eyes. This guitar means everything to him.

"How long have you had it?"

"Since I was a kid. One of my mom's *boyfriends* left it behind when they broke up, and I hid it before she could sell it. I've had it ever since."

I sense similarities between our mothers, but I don't quiz him on it. We're done with the heavy for today. "Sweet." I run the tips of my fingers over the cool, glossy wood. "She's a thing of beauty all right."

"Have you ever played?" he asks, staring straight into my eyes, highlighting how close we are to one another.

His eyes are more of a yellow-green color today but no less mesmerizing. I have to physically tear my gaze from his in order to form a coherent sentence. "No. I always wanted to learn how to play a musical instrument, and my sixth-grade teacher begged my mom to let me take lessons, but we didn't have the money." I shrug, like it didn't almost break my heart. "My teacher said I had a good ear, and I've always felt a real connection with music, but I guess it wasn't meant to be."

"There's still plenty of time," he reassures me. "And I could teach you how to play, if you like?"

"In here?" I glance around the room. While most of the other kids are occupied, playing board games, reading, chatting, or watching TV, more than a few heads are observing our interaction. "No thanks. I want to blend into the background, not become the center of attention."

"Like I already said," he says, smiling as his gaze darts to my lips. "There isn't a hope in hell of you fading into the background. You're way too pretty and far too interesting to go unnoticed."

"Are you deliberately flirting with me?"

"What would your answer be if I said I was?" He cocks his head to the side, and waves of dirty-blond hair fall into his eyes. I dig my fingers into my thighs to resist the urge to run my fingers through the messy strands.

"That I'm not in the market for a hookup, so if that's your

game plan, you might as well give up now." It's my usual mantra when I'm being hit on, and the words leave my mouth before I've had time to form a different response, because, in all honestly, I don't think I'd turn him down if he was flirting with me.

"That's not my M.O.," he protests. "I like talking to you, and it's just so … fucking refreshing to meet a girl with smarts and no hidden agenda."

"How do you know I don't have an agenda?" I quirk a brow, trying to ignore the fact that his knee is now brushing against my thigh.

"You're not the only one with sharp observational skills."

"Is this the part where you say you see the real me and we share a connection you've never shared with anyone before?"

Oh. My. Fucking. God.

Could I be any more lame?

I'm literally spouting shit from books now. Maybe the air's too thin in here, and it's depleting my brain cells. Or this guy is messing with my head in a serious way.

He laughs, and it's a deep full-bellied laugh that does funny things to my insides. "I can honestly say, Zeta, that I've never met a girl who intrigues me as much as you do."

"That's only because the pickings are slim around here. Trust me, I'm not that interesting."

"I think we'll have to agree to disagree." His eyes twinkle as he looks at me, and I get lost in their hidden depths and the warmth of his gorgeous smile. The air subtly changes, and that frisson of electricity I've felt in his presence before sparks to life, humming like a tangible thing. "Zeta," he whispers, never taking his eyes off my face.

I love the way he rasps my name, and a throbbing ache starts building between my thighs. "What?" I whisper back.

"I think I need you in my life." His eyes burrow deep into mine as he lifts his hand, extending it toward me. "Friends?"

There's no hesitation or indecision on my part. I place my

hand in his much larger one, and it feels like my heart might beat clear out of my chest. "Friends." I say it with confidence and determination born of some innate sense that tells me Ryder is going to be an important part of my life.

I've never believed in fate, or karma, or any of that superstitious nonsense, but as I sit on the cold floor, beside a boy I've only just met, a boy I scarcely know, I get a strong sense that I was meant to come here, that I was meant to meet him, and that we're meant to be friends.

And, quite possibly, something more.

5

RYDER

Zeta's been here a month, and already I'm having trouble remembering what my life was like before she arrived. I've never had a friend who was a girl before, so I don't have anything to compare our friendship to, but her presence in my life has been transformative, and she already means so much to me. It's not anything like the friendship I have with Luc, and while I don't want to knock my young friend, because he means the world to me too, my friendship with Zeta is already so much more.

I look forward to waking up every morning, knowing I'll get to spend my days with her. We laugh over breakfast, share notes and partner for assignments in class, discuss books we've read at length, often getting into a heated debate—which I love—jog around the yard together while trying to trip one another up, and watch movies and TV shows whenever she's not pleading with me to play for her. We even have a lot of similar musical tastes. When she told me she loved Green Day and Clapton, I almost declared undying love.

She's so unbelievably easy to talk to, and there's never any awkward moments or stilted conversation. The only topics we haven't discussed are our pasts, our families, and the reason why we're in here.

Thanks to Valeria, I know Zeta's been convicted of killing her mom. It was voluntary manslaughter, and she's been put away until she's twenty-five, apparently. Watson should have his ass fired for disclosing that information to Valeria while she was on her knees, no doubt. It didn't, for one second, alter my opinion of Zeta. I like to think I'm a better judge of character now, and I know she's not a bad person. I can't prove it, but I just know she's a good person caught in a shitty situation. It's the only explanation that makes sense.

And it'd be hypocritical of me to judge her harshly given my past actions. If I don't want to be defined by the mistakes of my past, then I have no right casting judgment on anyone in here because of theirs.

I could ask her what happened, but then I'd have to open up to her too, and I don't want to lie to this girl. So, we avoid conversing about our existence pre-juvie, and I'm happy to live in the land of denial, if it means I get to spend time with her.

"You tapping that yet?" Lopez asks, casting a quick glance at Zeta as she walks in single file with the other four girls, heading toward the school annex. Us boys are facing the wall, with our hands behind our back, waiting for the routine morning inspection to finish.

"Mind your own fucking business," I hiss under my breath. "And shut the fuck up before he catches us." Price is the officer on duty today, and while he's not on the Watson scale of assholery, he's been known to have his moments, so I want to stay off his radar.

"If you're not up to the job, I'd be happy to take her off your hands," he says, completely ignoring my wishes.

And what a fucking joke. As if I'd let Lopez anywhere near her. "I'm officially calling dibs." I cringe as I say it, knowing how hurt Zeta would be if she knew of this conversation. But I've watched Lopez leer at her for long enough. If I don't officially stake my claim, he'll go after her with all guns blazing, and just the thought of him putting his hands anywhere near her has me shaking with rage.

Despite the "Cage your Rage" program I've attended for years, I'm still prone to bouts of uncontrollable anger. I'm pretty good at removing myself to my cell when the frustration and aggression descends, but I doubt I could restrain myself if Lopez made a serious play for Zeta. So, I'm doing what I have to do to stop that from happening. And to keep her protected. Valeria hasn't done much more than toss out insults and scathing looks, but that would change if Lopez dumped her to actively seek out Zeta.

"Only with my permission," Lopez smugly states as we start moving forward in a line. He's at my back, whispering into my ear, annoying the fuck out of me, but I grit my teeth and stick to the plan.

"I never ask you for anything, man, and I've put in the groundwork. She's primed for the taking." My stomach contorts in distaste, but I say what I need to.

He chuckles, clamping a hand on my shoulder when Price isn't looking. "I knew there was a reason I liked you." He thinks I'm toying with her affections this whole time just to get in her pants, and I let him believe it.

A surge of self-loathing crashes into me. While it's not an unfamiliar feeling, Zeta's presence in my life has been successfully keeping those emotions at bay. Even the nightmares and flashbacks have been less frequent. So, I hate that I'm betraying her trust and disrespecting her by pretending I'm only after her body. I loathe that I'm forced into playing it this way, but there's no other choice.

🎼

"Hey, I need to tell you something," I whisper to Zeta later that evening as we sit beside one another on the floor in the common room. Carefully, I lean my Fender against the wall so I can give her my undivided attention.

"Sup?" She tucks her dark hair behind both ears, peering into my eyes with obvious concern. My gaze drifts to her lush mouth, and I sit on my hands to avoid grabbing her face and sampling her lips.

I'm fucking obsessed with this girl, and I wasn't joking with my previous spank bank comment. She's all I see when I close my eyes at night. It's her lips I imagine on my heated skin, her body I imagine thrusting inside of, as I stroke my cock to powerful release.

"Ryder?" She places her soft hand on my arm, and it takes colossal willpower not to pull her close and kiss her.

I snap out of it, remembering why I brought this up. "I had to say some shit to Lopez today to stop him making a play for you."

"What kind of shit?"

I clear my throat, scrubbing a hand over my stubbly chin. I hate telling her this, but it's not right to keep her in the dark either, so I made myself a promise that I'd fess up. "I insinuated I was only pretending to be your friend so I could fuck you."

"Oh."

Zeta is good at masking her feelings, but I can usually see behind it, because, in a lot of ways, she's a lot like me. My statement has upset her, and I need to make this right. "But it's obviously a total lie, and I'd never do that to you, so you don't need to worry." Now she looks even more hurt, and I can't figure out what I've said that's offended her. "But I'll need you to back me up if anyone asks."

She's quiet for a moment. Then she turns to me, a muscle tensing in her jaw. "I just want to make sure I got this straight." She narrows her eyes as she drills a piercing look at me. "You *are* my friend, and you've no interest in hooking up with me, but you want me to tell everyone we're not friends, and we're just fucking, if they ask?"

I bob my head. "That's pretty much it in a nutshell."

"Right. Got it." Her tone is icy cold as she scrambles to her feet.

I jump up. "Where you going?"

"Back to my cell. I have stuff to do."

"What stuff?"

"Just stuff." She stalks off, her long legs making quick work of the room.

I'm rooted to the spot, completely confused over what the fuck just happened. Snapping out of it, I take off after her, catching up to her just outside the room. Valeria and the other girls have her surrounded, and they're pushing her around, taking advantage of the fact Powell and Price are in some kind of heated argument back in the common room, unaware we've left, and Watson is talking with someone on his walkie-talkie, his chin down, not paying attention to what's going down out here in the hallway.

"Back the fuck up." I push my way in between Valeria and Zeta.

"Oh, look, it's lover boy to the rescue," Valeria taunts, and Sam, Camila, and Sofia laugh, like they're sharing some inside joke.

"It's such a shame," Camila adds, stepping into me and running her hand up my chest. "Such a fucking hot body, and no clue what to do with it."

The girls laugh again, and Zeta steps out from behind me, taking hold of Camila's wrist and thrusting it away. "Keep your fucking hands, and your stupid insults, to yourself."

"Possessive, isn't she?" Valeria sneers at me.

"You'd know all about that. The way you chase after Lopez is pathetic," Zeta coolly retorts.

"You know, you could've just taken me up on my offer."

Valeria ignores Zeta, pushing her chest into mine and reaching down for my cock. "I know how to show a man a good time. The offer's always open for you, gorgeous." I grip her wrist before her palm touches my dick, grimacing as I push it away. Zeta flinches, and I instantly step back, tugging her with me. On instinct, I take her hand, holding it firmly so she can't let go.

"I'm not into you, and I never will be," I tell Valeria, and I'm playing nice by not telling her what I really think.

Valeria laughs, as if the idea of anyone turning down her pussy is ridiculous.

"Are you scared of pussy, or you swing the other way?" Sam asks, grinning as she roams her gaze all over me.

"Let's not play games." Valeria flashes Zeta a smug look before fixing her gaze firmly on mine. "I know why you're hesitant. I know you fed Lopez a load of bullshit he bought, but the truth is, you're still rocking your V-card, aren't you? There's no shame in that, Ryder. I think it's kinda cute."

"I think it's fucking lame," Camila says, sending me a derisory look. "There's something clearly wrong with you."

"Why?" Zeta injects herself into the conversation while squeezing my hand. "Because he has enough self-respect to avoid sleeping with skanks like you?"

"Who da fuck are you to look down your nose at me?" she barks. "And weren't you the one who said you'd had more cock than hot dinners."

Zeta rolls her eyes. "If you're going to throw shade at someone, at least remember to do it correctly."

"Interesting," Valeria says, yanking Camila back. "You meant what you said literally." A sly smile creeps over her face, and then she cracks up laughing. "Oh, this is priceless. You're a virgin too?"

I'm tempted to look at Zeta, to see her reaction, to know if it's true, but I don't want to give Valeria the satisfaction of knowing she's right, on both counts, so I keep my gaze trained on the fiery bitch in front of me.

"Lopez is sure gonna love that," Sam pipes up, earning her a vicious look from Valeria.

"No one is breathing a word to Lopez." She shoves Sam. "Say anything to him and I'll fucking slit your throat in your sleep."

Sam pales, smiling weakly. "I was only kidding."

"Watch it." Valeria slants her a threatening look, and Sam meekly nods. When Valeria turns back around to us, that smug look is transparent on her face again. "I don't give a fuck what you two are doing or pretending you're doing. Just keep that shit to yourself, and I won't tell him either."

"Deal," Zeta answers before I can. "Now fuck off and leave us alone."

Valeria flips her the bird before walking in the direction of the sleeping pods. Watson leers at Valeria, openly groping her ass as he walks the girls back to their cells.

Tension is thick in the air as Zeta and I stand silently on the spot, both of us struggling to find something to say. "Is it true?" she asks in a hushed tone a few beats later. I inwardly curse Valeria for bringing the subject up. When I don't instantly reply, Zeta twists around so she's in front of me. Our hands are still interlocked, and if I could glue her palm to mine, to keep her skin attached to mine, I'd do it in a heartbeat. She peers up at me through hooded eyes, a shy smile on her face. "I'm a judgment-free zone, and I won't think any less of you if you are or aren't."

"I've never had sex," I blurt as the words burst free.

"Neither have I," she admits with a wider smile.

"You haven't?" I arch a brow. "I presumed you were beating guys off left and right."

She giggles, her tinkling laughter filling the empty space. "Let's not exaggerate my charms. Guys have hit on me, but it's not like it's a daily occurrence."

"Why the hell not? What's wrong with the guys in Garden Grove? Are they fucking blind, or their balls haven't dropped yet?"

She laughs harder. "Oh, their balls have most definitely dropped. The guys in my school are complete horndogs, and they have sex on the brain twenty-four seven."

"Then how did you manage to avoid caving?"

"It's quite simple. I don't want to be a notch on some douche's bedpost or give it up in a sweaty drunken encounter at a party or a grope fest under the bleachers. I want my first time to be special. To be with someone I care about. I don't want it to just be a physical encounter because then I'm no better than—" She abruptly cuts off, but I think I know what she was going to say.

No better than my mom.

I have a feeling Zeta's mom had plenty in common with mine. The thought makes me unbearably sad, and I wish I had a time machine so I could go back and erase both our histories, forging another way for us to meet.

"That only makes me respect you even more," I say, letting her know I'm not going to pry. If she wants to talk about it, she knows I'm always here to listen. "And it pretty much matches how I feel." If I wasn't incarcerated in here, I'm sure I'd have given it up a long time ago, and despite how fucking horny I am, all the damn time, I have zero interest in a rushed, fleeting moment with the threat of discovery looming over us.

I almost caved, last year, when this student intern working with Dr. Blaufeld came on to me after a session, suggesting we take a detour into the laundry room on our way back to the pods. I only turned her down because I'm afraid once I get a taste for sex I won't be able to stop, and I'd rather choke on my own cock than fuck any of the girls in here.

At least, that's how I used to feel.

With Zeta here now, it's completely different.

Now, I want to have sex. With her. But I still won't.

Because if I'm ever lucky enough to share that experience with her, it sure as hell won't be a sweaty, rushed fuck behind the guards' backs.

No, if that's ever in the cards for us, it will be outside of this place.

Somewhere incredible so I can give us both a memory we can cherish forever.

6

ZETA

I turn over in the bed, my body covered in a light sheen of sweat, my sleep top and shorts sticking to my skin like adhesive. A ticklish sensation brushes up my leg, and my body spasms, almost dragging me completely from sleep. I bury my head in the pillow, my eyelids heavy with exhaustion. The sensation on my leg intensifies, creeping higher and higher, and a familiar pressure settles on my chest. Adrenaline courses through my body, and my breathing becomes labored. Behind my closed eyes, I'm slowly adjusting to reality. The pressure on my leg solidifies when it reaches my thigh, and I freeze as tendrils of fear rip up and down my spine. My heart is thumping behind my chest, and then I'm aware of the heat on my stomach and I—

Agghhh!!

I bolt upright, crying out as I scramble up the bed, flattening my back against the wall, my gaze darting wildly around the room.

Slowly, my vision clears, my small cell coming into focus, and my panic starts to subside. A loud sob breaks free of my chest and I'm gasping for air. Tears stream down my face as I scan the gray block walls, cold concrete floor, stainless-steel toilet with no seat, and small sink. The only other fixture in the room is a small bedside table where I store my clothes and the few toiletries I'm permitted. It's bolted to the floor in the windowless room. Fixating on my surroundings always helps ground me after a nightmare. Gradually, my breathing recalibrates, and I push knotted clumps of hair back off my face. Sweat glistens on my skin as I stand on wobbly legs.

It was only a nightmare, I tell myself repeatedly, as I strip off my damp clothes, splashing water over my overheated skin. Redressing in my spare bra and underwear—the only spare clothing I have—I climb back under the covers, shivering in spite of the humidity in the room.

The nightmares have been frequent and brutal since everything went down, but I haven't had any for a week, and I thought they were passing, but I guess I was wrong. This was the worst one yet. Squeezing my eyes closed, I immediately see his face. I cry out again, loud, anguished sobs birthed straight from my soul. Blinking my eyes open, I curl into a fetal position as more tears sneak from my eyes.

"Shut the fuck up, bitch!" Camila—I think—shouts, banging on the wall from the cell she shares with Sofia. "Some of us are trying to sleep."

I block her out, forcing my eyes to remain open as I consciously avoid sleep. Even though I suspect Dr. Reynolds will quiz me about it at my therapy session later, I'd rather endure her prying questions over another one of those nightmares.

I can hardly keep my eyes open at breakfast, and my mouth is open in a perpetual yawn. "You look like shit," Luc says, plopping down on the chair beside me.

Ryder swats the back of his head. "There are much nicer ways of saying that."

"Like what?" he questions over a mouthful of rubbery scrambled eggs, looking perplexed.

Ryder leans across the table, fighting a smile. "You look tired today, Zeta. Did you have trouble sleeping?"

I burst out laughing, can't help it, and he grins, offering me a cheeky wink before shoveling a forkful of eggs into his beautiful mouth. "You were definitely right, Luc," I say, smiling at my only other friend. "Ryder's got good game."

"All joking aside," Ryder says, a split second later, "are you okay?" His face oozes concern, and warmth floods my chest cavity. It's been so long since anyone cared that I'd forgotten how amazing it feels to know you're not alone.

I want to tell him but not here. Not in front of Luc and in earshot of the cafeteria. "I'm good. Thanks for asking." I pin him with a look, and he nods, instantly dropping it. It's so strange how in tune we are with one another. It constantly freaks me out but in a good way.

"So, what's up?" Ryder asks me when we're in the library a couple hours later. This has become our "place." We get an assigned half hour in the library daily, during schooltime, and most of our classmates do a snatch and grab leaving us in virtual privacy. Sometimes, a couple of the other boys loiter to read, but they barely pay us any attention. Ryder and I have had some of our best chats in this room.

"It's no biggie," I start, trying to downplay it. "I just have nightmares, and it was a particularly bad one last night. I couldn't go back to sleep."

"Are they random nightmares or the same recurring ones?" He takes my hand, walking us toward the small desks at the back of the room.

I don't think he's noticed, but he's been holding my hand a lot lately. Not that I'm in any way complaining. I love the feel of his big hand engulfing my smaller one, and it never fails to cause a flurry of butterflies in my chest.

"Recurring nightmares," I admit, sinking into the chair with an audible sigh. I slump forward on the desk, laying my head on my outstretched arms.

"Related to previous events in your life?" he quietly asks, leaning toward me and keeping his voice low. I slowly nod. Silence envelops us for a few moments. "I get those type of nightmares too," he whispers.

I'm surprised he admitted that, because he's notoriously cagey anytime anything about our pasts comes up in conversation. I won't lie and say I'm not curious about his past. Specifically, what landed him in here. But he respects my privacy, so I want to show him the same respect. Besides, there's a teeny tiny part of me that worries I'll think differently of him once I know. Which is stupid really, because whatever he's done is in the past, and we all make mistakes. I know he's a decent guy, and that's the only thing that matters. I haven't had a real friend since kindergarten—Mom's rep and my stepdad's "job" made sure of that—and I'm enjoying Ryder's friendship too much to risk it by digging into his past. So, I let sleeping dogs lie, telling myself it's inconsequential anyway.

"How do you handle them?" I stifle another yawn.

"I've worked out some strategies with Dr. Blaufeld. Once I have a routine, and I feel more in control of things, my mind is less troubled." He looks up at the ceiling, and his chest heaves, almost painfully. When he lowers his head and fixes his gaze on me a few minutes later, his torment is laid bare. His willingness to expose his vulnerability to me only makes me appreciate him more. He's trusting me in a way he doesn't trust anyone else. Not even Luc, and those two are close. But what we share transcends that.

"But there isn't really anything I can do to stop them altogether," he quietly adds. "Only manage the outcome in a more controlled way." He rests his head on his arms, mirroring my position, and our faces are so close they are almost touching. We stare at one another with so much left unsaid, but sometimes, words are redundant, and there is more meaning in understanding without anything being verbalized. In this moment, his pain is my pain and vice versa.

We don't need to articulate it. That truth resonates between us as if we had spoken the words out loud.

I can honestly say I have never felt more connected to another living soul than I do to Ryder in this moment.

I'd do anything to alleviate his pain, and I know, unquestionably, that he would do the same for me.

My eyes wander to his lips, and my heart rate kicks up a gear. I wonder what he would do if I leaned over and kissed him. Would he kiss me back or reject me? Sometimes, I think Ryder shares the same intense desire I do—a desire to push us beyond the realm of friendship into something more. Other times, he seems so casual that I'm sure he just sees me as a good friend. And, let's be honest, in a place like this, it's easy to latch onto someone, to indulge *anything* that makes it feel like less of a solitary experience, and it's easy to make that into something it's not.

"Zeta." His whisper drags me out of my head. I realize I've been lost in thought, just staring at his mouth. Thank God, I'm not the type to blush, or my face would probably be scarlet right now.

"What?" My voice sounds all hoarse, like I've developed an instant sore throat.

"Have you ever been kissed?"

I blink profusely, and my lips stretch into a soft smile. "I'm seventeen not seven, Ryder. Of course, I've been kissed."

His brow furrows, his eyes crinkling at the corners. "You mean sixteen, right?"

I shake my head. "No, I mean seventeen. It was my birthday last week."

"What?" He jerks his head up, sitting upright in the chair. "Why the hell didn't you say anything?" He looks profoundly unhappy.

I shrug, straightening up too. "What's the point? It's not like you could make me a cake or take me out to celebrate."

"Your birthday is definitely something to celebrate, and I

… I have a present for you," he sheepishly admits as his shy alter ego makes a reappearance.

I tilt my head to the side. "You do? How?"

His eyes spark to life, and I'm pleased to see a smile forming on his mouth. "I'll show you later, after you're done with your session. You'll be back at your usual time, right?"

"Of course." Ryder is almost regimental about time and routine, and anything out of the ordinary really throws him for a loop, I've noticed. "Where else would I go?" I reassure him.

"What was the nightmare about this time?" Dr. Reynolds asks me during our scheduled therapy session. I swear she was a spy or an interrogator in a previous lifetime. Her ability to manipulate me into telling her stuff I had no intention or desire to disclose is hugely impressive even if it worries me enormously.

Part of me wants to tell her the truth in the hope she might have some insight on my options, but there's a bigger part of me that's still too fearful to open up. With her mad manipulative skills, I feel it's only a matter of time before the inevitable happens.

"It was the same one," I lie. "About that night."

"Talk me through it again."

"I don't want to. It only puts me in a bad mood."

"You need to talk about it. It's not going away until you process all your feelings related to your mother and that night." She stands, rounding the desk and hovering over me. "I know it's not easy to relive these things, but you can't focus on the future until you've dealt with the past."

Pain stabs me in the chest. "It hurts too much to relive it, and I really don't see how it will help. It's not like it can change what happened."

Her facial expression softens, and she walks toward me at a slow pace, grabbing a box of Kleenex from her desk on the way. "Please, sit with me." She motions toward the couch propped against the wall.

Perching on the edge of the couch, she smooths a hand over her tailored, black pencil skirt before patting the empty space beside her. I sit down, keeping reasonable distance between us. "I'm going to be direct, because you need to hear this. You come in here, Zeta, and you play a part. This is our fifth session together, and I have no understanding of who you are. I can't help you if you don't open up to me. Whatever we discuss in this room is confidential, and you can trust me with anything."

"Trust has to be earned. It's not something that can be freely given."

"Have I ever given you any reason to doubt me?" She waits for my reply, but I don't say anything. Fact is, she's been nothing but pleasant to me. The reason this isn't working is all down to me. She sighs. "I'm on your side. I just want to help."

"I can't discuss that night. Not yet. Please don't force me to." I pull my knees into my chest, wrapping my arms around my body to ward off the chills snaking through me.

"I would never force you to do anything you didn't want to do." Her earnest expression goes a long way toward reassuring me. "Let's talk some more about your relationship with your mother. The last time, you told me how sad she was after your father died and how everything changed then. Do you feel comfortable sharing what happened after that?"

I wet my dry lips, nodding. "I was six when my dad was killed in Afghanistan. I remember feeling so sad and wanting my mom to comfort me, but she just sat around in her pajamas all day, crying. Then we had to move, and we relocated to a new town where we knew no one. I was so upset because she took me away from all my friends. I started at a new school, and I hated it because the kids had all grown up together and I was the outsider. They made fun of me because my mom showed up at the school gates in her slippers and PJs, usually drunk and babbling shit no one wanted to listen to. No one wanted to play with me, and I was ostracized. I used to cry myself to sleep every night, praying she would hear me and come comfort me. But she never did. I might as well have been invisible."

"How did that make you feel?"

I shrug, briefly pursing my lips. "Lost. Scared. Lonely. Unlovable. Unloved." The words glide off my tongue without hesitation, because that pain is always with me. Piercing pain presses down on my chest. I might have only been six or seven, but the feelings were so intense I have no trouble recalling them again.

"Did things change when she met your stepfather?"

Every bone in my body turns rigidly still. Bile floods my mouth and my stomach churns violently. "Yes, but not in a good way."

Her eyes penetrate mine, and she holds my gaze as she asks her next question. "In what way did things change after he came into your life?"

I draw a huge breath, carefully composing my words. It'd be so easy to let it all pour out, but I've got to be cautious until I know I can trust her completely. "He was very controlling, and Mom just let him get away with it. Of course, he wasn't like that at the start. They dated, and he romanced her good. At first, things were looking up. She didn't drink so much during the day, and she stopped going out in her sleep clothes. She made an effort to shower and look presentable, and she started paying more attention to the house and to me. But then she moved him in, and gradually, she started changing again."

"How old were you then?"

"I had just turned eleven." I pick at a loose thread on the hem of my polo, fighting the surge of unpleasant memories.

"Is your stepfather the reason your mother turned to prostitution?"

My mom's sordid lifestyle had featured heavily during the court hearing, so she's aware Mom sold her body for money. Gulping over the painful lump in my throat, I nod.

"When did you realize she was sleeping with other men for money?"

"When kids at school started teasing me about it. I'd often come home from school to find strange men leaving the house, and when I asked her, she'd say they were friends of my asshole stepdad. But as I got older, I realized they were men who were paying her for sex."

"How did that make you feel?"

"Ashamed and confused. I tried talking to her about it, and she was horrible to me. Told me I was a naïve little girl who didn't understand. After that, she didn't try to hide what she was doing, and more and more men were hanging around the house. I saw stuff I didn't ever want to see. And it wasn't just sex. They were all abusing drugs and alcohol, and our house became known for wild parties and raging orgies."

"How did that impact you at school?"

I squeeze my eyes shut, trying to ignore the memories swamping my mind. I'm tightening my fists into balls when I find the courage to reopen my eyes and continue unloading. "I was propositioned constantly by boys. They seemed to think it was acceptable to grab and grope me, and I was always fighting them off. But the girls were the worst. They disliked the attention I got, and they bullied me and picked fights all the time. I was constantly in the principal's office for fighting even though I never started a single fight. It was always self-defense."

"Why didn't you tell anyone what was going on?"

"I did. I told the principal, and you know what she did?" I bark out a laugh. "She called my mom and stepdad in for a meeting and made me tell them everything I'd told her. They refuted it all, of course, and told her a bunch of lies regarding *my* unruly behavior and how they were struggling to tame *my* wild ways."

Anger churns in my gut. "The principal swallowed it all and told me to never darken her door with such heinous lies again. It didn't seem to matter that I was top of all my classes, didn't screw any of the boys, and that I never *started* any fights." My breath oozes out in painful spurts as renewed anger fuels the blood flowing in my veins. The system has constantly failed me, so is it any wonder I lied under oath? They would never have believed me even if I'd told the truth.

Anger underscores my words as I tell her how it went down. "The principal had her mind made up that I was the troublemaker, and nothing I said swayed her mind. Mom was furious with me, and she locked me out of the house for a few days, forcing me to sleep in the garden shed. After that, I gave up on adults. What was the point telling the truth when no one ever believed me?"

7

RYDER

Zeta is uncharacteristically quiet when she joins me after her therapy session. I'm guessing it was a grueling one, and I empathize. I've spent hundreds of hours in therapy, and opening up old wounds that continue to fester is never easy.

Dr. Blaufeld is aware of my real history, and he has tried diligently to help me move past my self-loathing and anger, but it's an impossible task. I don't see how I can ever forgive myself for what I orchestrated. And I don't believe I deserve to be forgiven. That's the crux of the matter and the main argument between me and the good doctor. He tells me I need to forgive myself in order to love myself and if I can't love myself, then I will never be able to love someone else.

But he just doesn't get it.

I don't deserve any of that.

I'm not worthy of love, and I shouldn't be entertaining this so-called friendship with Zeta, because we're skating on thin ice, and we both know it's way more than that, and she deserves so much better than me.

I look over at her, and it's clear she's a million miles away. Her cheeks are flushed, her eyes distant, and it's obvious she's not really present. My desire to erase her sadness and eliminate her pain is the main reason I stick to my plan despite the competing desire that says I should let her go and end this before we both get hurt.

"Hey." I gently cup one side of her face, forcing her gaze to mine. Her skin is so soft and smooth under my touch that I struggle to draw my hand away, but I do, because she doesn't like to be touched, and I'm crossing too many boundaries with how often I'm touching her lately. "You want to talk about it, or you want me to help you forget about it?"

She has the saddest expression on her face, and I've never wanted to pull her into my arms and comfort her as much as I do right now. "Help me forget?" she whispers, scooting a little closer to my side.

Despite my better judgment, I lean down and press a soft kiss to the top of her head. Her hair smells like the standard issue shampoo, but on her, the sickly strawberry scent smells pleasant, not nauseating. She doesn't push me away, and I continue to rest my chin on her head, with her pressed up beside me, enjoying the close human contact, until I notice Lopez and Torres staring at us. Reluctantly, I pull away, sliding my guitar over my shoulder, and I start plucking the strings, limbering up.

"I wrote this for you," I tell her quietly. "Happy birthday, Zeta."

I keep my eyes pinned on hers as I play her the song. I don't sing to her, except in my head, because the words are too personal, and they'll give my feelings away. Plus, if I start singing, I'll garner the attention of the room, and I don't want anyone listening to this but her. By now, everyone is used to me sitting in the far corner, strumming away, and most of them have learned to tune me out. Young regularly joins us, and a couple of the other guys sometimes hang out with us, but mostly, we're left to our own devices which suits me perfectly.

I pour my heart and soul into the music, humming along

softly, never taking my eyes from hers. So many emotions flit across her face as she dutifully listens. Her eyes seem sunnier, and my heart soars as her mood elevates. I have her full attention and it's a hugely private moment despite our surroundings. She peers deep into my eyes, and I drown in the exquisite depths of her beautiful brown eyes, that reddish-amber hue flaring brightly as we cocoon ourselves in a solitary bubble where nothing or no one else exists.

I imagine we're sitting cross-legged on an empty beach as I play. Waves are lapping the shore behind us, and the sound is the perfect accompaniment to my guitar. She's wearing a casual white sundress that billows in the gentle breeze. She's wearing no makeup and her hair is long and loose, like it is now, blowing softly across her exuberant face. Sun glints off her face highlighting her natural beauty and I sing my heart out, not worried in that imaginary setting about anyone else hearing. When I'm done, she throws herself at me, wrapping her arms around my neck as she brings her lips down onto mine. Her mouth is soft and warm against mine and I wind my fingers through her hair, pulling her face even closer, desperate to get as close to her as possible.

"It's beautiful." Zeta's awe-struck voice drags me kicking and screaming out of my daydream. Disappointment slams into me and I could cry at the loss of that imaginary kiss.

Fuck. I've got it bad.

Rapidly composing my features, before she guesses where my head went to, and runs away screaming from the crazy dude daydreaming of serenading her on the beach, I drape my arms on top of my Fender and smile. "Did you genuinely like it?"

"Like it?" Her eyebrows climb to her hairline. "I absolutely loved it. I can't believe you wrote that for me. Thank you so much. It's the best birthday present anyone's ever given me."

"While that makes me unbelievably happy, I'm seriously hoping that's not true."

A look of abject sorrow sweeps over her face, and I know she's telling the truth. Fuck. I hate that her background seems as lacking as mine. "I've got another present for you," I blurt, totally improvising. I just want to put a smile back on her face.

"You do?"

Removing my guitar, I rest it carefully beside the wall and tentatively open my arms. My heart is somersaulting in my chest, and my stomach roils with nerves. The look on her face is priceless. She looks half mesmerized, half terrified, and I can relate. "Everyone deserves a hug on their birthday. Come here." She looks anxiously at me, biting down on her lower lip in a totally sexy way. "I don't bite, Zeta. It's a hug. That's all."

Her chest inflates, and an exuberant smile creeps over her lips as she scoots over, softly laying her head on my chest. My arms go around her as if it's the most natural thing in the world. When her hands slip around my waist, encircling my back, a little sigh of contentment escapes my mouth before I can stop it. I rest my chin on top of her head, savoring the warmth of her body flush against mine.

If there were awards for best hugger, Zeta would win, hands down. Her hold on me is firm yet tender, and as she slowly runs her hand up and down my spine, I allow myself to fall.

My heart is ricocheting around my chest like it's dancing a tango. With her ear pressed so close, I'm sure she's aware of every overactive beat, but I don't care. She's finally in my arms, and it's everything I've been dreaming about.

"Aw, isn't this cute." Valeria's sneering comment brings me harshly back down to Earth. Lopez, Torres, Sam, Camila, and Sofia stand over us, and I fucking hate this damn place and the complete lack of privacy. Zeta slowly eases off me, and I want to ram my fist into Lopez's face and wipe that smug, condescending look from it. Zeta climbs to her feet, and I follow suit. "Puppy love at its finest," Valeria adds in a derogatory tone.

"Don't you have places to be and people to screw," Zeta retorts.

Lopez chuckles. "You've got some fire in your belly, baby doll."

"Do. Not. Call me that." Zeta glares at him. "I'm not your baby or your baby doll or your anything."

His eyes move slowly over her body, and my hands ball up at my sides. A familiar surge of anger creeps up on me, and I know I won't be able to keep it in check if that douche keeps leering at my girl.

"How 'bout you and me take this someplace else, and I'll give you a birthday present you'll never forget." Thrusting his hips forward, Lopez grabs hold of his crotch, making sure the offer is crystal clear. Zeta glances up at me, and I tell her with my eyes that it wasn't me. I would never tell that asshole anything about her.

"Are you for fucking real right now?" Valeria fumes, slamming her hands into Lopez's chest.

"Get lost, V," Lopez says, not taking his eyes off Zeta. "I never promised you exclusivity."

A cunning gleam flickers in Valeria's eye as she spins around, facing me. Before I've had the chance to consider her next move, she's on top of me, her ugly mouth slanting against mine while she presses her tits into my chest.

I push her off me the same time Zeta grabs hold of the back of her polo shirt. Losing her balance, Valeria's arms flail about as she falls back, taking Zeta with her. Zeta's head slams into the ground with an audible thud as she lands first with Valeria sprawled on top of her.

Horror washes over me like a bucket of cold water. "Get the fuck off her!" I roar, grabbing Valeria by the wrists and pulling her off Zeta. I drop to my knees beside her, but she's unconscious, and an icy hand has a vise grip on my heart.

"Zeta." I place my hands on her cheeks, leaning down close to her ear. "Zeta, baby, can you hear me?"

Lopez crouches over her from behind. "Shit, dude, is she okay?"

"What the fuck does it look like!" I yell. "This is all your fucking fault. Just leave her the fuck alone!"

"Step aside." Powell's voice is commanding, and the assembled crowd parts, letting her and Price through. Powell kneels beside me, pressing her finger to Zeta's neck before placing her palm over her forehead. "Get hold of Carina. Tell her to bring her first aid kit," she instructs Price. He walks off with his mouth pressed to his walkie-talkie, and a few minutes later, the nurse comes rushing into the room.

"I need some space," she says, pointedly looking at me. Price and Watson have already cleared the room, escorting everyone else back to the pods, where they're on lockdown, but I begged Powell to let me stay, and surprisingly, none of them argued with me.

"Ryder. Let Carina check her out." Powell pulls me to my feet, pushing me back a little as I watch the nurse check Zeta's vitals.

"She might have a concussion. I'd like to keep her in the infirmary overnight so I can watch over her."

"Should we organize an ambulance?" Powell asks, causing shards of terror to run riot inside me.

Carina shakes her head. "I don't think it's necessary, but if anything changes, I'll let you know."

I'm forced to watch as guards slide Zeta onto a stretcher and carry her out of the room. I begged Powell to let me sit with her, but there's only so many times she can bend the rules for me. She's adamant that I need to return to my cell, but she promises to stop by later to update me on Zeta's condition.

Nighttime has fallen, and there's still no word. I'm going out of my mind with worry. Grabbing clumps of my hair, I pace back and forth across the tiny cell, grateful we're not at full capacity right now and that I have my own space. I've had to share a cell countless times in the past, and it's not always a pleasant experience. Sometimes, having company is nice, provided the guy isn't a total asshole, but other times, like now, I'm glad there's no one else in this room to witness me falling apart.

This is all my fault. All I do is hurt people. If Zeta wasn't my best friend, and the girl I'm crazy about, Lopez's interest in her would've faded by now. But he continues to sleaze over her to mess with my head. What happened this evening would never have happened if Zeta was blending into the shadows like she'd planned all along.

The image of her lying on that floor, her face pale, eyes closed, body unmoving, plays repeatedly in my head, fueling my self-hatred, anger, and frustration.

I lash out, needing to feel physical pain, welcoming the raw, throbbing ache as I pound my fists into the concrete wall, ripping my knuckles, my skin bleeding. I pummel the wall, imagining it's Lopez's face, until I'm breathless and spent, my limbs exhausted, my body sweaty and limp as I fall to the floor, consumed in a blanket of remorse.

And, as I scream out in my sleep, assaulted by images I've managed to avoid these last few weeks, I know this is my punishment for daring to hope.

8

ZETA

My head still hurts like a bitch, and I have an obvious raised lump at the back of my skull, but I'm lucky it's only a mild concussion and not anything worse. Guess I should be grateful I've a hard head. Carina, the nurse, summoned a doctor to the facility to ensure I didn't need hospitalization. He prescribed strong pain meds and two days of bed rest, so today is the first day I'm returning to a normal routine.

I'm well used to my own company, and I spent most of the time sleeping or reading in bed, but I have little concept of time in here, and the two days felt more like two weeks. I've really missed Ryder, and I'm so looking forward to seeing him as I make my way over to our usual table in the cafeteria.

I'm the first one here, so I flop into a chair, keeping my head down as I eat my breakfast. "You're alive!" Luc quips, pulling out the chair across from me and sitting down. "Are you feeling okay?" he adds more solemnly.

"I've a killer headache, but I'm fine otherwise." I look up at the counter and over my shoulder. "Where's Ryder?"

Luc's Adam's apple bobs in his throat and he squirms in his seat. "He, ah, he's not sitting with us today."

A bad feeling sweeps over me and my stomach dips to my toes. "Why not?" Is he mad I tried to yank Valeria off him? I'm pretty sure he wasn't happy about her kissing him although, in the moment, I just reacted on instinct, rage spurring me on. The image of her kissing him made my blood boil, and I didn't like to think of her taking advantage of him like that either. But maybe I read it wrong? No. No, I didn't read it wrong. I know Ryder doesn't like her and that he'd never willingly kiss her.

"Because he's an idiot," Luc replies, shooting me a sympathetic smile.

Just then, I spot Ryder's messy blond head over the far side of the room. My appetite vanishes as hurt and anger spear me on the inside. He's back at the table with Lopez, Valeria, and their crew, looking like he never left. "He chose them over me?" I'm unable to keep the note of betrayal from my voice.

"He thinks he's protecting you by staying away. Like I said, he's an idiot." Luc reaches across the table, squeezing my hand.

"I don't understand."

"I don't really either, Zeta. Ryder's deep, you know?" His nose scrunches up. "And that's as much as he told me."

"Why are you here?" I ask, my tone harsher than it should be. Luc isn't the one I'm mad at. He's just the one caught in the firing line.

"Because I'm your friend."

"You're *his* friend, and you should go sit with him. I don't need you. And I don't need *him*," I hiss, drilling my eyes into his sad ones. I don't mean it, but it's the anger speaking, and pushing him away before he chooses to leave will hurt less in the end.

I was foolish to think things would be different in here. Once a loner, always a loner. I know how to deal with that because I've had plenty of practice.

But this?

This cold, cruel rejection is something I'm not equipped to deal with, especially with the pounding pain pummeling my skull.

"I'm not going anywhere," Luc stubbornly proclaims, picking up his plastic fork and pinning me with a determined look. "I don't care if you want that or not. I'm staying right here."

Over the course of the next week, Luc is like a faithful little puppy, and I both love and hate him for it. I don't want him falling out with Ryder on my account, but that's exactly what's happened. After my initial anger faded, I tried to speak to Ryder the next day, but he brushed me aside, telling me he didn't want to hang with me anymore. Luc was furious with him, and they almost came to blows.

I wish now that I'd never befriended Ryder, because having his friendship and then losing it is ten million times worse than never having known it at all. My life is gray and monotone without his larger-than-life presence in it.

Boredom is a real problem, because I've got so much spare time on my hands, and I hate how my mind wanders when I'm not occupied or distracted. I've stopped going to the common room in my free time because it hurts too much to see him in the corner by himself, playing his guitar and purposely ignoring my gaze.

Valeria sends smug smiles my direction any chance she gets, and it takes enormous willpower not to fly at her in retaliation. But I keep my head down and withdraw into myself, like I should have done from day one.

Luc still sits with me in the cafeteria despite the nonexistent dialogue between us. I admire his loyalty and wish I could tell him how much I appreciate it, but I just want him to patch things up with Ryder and leave me to lick my wounds by myself.

I'm feeling so many different things, and I return to my usual form of venting. Emotion pours out of me in the form of words, and I'm furiously scribbling lyrics into my notebook any chance I get. It's always been one of my coping mechanisms. Anytime I needed to retreat from the real world, I buried myself in music, and I'd write song after song after song, my agony bleeding onto the pages. I've written hundreds of songs over the years, but I've no idea what happened to my notebooks. Whether they're still back at the house with him, whether they were confiscated as evidence, or whether he threw them out along with the rest of my stuff. But at the rate I'm going, I'll have them replaced in no time.

The song Ryder wrote for me plays in a continuous loop in my brain, and I've now written lyrics to it. At night, when I miss him the most, I lull myself to sleep with those words reverberating in my subconscious.

My nightmares are a nightly occurrence again, and I don't get more than a few hours' sleep before I'm jolted awake crying and screaming. I know I'm spiraling into a dark place, and I'm not sure I have the resilience to fight it this time.

"You look exhausted," Dr. Reynolds says as I walk into the room for our weekly session.

"Hello to you too," I deadpan, collapsing onto the couch with a sigh.

"How much sleep are you getting at night?" she asks, pulling open a file on her desk.

"About three or four hours," I truthfully admit, too fucking tired to lie.

"You can't function on that little sleep, Zeta. You're dead on your feet."

I know what's coming next, and I prepare myself for it.

"And the only way you're going to get a handle on your nightmares is if you discuss what happened that night."

"No." I cross my arms over my chest, jutting my lips out in a pout.

"What is it you're so afraid of?" She leans forward on her

elbows. "I've read the court transcripts. I know what happened—"

"So why do you need me to say it?!"

"Because I want to hear it from you. I want to understand exactly how it happened."

"I was arguing with my mom because she was a slut who paraded a line of foul-mouthed assholes through our house every fucking minute of the day and night, and I was so sick of it! I just wanted it to stop!"

"So you stabbed her with intent? To make her stop?"

"Yes!" I lie, throwing my hands into the air.

She clasps her hands in front of her. "I don't believe you. I know there's more to it than that."

"Believe what you want," I snap, standing. "I'm done for today. I want to return to my cell."

I SOB into my pillow that night, and it feels as if there's an endless pool of tears growing inside me that will never be exhausted. My feelings when it comes to Mom are so conflicted. I hated her, but I loved her, and I hated that I loved her.

She wasn't always a bad mom.

When I was younger, when my daddy was still alive, she used to adore me, and I was as happy as little girls should be. It all changed after Daddy was killed in action. I know now she was depressed and grieving, but I didn't understand that as a kid. It felt like abandonment. And after she met my jerk of a stepfather, she completely changed.

I can see now how it's all his fault.

He preyed on a vulnerable woman.

Got her addicted to drugs and started pimping her out.

I hated Mom for being so weak, and I never had a kind

word for her, but she was too heartbroken to fight for herself or me. I hate that she died thinking I thought the worst of her.

I can't take any of it back now, and I wish I could. Because she deserved my love and my understanding. My support. Maybe if I'd taken the time to look behind my hurt and my anger, I'd have seen the truth.

She's a victim as much as I am.

And she paid the ultimate price with her life.

I vented and raged at the wrong person.

My stepfather is the one who deserves all my anger. He ruined my mom's life, and now I'm letting him ruin mine.

I want to make this right.

For Mom and for me.

But I'm terrified that in trying to make it right I may only make it a thousand times worse.

9

RYDER

I t's been one month since I last spoke to Zeta, and it's feels like a lifetime. To say I'm missing her is a complete fucking understatement. I've never known loss quite like this. Every day, I'm tempted to throw caution to the wind. To say the hell with it and beg for her forgiveness. But then I remember her ashen face on the floor, and I'm reminded of why I'm doing this.

Associating with me will only get her hurt. This way, I won't have the chance to ruin her life, and I can keep both Lopez and Valeria off her back. It hasn't been easy, and the lies I've told have stuck in my throat as I'm saying them, but if it keeps her safe, then I'll repeat them as often as I need to.

Doesn't mean I don't regret it or wish things were different because I do.

"Still can't believe she's got the clap," Lopez mutters, looking forlorn, as he watches Zeta jog around the yard.

"Tell me about it. It sucks," I agree, keeping the lie alive.

"At least you found out before she gave it to you," Valeria says, cutting into our conversation. "And if you're lonely, sugar, I can help take the ache away." She runs her hand up my chest, and I puke a little in my mouth.

Lopez glowers at her, snatching her hand away from me. "Like hell you will." He slaps her butt. "This ass is mine." He grabs her crotch. "This pussy is mine."

He seems to have forgotten Officer Watson in his little assessment. He made a deal with him last year that is still in play. If Watson leaves the laundry room unlocked and distracts the other guards while Lopez and Valeria are fucking in there, then he gets a ride or a blowjob for his efforts.

Valeria swats Lopez away. "You were the one who said we weren't exclusive."

Lopez hauls her into his chest. "That only applies to me. You're not allowed to fuck around."

He's a fucking dog, but I've got to hand it to him—he sure knows how to wind her up.

She wriggles against his chest, and steam is practically billowing out of her ears as she tries to break free of his hold. "You fucking asshole. I'm done with this. Done with you."

"You'll be done when I say you're done." Popping the button on her shorts, he slides his hand into her panties, and thirty seconds later, she's panting and squirming against him. I look away, not wanting to witness him fingering the fuck out of her in broad daylight.

He's lucky he has Watson on his side, or he'd never get away with half the shit he pulls. The moans and cries coming out of her mouth sour my stomach, and I wish I could walk away. "And, if I want to fuck other girls, I'll fuck other girls," he adds, a couple minutes later, plonking his butt down on the bench beside me as Valeria cries out in a fit of rage.

Her heavy breathing sputters out, and it's clear he didn't let her finish as a form of punishment for daring to challenge him. She stands in front of him like a time bomb ready to explode. "I fucking despise you. Go screw the disease-ridden bitch, and see if I care." She storms off, dragging the other girls with her, as Lopez chuckles.

"If you're no longer—" Torres doesn't get to say any more than that.

"No!" Lopez snarls. "V's off-limits."

"Ah, come on, man. That's hardly fair," Kelly cuts in, like the brainless dimwit he is. "Pussy's in limited supply around here. If you don't want to fuck her anymore at least let one of us."

"Are you totally fucking brain-dead?" Lopez sneers, rising to his feet.

I stand, ready to intervene when some innate sense drags my gaze to the far end of the yard, just in time to watch Valeria kick her leg out as Zeta runs past. Zeta trips over, falling face-first toward the ground. I'm already running before my legs have registered the movement. I watch, aghast, as Zeta faceplants the asphalt with nothing to cushion her fall.

Powell blows her whistle, and I spot her running toward Zeta out of the corner of my eye. I reach her first though. She's curled onto her side on the ground, whimpering and rocking gently as she cradles her face in her hands. Blood trickles through the gaps in her fingers, causing my heart to stutter.

"Zeta." I drop to my knees as déjà vu hits me hard. "Let me see." I place my hand over one of hers, gently unfurling her fingers.

"Get away from me," she cries.

"Let me through, Ryder," Powell demands, crouching down beside me.

Reluctantly, I step aside. Powell helps her sit up, and my stomach twists into knots when I see the state of Zeta's face. Blood pumps out of her nose, and it's clearly swollen—it might even be broken. Cuts and scrapes cover her beautiful face, and blood drips down her chin, soaking her white polo top.

"Oh, dear. Look what a mess you made of your pretty face," Valeria taunts.

I'm all up in her face before she notices. "Shut your mouth, you stupid bitch!"

"Ryder!" Powell sends me a cautionary look as she helps Zeta to stand. "Stand down."

"It was *her* fault." I jab my finger into Valeria's chest. "She deliberately tripped Zeta up."

"It was an accident, jerk face," Valeria spits, keeping up the pretense.

"Don't make it any worse for yourself, girl." Powell eyeballs her. "I saw the whole thing go down."

Price arrives then, grabbing hold of Valeria's elbow. "Time for a little solitary confinement."

A satisfied smile spreads over her mouth. "It was worth it," she sneers before being led away.

"Let me help," I say, returning my attention to Zeta. She has one arm slung around Powell's shoulders, and she's hobbling, pain evident in her grimace. Both her knees and her shins are cut, blood seeping down her legs.

"Don't touch me." Her eyes flash with hurt. "We're not friends anymore, and I don't need or want your help. You've done more than enough."

I deserve that. I truly do. But it still cuts like a bitch.

"Fuck, her face is seriously messed up," Lopez says, appearing at my side.

"Shut the fuck up," Luc says before I've had the chance to. "This is all your fault for riling Valeria up."

"Da fuck you say to me, boy?" Lopez whirls on him, but I grab Young, shoving him behind me as I act as a barrier between him and the dickhead. Powell escorts Zeta across the yard, and she's limping the whole time.

I eyeball Lopez, working overtime trying to contain my rage. "He may be out of line, but he's not mistaken." I grind my teeth hard, and my jaw clenches painfully. "Valeria has it in for Zeta, and we all know it's because you want in her pants. You need to fix this."

"How the fuck is this my problem?"

"It will be your problem if she goes near Zeta again because I won't hold back next time."

Lopez leans against the fence, scrubbing a hand over his jaw. "I'll get her to play nice," he says after a few beats. "But it'll cost you."

"Name your price. It's yours."

A cunning look slides over his features. Stepping up to me, he grins. "The Fender, man." All the blood drains from my face. "Give me your guitar, and I swear your girl won't have any more problems with V."

"You can't even play," I murmur, blood thrumming in my ears.

"I want to learn. How hard can it be? If you taught yourself how to play, it'll be a cakewalk," he arrogantly adds.

"Ryder, no." Luc tugs on my elbow. "Zeta wouldn't want you to do that."

"Butt out, Young." I shove his hand off. Pinning dark eyes on Lopez, I force my frustration aside as I enter into negotiations. "Both you and Valeria will leave her alone. No more leering, no more sleazy comments, and you keep your hands to yourself. Valeria will refrain from even looking sideways at Zeta. No taunting, no bullying, no physical assaults." Lopez nods, and I don't trust the sly smile playing on his lips. "For as long as she's in here." I tack on the end, because I'm not always going to be around.

"I feel like I'd be justified in asking for your firstborn too." Lopez smirks. "Anything else, or we have a deal?" He spits on his hand and holds it out to me.

"Valeria quits hitting on me."

Lopez laughs but his jaw is tense as he nods his agreement.

I spit on my palm and we shake on it.

I've just made a deal with the devil and I have a feeling it's going to come back and bite me in a big way.

"WHY THE HELL does Lopez have your guitar?" Zeta demands, the following day, standing over me as I face the TV in the common room, attempting to pretend that my heart isn't destroyed inside my chest listening to that asshole butchering my baby as he tries to play.

"Never mind that. How badly are you hurt?" I inquire.

I was happy to see her walking into school this morning, grateful she hadn't broken any bones in the nasty fall, but that happiness was short-lived when I took one look at her face. Her nose is swollen to twice its size, and her skin is littered with bruises and cuts. Her lips are cracked and dried, and there's a small cut on her bottom lip which looks sore. Scabs and bruising cover her knees and lower legs too.

Rage like I haven't felt in years swelled up inside me, and I sat on my hands to resist the urge to hit something or someone.

"I ache all over, and Frankenstein's bride was staring out of the mirror at me this morning, but I'll live. Now stop deflecting, and answer my question," she demands.

"No."

"No?" She plants her hands on her slim hips.

"No." I elongate the word for extra effect, arching a brow. "We're not friends anymore, remember?"

"You decided that. Not me."

"You didn't seem unhappy about that yesterday."

"Because I was fucking hurting! And I'm not just talking about my obvious injuries."

The mournful look on her face causes me actual physical pain.

I want to take it all back.

To fess up and tell her the truth, but that little voice in my ear reminds me of how destructive I am, of how I always mess things up, and it renews my resolve.

I harden my heart, silently begging her forgiveness as I twist my lips into a sneer. "Whatever. Like I care."

Her nostrils flare, and her eyes darken as she glares at me. "I can't believe I ever fell for the nice-guy act. You're just like every other asshole I've ever known. Only interested in one thing, but you were just cleverer about it." Her words cut a line straight through my heart, but I school my features into a disinterested expression, ensuring she has no clue how much it kills me to hear her proclaim what we shared as fake when it's the most real thing I've ever known. "I don't ever want to speak to you again."

She storms off, and I watch her leave with a lump of stone in my chest in place of where my heart should be.

"Man, you're totally fucking up," Young supplies, shaking his head. "She's going to figure it out, and she's gonna be so mad at you."

"Not now," I bark, rubbing a tense spot between my brows. "You know why I did it, and I have no regrets. She might hate me, but at least she's protected."

"I hope you're right, dude, and that it's worth it."

The next few weeks are some of the worst of my life. Without Zeta and my Fender, I've lost the will to live.

Flashbacks and nightmares assault me on an almost daily basis, and I'm sinking back into dangerous territory. It's a timely reminder there's no long-term solution to my problems. This is something I will live with for the rest of my life, and every time something traumatic or upsetting happens in my life, I risk falling into that black hole again.

Dr. Blaufeld has noticed, and when I wouldn't open up, he went digging on his own. Powell clearly tattled about the guitar and Zeta, but I keep my lips sealed as he attempts to coax me into talking. There's no way I'm telling him what went down because blabbing to authority figures never ends well. I know better.

Zeta's face is almost fully healed, and Lopez has remained

true to his word, ensuring she's left alone, so that provides me with some comfort at times when Zeta glares at me like she hates me most in the world.

To have had a shot with the girl of my dreams ripped from me in such a cruel way is also a timely reminder.

That I don't deserve happiness.

That I will always be lonely and alone.

That I'm stupid to harbor any hope because I already know what fate has in store for me.

But none of that could prepare me for what I learn next.

Zeta's been shooting daggers in my direction for weeks, which is how I notice the difference almost immediately. She's gone from glaring at me any chance she gets to avoiding looking at me, at all costs. Both reactions hurt, but at least with the former, I still got to look at her beautiful face. Now, she hangs her head, avoids the common room like the plague, and flees the library with the first book her hand lands on before I've had time to even glance in her direction.

The second strange instance occurs a few days later when Lopez hands my guitar back to me. "Why?" I ask, suspicion underscoring my tone.

"Relax, dude." He clamps a hand down on my shoulder. "I won't renege on the deal. I'm just bored with it. I know how much you love it, man, so have at it. It's yours. Knock yourself out."

I'm suspicious as fuck of his motives, but I've missed my baby too much to challenge it, so I head to my corner and play for hours until my fingers bleed and my free time is up.

That night, for the first night in months, I sleep without interruption.

I'm in a fucking brilliant mood the next day after school, because my heart is lighter now I've got my guitar back; plus, I've decided to come clean to Zeta. I only have a few more months left in here, and I don't want to waste it deliberately ignoring her when I crave her company so much. The threat posed by Lopez and Valeria has passed, and there's no imped-iment to our friendship.

Except for the truth.

I expect she'll be mad, but once she's calmed down, she'll realize I did it all, said it all, to keep her safe.

I'm planning on approaching her in the common room after our physical activity hour has ended. I'm whistling, with my hands shoved into my pockets, as I stroll across the yard toward the guys. The hot August sun is gloriously warm on my arms, and I'm feeling on top of the world. I'm nervous about Zeta's reaction, but I trust in our bond, and I know we can reclaim what we had. That fact, and the fact I can almost taste freedom, has buoyed my spirits in a way I haven't felt in ages.

Lopez, Torres, and Kelly are in a huddle, talking and laughing as I approach. Kelly reaches over, slapping Lopez on the back. "You the man, bruh."

The second they see me, they stop talking, trading knowing glances at one another. "Sup?" I ask with a frown.

"Nothing, dude." Lopez's grin is smug in the extreme, and goose bumps sprout on my arms.

"What were you talking about?" Lopez purses his lips, but he's struggling to contain his smile. Torres and Kelly exchange amused grins. "What the fuck is it?" I snap, my patience stretched thin.

Kelly coughs, shooting Lopez a fake apologetic smile. "Did you seriously think he'd just hand back your Fender for nothing?"

"What the hell are you saying?" A line of sweat coasts down my spine, and I just know I'm not going to like this.

"Zeta must really have a thing for you." Kelly smirks. Bile swims up my throat, and my stomach twists into painful knots, as my mind goes somewhere I'd rather it didn't.

"Or she has a thing for Lopez's cock," Torres says, snickering.

All the blood leaches from my face. "What the fuck did you do?" I push my face into Lopez's, and a vein throbs in my neck as fury trundles through my veins, pumping me full of testosterone.

"Dude, chill." He holds up his palms. "It was all her idea, so if you want to point the finger of blame, you can point it at her."

"*What* was her idea?" I shout. I know I'm playing into his hands, but I'm beyond the point of caring. I just need to know.

"She said she'd blow me if I gave you back your guitar."

I stagger back as if he's just sucker-punched me. All the air flees my lungs, and pain smashes into my chest, making mincemeat of my heart. "She followed through?" I have no idea how my voice manages to sound so restrained. Not when I want to pound my fist into his conceited face.

"Hells yeah." He rubs a hand over his crotch, and I'm sickened to see the bulge tenting his shorts. "Baby doll sucked me good too, and she swallows like a pro. I would've fucked her, but I don't want to get the clap. Val would cut my cock off if I gave her an STD."

I slam my fist into his face, enormously satisfied when blood spurts from his nose and he stumbles back, falling to the ground, caught completely unawares. Then I jump on him, pummeling his face and his body with blow after blow, easily swatting Torres and Kelly away as they attempt to drag me off him, fueled by an aggression I haven't felt in years. Vaguely, I hear a whistle sounding in the background, but I'm lost to the rage, and I keep at it, hitting him over and over through the red haze coating my eyes.

Someone tackles me to the ground, and I lash out, arms and legs flailing as I shout obscenities at Lopez. "I'll fucking kill you if you ever touch her again! I'll gut you, you mother-fucking asshole! I won't stop until—"

"Ryder!" Powell slaps me hard on the cheek, and the

stinging pain brings me back to the moment. "What the hell is wrong with you?" she asks, shaking her head, a look of disappointment etched on her face. "You're on the home stretch, boy! For your sake, I hope you haven't inflicted any serious injury." Watson hauls me up off the ground, roughly cuffing my hands behind my back.

My eyes lower to the ground, and I suck in a breath as my gaze skims over Lopez. He's out cold although it's hard to tell because both his eyes are swollen shut and blood covers most every inch of skin on his face. His shirt is stained with so much blood you can't tell it's white. Torres and Kelly look at me with a mix of fear and respect in their eyes. The assembled crowd starts to break up, and my head whips sideways, as if pulled by an invisible force.

My eyes lock onto Zeta's, and I read every emotion on her naked face.

But it's too late.

I'm sickened and disgusted at what she's done, and the heated stare I level in her direction conveys all that and more.

A tear trickles out of the corner of her eye as I'm escorted past her in handcuffs, but I'm numb to it. Anger and rage have done a number on my insides, and I'm immune to her baleful eyes and her pleading expression.

Whatever we had is over before it's even begun.

10

ZETA

I have no one to blame for my current predicament but myself, yet it doesn't make things any easier to swallow. I knew it would come back to haunt me, but I still did it. After Luc told me everything Ryder had done to protect me, I was overwhelmed with emotion, and so consumed with love for him, that all I could think about was getting his beloved guitar back. I still can't believe he traded it in exchange for my safety. No one has ever done anything like that for me before and it blew me away.

I spent a couple days wondering how best to approach this, but I had nothing to offer Lopez except my body. There's no way I was giving the douche my virginity, but I knew Ryder had told him I had the clap, so I used that to my advantage, knowing he'd knock my offer to fuck him on the head but ask me to blow him instead.

It's not like I wanted to do it, because I'm nauseated every time I think of it, but it was the only way to get Ryder's Fender back, so I swallowed my pride, and my distaste, and dropped to my knees for him.

I was strangely numb the whole time, successfully blocking out what I was doing, which was the only way I was able to do it. I'd seen Mom do it enough times to know how it needed to be done, but I hate that the memory of that first is forever tarnished for me.

It's definitely not my proudest moment, and despite the fact Lopez went back on his word and blabbed to Ryder, I'd still do it again, because it means Ryder isn't without his guitar, the one thing helping him keep his sanity in here.

Ryder has been placed in solitary for a week. Thankfully, Lopez didn't suffer any broken bones or serious injuries, so Powell says it's unlikely it will affect Ryder's release date, especially when his record is squeaky clean until now. And in one piece of good news, Lopez has been transferred. He won't be coming back here after he's been discharged from the hospital because he's been relocated to the Orange County Central Men's Jail. I felt like throwing a party when I found out.

Valeria is hopping mad and mouthing off any chance she gets. She and her posse take any and every opportunity to push me around, and it's only a matter of time before we come to blows. But I'm expecting it, and I'm on my guard.

When Ryder arrives back at school, he returns to ignoring me. I'm not surprised, but I am disappointed. I had hoped he'd understand why I did it, but he's giving me a wide berth. I allow him a couple of days to calm down, but when he's still avoiding me, I decide it's time to take matters into my own hands.

I corner him in the library, putting myself directly in his path so he'll have no choice but to speak to me. "Ryder, can we talk? Please." I plead with my eyes, willing him to at least look at me.

A muscle pops in his jaw as he lowers his face to mine. Pain glimmers at the back of his eyes. "I have nothing to say to you," he says in a clipped tone.

He moves to go around me, but I place my hand on his arm, stalling him. "I didn't want to do it," I whisper. "But I'm not sorry I did because you have your Fender back, and that's all I wanted."

"You think I wanted it back like that?" he snaps, hurt transforming to anger.

"I know how much that guitar means to you, and I know what you did for me, and I wanted to show you how much I care for you, how much I miss you."

He snorts. "By sucking another guy's cock?" His tone screams disbelief as he shoves my hand away. "You have a really fucking warped way of showing you care."

"Please, Ryder." Tears prick my eyes. "I know I messed up, but can't you find it in your heart to forgive me? I forgave you for all the shit you said about me and all the pain you put me through. Why can't you do the same for me?"

"Because I didn't get down on my knees like a fucking whore!" he barks, loud enough for everyone in the room to hear.

I jerk back as if slapped. The truth of his words rips through me, and I'm devastated as I finally let the thoughts lingering at the back of my mind free.

I'm exactly like my mom, and it's no wonder Ryder has lost respect for me. As I note the look of disgust in his eyes, I know he's never going to forgive me.

I've lost him, and there isn't anything I can do to change that.

I sink into a bottomless pit after that. Luc is an absolute sweetheart, trying his best to remain loyal to both of us, attempting to act as peacemaker, but I tell him to let it go. I don't harbor any grudges against Ryder, and I understand why he can't get past this. Last night, after I woke up from another nightmare, I imagined what it would be like if he'd gone down on Valeria in a deal to keep me safe, and it sickened me to my stomach.

So, I get it. I don't like it, but I get it. I fucked up spectacularly, and now I'm paying the price.

Valeria has made it her mission to torment me every chance she can, and that includes draping herself over Ryder any opportunity she gets. He doesn't encourage her in any way, and he's constantly rejecting her advances, but it still kills me, and she knows it, so she continues to do it. According to Luc, she's fucking Kelly and Wright now that Lopez is gone, and she's still bouncing up and down on Watson's cock too, and while I hope she'll get bored of heckling me soon, I'm not naïve enough to believe she isn't planning something.

I'm watching her watching me as I perform my usual jog around the yard the next day. I've never been able to relax out here, constantly feeling eyeballs glued to my back, fully aware that the hushed whispers and pointed fingers are leveled in my direction. Although exercise is supposed to loosen the muscles, mine are permanently locked tight out in this yard, as my entire body stays on high alert.

The thirty-foot chain link fence topped with barbed wire, and the guard tower, reminds me I'm in a serious predicament, and that doesn't help my mood either. I'm in a particularly pissy frame of mind today, and Valeria's suspicious behavior has me on edge.

She's whispering in a corner with Sam and Sofia, and every few seconds, they cast a glance in my direction. All the tiny hairs lift on the back of my neck as I wonder what they are plotting. I slow my pace a little, not wanting to exhaust myself if they are planning to strike today.

Shouting at the far end of the yard draws my attention, and I slow down to a stop as I watch a fight erupt between Torres, Kelly, and Wright. Fists are flying in all directions as a few other boys join the melee. My eyes scan the group for Ryder and Luc, and I breathe a sigh of relief when I spot them standing back by the fence watching shit go down.

"Zeta."

I spin around at the sound of Valeria's voice, instantly on my guard.

I suck in a gasp as intense pain slices across my belly, ripping through my insides like a deadly tornado. I'm instantly light-headed, swaying on my feet as an icy-cold chill tiptoes up my spine. My breath catches in my throat, and I'm gasping for air as my hands instinctively move to my stomach.

Valeria's glare is evil incarnate as she stands right in front of me, flanked by her posse of bitches. "That's for blowing my boyfriend," she snarls. She twists the knife in deeper, and warm liquid bubbles up my throat. "And that's just for being you."

My eyelids flicker open and shut, and I stumble backward, my hands cradling my stomach. I glance down, barely hearing their laughter as horror engulfs me at the sight of so much blood oozing from the deep wound.

She roughly yanks the knife out, and I scream as indescribable pain rips through my body. Blood gushes out of my stomach like a river overflowing its banks, and I crumple to the ground. I land on my side with a thud, my head slamming painfully into the asphalt.

Blood leaks out of my mouth as I frantically clasp my hands over my stomach, desperately trying to stem the blood loss. In the background, the sound of approaching footfall mixes with the shrill ring of a whistle, but over it all, I hear Ryder repeatedly shouting my name.

My eyelids shut, and I shiver as a cold, bristling wind washes over me, freezing me from my head to my toes. Darkness is calling, beckoning me with a seductive promise of no more pain.

Before I black out, I feel his hands on my face. "Baby, please open your eyes." His voice is riddled with torment. "Stay with me, Zeta. Open your eyes." Forcing my eyes open, because I hate to hear the pain in his voice, I feel an immediate sense of peace as I stare into his beautiful yellow-green eyes. Tears spill down his cheeks as he whispers my name.

"Ryder." I try to speak over the blood frothing in my mouth, but my voice is muffled and indistinct. "I'm sorry."

"Baby, shush. Don't try to speak."

A gurgling sound emits from my throat, and I'm struggling to breathe. My eyes pop wide with fear as it dawns on me that I'm dying. Tears seep from my eyes as I stare at him, wanting his face to be the last thing I see, knowing it's the only comfort I can take in this moment.

"Don't give up, Zeta," he begs, his voice breaking. "I need you to fight because you are everything to me." A look of determination ghosts over his face. "I love you. I love you so much. Please don't die because I can't exist in a world without you in it."

Darkness encroaches, summoning me with an invisible reach I can't avoid. I try to fight it. I try to force the words from my mouth to let Ryder know I love him too, but I'm not strong enough to resist.

The last thing I hear as my world turns black is the sound of Ryder crying and pleading with me not to die.

11

RYDER

The car ride from juvenile hall to the hospital seems to take forever, and my anxiety increases with every second that passes. My feet and hands are handcuffed, and I'm sitting stiff as a poker in the back seat alongside Powell. That dickhead Watson is driving. I'm only here because Zeta begged that I be permitted to visit her. Apparently, she had a bit of an episode when her stepfather showed up at the hospital earlier today, and her therapist, Dr. Reynolds, spoke to the administration, explaining my presence would help calm her down.

I can't wait to see her. I spent several hours last night thinking she was dead, and I almost lost my fucking mind. I paced my cell nonstop, in between bouts of crying and futilely hitting the wall with my bare fists. My knuckles are torn to bits, but I welcome the pain. All night, I've been beating myself up for pushing her away for so long. Chastising myself for my jealous, bitter feelings. I know she did what she did for me, but every time I've closed my eyes, I see her—on her knees, sucking his cock into her beautiful mouth—and I'm enraged.

But her almost dying puts things into perspective.

We can't change the past, but we can salvage our future.

A future that was almost torn away when she nearly died.

I'm done punishing the both of us, and I hope she'll give me the chance to make it up to her.

"Ryder!" She calls out to me the minute I step foot into the room, her face lighting up as I shuffle toward her as fast as I can with my leg restraint.

She's wearing a hospital-issued gown, sitting up in the bed, propped against a bunch of pillows. She looks pale and drawn, but she's still the most beautiful girl I've ever seen.

"Zeta," I rasp, my voice overcome with emotion. I want to hug her, but I'm restricted by my cuffs. I pin pleading eyes on Powell.

She walks toward me with a wary expression. "Don't make me regret this."

"You won't, and it's not as if I can do anything with you in the room."

"You're unpredictable, lately," she murmurs, unlocking the restraints from my ankles before moving to my wrists.

"I'm here for Zeta. There's no other agenda. I swear."

"Very well." She turns her gaze on Zeta as I sit down on the chair, pulling it in close to the bed. "I'm glad you're okay. You gave us all a fright last night."

"Thank you for getting me here in time." Zeta reaches out, clasping Powell's hand.

"I can give you an hour, no more. This isn't exactly standard protocol."

"I appreciate that," Zeta says, casting a quick glance at me. "Thank you for bringing him here."

Powell pops earbuds in her ears. "I can't leave the room, but I'll give you as much privacy as I can." She drags a chair over to the door, facing it to the wall, and sits down, plugging her earphones into her iPod, giving us space to talk alone. Not for the first time, I'm so grateful for that woman and all the ways in which she's tried to help me over the years. I don't know why she does it. Maybe she's just a fucking awesome human being, but I know my juvie experience could've been hella worse without her presence in my life.

I give Zeta my full attention. "Are you okay?"

"I am now," she whispers, smiling softly.

I take her hand in mine without hesitation, mentally fist pumping the air when she threads her fingers through mine. "How much pain are you in?"

"They've given me strong painkillers, so it's not too bad. I'm trying not to move too much, because my stomach feels like it's ripping in two every time I reposition myself."

"I thought I'd lost you." My voice cracks and I take a second to compose myself. "And I had so many regrets. For being such an asshole. For not accepting your apology. For continuing to let Lopez and Valeria come between us. But mostly for not telling you how much I miss you." I swallow over the nervous lump in my throat. "How much I love you," I whisper.

"I thought I dreamt that," she murmurs, her face slightly flushed.

I smile. "No, I'm pretty sure the whole yard heard me declaring my love."

Her eyes are brimming with emotion as she tightens her grip on my hand. "Ryder, I love you too, and it terrifies me."

My heart soars. "I know the feeling." I rub my thumb in soothing circles across the back of her hand. "I've never told anyone that before or had anyone say it to me," I admit.

"I've never loved any other boy but you," she confirms, and I want to kiss her so badly. "But my parents used to tell me they loved me all the time when I was little, before everything turned to shit."

She averts her eyes and I sit up on the edge of her bed, careful not to hurt her. "Hey." I brush my thumb against her cheek. "I'm always here for you if you want to talk about it."

The look of anguish in her eyes when she meets my gaze

almost undoes me. "I'm frightened, Ryder, and I don't know what to do."

"Talk to me. Let me help you figure it out." I continue rubbing her cheek with my thumb, and she seems to draw comfort from it. "Is this something to do with your stepdad coming here earlier?"

She nods. "He's my guardian and the reason I got put away for my mom's death."

I peer into her eyes, seeing everything she wants me to see. "You didn't kill your mom, did you?" She shakes her head. "He did it? Your stepdad?"

She pauses for a beat and then nods. "I haven't heard from him since that night, but he showed up here this morning because he's listed as my official guardian and he was notified by the warden." Her lips pull into a thin line, and her eyes flash with anger. "He only came to warn me to keep my mouth shut."

A whole heap of confusing emotions rushes me in that moment, but I focus on Zeta. This isn't about me; this is all about her. "Why are you covering for him?"

"Because I was afraid if I told the truth that he'd get away with it and I'd be forced to live with him until I turned eighteen. That night, when it all went down, being sent to juvie seemed like the lesser evil, but I didn't realize they'd convict me of voluntary manslaughter and that it might mean transfer to an adult prison. I don't want to go to jail, Ryder, but I don't know how to fix the mess I'm in."

"Do you feel up to telling me about it?"

She leans her head back against the bedframe, sighing deeply. When she pulls her eyes back to me, she nods, her chest heaving. "I want to tell you. I need to tell someone, because it's eating me up inside."

"You can trust me. I promise I won't tell anyone."

"I already know that." She smiles, reaching up and cupping my face. My hand drops down to the bed. "Before I start, I want to thank you. For looking out for me from day one. For being my friend and giving me a reason to open my eyes every morning. For giving up your guitar for me. I know that guitar means everything to you, and I still can't believe you did that for me."

"My Fender doesn't mean everything to me." I plant my hand over hers on my face. "*You* mean everything to me. You're my entire world, and whatever we need to do to fix this, we're doing it, because I want us to be together, to build a life together outside those damn walls."

"I would love that too, but I don't know if it's possible. How can I get anyone to believe I'm telling the truth when I've lied under oath?"

"Because you were scared, and your mom had just died."

"Will that be enough?"

"We won't know until you try." I lean forward, pressing a kiss to her forehead. "Tell me what happened, babe."

She drops her hand to her lap, and I thread my fingers in hers again. "Mom wasn't always a bad mom, but after my dad was killed in action overseas, she changed. She was heart-broken and incapable of looking after me. I was only six, but I had to grow up fast. We'd been living in a house the military provided, so we had to move. I know it wasn't her fault, but she took me away from everyone and everything I knew and loved. I had no friends at my new school, and I was bullied because Mom was such a drunken mess. Then she met Bob." Her face contorts into a grimace, and she clenches her jaw tight.

"Your stepdad?"

She nods. "He was nice, at first. Brought Mom flowers, brought me candy, whenever he came for dinner. Joked around with me, and he put a smile back on Mom's face. I didn't want a replacement Dad, but things were better for a while. However, it all changed after he moved in, and especially after they got married. Then he showed his true colors."

A tear trickles down her cheek, and I smooth it away with my thumb.

"He was a pimp, and he got my mom addicted to drugs and coaxed her into prostitution. I was too young to know exactly what was going on at first. All I knew was that something wasn't right. All these strange men coming and going from my house scared me. When I was thirteen, one of the boys in school propositioned me. He said he wanted to know if I was as good a fuck as my mom."

My heart hurts for her, and I squeeze her hand tight.

"He took great pleasure in telling me how his dad had paid for her to take his virginity. He was *fourteen*, Ryder. Fourteen." She shakes her head. "I was sickened, but I didn't deny it, because everything slotted into place. I confronted her when I got home, and she belittled me. After that, she made no attempts to hide anything. Assholes were constantly in my house doing drugs, getting drunk, throwing parties, and fucking my mom and other women."

Tears cascade down her face, and I wish I could take her pain away. "When I came home the day of my fifteenth birthday, Bob was waiting for me; said he had a birthday surprise lined up." Her eyes burn with anger. "His present was to force me to watch three guys fucking my mom while she was coked out of her head. He watched me the whole time, grinning as I trembled in fear and disgust."

My stomach lurches unsteadily as I guess where this story might be going.

"He told me my present was the fact he would allow me to wait until I was sixteen before I joined the family business. He said he'd let me live under his roof for free if I watched and learned."

Her lower lip wobbles. "I ran away that night, but he found me sleeping rough under the bridge two nights later and dragged me back. He beat me black and blue and said if I tried that again he'd kill me. He told me I belonged to him and to get used to it."

"Shit, Zeta." I gently lean in and hug her, careful not to press against her stomach. "I'm so sorry you had to live with that." I understand what it's like, more than she realizes. "Didn't you have any other family you could turn to?"

She rests her head on my shoulder. "Mom's parents died in a car accident when she was twenty, and my dad's parents are old, and they live in Florida. I hadn't seen them in years, and I didn't feel I could approach them with this. The only one was my mom's younger sister, but they'd had a big falling-out when I was a toddler, and I didn't know her at all. All I knew was she worked overseas, and her name was Jillian Roberts. There was no one. I was completely alone."

She looks off into space, and I can only begin to imagine the horrors toying with her mind. She shakes herself out of it a few minutes later, continuing. "I threw myself into school and my studies because it was the only way I could avoid the horrors that played on repeat in my mind. Every day, I was forced to watch and listen to mom as she fucked an endless stream of different guys. And they leered after me, some of them tried to touch me, but Bob always kicked them out. I was under no illusion. I knew he wasn't doing it out of the goodness of his heart, and that terrified me."

I'm struggling to keep my emotions in check listening to her. I hate that she grew up like that. That she's been deprived of love. It's no wonder we felt such a strong connection to one another the first time we met. We have so many similar experiences. I run my fingers through her hair, pressing a kiss atop her head. I just want to bundle her up and protect her from all the evil in the world, but I know I'm too late.

She's already seen more than her fair share.

She places her hand against my chest, peering into my eyes as she continues explaining. "I couldn't eat for weeks in the run-up to my sixteenth birthday, and I thought about running away again, but I had nowhere to go, and I knew there was a chance he'd make good on his threat to kill me, so I felt trapped. I pleaded with Mom. Begged her to leave him, but I didn't even know if she heard me. She lived in a permanent drugged-up state, and I had given up all hope."

I stroke her cheek, needing to touch her, to comfort her.

"But he didn't come near me, and as weeks turned into months, I gradually started to relax. He still made me watch, and I knew it was only a reprieve, but I took the wins where I could. I signed up for self-defense classes after school, and I also fitted a lock on the back of my bedroom door because, more and more, assholes were wandering into my room while I was sleeping."

A shudder works its way through her, and her face twists in pain. I feel sick to my stomach at the thought of what she's remembering, and I want to pound my fist into those skeezy bastards for daring to make her feel unsafe in her own home.

Shaking the memories aside, she rests her head against my shoulder again, loosely draping her arms around my waist. She's trembling against me, and I can almost smell her anxiety scenting the air. I run my hand up and down her back. "You don't have to go on if it's too painful."

She clings to me, and I close my eyes, savoring the feel of her body warming mine.

"It all came to a head that night," she whispers, pulling back and eyeballing me. "I woke in the middle of the night to a strange man running his hands up and down my bare legs." She squeezes her eyes shut, and she's shaking all over. I hug her to me again. "My stepdad was in the corner of the room, and he said it was time to give up my V-card. That he'd auctioned my virginity to the highest bidder, and this man was here to claim what was his."

A piercing sob flies out of her mouth, and I hold her closer, scarcely able to breathe for fear of what she's going to say next.

"He was disgusting, Ryder. At least forty, overweight and ugly, with a combover and bad breath. He was completely naked, stroking his cock and licking his lips as he tried to pull me down the bed to him. I kicked at him and screamed at the top of my lungs. Bob grabbed me by the hair and slapped me so hard in the face I almost blacked out. He ripped my clothes off and pinned my arms down. I was screaming for help, crying for my mother, begging her to rescue me, even if I knew it was futile. But then she was there, standing in the busted doorway, holding a knife, and shouting at them to leave me alone."

Her sobs transform to full-blown crying, and Powell comes over, alerted by her distress.

"I'm okay," she tells her. "I promise. I just… This is hard to relive, but I want Ryder to know."

She nods, silently filling a paper cup with water and handing it to her. Powell's eyes meet mine as Zeta takes sips, and I see nothing but compassion there. She's the only guard who has ever shown me any kindness, the only one who has looked out for me, the only one willing to look beyond my crimes and see something more. "Thank you," I mouth at her over Zeta's head, and she nods before returning to her seat and her iPod.

"Your mom came through for you in the end," I say, tucking her hair behind her ears.

"She did, or at least she tried. I also suspect she was the reason why that hadn't happened on my sixteenth birthday. I guess there was still some part of her trying to protect me, even if she wasn't coherent or sober most of the time. She told the john to get off me, and I scrambled off the bed, going to her side. Bob was trying to placate her, all the while inching toward her. Her hand was shaking, and I knew she wasn't strong enough to fight him off, but she surprised me. When Bob lunged at her, she put up an impressive struggle. I was rooted to the spot, terrorized and incapable of moving. They fought, but she held onto the knife even as he pulled at her wrist, trying to get her to drop it. The john decided now was a great time to get the fuck out of there, and he shoved them aside in his haste to get out the door."

Tears spill down her cheeks. "I'm not quite sure what happened, because as the asshole fled, I saw Bob's best friend Clive lounging in the hallway, quietly watching everything go down. He'd made no secret of his desire for me, and fresh panic raced through me. His eyes were roaming my naked body with obvious intent, and I was terrified all over again. Then Mom screamed, and it was the worst sound I'd ever heard. Nothing else mattered then. I turned around and froze. Somehow, she'd lost the knife, and Bob made a grab for it as she turned toward me. I'll never forget her screams as the knife embedded in her chest. She howled in pain, dropping to her knees, turning white in the face. Blood gushed from her chest, and I couldn't stop screaming."

She pauses for a few seconds, drawing deep breaths and swiping at her tears. "I was crouched over her dead body, sobbing, a couple minutes later, when the police arrived. One of the neighbors had heard my earlier screams and called the cops so Bob hadn't had time to get out of there. He fed the cops a pack of lies, and when he told them I did it, I didn't refute his claims because I didn't think they'd believe me. And I thought I'd be safer in juvie."

She looks down, sliding a hand across her bandaged belly. "But I'm not safe anywhere." She looks up at me with forlorn eyes. "And now I'm trapped. That one lie is going to ruin my life, and I don't see that I have any way out."

12

ZETA

"You've got to fess up, Zeta," he tells me. "Talk to your attorney, and tell her what you told me."

"She's useless, and I have no faith that she's on my side. She hasn't even bothered to update me on whether she located my aunt or not, and I'm not sure she cares enough to hear the truth."

"What about Dr. Reynolds? Does she know the truth?"

I shake my head. "I wanted to tell her, but I wasn't sure I could trust her. And what if I tell the truth and he gets away with it? He's still my guardian, and I'd be sent back to him. I'd rather rot in a jail cell for the next eight years than go back to that house."

He scrubs a hand over the thin layer of stubble on his jawline. "I guess that's a risk, but if you tell them everything, surely they'll investigate him, and I can't imagine it would take much to verify he's a pimp." He gently cups my face. "I know it's not my call to make, but I'd take the risk."

"And what if I tell her and it changes nothing? I don't want to go to jail."

"I'm not going to let that happen." He kisses my head again, and the gesture makes me feel so loved.

"You won't be able to stop it."

"I'm getting out in three months' time, and I can help. I'll find your aunt and get you a new attorney."

"You probably won't even remember me once you get a taste of freedom."

Hurt glimmers in his eyes. "How can you say that?" He holds my face in both his hands. "Do my words mean nothing? Don't you realize the strength of my feelings for you?"

I place my hands over his. "I can't ask you to wait for me. You have your whole life ahead of you, and I could be stuck in prison for years. I can't ask you to put your life on hold for me."

He leans in closer, and his warm breath fans across my face. "You're not asking. I'm telling you I'll wait for you, because you're my girl, Zeta. I love you, and I don't want anyone else. I will do whatever is necessary to set you free. You can count on it."

"I don't deserve you. Not after what I've done." I hang my head. "I'm just like her, aren't I? Maybe Bob knew what he was doing, forcing me to watch." I tap my temple. "Maybe it's ingrained in here subliminally, and there's nothing I can do to avoid my fate."

"No, babe." He shakes his head, tracing his finger across my lower lip. "You're not your mother. It was a mistake, a bad judgment call, but your heart was in the right place. If you were just like her, you wouldn't still be a virgin. You wouldn't be holding out for the right person."

His eyes drill into mine, and I get lost in the tenderness and love there. "Our environments, and our pasts, only define us, if we let them. We choose how to deal with the consequences, and you're a fighter, a survivor, a good person, through and through. There is greatness in your future, Zeta. I truly believe that."

"Ryder." My voice is choked, my heart swollen with love for this amazing boy who has entered my world and turned it upside down. "I've never felt this way about anyone before, and I've never had anyone believe in me the way you do."

"I know the feeling." He brings my hand up to his mouth, kissing my knuckles, and I feel it all the way to the tips of my toes. In this moment, there's no pain, only longing.

"You're the other half of my heart and soul, Zeta. We belong together. Of that, I'm sure."

The biggest smile spreads across my mouth at his words. "I feel the same way. From the moment I met you, I knew you were different and that you were going to be important to me."

"I think about you all the time," he whispers, his eyes drifting to my lips. "I think about holding you, kissing you, touching you, loving you." My mouth turns dry, and my eyes drift to his lips as he leans in closer until there's barely any space between our mouths. "I think about building a life together when we're free. You bring out the best in me, Zeta, and I don't ever want to be without you."

He closes the tiny distance between us, pressing his lips against mine. His kiss is soft and tender and everything I'd dreamed it would be and more. He holds my face in his hands as I tilt my neck, allowing him to deepen the kiss. Our lips glide effortlessly against one another, and my heart is fit to burst in my chest, my body coming alive under his touch.

"Ahem." A throat clearing breaks us apart, and I know my face is flushed, my eyes swimming in love and lust. "I'm sorry, but it's time for Ryder to leave." Powell pats the top of my head. "You have one minute to say your final goodbyes, and then we'll be on our way."

Ryder presses his forehead to mine. "I love you." He kisses me sweetly. "I love you so much."

"I love you too." I kiss him back, carefully circling my arms around his neck. "And I know it's crazy, because I'm in pain, and I'm still facing years in jail, but I am so happy right now I could sing it from the rooftops."

A goofy smile graces his lips. "I'm right there with you. I can honestly say I've never been this happy in my entire life. You mean everything to me, Zeta. You're everything." He kisses me one last time before standing. "Hurry back to me. I'll be counting down the days until I see you again." Powell smiles as she fixes his leg restraints before moving to cuff his hands. "Goodbye, beautiful. See you soon." His smile is a mix of happy and sad as he shuffles toward the door. Stopping, he casts one last glance in my direction, and I blow him a kiss, sinking back into my pillows and sighing contentedly as he's led away.

AFTER ANOTHER FEW nights in the hospital, I'm eventually released. Then I'm on bed rest for a few days with Carina checking in on me at regular intervals. I'm on pretty heavy-duty pain meds, so I spend most of my time sleeping, but I still miss Ryder and hate that I'm not allowed any visitors.

Moments when I'm not thinking of him are spent thinking about how I almost died. There was a time when I would have welcomed that, but not now. Now, more than any other time in my life, I have something, some*one*, worth living for, and I'm glad Valeria didn't succeed. Buoyed up by Ryder's fighting talk and words of love, I'm determined to fight for my innocence and my freedom.

Powell came to see me last night, confirming I can return to school tomorrow. She knows how serious I am about getting my high school diploma, and I have a couple of online assignments due soon that I need to work on. She explained that Valeria has been transferred to the women's jail, and she's being prosecuted for attempted murder. I'll have to make a formal statement and attend trial at some point, but I'm just relieved I won't have to watch my back so closely anymore. I wonder which one of her posse will take her place and whether they'll still have it in for me. I guess time will tell.

$$\oint \text{♫}$$

"I MISSED YOU," Ryder whispers in my ear before slipping into the seat across from me.

"I missed you too," I whisper back, unable to stop a massive smile from breaking free on my face.

He leans across his desk to me, ignoring the pointed stares of our classmates. "I've been fantasizing about kissing you again."

Strands of messy, blond hair fall across his forehead, and my fingers twitch with the craving to touch him. The brown in his eyes is more pronounced today, and I'm captivated by the little flecks of green and gold which make his eyes smolder. I could stare into his eyes all day long and completely lose sense of time and reason.

"Babe." Glancing quickly at the top of the room, he reaches out, sweeping his thumb along my jawline, sending a flurry of delicious tingles ricocheting all over my skin. "You doing okay there?" I hear the amusement in his tone, and he totally knows the effect he has on me.

"You're not the only one fantasizing," I whisper back. "And I have a tendency to zone out whenever you're near. It's like you've cast a spell on me."

"If that's the case, you've definitely cast one on me too." His features soften, and the look on his face is one of pure happiness and sheer adoration. I feel a sudden, uncharacteristic, urge to jump up on my desk and scream out how much I love him.

Yanking his hand back when the teacher calls for quiet, he settles back in his seat with a lopsided grin.

All through class, we cast sly glances at one another, and the tension in the air is building and building until I feel like

I'll combust. I'm hyper aware of him—of every cross of his legs, every tap of his fingers off the desk, every time he rolls his head from side to side, and every time he squirms in his seat. I adore the way he casually runs his hand through his hair and the way his eyes twinkle with hidden promise when he stares straight at me.

My eyes are glued to the clock on the wall, willing it to speed up. Eventually, after what feels like forever, it's library time, and chairs scrape noisily as everyone gets up. Ryder is by my side in a flash, placing his arm around my back and carefully helping me out of my seat. I loop my arm through his, playing up the invalid card so the teach doesn't reprimand us for touching. Ryder's arm around my waist tightens, and I press myself up against him more closely, determined to take advantage of the situation. His lips ghost over the top of my head, and a happy sigh slips from my mouth. "I hate that we have no privacy," he whispers in my ear.

"I know, but we'll just have to sneak moments whenever we can."

"I love your way of thinking," he purrs in my ear, sending a shot of liquid lust straight to my core. I sway on my feet, and my stomach pulls a little, causing me to wince.

"Shit, sorry." He stops just inside the entrance to the library, turning to face me. "You shouldn't be back at school if you're still in pain."

"I'm fine. I have assignments to catch up on, and I didn't want to be away from you any longer. I missed your ugly face," I tease, batting my eyelashes at him.

He grins, tweaking my nose. "Cute, but such a lie."

"Cocky much?" I tilt my head to the side, smirking.

His eyes burn with lust, and I gasp when he leans down, moving his face in close to mine. "Around you? Always."

I practically melt into a puddle at his feet, and with the way he's devouring my mouth on sight, I'm dying to kiss him again. I've never felt such intense desire before or the need to touch someone so bad my skin feels like it's burning. "C'mon." He offers me his arm again, grinning knowingly, and I can tell he knows every thought running through my mind right now. "I think you should hold on to me, you know, in case you faint."

I roll my eyes. "Wow, someone's ego appears to have multiplied while I was gone."

He chuckles. "I'm just calling it like it is. You're crazy about me, and that's nothing to be ashamed of. I *am* a spectacular catch."

"Spectacular egomaniac, more like," I joke, looking up at him through hooded eyes. "But once you're *my* egomaniac, I'm okay with that."

Ryder walks us over to the far corner of the small library, tucking us into the crevice, away from prying eyes and ears. His arms go around my waist as his mouth lowers to mine. "I'm yours, Zeta. I'm all yours. Now and always. You never have to doubt that."

13

RYDER

For years, I wished to speed up time, and now all I want to do is slow it down. The next few weeks with Zeta are some of the best weeks of my life. And I don't say that lightly. Because we're still in juvie, with nonexistent privacy and minimal opportunities to be a normal couple, but just sharing the same airspace as her has me floating on a cloud.

I'm well aware I sound like a total pussy. But I couldn't give a flying fuck.

For the first time, ever, I am fucking happy. Even Dr. Blaufeld has noticed the changes. And, while he's happy for me, especially because my nightmares and flashbacks are becoming more infrequent, he's cautioned me about relying too heavily on my girlfriend, telling me I have to take responsibility for my own happiness, because learning to control and manage my mental health shouldn't be based on how someone else makes me feel. I get his concern, and I know it's coming from a good place, but no one is taking this away from me.

Zeta and I spend as much time together as we can, and now that the threat of victimization has been removed, we're both much freer. My mini meltdown in the yard, when I pummeled the shit out of Lopez, was enough to convince everyone to stay away from me, and now that Zeta's my girl, that protection applies to her too. But that's not the only reason for her newfound optimism.

Zeta confessed to Dr. Reynolds, which proved to be a good judgment call, because the doctor always believed there was more to the story, and she didn't hesitate to believe this new version of events. Having her support has bolstered Zeta's confidence, especially because her attorney failed her, refusing to accept the truth and advising Zeta against appeal. With Dr. Reynold's help, Zeta has filed new paperwork to have her attorney replaced. But, because it's court-appointed, and there's a ton of red tape to go through, it's going to take time before a new attorney is assigned to her case, and there's no guarantee he or she will be any better than the previous one, but at least it's some progress.

"These lyrics are so good," Zeta says, handing me back my notepad.

"That's only because I have the best inspiration," I say, pecking her lips superfast before any of the guards on duty in the common room notice.

"I'll never be as good as you, and that makes me so envious." A little crease appears between her brows. "Is it normal to be jealous of your boyfriend?"

"When he's as hot, sexy, and supremely talented as me, I'd guess that'd be a yes." I have no clue how I manage to say that without laughing. Winding her up is way too easy.

She thumps me in the chest. "What have I told you about reining in that ridiculous ego of yours?" She's shaking her head, attempting to smother her grin. She's as good at goading me as I am her, and it's just another thing I love about her.

"It's not ego if it's true."

"Says the egotistical one."

I glance over at the guards quickly before capturing her

mouth again, only this time I can't keep it brief. Man, I love kissing her, and I wish we could take things further, but I'm not about to do that in here, because Zeta deserves more than a quick fuck behind the guard's back, and I'm determined to make our first time as special as it can be. But it's hard to hold back, not knowing how long I'll have to wait for her, especially when she turns me on so much jerking off twice daily has become the norm.

Watson, predictably, blows his whistle, stomping toward us like a herd of elephants. I brace myself for it. "No kissing. No touching. You know the rules," he snaps, glaring at me, before his eyes drop to Zeta's tits. Her gaze darts to mine, and she cautions me with one of her looks.

"Sorry, Officer Watson," Zeta says, smiling sweetly at him. "It won't happen again."

"It better not. I'd hate to have to separate you on a more permanent basis." Every so often, when we lapse and indulge in PDAs, Watson makes a point of separating us as punishment. It makes me so fucking mad, because he's gotten away with screwing the female inmates for years. But I know his threat is an empty threat, so I grit my teeth and wait until he's walked away before unclenching my fists.

"Babe, stop letting him get to you," Zeta says, discreetly tangling her fingers in mine while Watson's back is turned. "He wants you to hit him just so he can get your release delayed. Don't give him the satisfaction. He's not worth it."

"I know that, but the way he looks at you fills me with so much rage."

"He can look all he wants, but the only one who'll ever be touching me is you." She drills me with a suggestive look, and it almost works to distract me.

"If he comes near you after I'm gone, I will not be responsible for my actions." It's one of my biggest fears—what will happen to her when she's in here by herself.

"That's not going to happen. Powell won't let it. She gave you her word, and I know you trust her."

I finally caved and went to Powell about Watson. It was risky, but I'm sick of watching him leer over my girlfriend, sick of him bending the rules, and getting away with it. Powell told me she's always suspected him, but without concrete proof, the administration will not investigate any claims. Instead, she keeps him in line by threatening to report him. She's promised to ensure he goes nowhere near Zeta after I leave, and I trust her to keep my girl safe. Doesn't stop me from worrying though.

"I know, but I still worry." I pluck at the strings of my guitar, a new melody floating through my mind.

"Well, stop, because I know how to defend myself, and I honestly don't think anyone is going to mess with me after you're gone. And I have Luc."

I stop playing, slanting her a look. "Luc couldn't protect a fly. Kid's way too soft. If anyone's doing the protecting after I'm gone, it'll be you protecting him."

"I think you underestimate him."

"Babe, I love Luc like a brother, so don't think this is me criticizing him, because I'm not. I love that Luc has a big heart, and I hope he never changes."

"Is that something new?" she asks, narrowing her eyes in concentration. I didn't realize I'd been absently playing as we spoke.

"It's just come to me."

"Give me the notepad." She holds out her hand for it. "Keep playing," she encourages after I give it to her, and I let the melody take control, closing my eyes as she starts scribbling furiously.

When I've finished, I open my eyes, and my heart melts at the excitement on her face, the passion shimmering in her eyes, as she logs words in my notepad. I've always believed

Zeta and I were kindred spirits, but discovering she writes songs in her spare time just blew me away.

This girl speaks to me on so many different levels.

When she showed me all the songs she's written, it was clear she has enormous talent, and that made me giddy with excitement. While I know it's a pipe dream, my goal is to make my living from music one day. I imagine myself up on a stage, fans screaming, lights blinding, and the rhythmic beat of my band, and it's everything. Music and Zeta are my life, and once I have both, I'll be a happy man. Discovering the love of my life shares this creative streak with me gave me the hardest boner of my life. I swear I jerked off four times that day just thinking about it.

Now, every afternoon, when we're not chatting or stealing sneaky kisses, we work on songs. I write the music, and she writes the lyrics, and then we tweak them together.

It's the highlight of my day.

Knowing we're a team, in every sense of the word, only reaffirms my belief that I've found the person I'm meant to share my life with. I know she's my first girlfriend, my first everything, but I don't need vast experience with the opposite sex to know she's the one for me.

I feel it in every part of my being with all that I am.

Zeta is the only girl for me, and I'm going to work tirelessly to get her conviction overturned, because living my life without her in it just won't cut it. She belongs with me, like I belong with her, and I'm going to make it a reality.

There's only one thing playing on my mind that has the potential to derail what I've got going with Zeta, and that's my past. She's opened up to me, and I want to return her trust and faith, but I can't. Because I'm terrified if she knows who I really am that she'll walk away. At the same time, how can I expect her to commit to a life with me if she doesn't understand the darkness that resides inside me? I've been puzzling over how to handle this as our weeks together start dwindling at a rapid pace, but she ends up taking the decision from me.

It's four weeks until I'm released, and we're in the library by ourselves, when she broaches the subject. "Ryder?" I lift my head from its resting place on her neck, hearing the uncertainty in her voice.

"What's wrong?" I scrutinize her face, looking for evidence of what's bothering her.

"Nothing's wrong, it's just I need to ask you something, and I think you might get mad."

I wind my fingers through her hair, clasping the back of her neck. "You can ask me anything, Zeta. You should never be afraid to tell me what's on your mind." I say that, and I mean it, even as my heart starts thumping in my chest as anxiety rears its ugly head.

"You know why I'm in here, and I just wondered what your story is." She bites on her lower lip in a way that always has my cock twitching in my pants. "It won't change anything between us," she assures me, "but I'm curious about your past because you've said some things in passing, and I think we had similar upbringings." She pauses for a beat, squirming a little in her seat. "This isn't coming out how I wanted it to." She sighs. "Just that you've helped me a lot, and I want to help you. I know you have stuff on your mind, and I want to understand so I can help."

I see the truth of her statement written all over her face. There isn't any ulterior motive here. She just wants to understand me more, and I get that. I want to tell her but the risk of losing her is too great, so I tell her as much as I can, convincing myself it's not lying if you conceal parts of the truth.

"My story isn't a pleasant one. You sure you want to hear it?" I give her one last out.

"I want to know everything there is to know about you," she quietly confirms, pecking my lips. "And there is nothing you can say which will make me love you any less. I love you to the ends of time, Ryder. I will never not love you."

I slam my mouth down on hers, kissing her passionately, pouring everything I wish I could say into the kiss. When I pull back, we're both panting.

"God, I want you so much," she whispers. "I ache for you, Ryder."

"I ache for you too, babe, and we'll get there. Once both of us are free of this hellhole."

She nods, completely in agreement with me on this even if she craves my body as much as I crave hers.

I lean back in my chair, taking her hand and locking her fingers in mine as I start explaining. "I never knew my dad. He was just one of a number of random men my mother fucked. I don't understand why my mother kept me. Why she didn't abort me or give me up for adoption, because a kid didn't mix with her lifestyle." I meet her gaze. "My mother was a prostitute too, except, unlike your mom, no one forced her into it. I basically raised myself. Spent much of my youth hanging around the streets, anything to avoid going home. I saw a lot of the same things as you, and I hated being there. We grew up in a poor neighborhood, and I fell in with the wrong crowd, joined a gang, and started doing all kinds of illegal shit."

This is the part I need to fudge, and I hate that I'm not being wholly truthful even if I don't have a choice. It's better she doesn't know what I'm truly capable of. And, I firmly believe, with her by my side that I can put that behind me and be a better man. If I didn't, I wouldn't entertain any notion of "us."

"What happened?" She rubs my arm in a soothing gesture.

"It was a robbery gone wrong and … and someone died. We were responsible, and we all went down for it."

"Oh." Her voice is quiet, and I wonder if I've said too much even if I haven't said enough.

"Do you hate me now?"

"What? No! Of course not." She kisses me. "I love you. I could never hate you."

"Famous last words," I murmur, feeling sick to my stomach.

"Ryder, look at me." She forces my face to hers. "I don't hate you. At all." Her nose scrunches up as she tries to find the right words. "I just hurt for you." She strokes my face, and I lean into her touch. "I know you're a good person, a good man, and I understand now why you disappear into your head sometimes. I've seen my mother killed, and it's something that will never leave me. I know I'll be dealing with it for as long as I live."

"Me, too. I used to see his face every time I closed my eyes but not so much lately." I raise our conjoined hands to my mouth, kissing her knuckles. "You make everything better, Zeta. You make me believe I'm capable of being good, of being worthy of love."

"Oh, Ryder. You are both of those things and so much more." Tears stab her eyes, and she looks at me with so much love in her heart it almost undoes me. "You were only a kid. A kid left to fend for himself. Is it any wonder you made some bad choices?" She rubs her thumb across my mouth. "A very talented, very hot, very wise man once told me we're not defined by the mistakes of our past, only how we choose to deal with the consequences."

I told her that one time, when I was trying to make her feel better about her mom, but I've never thought that about myself.

Maybe it's time I started practicing what I preach.

Although I have no idea how I even begin to move on from my past in order to do it.

14

RYDER

"Don't cry, baby. Please. You're killing me." I wrap my arms around Zeta, holding her close. Powell arranged for us to say a private goodbye in one of the rooms usually reserved for attorney visits, and although she's in the room, it's much better than doing this in front of everyone. Like that time in the hospital, she has her back to us and her earbuds in, so it's easy to pretend she's not here.

"I'm going to miss you so much," Zeta sobs.

"I'll come visit every week. I promise, and I'm going to miss you every bit as much as you miss me." Powell came through for us again, appealing to the warden and securing my name on Zeta's visitor's list.

"What if you change your mind? What if you forget about me once you settle back into normal life? You're the only reason I've been getting through this. The thought of you not being in my life …"

I hate that she's having last-minute doubts when she's been so strong and so positive these past few weeks as we prepared ourselves for this day.

"Zeta." I turn her face to me, pressing a firm kiss to her forehead. "I'm not going to change my mind or forget about you. That's an impossibility. I *love* you. Only ever you, and that's a promise."

She clings to me, circling her arms around my neck and pressing her warm lips to the underside of my jaw. "I'm sorry," she sniffles. "I'm being selfish." She sits up straighter, swiping at her tears and forcing a smile on her face. "This is a great day for you, and I'm ruining it by acting like a needy, whiny girlfriend." She cups my face. "I'm really happy for you. You've been here a long time, and you're finally free!"

"You're not being selfish, you're just being human, and I'd rather you tell me how you really feel than pretend with me." Grabbing her face, I pull her mouth to mine for a long, slow, deep kiss. My tongue flicks against the seam of her lips, and she willingly opens for me. I run my tongue around her mouth, memorizing every taste, every touch, knowing I will need it to keep me going on lonely nights.

When Powell tells me it's time to leave, I reluctantly break the kiss, pressing my forehead to Zeta's. "I love you. I love you so much it hurts. If you think our separation isn't killing me too, then you're mistaken. I'm sure I'd feel exactly the same if our situations were reversed, but please don't doubt me, baby." I peer into her gorgeous brown eyes. "I'm yours. And you're mine. And this is only temporary, because I'm going to do everything in my power to see that you're set free. If you want to focus on one truth, focus on that, because I'm not giving up until you're by my side."

REArDJUSTING to life outside is harder than I anticipated. A lot has changed since I've been in juvie, and I'm feeling more than a little out of my depth.

I managed to graduate with my high school diploma, and Powell hooked me up with Stan, a buddy of hers, who owns a restaurant. He took a chance on me, and I've been working as a kitchen hand for the last month. He even rented me the tiny studio apartment above the restaurant, taking rent from my paycheck and giving me a subsidy on meals. I don't have much left over, but anything I do have, I'm putting away, because I want to save up for a bigger place for when Zeta gets out. I can't thank Stan or Powell enough for helping me get back on my feet.

Another advantage is the proximity to the juvenile hall. It's only a thirty-minute bus ride, and I make the trip once a week. I'd be there every day if they granted me daily visitation rights, but I'm lucky they allow me to visit her at all, as that's usually only reserved for parents and guardians. At this point, I'm considering nominating Powell for sainthood for all she's done for us.

Zeta is doing well, and I'm proud of her for holding it together. Every visit, I have to force my feet to move once our time is up, and I'm always melancholy on the trip back to the city.

I'm missing her hella bad, and it feels as if I've lost half of myself. I try to keep myself busy in my free time so that I don't fall back into dark times. I do a few extra shifts at the restaurant when they're available, I jog at least five miles a day, work out at the local public gym, and spend hours playing my guitar and writing new music, and the rest of my time is devoted to tracking down Zeta's aunt.

I'm practically bouncing into the juvenile center the following week, bursting to tell her the good news.

"Someone looks happy," she says into the phone.

"I'm always happy to see you. How are you, baby? I missed you." I blow her a kiss, wishing I could kiss her properly, but the plexiglass separating us prevents that.

She places her hand on the glass, and I line my palm up with hers. "I'm hanging in there. My new attorney submitted the appeal paperwork, and he's hoping to hear of a court date next week."

"That's excellent news. And I have more."

She arches a brow. "Don't keep me in suspense."

"I located your aunt Jillian, and I've spoken to her."

Shock splays across her face as she gasps. "How did you find her?"

"It wasn't actually that hard. I found several women named Jillian Roberts on Facebook, and I just reached out to all of them until I found the right Jillian. She didn't know, Zeta. She didn't know your mom was dead and that you were in here."

"That bastard," she spits out, her face instantly hardening. "Although I don't know why I'm surprised. Of course, Bob wouldn't tell my mother's only other living relative that she had passed."

"She was really upset," I explain. "And horrified to hear what your stepdad did to you. She feels terrible for not keeping a closer eye on you. She's been in Australia for years, but she's coming home, Zeta. She's coming home for you."

Tears well in her eyes. "For real?"

I nod, and I can't contain my grin. "She didn't hesitate, baby. As soon as she heard you were in here, she dried her tears and said she would make arrangements to return to the US as soon as possible."

"I can't believe it." She's smiling through her tears.

"She told me she was planning on coming home within the next year, but this has just given her incentive to do it quicker." I waggle my brows, grinning. "And there's more. She's already filed paperwork to be granted guardianship of you, and she's lined up a meeting with a top attorney. She's determined to get you out of here."

Zeta sobs, her shoulders heaving as months of stress unload. I want to bundle her into my arms and comfort her, and I hate that I can't.

"I'm in shock," she says, half laughing, half crying. "I can't believe this is really happening."

"It's happening, babe. You're going to get out of here, and we're going to be together."

I'VE BEEN on a countdown the last couple of months, trying not to get frustrated at how long it's taking Zeta's new attorney to get her conviction quashed. I've met her aunt Jillian several times, and she's also been in to visit her niece. She seems to care a great deal about Zeta, and she's gone out of her way to set things up so Zeta has a loving home to return to now she's been awarded guardianship of her niece. They are slowly getting to know one another, and while Jillian isn't privy to all the facts of Zeta's unhappy childhood, she's smart enough to fill in the gaps. I can tell she feels tremendous guilt for abandoning her niece, and I think she'll go out of her way to make it up to Zeta.

Zeta doesn't turn eighteen for another four months, which means she won't be able to live with me from the outset of her release, but I can wait. At least, I'll be able to see her every day, and it'll give me more time to save for a nicer place. I've managed to get extra shifts in the restaurant most weeks, and I've been busking every Saturday afternoon in the city center, gathering a loyal little following who are happy to throw some cash my way. Every cent counts, and I take very little for myself, putting as much as I can aside so that I have enough to look after my girlfriend when she gets out.

Jillian called me while I was on the bus en route here telling me the good news, and I'm so fucking excited to see my girl, knowing she's going to be out soon. I have the goofiest grin on my lips as I sit down in front of the plexiglass screen, picking up the phone.

"You heard the news?" Zeta is smiling and staring at me with so much joy on her face.

"Two weeks, baby! You're going to court in two weeks, and

your aunt said the attorney is one hundred percent certain you'll be granted release straightaway."

"Thanks to you." She places her palm on the glass, and my hand instantly lines up on this side.

"Fuck. I need to kiss you so badly. I've missed kissing you so much. I've just missed you. Period."

"I've missed you too, and when I get out, I'm never going to stop kissing you."

"You say that like it's a bad thing," I tease.

"Thank you, Ryder." Her eyes well up. "I know you found Clive. I know you were the one who convinced him to tell the truth about what happened that night."

I shrug. "I told you I'd do anything to get you out of here, and I meant it. Clive knows he'll get control of Bob's business once he's locked up, so he didn't take much convincing. He was outside the door long enough to hear exactly how it went down, and he saw what Bob did to your Mom. It's open and shut now."

Tears spill down her cheeks. "Do you have any idea how much I love you, Ryder Stone? There are no words in existence in the English language to adequately describe how full of love my heart is for you. I can never repay you for this."

"Sure you can. You can agree to be my wife." I wasn't planning on proposing, but I've thought about it a lot. Her mouth hangs open and shock splashes across her gorgeous features. "I'm not saying I want us to get married straightaway," I rush to assure her, "because I'm not in a position to provide for you yet, but as soon as I can give you the lifestyle you deserve, I'm putting a ring on it unless you tell me you don't want that with me?" A sharp ache pierces my chest as I wait for her to respond.

"Of course, I want that with you! Nothing would make me happier than to be your wife."

I press my lips to the glass, and she does the same. Closing my eyes, I can almost pretend that I feel her mouth moving against mine. "I can't wait to bury myself balls deep inside you," I whisper into the phone. "I'm going to worship every inch of your body and make you scream my name all night long."

She shudders and her pupils darken. "I want you so much I ache all the time."

"Believe me, baby, I know. But we don't have long left to wait."

We make plans for the day she gets out, and I promise I'll be outside those gates, waiting to swoop her up into my arms. Then I tell her over and over how much I love her before Powell has to physically drag me from the room.

I'm whistling as I make my way out of the gates, walking in the direction of the bus stop, feeling on top of the fucking world. Nightfall is encroaching, and the darkening sky casts shadows on the sidewalk as I advance toward the bus stop with a new spring in my step.

Without warning, I'm yanked sideways into an alley and shoved hard against the wall. "Well, well, would you look who it is," says the voice from my nightmares. He grabs me around the throat with both hands before I have any time to react.

My lungs constrict, and I'm gasping for air as his choke-hold tightens. He slams my head back into the brick wall, rattling my bones. "I've been waiting for this day for years." His lips are curved into a sneer, his pungent breath slapping me in the face as he opens his mouth, flashing his yellowed teeth. "I should fucking end you right now." Hatred burns the backs of his eyes as he bores a hole in my skull.

My lungs are seizing up, and my limbs twitch as I struggle to get free. He drops me abruptly, and I slump to the ground, banging my hip off the hard stone although I barely feel it, because I'm too busy sucking air down. "Get up, asshole." He kicks me in the gut, and when I don't stand, he grabs hold of my shirt, yanking me up.

"Fuck you." I push at his chest, grateful I've been lifting

weights and have decent upper body strength. We face off, both of us glaring at one another. "What the fuck do you want, and how the fuck did you find me?"

"Payback, and that's for me to know."

"Payback?! Are you kidding me?" My nostrils flare up.

He slams his fist into my gut, punching me several times, winding me. "Do I look like I'm fucking around?!" he snarls. "You screwed us all over, and now it's time to pay up."

"Get lost, asshole. I owe you nothing," I pant. Straightening up, I summon strength from somewhere, shoving him in the chest repeatedly, snarling in his ugly face as I push him back down the alley. "The terms of our release were conditional on staying away from one another. I can report you and have you locked up just like that." I click my fingers in midair.

He rams his fist in my face, and blinding pain lances through my skull as I stumble back, clutching my bloody nose. "I wouldn't go slinging threats around if I were you." The look he pins on me is pure evil, and chills tiptoe up my spine. Extracting a cell from his back pocket, he thrusts it in my throbbing face. "Wouldn't want your girl paying the price for your mistakes, now would we?"

My stomach flip-flops as I stare at the image of Zeta in the yard. It's date-stamped this week. Adrenaline courses though me, fueled by anger and fear. Grabbing him into a headlock, I slam him into the wall, rage pummeling my insides. "You leave her the fuck out of this!" I shout. "If one hair on her head is harmed, I will fucking end you!!"

He jabs his elbow into my rib cage, and all the air flees my lungs. Pushing me back into the wall, he wraps his hand around my throat again. "You're in no position to make demands."

"What do you want?" I splutter, grabbing hold of his arms and trying to loosen his grip on me.

"Everything. I want everything. I own you, *Ryder*."

"Not the girl," I rasp, feeling the last trickle of air squeeze out of my lungs. Blood drips down my chin from my nose, creeping under the collar of my shirt. He eyeballs me with those cold, unfeeling eyes of his before letting me go. I rest against the wall, sucking greedy mouthfuls of oxygen into my lungs as I fight to keep my limbs upright. "I'll do whatever you want, just leave her out of it. She doesn't know anything." My tone is resigned.

He stares at me, a muscle ticking in his jaw, as his brain goes into overdrive. "We can make a deal and leave the girl off the table. But if you mess up, if you say no to me, if you try and trap me, the girl takes a bullet."

15

ZETA

"Good luck to you, Zeta. Good luck to you both," Powell says as she unlocks the gates and steps aside.

On instinct, I fling my arms around her in a hug. "Thank you. For everything."

"I'm glad it's worked out, and I hope you're both very happy, because you deserve every happiness. Look after my boy."

"I will," I promise, slinging my bag over my shoulder and waving at her. I run toward the parking lot, such is my desire to see my boyfriend, but my aunt's smiling face is the first familiar face I see.

She pulls me into a tentative hug and promptly bursts into tears. "I'm so happy you're free of that place," she says, laughing a little in between her tears.

I slip out of her embrace, a little uncomfortable. While Jill has visited me every week since she returned to the US, we are still virtual strangers. It's going to take a while for me to feel natural around her even if I'm hugely grateful to her. "Thank you so much for everything you've done for me. I don't know how I can ever repay you."

"Sweetheart." She tenderly cups my face, dropping her hand when I shrink back a bit. Her smile falters, but she hides it fast. "We're family. No thanks or repayment is necessary. I just want you to live your life and be happy. God knows you've earned it." Her lower lip wobbles. "I'm so sorry I wasn't there for you growing up. I'll never forgive myself for abandoning you."

I wet my dry lips. "It's okay. You didn't know. She forced you out of our lives and ignored every attempt you made to patch things up. What happened is not on you."

She swipes a tear away. "I know you haven't told me the worst of it, and I can't imagine what you lived through. I hate that I was off on the other side of the world living my life in blissful ignorance while you were being neglected and abused. I don't know how you can bear to look at me."

"You came through for me when I needed you. That's all that matters," I quietly admit.

Jill gave up a lucrative job in IT management to come back to the US. She dropped everything without a moment's hesitation once she found out my predicament. She's since bought a house, in Newport Beach, and secured a fancy, new position with a leading technology company.

She takes my bag, smiling again. "C'mon. Let's go home. I'm dying to show you your bedroom, and Liam is so excited to meet you."

"We have to wait for Ryder. He promised me he'd be here."

"Yeah, look, about that." She shoots me an apologetic look, and my stomach dips to my toes, then somersaults up to my chest and back down again. "He was really upset when he called, but he had to work a double shift, and he couldn't get out of it. He promised he'd drop by later."

"Oh, that's too bad." I draw a deep breath, forcing my sudden surge of anxiety to settle back down. Naturally, I'm disappointed he's not here. I had visions of him waiting with outstretched arms and me racing toward him like the pathetic, lovesick fool I am. He didn't visit last week, because he was working too, and it's the first time I've gone this long without seeing him. I honestly can't wait a minute longer. "Could we drop by the restaurant on our way home? I want to surprise him."

"No problem. Let's go."

Jill chats animatedly in the car about the new house and her new job in between asking me what my plans are. I graduated with a high school diploma the same time Ryder did, and I always dreamed of studying music, with a major in songwriting, but I never thought it would ever be possible.

Now she's offering me the opportunity to go to college, and it's like everything I've ever wanted is right there for the taking. It's a bit overwhelming, if exciting. I want to talk to Ryder before I make any decision, because I know he's been making plans for us too, and I won't agree to anything without discussing it so I know we can make it all work.

Not that I think he'll discourage me from going to college. Quite the opposite, but I want to include him in my plans, because that's the way relationships should be. I smile as I stare out the window. Listen to me, acting all grown up and shit.

The restaurant is much nicer than I was expecting it to be. It's an old-school-type steakhouse with leather-backed booths, low lighting, and country music playing in the background. I'm a little nervous as I step inside, but the nice man at the front desk smiles broadly at me and Jill, helping to settle my nerves. "Table for two, ladies?" he asks, pulling out a couple menus.

"Oh, no. We're not eating," Jill corrects him.

"I just dropped by to say hi to Ryder, if that's okay," I say, smiling.

His whole demeanor changes, and he looks a little flustered. He clears his throat. "Hold tight for a minute." I watch him retreat across the room, entering into a door marked Staff Only with a renewed surge of anxiety. All the tiny hairs lift on the back of my neck, and an ominous black cloud descends, pressing down on me, elevating my anxiety to coronary-inducing levels.

Something is wrong.

Something is very wrong.

I just feel it in my bones.

An older man with a mop of jet-black hair and a matching thickset mustache approaches us. "You must be Zeta," he says, and I can only nod. "I'm Stan, and this is my restaurant."

"Nice to meet you." I shake his hand, while trying to quell my rising hysteria.

"Ryder left this for you." He hands me a white envelope with my name scrawled on the front in Ryder's messy handwriting.

"Left it for me?" My voice comes out all high-pitched and squeaky, but I'm freaking out too badly to care.

His features soften. "I'm guessing he didn't tell you."

"Tell me what?" My heart is slamming against my rib cage, and butterflies are going crazy in the pit of my stomach. I feel like I'm going to throw up.

"He's gone, sweetheart. Barely gave me any notice."

"Gone where?" I whisper, sure shock and horror is fully displayed on my face.

"He didn't say, just that he had to leave. I was mighty sorry to see him go. He was a hard worker, and we miss him around the place."

Blood thrums in my ears, and I'm struggling to hold my tears at bay as I run my fingers across the lettering on the front of the envelope in my hand. I vaguely hear my aunt thanking the man before she wraps her arm around me, escorting me back outside to the car.

I'm in complete shock as I buckle my seatbelt, swiping at the tears silently leaking out of my eyes.

"Don't react yet," Jill says, reaching over and squeezing my hand. "Not until you've read the letter."

"He's left me." I stare straight ahead, barely able to see through the tears blurring my eyes.

"Zeta, honey. Look at me." She forces my gaze to hers. "I'm sure there's a reasonable explanation for this and that he hasn't left you. At least not permanently. I know him well enough by now to know that young man adores the ground you walk on. I've never seen anyone more devoted or so in love. I'm sure it's fine. Why not open the letter and find out?" she suggests.

I shake my head. "I'd rather wait until we get home." So that I can break down in the privacy of my own bedroom if this letter says what I think it's going to say.

She switches on the radio, working hard to keep my spirits up as we drive to Newport Beach, but I'm lousy company, and I barely even acknowledge her chatter.

The house is a beautiful big family home on a prime site overlooking the magnificent beach, but I barely take in my surroundings or properly acknowledge Jill's fiancé, Liam, as we meet for the first time. He's made dinner, and I have to force myself into eating it so I'm not rude. Afterward, I insist on cleaning up, and then Jill shows me to my bedroom.

It's gorgeous. Painted in duck egg blue and cream with a gigantic four-poster bed, huge walk-in closet, en suite bath, and my own couch and TV, it's like something from a show-house or a posh hotel. I thank her, reassuring her that I love it when I see the skeptical look on her face. Before she leaves, she tells me to come and get her if I need her for anything.

I set the envelope down on my bedside table, strip off my clothes, and take a long, hot shower, but I can't even enjoy the luxury of it because I can't get the letter off my mind, and I can't eradicate the horrible sense of dread I feel.

But I can't avoid reading it forever, so once I'm in my pajamas, tucked up in bed, with a cup of chamomile tea—courtesy of my thoughtful aunt—I slide my finger under the flap of the envelope and remove the contents.

I stare at the folded piece of paper in my lap until my tea turns stone cold. My heart is in my throat as I finally pluck up the courage to open it. With shaking fingers, I start to read.

ZETA,

Writing this letter is one of the hardest things I've ever had to do. There is no easy way to tell you this, but I've left Orange County, and I'm not coming back. I'm sorry I've broken every promise I ever made to you, but you were right—things have changed. I've changed, and with time and distance, I've realized the things I want are different from the things we planned together. I will always love you and always remember our time together as a happy period in my life, but I've moved on. I've met someone else, and I'm moving to be with her. The last thing I ever wanted to do is hurt you, and I hate myself for that. You're destined for great things, Zeta. I know you're going to have an amazing life. Be happy because you deserve all the happiness in the world.

RYDER.

I STARE AT THE LETTER, rereading it several times, until I can no longer see through the tears coating my eyes.

I don't understand.

Everything was fine two weeks ago. When he was declaring his love for me and proposing marriage. Was it all a lie? Did he mean anything that he said? Or was it just pity that drove him to help me?

I'm so confused and still in a state of shock. I half-expect him to jump out from under the bed, laughing at my distress, like it was some sick, perverted joke. Or a test to prove my loyalty, but I know that's just my stupid foolish heart speaking.

I can't believe he's fallen for someone else so soon, but is it really that much of a surprise? Maybe he's one of those guys who falls in love at the drop of a hat, moving from girl to girl, professing undying love until someone new captures his eye. That's the only explanation that holds any weight and the more likely scenario. I prefer to think like that than accept he never loved me at all.

Fat teardrops drip onto the page, smudging his messy handwriting. I curl into a ball under the covers, wrapping my arms around my body tight, as if that will somehow hold the heartache at bay. Wracking sobs heave my chest, and I bury my face in my pillow, trying to muffle the sound of my pain. I cry until my throat is raw and my eyes sting.

Today should've been one of the happiest days of my life, but Ryder has managed to destroy every joyful feeling.

At some point, Jill slips into the room, crawling into the bed with me and wrapping her arms around my frozen body. She whispers reassurances, telling me how much she loves me and that she's here for me, but there's no comfort she can offer that will fill the huge gaping hole in my chest. I've never experienced such heart-crushing pain before, and the ache in my chest penetrates cell deep, invading every part of me, ensuring no organ, no tissue, no cell, is left unscathed. The scars on my heart run wide and deep, and I know I'll carry them with me forever.

Ryder is gone, and he's taken part of me with him.

The part that believed in the dream.

In the healing power of love.

His love may have been fleeting, and he may have gotten

over me and moved on, but I know, without a shadow of doubt, that he is my one true love, and I will never, ever get over him.

And, for as long as I live, I will never forgive him for destroying me like this.

PART II

Eight Years Later

RYDER

I slowly come to, conscious of something hot and heavy pressing down on my back. Ignoring the dull pounding in my head, I lift my upper body, glancing over my shoulder and scowling at the naked girl using my back as her own personal pillow. She's snoring and drooling onto my skin, and a nasty shiver works its way through my body as I slide out from under her.

"Mike," I croak, my throat rasping from the aftereffects of last night. "Mike," I yell, louder this time, while swinging my legs over the side of the bed and reaching for the bottle of water on top of my bedside table. The girl groans, turning over onto her back, blinking her eyes open.

"Hey, sexy," she purrs, sitting up while stifling a yawn. Smudged, thick, black mascara rims her bloodshot eyes as she fixes them on me. Bile mixes with the nasty sandpaper-like taste in my mouth when she crawls on her hands and knees toward me, licking her lips and scanning my naked body with hungry eyes.

"You looking for me, boss?" Mike pops his head through the bedroom door.

"Get rid of her!" I snap, pissed that she's still here.

My bodyguard narrows his eyes as he steps into the room. "And the two on the floor?" he asks, raising a brow.

I look over the other side of the bed and cuss at the sight of the curvy girl with short blonde hair being spooned by the leggy redhead. Both of them are naked and in a deep sleep.

"Get rid of *all* strays. You know the score." Spotting a bottle of JD tucked down the side of my bed, I snatch it up and take a swig, welcoming the burn as it slides down my dry throat.

The girl on the bed grabs hold of my ass as I stand, and I see red. "Get your fucking hands off me, and get the hell out of my penthouse." I shove her hands away, picking up an article of women's clothing off the carpeted floor, tossing it at her. "Don't forget this. Would hate for you to do the walk of shame without any clothes on."

"You're a fucking asshole," she spits, clutching the dress to her chest.

I smirk. "You think that's news to me, darling?" Her nostrils flare, and I laugh as I walk toward my en suite bathroom. "I'm taking a shower, and I want them gone by the time I'm done."

"I'm working on it," Mike huffs out, shaking both girls on the floor by the shoulders in an attempt to wake them up.

I decide to help him out. Grabbing an empty pitcher from the table by the wall, I fill it in the sink in the bathroom and return to my bedroom, throwing cold water over the two comatose girls without a moment's hesitation. They bolt upright, screaming and shrieking, glaring at me as they push strands of sodden hair back off their faces. Mike gives me the evil eye, tugging at his soaking wet shirt, looking like he wants to murder me in cold blood.

I toss the empty pitcher on the bed and saunter toward the bathroom without a backward glance.

Standing under the steaming hot water, I close my eyes and picture *her* face.

The only woman I've ever loved. The only one I ever will.

No matter how hard I try, I can't forget the woman I was forced to walk away from even though it fucking destroyed me leaving her behind. It's been eight long lonely years without Zeta by my side. I thought it'd get easier, but it's only getting fucking harder. I'll never stop missing her. Stop wanting her. Not until my dying breath.

Propping an arm up against the wall, I slide my other hand down my body, stroking my rock-hard cock as Zeta's stunning fiery brown eyes stare back at me through my mind's eye.

I permit myself to think of her every morning when I'm showering. To give myself this one indulgence.

I imagine I have her pinned up against the wall, her legs wrapped around my waist, and she's writhing and moaning as I thrust into her hard, fucking her like she's never been fucked before. I can almost hear her cries and screams as I bring her to release, and it's not long before I'm jerking hard in my hand, cum spraying everywhere.

I lean against the wall, pressing my forehead to the cool tile, wishing the dream was a reality even though thinking like this always sends me into a spiral.

Is it possible to love someone so much it feels like I'm dying every day I spend on this planet without her in my arms?

"Boss, you okay?" Mike's concerned eyes meet mine through the steamed glass doors.

I push off the wall, turning the shower off with a sigh. "I'm peachy. Just fucking peachy, Mike."

"Heads-up. Rod's on his way. ETA in forty minutes."

He hands me a towel, and I wrap it firmly around my waist. "Thanks. He's going to lose his fucking nut when he sees the state of the place."

"Don't sweat it. Maggie has already worked her magic."

"Remind me to give that woman an increase in pay." I

move past him, grateful at least my housekeeper knows how to do her job. "And to reduce yours," I add, narrowing my eyes to slits.

"Don't fucking pin that shit on me, Stone." Mike crosses his arms, challenging me with his stare. While Mike is the consummate professional, he's also one of my closest friends, and sometimes, the lines blur. He's way too familiar with me, and I should probably pull him up on that, but I value his role in my life too much to risk going there. Besides Rod, he's the only other person who gets through to me although most of the time I ignore both their advice, hence why my life is one messy clusterfuck after another.

"What the fuck were they still doing here?" I grab my toothbrush and start vigorously brushing my teeth.

Mike's been my personal bodyguard long enough to know the drill. The girls *never* stay the night. As soon as I fuck them, I want them gone. I want no reminder of the encounter, and I never go back for seconds. It's a pure physical release. A way to block out the destructive thoughts in my mind and nothing else. The last thing I need is to wake up beside a woman. Because if she isn't Zeta, then she has no business being in my bed.

"Why do you think?" he says, just as other voices start making a ruckus outside.

"Fucking Garrett," I grumble, wondering how I let my bandmate talk me into the impromptu session last night.

You know why. I punt kick that troublesome inner voice to one side.

I need to focus on looking semi-human before our manager gets here, because if he finds out I'm partying hard again, he'll string me up by my balls. Or send me to rehab again.

Rod is the best fucking man I know. He literally saved me single-handed, and our band, Torment, has received worldwide fame thanks to his expert management and savvy business skills.

I owe him so much.

I owe him everything.

As messed up as I am, I shudder to think of how much worse it would be if he hadn't found me busking that day. If he hadn't taken a chance on me. If he hadn't whisked me away to New York and given me so many opportunities.

Letting him down only adds to my guilt, and I wish I could say I never do, but I'm locked in a vicious cycle where guilt and remorse drive my actions, only adding more shit to the pile.

I have the music career I've always wanted, wealth beyond my wildest dreams, and women throwing themselves at me everywhere I go. I should be on top of the world, yet I feel like I'm stuck at the bottom of the ocean, my feet harnessed to the ocean floor, my mouth open in a silent scream, gagging as I drown in a sea of self-hatred, my body bucking as I'm sucked downward into an endless dark void that refuses to let me go.

"He's still out there with his fuck buddies," Mike supplies, dragging me back into the moment.

My anger instantly flares. "Do you actually *want* to be fired?" I roar, shoving past him out into my bedroom.

"I tried to get them to leave, and one of them screamed I was manhandling her. Garrett just sat on his ass and laughed." He, at least, has the decency to look apologetic. "You know I won't touch that."

My anger fades instantly. We had an incident, a couple years ago, just before I went completely off the rails, when Mike was accused of assault by one of the groupies after a party in my L.A. pad. All he'd been trying to do was help the girl to leave, but she was fucking smashed, and she fell over as he was escorting her down the hallway. The top half of her dress had fallen open in the process, and she screamed bloody murder, accusing him of undressing her with intent even though he hadn't laid a finger on her. I wrote a check and made it go away but Mike's wary of touching any of the girls now, and I can't say I blame him.

I storm into my open-plan living room, my skull protesting at the noise blaring from the wall-mounted TV. Garrett Jones, guitarist and backup vocalist for Torment, my usual wingman and closest friend, is sprawled across my leather couch, in just his boxers, with a scantily clad girl on each arm and one on her knees between his feet.

Yanking the remote off the table, I mute the TV and stalk over to my buddy. "Get them the fuck out of here now!" Gar knows how I feel about this, and I'm pissed he's taking advantage. "Rod's on his way here."

I claw a hand through my hair, forgetting it's so much shorter now, instantly grieving the loss of my longer tresses. "Are you fucking insane? He will rip us a new one if he knows what went on here last night."

"Dude. Relax." Garrett steps over the girl at his feet and clasps hold of my shoulders. "He won't hear about our eightsome from me." His piercing green eyes are laughing as he raises his hand for a knuckle touch.

Ignoring him, I collapse on the couch behind me, shaking my head. "Fuck. Me."

That's a new record even for us.

I swore I was giving up the orgies after the last one. One of the girls had secretly recorded footage on her cell, and she wasted no time releasing it. It went viral in minutes and crashed Twitter. Shit like that does wonders for the band, but I cried like a pussy that night imagining Zeta watching it. Not that it should matter. She must hate my guts after the way I ended things, deserting her like that without another word.

"Been there, done that, and have the aches to prove it," the brunette in the black lacy panties and bra says, sitting down beside me and running her hand up my chest.

I slap her hand away, more irritated than usual. "Get the fuck out now."

"Dude." Gar pulls his mouth away from the blonde he's currently locking lips with, looking over at me. "Relax, it's not like Rod doesn't know you've fallen off the wagon. And the redhead Mike just kicked out has already posted pics online."

I bury my head in my hands, groaning. I know I'm going to get the rehab speech now.

"Just get them the fuck out of here, Gar. I mean it. I want them gone."

I storm back into my bedroom, violently slamming the door behind me. My hands ball into fists, and I really want to hit something.

Controlling my frequent bursts of anger is becoming more challenging. Every little thing seems to set me off these days, and I know I'm losing my grip on my sanity.

Stepping into my walk-in-closet, I drop the towel and spend fifteen minutes beating the shit out of my punching bag. After another quick shower, I pull some clothes on, and when I emerge from my room, Garrett is dressed, sipping a coffee as he flirts with Maggie in the kitchen. It doesn't bother him that she's in her late fifties with children older than us—he still flirts up a storm any chance he gets.

"Here," Maggie hands me a cup of her special honey and lemon concoction the instant my foot hits the kitchen floor. "I'm guessing you need that."

"Thank you." I kiss the top of her head. "And thanks for cleaning up the place."

She cups my cheek. "You don't want to do this again, Ryder. Remember what happened last time. You might not be so lucky again."

My stomach drops to my toes at the memory, and I hate that I've let her down too.

She came to work for me shortly after I bought this place, seven years ago, and she's put up with a lot of crazy shit over the years, but she never judges. She just cares. She's the closest I've ever had to a proper mother figure in my life, and I don't like disappointing her even though it's a regular occurrence.

I don't get a chance to offer false platitudes we both know are lies because Micah and Scott choose that moment to make a grand entrance. "Sup, assholes?" Micah shouts, grinning as he enters the room like he owns it.

"Why you all sunshine and rainbows?" I ask, sipping on the delicious honey drink, feeling it soothe the ache in my throat.

"Bella finally let me take her ass last night. Hottest fucking fuck of my life."

Gar reaches over to Micah for a knuckle touch as Scott wraps his arms around Maggie, hugging her while shaking his head at me. I thump Micah in the upper arm. Hard. "You can't say shit like that in front of Maggie. Show some respect."

"Maggie, sweetheart." He slings his arm around her shoulder, drawing her away from Scott. "That was out of line, please excuse my excitement and accept my most heartfelt apology."

"You boys will be the death of me," she murmurs, pinching his cheek and ruffling his blond hair. "And I hope you're treating that young lady right. She's a sweet girl. Don't lose this one." While Gar and I are the stereotypical manwhores of the band, Micah bounces between groupies and girlfriends when it suits him. Scott is the only one tied down. He's been with his wife Linda since high school, and they recently welcomed their first child. He doesn't know it, but I'm so fucking envious of him.

We shoot the shit for a few minutes over coffee and pastries until Rod arrives.

We reconvene to the living room as Maggie makes fresh coffee. The others take seats on the couches, but I prop my butt on the edge of the sideboard near the floor-to-ceiling window that offers magnificent views of New York City in the distance. I love living in Greenwich Village although I'd live full time in my house in the Hamptons if I had a choice. But this place is closer to the studio and the airport, so it makes more sense to live here, although I escape to my beachfront property every chance I get.

Rod is all business-like as we discuss plans for recording our next studio album in the coming months, along with a few event dates scheduled for the next couple weeks. I perk up when the subject of our forthcoming biography pops up. "Have you given any more consideration to the idea?" he asks.

"I love it," I cut in first. "It's a different take on the usual rock bios, and I think it would work."

Rod pitched the idea at our last meeting. We already have an official biography of the band, written a year after we burst onto the scene, and it's your typical rags to riches tale, told in the same vein of every other rocker bio. This time, Rod is suggesting a more intimate look at the band with the focus on our professional lives and how our career has evolved over the years. He suggested we invite a journalist to watch us creating and recording our next album so the world gets a warts-and-all view of the entire creative process involved in producing a Torment album.

The other guys nod, and I know they are on board with the idea too.

"And you're all okay with having a journalist live with you while you're recording?"

"If it's still that hot chick from *RockOut*, Kayla, hells yeah. She can live in my room, no problem whatsoever," Gar offers, smirking.

"That's exactly what I'm afraid of," Rod replies. "If we go ahead with this, it'll be a strictly professional relationship, as in you're not allowed to hit on her. The schedule is tight, and we won't have time to find a replacement writer if you drive her away."

"He'll behave," I tell Rod. "And Kayla knows how to knock him on his ass if he tries anything."

"Don't be jealous, man. It's not my fault she kicked you to the curb in favor of my hotter ass," Gar says, smirking, reminding me of that one time he hooked up with the feisty blonde.

"I've never hit on her," I truthfully admit, and that's no word of a lie, even if she is gorgeous and alluring.

"Bullshit," Gar says, pretending to cough.

"Whatever, man." I eyeball Rod, done with all the posturing. "Kayla knows us, and she's a cool chick, as well as a shit-hot reporter. She can use the guesthouse, so I don't see it as an issue."

I'm determined we give this gig to *RockOut* magazine as I know they need the business. Rod partly understands the reason for my allegiance, but I've never told any of the guys in the band about Zeta, and I intend to keep it that way.

Rod puts his iPad back in his briefcase along with some papers. "If we're in agreement, I suggest we propose it to Kayla at the press conference. I think it's best to sound her out first, and then we can officially present it to Harrison Meadows at *RockOut*."

We all concur, and then the guys head home to pack a bag before our flight this afternoon. Rod hangs back, but I knew he would.

"I'm worried about you," he says once we're alone, seated on my rooftop terrace, sipping the iced tea Maggie prepared before she left for the day.

"I'm fine."

"This is not fine." He shoves his cell in my face, and I glance at the pic of me lying naked, sprawled facedown on my bed.

That fucking bitch.

I guess I should be grateful the photo doesn't show any

evidence of the coke we shoveled up our noses or the lines Gar and I snorted off the girl's tits. "This is you relapsing."

"I'm not relapsing." I dig my nails into my thighs. "You know why I needed a blowout. Once the gig is over and I'm back in New York, I'll stay clean, I swear."

"Don't treat me like I'm stupid. This is *me* you're talking to. The guy who found you busking on the street when you were homeless without a dime in your pocket or any food in your belly."

"Trust me, I haven't forgotten."

"Could've fooled me." He twists around in his chair until he's facing me. "You're like a son to me, Ryder. Cindi and the kids adore you and consider you part of the family. I know what demons you have, and I know how much you struggle with your past and with what happened to Lucas—"

"Don't. Please don't go there. I can't do this today." I walk off back into the house, pouring myself a large whiskey neat.

Rod appears at my side, dragging a hand through his graying hair. "I know you don't want to play the venue in Orange County, but it's one night only, and it's for charity. I'll charter the jet to take you straight home."

"You don't need to change the plans. Gar and Micah will want to go to the after-party, and Scott and I have already agreed to hang out with Sawyer Weston at his brother's bar. We'll crash at Sawyer and Noah's place and then meet the guys at the airport the next morning."

Sawyer and Noah Weston are fraternal twins who make up one-half of Bastards and Dangerous a.k.a. BAD. They hit the scene around the same time we did, and while there's a certain competitive rivalry between both bands, we all get along and enjoy socializing after group festivals and events.

Sawyer and I struck up a closer friendship, a couple years back, and I've been promising to visit Just an Illusion, the bar his brother Jordan owns, for some time. Tonight's the perfect opportunity to take him up on his offer, because I loathe being back in Orange County, and I want to get the hell out of there as soon as the show is a wrap. Jordan's bar is in southern California too, but it's in L.A. County and gives me the distance I desperately need.

"Okay." Rod grabs his things. "But when you come back, I want you to schedule an appointment with Dr. Fleming. I know you've stopped going to therapy, but you need it, Ryder. You know you do."

"Therapy isn't going to fix the mess in my head. We both know that. I'm fucked up, and it's my penance. It's the punishment I'll live with every day of my life, and I've already accepted that." I knock the whiskey back, draining it in one go.

There's only one person who's ever been able to bring me any measure of peace, and she's the one person who's completely off-limits to me.

17

ZETA

"**Y**ou look like you're about to topple over. You sure you still want to go out?" I ask Kayla for the umpteenth time as we titivate ourselves in the compact bathroom of my eleven-hundred-square-foot condo in Queens.

"I'm pregnant, not incapacitated," she protests, elbowing me out of the way so she can get at the mirror, and I grin.

Pregnancy has *not* changed my best friend—my *only* friend—not a bit.

Well, except for her altered physical features.

Mikayla is a teeny, tiny little thing, and I have no clue where she got that ginormous baby bump from. Or how she continues to wear skyscraper heels and still manages to maintain her balance. I tease her constantly that she's carrying twins or triplets, and she shoves her scan photos in my face every time, pointing at the only baby growing in her womb.

Although I'm undecided about kids, I'm super excited for Kayla and Gage's baby boy to make his entrance into the world. She's due in a month, not that she's letting that slow her down.

We met at *RockOut*, the magazine where we both work as

157

music journalists, four years ago. Kayla was employed the year before me, and I was recruited straight from college. We clicked the second we met, and we've been joined at the hip pretty much since then.

That's not usual for me.

I don't make friends easily, and I always have my guard up.

There have only been two occasions in my life where I willingly dropped my walls to let someone in. After the first time ended so badly, I swore I was never opening up to anyone ever again, but Kayla challenged my conviction the instant I met her, and with her determined personality, I never stood a chance.

"I haven't missed any of Gage's performances to date, and I don't intend to start now." Gage is her baby daddy and fiancé, and he's also the front man for Savage Mania, an up-and-coming rock band our magazine has been supporting for the past year.

I was with Kayla the night she met Gage. It's important that we keep our finger to the pulse when it comes to the indie rock scene, so we go out to smaller venues and bars, scouting fresh talent to watch, at least a couple times a week, as well as attending all the bigger musical events and rock concerts which we're required to report on. Even though I've long since given up on my songwriting dreams, as jobs go, I'm lucky, because I'm surrounded by music twenty-four seven, and not many people can say they get to pursue something they're passionate about.

"Does he know you're coming?" I ask, leaning into the mirror as I apply a final layer of lip gloss. Gage has been a tad overprotective these last couple months, and I can't believe he's happy for Kayla to attend the gig tonight. The crowd tends to be rowdy.

"He's expecting us, and he said he'd reserve a section near

the stage for us." She runs her fingers through her cropped blonde hair, giving herself one last look over in the mirror.

"Sweet." I smack my lips against her cheek. "Ready to go, or you need another minute to pee?"

"Do you even have to ask?" She rolls her eyes. "I swear this kid is sitting right on my bladder. I need to pee at least four times an hour."

"At least you don't have to suffer for much longer, and you've had a dream pregnancy. When Jill was pregnant, both times, she had horrible morning sickness that lasted all day, and when that passed, she got really bad heartburn that kept her awake at night. It's the reason why her and Liam have drawn the line on any more babies."

"That reminds me," she says, tugging down her black leggings and panties and sitting on the toilet seat. "I need to send her a card to thank her for all the baby stuff she gave me. It's saved me a fortune."

I lean back against the bathroom counter, smoothing a hand over my black leather leggings, enjoying the feel of the material against my skin. "She was just happy to have someone to give it to. I think she finally understands I'm serious about never getting married."

"Never say never, babe. I used to think the same. And now look at me." A goofy smile appears on her face, and it's the same dreamy look she always wears whenever she thinks about her man.

"You did good, girlfriend. Gage is a real catch, and I'm so happy for you."

"Your time will come," she says, a more serious note in her voice.

"You know my thoughts on that, and it's not something I want to dwell on tonight. Let's just go out and let loose and have some fun."

The bar-slash-club is hopping by the time we arrive, and

I'm grateful Gage reserved a section for us because there's no way Kayla could stand on her feet all night in this place. I push my way through the boisterous Friday night crowd, clearing a path for my bestie, as I head toward the front of the room. Gage is performing a soundcheck up on stage with the rest of the guys, and as soon as he spots us, he jumps down, making a beeline for his fiancée.

Kayla shrieks as he scoops her up into his arms, cradling her protectively against his massive shoulders as he walks toward the section he reserved. "Thanks, baby." Kayla grabs him into a deeply passionate kiss as he places her carefully down on a seat, and a pang of longing runs through me. Kayla and Gage are so fucking hot for one another, and extremely open with the PDAs, and, sometimes, I find it difficult to be in their company even though they're two of my most favorite people in the world.

I slide into the booth and shrug off my leather jacket, reminding myself how happy I am for my friend. It's just that, looking at how close they are, how much in love they are, reminds me of how good it was with Ryder, and those feelings are always bittersweet.

"Grabbed you a beer, princess." Gus—Gage's brother and drummer with the band—says, leaning across the back of the booth, and reaching down to hand a cold bottle to me.

"Thanks for the beer, and quit with that princess shit. I'm about as far removed from a princess as you can get." I gesture at the tattoos on my arms, my oversized Jim Morrison T-shirt, leather leggings, and studded knee-high boots. With my dark hair, smoky eyes, and red lips, I'm in no way a girlie girl.

"I don't know about that," Gus says, blatantly staring down the front of my top. "You're definitely my kind of princess."

I shove him back. "Stop staring at my tits, and go finish your soundcheck."

"But I like looking at them," he pouts. Coming around the front of the booth, he plants his large hands on the table—hands that have explored my body intimately—and leans forward, pressing his mouth up to my ear. "You have the best tits, and I really want to fuck them again." He stares at me, his eyes darkening with lust. "C'mon, babe. One more night. No strings attached. You know you want to."

For the first time in a long time, I actually kinda want to go back for seconds. I'm strict with my one-time rule, and I've only bent it for one guy—Brody from work—but that was a bad judgment call, because now he won't stop pestering me for dates. But I'm seriously tempted with Gus, because he was a terrific lay, where most times the hookups I engage in are usually a disappointment.

Sex and I have a checkered history, and I know my predilection for casual hookups and one-night stands isn't the norm—hell, it's basically frowned upon by society—but I have a strong sex drive, and no desire for a relationship, so how else am I expected to meet my needs? And why is it okay for guys to fuck around, but girls are called sluts when they try to take control of their sex lives? I'm always safe, the sex is always consensual, and I make it clear up front that it's a one-time thing, so I don't see that I'm doing any harm.

I know Aunt Jill is concerned about me, and my therapist agrees it's related to my upbringing and my past, but I'm not my mom, and I won't let anyone else make me feel like I'm doing something wrong. I'm not charging men for sex, and I'm the one who's always in control.

"I know you're into it," Gus adds. "And you know I'm not looking for a relationship either. With the band going places, I fully intend to take advantage of all the pussy that comes my way." He winks, rubbing his thumb across my bottom lip.

"Spoken like a true rock star," I tease, knowing full and well how hedonistic the lifestyle is.

"Don't make me beg, babe. Say you'll spend the night with

me tonight, and I promise you won't regret it." He pins me with puppy-dog eyes, which just looks ridiculous on his broad six-foot-four frame. But I've got to hand it to the man—he's charmingly persistent.

"Gus, stop bugging, Zeta," Gage interjects, slapping his brother on the shoulder.

"I'll think about it," I say, and, without warning, Gus grabs my head and pulls my mouth to his, kissing me deeply with a promise of more to come.

"We can leave right after the set." He slides his hand up the inside of my thigh. "I'm already so fucking hard for you."

"I didn't say yes!" I splutter.

"C'mon. We both know you did." With a quick peck to my lips, he saunters off with a cheeky smirk.

"Your brother just completely ambushed me," I complain to Gage.

He chuckles, pulling Kayla in closer under his arm. "Yeah, he seems to have that effect on women."

"Not on this woman," I protest, taking a healthy glug of my beer.

"I'll tell him to back off if you want," Gage offers in all seriousness.

"Nah, it's cool. I can handle your brother. Don't worry about it."

He turns to Kayla, smiling down at her like she hung the moon. "I've gotta go, babe. Remember what I said, no dancing. It's fucking crazy tonight, and I don't want anything to happen to you."

"Don't worry," I reassure him. "I'll keep a close eye on her."

"Knock it off, you two," Kayla argues, her dark gaze bouncing between me and her fiancé. "As much as I'm dying to get out there and shake my booty, I'd never do anything to jeopardize my baby, so you can both cut the crap talk. No one needs to mollycoddle or babysit me."

She puts her hands on her hips and juts out her lower lip, and I can't help laughing because she just looks so funny with her swollen baby belly and fierce expression. "I'm damn well able of looking out for myself and my unborn child."

"I fucking love you to bits, Kayla," Gage exclaims, kissing her softly as his hand tenderly rubs her stomach.

"And I love you too, stud," she says. "Now get out there and do your thing." He kisses her again before leaving, and Kayla practically melts into the seat.

"You two are nauseatingly in love. It's disgusting," I joke.

"We are puke-inducing, aren't we?" she proudly agrees, sipping her water.

"Yep. That you are." I hate the pang of longing that races through me. And I hate that my mind automatically returns to Ryder.

You'd think, after all this time, that I'd be over him, but there's no getting over that boy. I've tried everything, and I can't erase him from my mind. It doesn't help that his gorgeous face is plastered all over social media and our TV screens. His outrageous actions ensure him prime coverage, and even if I wanted to avoid any mention of him, it's virtually impossible.

I've lost count of the amount of sex videos and tell-all's he's been the subject of. Ryder has taken advantage of all the perks that come with being one of the world's hottest rock stars, and he seems so far removed from that deep, sweet boy I knew in juvie. The one who traded his guitar to keep me safe. The boy who visited me every week for months after he got out. I still struggle to accept the contents of that letter. To understand why he left the way he did.

"You should just talk to him," Kayla says, interrupting my troubled inner thoughts.

"To who?" I frown, playing dumb.

"You know who." She treats me to one of her intense stares. "Ryder."

I shake my head. "No good would come from that."

"You know that's bullshit. You need closure, Zeta, and he's the only one who can give you that."

"I can't just show up after all this time demanding answers." I fold my arms over my chest as the band kicks off with their opening number.

"Why not?" she questions.

Kayla knows about my past with Ryder, but she's sworn to secrecy, and I know I can trust her not to mention a word to anyone, especially not the man himself. "Because he's long since forgotten about me, and I'd only end up even more humiliated. We were just stupid kids, and it wouldn't have gone anywhere anyway."

She taps a finger off her lips, looking contemplative. "I think you're wrong." She eyeballs me seriously. "I've interviewed them every year for the past five years, as you know, and I've never seen a man so unhappy or more troubled than Ryder Stone."

When I first joined the magazine, I told Harrison—the CEO and my boss—that I had bad history with Ryder and that I never wanted to be assigned to anything to do with Torment. He wasn't happy about it at first, believing my connection with him could give us an in, but after their manager contacted the magazine, specifically requesting Kayla be assigned to report on the band, he backed down. Although it was something I'd asked for, because I didn't trust myself to be around *him* and not fall apart, I remember going home and crying myself to sleep that night.

"Anyone can see that, Kayla," I reply, because you only have to read the headlines and look at pictures of him falling out of clubs, completely smashed, with groupies hanging off his arms, to know he's not in a good place.

Even though he ruined me, it still hurts to see him hurting, especially knowing I can do nothing about it. Becoming the rock star he always wanted may have given Ryder fame and riches beyond his wildest dreams, but it seems to have tormented him on a personal level. I don't need to be an active participant in his life to understand that. "And it's got nothing to do with me."

"I wouldn't be so sure about that." She chews on the inside of her cheek, looking unsure of something, and that's rare for my outspoken best friend.

"Just say what you're going to say." I knock back the last of my beer and signal at the waitress passing by for another.

"He always asks me about you," she quietly admits. "Every single time I've interviewed them, he's pulled me aside at the end and asked me if you're happy."

My mouth drops open. "Why didn't you say anything?!" I shriek.

"Because he asked me not to." She sighs. "And because you are so reluctant to talk about him. I didn't know if you'd want to hear it."

"I don't know what to make of that," I honestly admit, feeling conflicted.

"Do you want to know what I think?" she asks, as the waitress appears with another beer and bottle of water.

I hand her a couple bills, telling her to keep the change, before refocusing on Kayla. "Always."

"I think he still thinks about you, possibly still loves you, but for whatever reason, he's not permitting himself to reconnect with you, but he wants to feel close to you, and that's why the band requested me as their assigned reporter and why he drills me for info on you every time we meet."

I can't deny or confirm her statement, and I can't talk about him any longer because it kills me every time. Kayla knows me inside and out, so she understands that, instantly dropping the subject of Ryder Stone.

We focus on enjoying the night, and when I leave the bar a

few hours later, with Gus's arms wrapped tightly around me, I toss all thoughts of my ex-love from my mind.

And, back at my apartment, as Gus thrusts in and out of me, I'm numb to everything but the pleasurable sensations he's drawing from my body.

RYDER

"You look like you need something stronger," Sawyer says, placing two glasses and a bottle of whiskey on the table in front of us. We left the stadium as soon as both our sets were finished and came straight to Just an Illusion. Scott didn't join me after all. His wife, Linda, made a surprise visit. She finagled her in-laws into babysitting and flew out to spend the night with her husband, so they're staying in some top hotel for the night, and we're all meeting at the airport in the morning.

I drain the last mouthfuls of beer and lean back in the booth. "It's that obvious?"

"You're tense, man. Figured you could use it."

I nod, watching as he pours generous measures into the two glasses. "Returning to southern California is always hard for me. Tonight, I just want to forget."

Sawyer knows my backstory or at least the version the press reports. My true identity remains sealed, along with the true nature of my crimes, and the only other person who knows the truth, outside of those who were involved and the authorities, is Rod.

"I can get with that plan." Sawyer grins, chinking his glass against mine. "You don't miss it at all?" he asks a couple minutes later.

"I miss the weather, and I fucking hate the rain and snow in New York, but it's my home now. I have a pad in L.A., but that's purely so I have a place to stay when we're here on business. The minute I don't need it, I'm selling it." I shove my feet up on the empty side of the booth, stretching out my legs. "Nice place Jordan's got here, and business looks good."

The large stage is the center attraction, as well as the sizable dance floor in front of it, currently occupied by an enthusiastic crowd, jumping around to the local band playing tonight. They've mainly stuck to playing covers, interspersed with some original stuff. They're decent, and the crowd seems to agree. Oversized, cozy booths and sleek, leather furniture round out the décor in the space. There are two bars, one on the left and right side of the rooms, and both are mobbed with customers lining up for drinks.

"This place is a goldmine. Jordan's a shrewd businessman even if you wouldn't think it looking at him." Jordan's tatted up like Sawyer, but he's shorter and stockier, and in his black shirt, worn jeans, and scuffed boots, he looks more like a customer than the owner. "Most everyone underestimates him, and he has a lot of self-doubt, but he's done good with the place," Sawyer adds with a note of pride.

Just then, the gorgeous female bartender approaches our table, fixing Sawyer with a look that would get most guys in trouble if they tried it. Her generous tits are almost spilling out of the tight-fitting corset top she's wearing, but she's still got nothing on Zeta. And, of course, my mind goes there again. It's been worse today because being back in Orange County always reminds me of her.

"I'll be back," Sawyer says, sliding out of the booth and shooting me a knowing look.

I unscrew the cap on the bottle of whiskey. "Take your time, man. I'm going nowhere."

"You could always join us," the pretty bartender says, eye-fucking me without shame.

I'm smiling as I shake my head. "Thanks for the offer, sweetheart, but I'm good right here."

I don't want to fuck anyone in the mood I'm in. Tonight, I just need to drink myself into oblivion. To blank all thoughts and memories from my mind.

I've drunk half the bottle by the time Sawyer returns, and I'm well on my way to achieving my goals. His hair has that just fucked look about it, but he doesn't look overly happy. "She a shit lay?" I ask, quirking a brow in surprise, because that woman looked like she knew how to show a guy a good time. I pour him a double, because he's got some catching up to do, and he takes the drink from my hand, knocking half it back.

"Sasha's a great fuck, and we tend to screw whenever I drop by the bar, but I'm just not feeling it tonight."

"I hear ya."

We don't talk for ages, and I get a sense Sawyer's got a lot on his mind too. We sit in companionable silence, drinking and listening to the music, slowly getting smashed.

"You ever been in love?" he asks me, a while later, completely out of the blue.

Reporters love to ask this question, and I always lie, but Sawyer's a buddy, and it's not like we usually sit around and talk about this shit, so I give him an honest answer. "I was in love once."

"What happened?" He crosses a leg over his knee, slouching a little.

"Fate fucked me over." I pour another shot of whiskey and knock it back in one go. The room spins, and I close my eyes for a second.

"Tell me about it," he murmurs, sounding as sad as I feel.

"And you?" I have a feeling I'm slurring my words.

He glances briefly over his shoulder before answering me.

"I think I might be in love," he confirms in a low voice, and I wonder if he's afraid of someone overhearing or if he's just afraid of admitting it to himself.

"Good for you." I throw back my drink.

"She'll never be mine," he adds, draining his own drink. "Fate fucked me over too."

"I'm sorry, man."

"Tell me it gets easier. Tell me I'll be able to move on," he continues, his voice laced with pain.

"You want me to lie or you want the truth?"

"Fuck." He buries his head in his hands, and we're both quiet for a few beats. When he lifts his head up, I spot the torment written all over his face. "How do you deal with it?"

I shrug. "I do everything I can to numb the pain. Bleed my emotions onto the page and infuse it into my music. Work nonstop. Fuck around, get drunk, get high more than I should, but nothing works." I tap my temple. "She's embedded so far into my psyche that I'll never be able to forget her, and there's a sick part of me that doesn't want to. A part that clings on even when there's no hope of anything changing. But it doesn't seem to matter. She's the love of my life."

I pause to draw a breath because I'm close to losing it, and this conversation is already weird as fuck. Sawyer and I don't usually do this, but I'm figuring he needed this night as much as me.

"I knew it the minute I met her," I explain, "and I know there'll never be anyone else. She's it for me, but she'll never be mine, and I have to live with that knowledge every fucking day, and every fucking day it almost kills me."

"Fuck me. I wish I'd never asked." Sawyer sighs, dragging a hand through his black hair.

"I never imagined you could have it all yet have nothing at the same time," I muse, resting my head back. "My success, my life, means absolutely nothing without her, and I don't know how much longer I can go on like this—just existing, not living." Pain is a heavy weight pressing down on my chest. "I just want to hold her and touch her and wake up with her lying by my side." I snort out a laugh, and Sawyer pins me with a questioning look. "I sound like a total fucking pussy."

He smirks, looking over his shoulder again. "Just making sure there's no reporters around. Imagine someone overheard us; we'd never live it down." He chuckles.

Mention of reporters makes me wonder if he knows Zeta. I'm sure he does. *RockOut* covers all the main events. But I don't ask him because he hasn't offered up the name of his mystery love, and I'd rather speak in hypotheticals. "I can see the headline now. *Bad boys of rock struck with the lovesick bug!*" I joke, even though there's nothing amusing about it.

Sawyer seems to agree as his smile fades. Silence engulfs us for a beat, and I sigh. "This fucking blows, man." He slides out of the booth, and I think I might've run him off.

"You going somewhere?"

"I'm not nearly shitfaced enough for this conversation." He jerks his head in the direction of the nearest bar. "I'm getting us another bottle."

ZETA

"Hell no." I shake my head. "No way." My boss has just summoned me to his office and informed me I'm to attend the press conference and private interview with Torment later on today. "Why isn't Kayla going?"

"Because she's gone into labor."

"What!?" I screech, jumping up and knocking the chair to the ground. "But she's still got two weeks to go!" My tone is borderline hysterical.

"All I know is her water broke an hour ago, and she was en route to the hospital when she called," Harrison says, and I bolt out of his office door, racing back to my workstation.

I shove papers off my desk onto the floor, desperately searching for my cell. I'd switched it off this morning because I was trying to finish an article for this week's edition, and I didn't want any distractions.

"What's wrong?" Brody asks from behind me.

I don't look up, grabbing my bag and rummaging through it. "Kayla's in labor, and I can't find my cell."

"It's right there."

I look over my shoulder, following his pointed finger. My

cell is sitting on top of the small printer on my desk, right where I left it. I hate feeling flustered, but I'm worried about my friend. I make a grab for it as Brody's hands land on my shoulders, and he starts rubbing the corded muscle he finds there. "Don't touch me." I shirk his hands off, still hating it when anyone touches me uninvited. And Brody's been very touchy-feely since we had sex, and it unnerves me.

"Relax, Zeta. I'm only trying to help." His blue eyes radiate sincerity, and I know he means well and that there wasn't any ulterior motive.

Brody is a nice guy, and he's hot, smart, and funny.

Perfect boyfriend-slash-husband material.

Maybe if I wasn't so hung up on a boy from my past, we might have a shot at something. I think it, but I don't believe it. Brody's never been my type. I prefer the moody, possessive, asshole rocker type. The type who promises you the world and then flees without a proper explanation, stomping on your heart and leaving you broken forever.

"I know, and thank you, but I've got it from here." I send him a tight smile, and he walks back to his desk, looking a little crestfallen.

I grab my cell and my empty mug and make my way into the staff kitchen. I skim over the missed calls and texts from Kayla as I switch the Keurig on, calling her back. She doesn't pick up, and my panic-o-meter cranks up a few levels. I call her again, and this time, Gage answers. "Hey, Zeta. Kayla's a little busy right now."

"Is she okay? Is the baby okay?" I ask as I hear muffled sounds of conversation in the background, and then Kayla's on the line.

"It's okay to be an only child, right? Because I'm never going through this again," she shouts, panting like she's running a marathon.

"But everything's okay though, right? There isn't anything to worry about?"

"Our boy thought he'd surprise us early, but everything's good, according to the doctor."

"Thank God." A layer of stress lifts off my shoulders. "I shrieked at Harrison and ran out of his office the minute he told me. I was freaking out so bad."

"My notes for the Torment interview are in the top drawer of my desk," she says, in between panting down the line.

"Don't worry about that. I'll handle it," I lie, not wanting to stress her out.

She bursts out laughing. "You're such a bad liar. Oh, my fucking God!" she screeches, and my ears protest in earnest. "You are never getting laid again!" she screams at Gage, I presume. "Zeta, babe, I've got to go," she pants. "I've got a little person to squeeze out my hoo-ha."

I roll my eyes, laughing. "I'm on my way. I'll see you soon. Good luck."

By the time I arrive at the hospital, Kayla has already delivered her son. He looks just like his daddy, something Kayla is not impressed with. She hasn't stopped lamenting how she did all the work and the child doesn't resemble her in the slightest. But I know she's only kidding, because the way she gazes adoringly at her beautiful son, and the way she swoons at Gage, tells me the opposite.

I rush out of there an hour later, heading to the hotel in Manhattan where the press conference is being held, trying not to lose the contents of my stomach on the way.

I stare out the window of the cab, trying to convince myself I can do this. But I'm a fucking nervous wreck every time I think about being in the same room as Ryder again. My hand is shaking, my leg won't stop jerking, and the butterflies in my chest are going haywire, making me even more on edge. I take deep breaths, telling myself I'm a grown-ass woman, a professional music journalist, and he's only another egotistical rock star with an inflated sense of self-importance. I've met my fair share of them over the last few years, so I can handle Ryder Stone, I lie to myself.

I touch up my makeup, run a comb through my long wavy hair, and spritz some perfume on my wrists and neck before smoothing the wrinkles out of the tight-fitting black minidress I'm wearing today. I've teamed it with my studded knee-length boots, and I brought my gray leather jacket and silk scarf with me too. I'm hoping if I look suitably composed that it might disguise the mess I'm hiding inside.

I flash my media card at the beefy bouncer standing guard outside the room in the hotel where the conference is taking place, and he opens the door for me. I say hi to a few reporters I know as I make my way through the room, hoping they can't tell I'm on the verge of a mini meltdown. Choosing the most innocuous seat I can find—in the middle, over on the far left —I'm hoping I can blend into the background and go unnoticed. I've already decided that I'm not asking any questions. The last thing I want to do is draw attention to myself while there are cameras around. I have no idea how Ryder will react when he sees me, and I'm not sure if he's been informed that I've replaced Kayla. I don't want anyone suspecting we have a past, because I like my anonymity, and I have zero desire to have my name connected to his or splashed all over social media.

So, I'll keep a low profile during the press conference and take advantage of the opportunity to get used to seeing him up close and personal again. Hopefully, by the time I speak to the band in private, I'll have gotten a hold of myself.

But I've either underestimated how delusional I am or I've forgotten the power that man holds over me.

Their manager opens the meeting, welcoming the assembled media audience and thanking us for coming. My knee is bouncing off the ground, and I press my free hand into my thigh, urging my body to cooperate. A little whimper flies out of my mouth when the side door opens and Garrett Jones steps into the room. I can see Scott White standing behind him and two more forms at his back. All the blood drains from my face and my stomach is churning so badly, I'm terrified I'm going to puke. The hand holding my pen and notepad is shaking like I have no control over my limbs.

The guy sitting beside me stares at me like I'm some dazed newbie or a crazy fan who managed to smuggle her way inside.

One by one, the band enters the room and steps up onto the podium. My heart is beating a hundred miles an hour, and I clamp a hand over my mouth as nausea swims up my throat.

Please don't throw up. Please don't throw up. I repeat it on a mantra as my body floods with nervous adrenaline.

I should've made Brody come in my place. I'm sure I could've sweet-talked him into it. Why the fuck didn't I think of that earlier?

Micah Rawlings is the third member of the band to walk into the room, and then I see *him*, just outside the door, not quite visible as he hangs back, waiting for his cue. My heart stutters, and the fluttering sensation in my chest intensifies. My eyes well up, and I silently beg my body to get with the program before I completely humiliate myself.

I glance over my shoulder, wondering if I can make a last-minute dash for the exit, but the room is packed to capacity, and there are rows of reporters standing behind the occupied seats, blocking the doors and squashing that plan on the spot.

I pinch my leg hard, trying to ground myself, as Ryder steps into the room, and I stop breathing.

The rest of the room disappears in an instant, and I only see him, walking with confidence toward the podium. His dark denims hug his long, lean legs, and his vintage Rolling Stones T-shirt is molded to his toned abs and impressive chest and stretched firmly around rippling biceps. Both arms are covered in tattoos, and one of his eyebrows is pierced.

When I first saw photos of him with his newly shorn hair,

I was disappointed he'd chopped off his long blond locks, but now I see how very wrong I was. Cut tight at the sides, and slightly longer on top, there is no more hair left to hide behind, and his flawless features are on full display.

Ryder remains, to this day, the most beautiful man I've ever seen.

He flashes his trademark smile, one I know is orchestrated for the public, because his eyes don't light up the way they used to when he smiled at me, but half the women in the room still visibly swoon, totally taken in by the act.

I'm in a daze as he takes his seat alongside the other band members, and I can't drag my eyes from him. It's as if I've been transported back into my teenage body, and every emotion I felt the first time I laid eyes on him is waylaying me again. That invisible pull I always felt in his presence tugs on my heartstrings, adding to my pain.

No amount of preparation could've equipped me for this.

"Are you okay?" The man beside me whispers, peering at me with a mix of concern and wariness.

It's only now I realize my entire body is shaking and a few tears have escaped my eyes. I swipe them away quickly, fixing a smile on my face. "I'm fine. I just got some bad news before arriving," I lie. He seems to buy that, turning away and refocusing on the press conference which has just kicked off.

I try to listen, to take notes, but my concentration is screwed, and my eyes keep returning to Ryder of their own volition.

He casually leans back in his chair, answering questions when directed to him, and his passion for music still comes across loud and clear as he discusses plans for their next album and tour. But his whole demeanor changes when anyone asks anything personal, and he instantly shuts down.

In between questions, he looks distracted, shifting on his seat in a way that makes me wonder if he's high. He continuously scans the crowd, his brow slightly furrowed, and I duck my head down on several occasions when his gaze wanders in my direction.

When their manager brings the event to a close, I glance at the page in front of me, groaning when I see the measly three things I've written down. The guys better give me something good in private, or Harrison will fire my preoccupied ass.

The band members leave the stage to a rapturous round of applause, and I hang back in the crowd until I'm sure they're long gone. This also grants me time to give myself another little pep talk. However, my nerves are still frayed as I make my way to the top of the room. At this point, I'd just rather get this over and done with. There is nothing I can do to stop this train wreck from happening. Not unless I want to lose my job, and I can't afford to.

Before I lose my nerve and run out of the place, I force one foot in front of the other and approach the podium. When I introduce myself to Rod Hemsworth, shock splays across his face, and that reaction tells me a lot. "I'm taking it Ryder doesn't know I'm standing in for Mikayla?"

He composes himself rapidly, thrusting out his hand. "Forgive me, Ms. Williams. It's a pleasure to meet you. I wasn't aware Ms. Evans wasn't joining us."

"She went into early labor," I explain, "so Harrison asked me to step in. I hope it won't be a problem, and I can assure you of my professionalism."

"I don't doubt that." His smile is kind and warm, and it helps to settle my nerves a little. "Ryder has told me a lot about you, and it's truly wonderful to meet you at long last." I can't mask my surprise, and he notices. "That surprises you?"

I nod. "I can't imagine why he would have discussed me with you or anyone."

He scrubs a hand over his neatly trimmed beard as he

considers how to respond. "You have been one of the most influential people in his life."

What a crock of shit, but I smile, like expected, nodding politely. "Should we get started?" I ask before I decide to jettison my career by hightailing it out of there.

"Absolutely." He ushers me forward, and we head out through the same door the band exited.

I've heard that Rod is one of the nicest managers in the business, and by the time we arrive at the suite where the band is waiting, I concur, even if half of what he said went in one ear and out the next. It's difficult to concentrate on conversation when my heart's about to take flight from my chest.

I wipe my clammy hands down the front of my dress as Rod escorts me into the presidential suite, repeatedly telling myself I'm a professional and I can do this, in the hope it might actually stick.

When we enter the main living area, only three members of the band are present. Ryder is noticeably absent, and a strange combination of relief and disappointment washes over me.

No wonder the guy downstairs was looking at me like I'm insane, because I'm so highly strung it feels like I'm about to snap.

Garrett Jones is the first to approach me, his eyes drinking me in with obvious pleasure as he steps forward, taking my hand without invitation and bringing it to his lips. I think I hear Rod sigh, but I could be mistaken.

Gosh, Garrett is really fucking hot in the flesh. The videos and pics I've seen of him do not do him justice at all.

With his cropped dark hair and piercing green eyes, he's working a completely different look to Ryder even if they share a love of tattoos and eyebrow piercings. "Aren't you a sight for sore eyes?" he says, by way of introduction, and I fight an eye roll.

"Aren't you a walking cliché," I retort, more calmly than I feel, clutching the strap of my bag like it's a lifeline.

"Never pretended to be anything else," he quips, gesturing at himself. "What you see is what you get." He leans in closer to me. "Liking what you see yet?"

Ugh.

"If you think those cheesy pickup lines will work on me, think again." I take a couple steps back, lifting my chin up and straightening my spine, hoping it hides how badly I'm shaking right now. I've faked bravado on more than one occasion, and I can do it again. Although I know it's easier because Ryder's not in the room.

"Can I get you anything to eat or drink, Ms. Williams," Rod asks, holding out his hand for my jacket.

"A bottle of water would be great." I remove my jacket and scarf and hand them to him. "And please call me Zeta."

I put that out there as a test because I want to see how the other members of the band react to my name. It's not that common, and I want to know if Ryder has told them about me too. But as I subtly peruse their reactions, I realize they have no clue who I am, and that relaxes me a little more. The only guy with a spark of recognition is the big guy standing in the corner of the room with his arms folded. Judging by the size of him, and his serious manner, I'm guessing he's part of their security detail.

"Where is Ryder?" Rod asks as he steps into the kitchen.

"He had some *business* to attend to," Garrett says, waggling his brows and enunciating the word so it's clear exactly what he means.

My face twists into a grimace. Really? He's that desperate to blow his load he couldn't wait till after our meeting concluded? A stab of pain slices through my heart, but I latch onto my anger instead, focusing on his lack of professionalism rather than the image of him fucking some random girl while keeping me waiting.

"Don't sweat it, boss," Micah says, smiling at me. "We'll take great care of Zeta while we wait for the slut to show his face." He pushes Garrett aside, leaning in to kiss me on the cheek. "I'm Micah, and you're beautiful."

"Flattery won't work either," I deadpan, and he laughs.

"Worth a try," he says, winking as he reclaims his seat.

Scott White is the last one to come forward. He shakes my hand firmly. "Take no notice of these d-bags. They still act like they're in high school."

"Don't worry. I've been around enough rock stars to know the score. And I'd put it more at middle school level," I joke, accepting a bottle of water from Rod with a smile.

"Mikayla isn't available because she's just had a baby," Rod explains. "Zeta also works for *RockOut,* and she has excellent credentials."

"That she does," Garrett cuts in. His eyes hungrily roam my body, lingering on my chest.

"I don't think Rod was talking about her tits, dude," Micah teases.

"Sweetheart, you have the best rack I've seen in a long time," Garrett blatantly says. "How about a little private show after we're done talking?"

"Not a chance in hell." I steel my eyes at him.

"You seem uptight," he says, his hands automatically going to my shoulders. "I can help you loosen up."

Shucking his hands off me, I give him a tight smile when I really want to knee the presumptuous prick in the balls and flip him the bird. "I'll pass. Thanks."

"C'mon, doll. I know you want to, and I'm horny as fuck." He rubs a hand over his crotch while Rod shakes his head, muttering under his breath.

I take it back.

Garrett may look hot on the outside, but his asshole personality completely diminishes his attractiveness. It's clear his rep has been well earned. "You're not seeing my tits. Or any part of me for that matter. Might as well put that out there now." I glare at him, struggling to maintain my professionalism.

"Famous last words, baby," he says, instantly dragging me back to a different time and place.

20

RYDER

Gar's words transport me back to juvie, and Lopez's voice echoes in my head as I hear him say the exact same thing to Zeta all those years ago.

I've stood in the hallway of the suite these past few minutes trying to make my legs move, but they're rooted to the marble floor, frozen in shock and disbelief. I thought I was hallucinating at first when I heard her sultry, seductive voice, and it wouldn't surprise me because she's been on my mind continuously since my visit to Orange County last week.

I've listened as Gar and Micah both hit on her, a proud smile ghosting over my lips as Zeta effortlessly deflected their piss-poor flirting attempts.

My heart is going crazy behind my rib cage, and I'm awash with emotions I've worked hard to bury. I'm torn between running in there and grabbing her into my arms or fleeing out the door.

She shouldn't be here.

I've gone to great lengths to ensure our paths never cross, but I suspect fate is fucking with me again.

Now I know why I was on edge throughout the press conference.

I felt her in the room.

I know I sound like a pussy again, but I swear I sensed she was there. I just couldn't pinpoint why every molecule of my body was on high alert, why static electricity was pulsing in the air, or why my eyes roamed the room, searching and seeking.

I know what'll happen when I step into that room. And I know I can't deflect it for much longer. I also know I have zero intention of fleeing this place. I'm not strong enough to walk away from her again.

As my mind's been churning, my feet have been moving of their own accord. I step into the living room as Gar's hand hovers over Zeta's chest. "C'mon, babe. Just let me cop a feel."

Red heat sweeps over me, and I'm two seconds away from charging the asshole when Rod rides to the rescue. "It's nice of you to finally join us, Ryder."

Zeta's facing Gar, with her back to me, and I watch her spine stiffen as the air crackles with electricity. Trailing my eyes over her curvy figure, I note she's still got beautiful long, dark hair, one hell of an ass, and those long, long legs, encased in a pair of fuck-me boots I wouldn't mind wrapping around my neck.

While I've been drooling, and Zeta's evidently distracted, Gar's made a move, and his hand now cups her left tit. Anger burns through my veins, and my hands curl into fists. "Get your fucking hands off her, Gar."

Gar removes his hand, smirking. Zeta drops her chin for a split second, and her chest heaves. Tension hovers in the space between us, and the urge to comfort her hits me hard and fast. I'm striding across the room toward her without hesitation.

Jerking her head up, she slowly turns around, and my world shifts sideways.

I slam to a halt, almost brought to my knees. I swallow hard as my heart swells to bursting point. Every single thing I've ever felt for her hits me like a bolt of lightning as we stare at one another. My heart thuds painfully, and it feels as if all the air is being squeezed from my lungs. A strange, strangled sound escapes my lips, and a single, solitary tear rolls down her cheek.

The guys trade puzzled expressions, watching the exchange between Zeta and me with avid curiosity.

I move toward her involuntarily as if some invisible string is drawing me in. "Zeta," I rasp, my voice choked with emotion. I can only imagine what's showing on my face.

My voice seems to snap her out of whatever shared emotional moment we're in. Thrusting her arms up in front of her, she holds her palms mere millimeters from my chest. "Stop right there, Rock Star."

There's not much space between us, and my eyes rake over her familiar features, while I drown in a host of competing emotions.

When I left her, she was still just a girl, but she's all woman now. I've seen photos of her during our separation, but a photo doesn't come close to the real thing. She's even more beautiful than I remember, having grown into her skin with flawless ease. She's the most stunningly gorgeous woman I've ever known, and the time apart has done nothing to dull my feelings for her.

She is still my everything.

Her smoldering eyes blaze with an indecipherable emotion, and I can't hold back. "I can't believe you're here," I croak, struggling to contain my feelings. "You look so incredibly beautiful."

A muscle ticks in her jaw and she purposely glances down my body. "Your fly's undone."

Her cold tone matches her icy expression, and I gulp over the lump suddenly clogging my throat. Gar snorts and Micah snickers while Rod and Scott look at me with the usual disappointment. Shame slays me as I zip up my fly, realizing she knows exactly why I'm late. I could tell her it's all her fault for putting me so on edge downstairs I needed the release.

When the reporter from *Blazing Trail* propositioned me in the hallway outside the conference, I didn't consider turning her down, letting her take me into the wheelchair accessible bathroom where she dropped to her knees and blew me so hard I shot my load right down her throat.

Something I'm now seriously regretting because the look of disgust on Zeta's face guts me to my core.

"It's not as bad as you're thinking," I blurt, wanting to remove that look from her face.

"Who you put your dick in is of no concern to me," she coolly states. "I'm here for one reason only, and that's for the interview. I'm on a tight schedule, so I'd prefer if we could get started. We're already behind."

My heart hurts. Like it's seriously fucking aching. I wonder if this is what it feels like right before you take a massive coronary.

"Sit down, Ryder." Rod sends me a loaded look, gesturing at the couch across from Zeta, and I move toward it in slow mo, dropping down beside Micah and Scott like I'm in a trance.

Of course, Gar has positioned himself right beside her with Rod seated in the chair in front of the fireplace. I glare at my bud, warning him with my eyes. The gloating smirk he sends me back does nothing to reassure me. I'm going to fucking kill him if he as much as looks funny at her.

Rod kicks off the meeting, explaining our idea for the new biography and confirming we had intended to offer the opportunity to Kayla, but as she's no longer available, we'd like to explore the possibility of Zeta backfilling the place.

His eyes drift to mine as he speaks, and I've got to say I'm surprised he didn't pull me aside to give me a heads-up. He knows she's my ex and she's important to me. He doesn't know the exact circumstances of how we broke up or that I'm still being blackmailed over my past. I know if I told him that he'd sic a P.I. or the police on it, and I can't take that risk.

They'd throw my ass in jail for breaking the terms of my release agreement, and then who'd protect my girl? *He's* always been very resourceful, and I'm taking no chances when it comes to Zeta's life, which is why we can't let her do this.

Or can we?

I tune out for a bit as I weigh it all up. If Zeta agreed to do this, she'd be living with us at my Hamptons house while we write and record our new album. I have the very best security system money can buy, and I can increase the security detail. There's no way he'd be able to get near her while she's there.

Excitement starts mounting as I think of this as an opportunity. If Zeta was living with me for the next few months, maybe we can reclaim what we lost. If she's willing to give me a chance, and if she still loves me as much as I love her, I'm prepared to man up and tell her the truth about my past and why I left her eight years ago.

I have the means to keep her by my side now and ensure she's well protected, something I wasn't able to do back then. It's a selfish, risky strategy, because I may have hurt her too much or left it too late, and there's no guarantee she won't hate me when she discovers the full extent of the sordid secret from my youth, but I've got to give it a try.

Because I'm sick of barely existing. Fed up of missing her to the point of constant pain.

The potential reward is worth the risk, because if it means I have a shot at having her back in my life, then I've got to try. I'll never forgive myself otherwise.

"Let's see if I've got this straight," she says, yanking me back into the conversation. "You would like me to live with the band, in *Ryder's house*"—she spews the words like they're poisonous—"for the next two to three months, to shadow them as they write and record their new album, and you'd like me to interview them together and separately during that time, to build up a bigger picture of their personal and professional evolvement over the years since the band started." She hasn't stopped for a breath, and by the way she's gesturing wildly with her hands and how her voice is elevating higher and higher with every word, I know she's severely pissed.

She's definitely not going to make this easy. But I've always loved a good challenge.

"And you want me to document it for monthly updates in *RockOut* and then to write a formal biography for worldwide publication," she adds.

"Yes." Rod nods, smiling at her as he leans forward on his knees. "That's about it in a nutshell. Obviously, you would be doing this as a *RockOut* employee, but we've prepared an offer which will pay your employer a lucrative sum for the magazine content, as well as covering your salary and all living expenses for the duration of the project, and you will get full writing credit for the biography. All royalties earned will be divided in the percentages specified between the band and yourself." He hands her an envelope. "Take your time to peruse the offer, but I think you'll agree it's a very generous one."

She hands it back to him. "Thank you, Rod. You've been very gracious, but I don't need to look at it." She stands. "The answer is no."

I jump up. "Baby, wait."

The look she gives me could cut glass. "I am *not* your baby."

"You were once." I dare her to disagree.

"You already fucked her?" Gar interjects, sending me a sour look. He's always been competitive with me, especially when it comes to women.

"Back the fuck off, Gar. This doesn't concern you." I grind my teeth to the molars, as frustration trundles through me.

Zeta turns to Gar. "For the record, he didn't fuck me. He dumped me before we got the chance."

"Are you fucking insane, dude?!" he exclaims, waving his

hands up and down her body. "At least tell me you fucked her tits."

I explode, jumping over the coffee table and lunging at him. I swing my fist, landing a right hook on the side of his jaw before Scott and Rod pull me away. Micah is doubled over, laughing like it's comedy hour. "You're fucking next if you don't shut your mouth," I growl.

"And you." I jab my finger at Gar. He's currently nursing a swollen jaw and shooting daggers at me. "Don't you ever speak about the woman I love like that."

Yep, I just blurt it out. My mouth has completely disengaged from my brain, and there's no telling what I'll say next. The guys emit a few expletives and shocked gasps, but Zeta is tellingly silent. I swing my gaze to her, and she's schooled her features into a neutral expression so I can't tell what she's thinking.

Clearing her throat, she eyeballs me with a derisory look I'd only reserve for enemies. "Nice try, Rock Star, but if you think that'll get me to say yes, you're sorely mistaken."

What's with all this *Rock Star* shit? Is she allergic to my name now? If she's trying to rile me up, it's working. "That's not why I said it." I rub a hand across the back of my neck. "Look, could we go in the other room and talk in private."

"I have nothing to say to you." She gathers up her belongings, stuffing them in her bag.

"Well, I have plenty to say to you."

"I'm not interested in anything you have to say." She slings her bag over her shoulder and purses her lips.

"Please, Zeta. Please let me explain."

"Your actions speak volumes." Sending me one last lethal look, she walks to Rod, shaking his hand. "Thank you very much for the opportunity, but I'll have to politely decline." She turns to the guys with a smile. "It was nice meeting you all. You should get some ice on that asap," she tells Gar.

"Call me." He thrusts a piece of paper with his number

into her hand. I can't tell if he's deliberately pissing me off or if he genuinely has an interest in her. Either way, it'll never happen.

Crumpling the paper in her fist, she hands it back to him. "Not if you paid me." Spinning on her heels, she ignores me as she walks toward the door.

A spurt of anger jumps up and bites me. "What? No goodbye for me?"

"I'll write you a letter," she spits out over her shoulder, slicing my heart in two all over again. I knew she probably hated me, but this level of anger speaks of deep-seated, entrenched hurt that's never healed. I desperately need a chance to fix it, and her doing this is the only way I stand a snowball's chance of getting through to her.

"You're going to do this, Zeta. This isn't the last you've seen of me."

Turning around, she plants her hands on her slim hips and fixes me with a glare the devil would be proud of. "There is nothing you can say or do that will *ever* get me to agree to this."

"You'll be eating your words soon. A little chat with your boss should do the trick." I can't help smirking because I know I've got her where I want her.

"You clearly don't know Harrison Meadows if you think you can bully him into anything."

"He'll agree if I'm his boss."

That shakes her.

"What?" she splutters

"I'll buy the fucking magazine if I have to, but mark my words, you're doing this, *baby*."

The expression on her face is classic. She looks like she wants to throttle me with her bare hands, and I'm fucking loving it. I feel alive, properly alive, for the first time in years, and I don't want to stop sparring with her, so I milk it a little longer.

Stalking toward her with a smug grin on my face, I say, "I'll get your bedroom ready, or we could just save ourselves all the back and forth, and you can move straight into mine."

I'm being an asshole. I know it. But I'll take her anger over indifference any day.

Her mouth drops open, veins thicken in her neck, and her face turns red with rage. I think she might actually hit me, but she restrains herself. "Buy the magazine, see if I care. I'll quit and get another job." Defiance glints in her eyes and as I get all up in her personal space, I want nothing more than to kiss the living daylights out of her.

My eyes drop to her lush mouth, and I'm reminded of how incredible it felt to kiss her. Before I get sidetracked, I deliver the parting shot. "Go for it, darling. I'll just buy wher-ever you move to. And if you move again, I'll do the same there. There's no way you can escape this or me." I sweep my thumb across her pouty lips. "Fate drove us apart, and now, it's bringing us back together. Stop fighting the inevitable."

"I hate you," she says, but she doesn't mean it. She doesn't even realize her body is arching toward mine, and her eyes keep lowering to my mouth. She can deny it from the rooftops all she wants, but she can't hide the truth from me. We never could shield our feelings from one another.

She still loves me.

I see it in her eyes, and as long as that truth remains there, I'm not giving up. I want her back, and this time, I'm going to fight tooth and nail to hold onto her.

"We both know that's a lie." I press my mouth to her ear. "If I slid my fingers inside you right now, how wet would you be?"

She shoves at my chest. "You...you...pig."

I chuckle, enjoying this enormously. She's all flustered, and that's my doing. I feel like patting myself on the back for a job well done.

"You can keep denying it, but we both know this is

happening. Get used to it, baby, because this is on." I slap her on the ass, and this time, I'm convinced she's going to swing at me, but she just storms out of the room, completely agitated, before returning two seconds later.

"Deny this, asshole," she fumes, violently flipping me the bird.

There's my girl, and this time, I'm not running away from her. If I have to be an asshole to ensure she's back in my life, then so be it. Because I'm not letting *him* scare me into pushing her away again. I'm going to protect her and keep her safe, and I'm going to prove to her that we are meant to be together.

I'm not giving up until she's back in my arms again.

21

ZETA

I cradle the phone under my neck while I use my free hands to open a bottle of wine, pouring a large glass and taking a quick sip. My plan is to get completely trashed so I don't even remember my name. Maybe that way, I can stop rethinking the shitshow that was my life today. "I really fucking hate him."

"No, you don't," Kayla calmly protests. "You love him. It's always been him. It's why you've never entertained the idea of a relationship with anyone else."

"Don't say that to me," I plead, gulping down wine.

"The truth hurts, babe, but it's time you faced up to it. And I knew he still loved you. I just knew it."

"I'm not buying that crap. It's a ploy to get me into his bed because he never made it there the last time. That's all this is."

"Well, you won't know unless you take a chance, and the opportunity is too good to pass up. Think of all the other offers that will roll in once you're a published author. And think of the money, babe. I wouldn't be too hasty to turn it down."

"Maybe you should do it. They were going to offer it to

you first, and you're the one with family responsibilities. You need the money more than I do."

"Girl, are you high? You really think Gage is gonna let me live with Torment knowing their reputation?"

I open my mouth to say they wouldn't hit on her knowing she's engaged and has a baby with her fiancé, but who am I kidding? Something like that wouldn't matter to Garrett Jones.

"And I very much doubt Ryder's going to back down now you've come barreling into his life again. He sounds determined."

"He couldn't really buy the magazine, could he?"

"Of course, he could," she unhelpfully confirms, yawning. "Those extravagant bastards can buy anything they want. Everything is available for a price."

Guilt slaps me in the face. "You've had an exhausting day, and I shouldn't be burdening you with my shit. Go be with your family. I'll come visit tomorrow."

"Zeta." She uses her adulting tone.

"What?"

"I know you're scared, and I know he hurt you, but maybe he's right. Maybe it *is* fate. Maybe this is where the last eight years have been leading. And if nothing comes of it, at least you'll get closure. And this could be amazing for your career. If you let it go, you could end up kicking yourself in the ass." She pauses, and I let her words settle in. "At least take some time to think about it. You can't make a logical decision when you're so emotional."

"I'll think about it," I promise. "Now go give that adorable little boy a big kiss from me."

I fall asleep on the couch midway through the second bottle of wine.

Sometime later, I'm woken by the incessant chiming of the bell. I glance at the time on my cell through bleary eyes. It's not even eleven. Guess the wine combined with my overwrought emotional state was enough to send me to sleep way before my usual bedtime.

I'm rubbing my tired eyes as I pad toward the door, yawning. I peer through the peephole and jerk back, the sight of Ryder standing in my hallway is enough to induce a rapid case of tummy flutters.

"Zeta, open up." He pounds his fists on the door. "I'm not leaving until you talk to me. I'll just sit out here all night." I think he's stubborn enough to do it too.

Ignoring the butterflies careening around my chest, I open the door and scowl at him. Well, it was either that or swoon, because he looks completely fuckable in his jeans, white tee, black leather jacket, boots, and beanie combo. He might as well have written Rock God on his forehead to complete the look. "What do you want?"

"Wow. Is that how you usually greet your guests?" His eyes twinkle with mirth, and his lips twitch.

"Only the unwanted ones." His smile drops, and I feel like a bit of a bitch. Someone opens their door across the way, and I sigh. "Come in." I step aside to let him enter because I don't want to have this convo with an audience. He bends down, retrieving a box I hadn't noticed on the floor before stepping into my modest condo.

"Cute PJs." His eyes do a quick one-over of my *Frozen* sleep shorts and tank top attire, and I curse my sleepyhead for opening the door without giving any consideration to my state of undress.

I cross my arms over my braless chest, and he works hard to keep his eyes on my face. I don't owe him anything, and it's probably best not to engage him in conversation, but I find my mouth opening anyway. "My five-year-old cousin Kendall loves *Frozen*, and Jill bought us matching pajama sets for Christmas because I was the one who got her hooked on the movie."

"How is Jill?" he asks, shutting the door with his booted

foot. I narrow my eyes at him, and he shrugs innocently. "It was drafty."

"She's great. She's married now, and her and Liam have a son too. Kyle is four and a real little monkey." I smile as I think of my two adorable cousins.

"I'm really glad things worked out there for you." He smiles, and unlike earlier today, it's warm and genuine, and it meets his eyes. I'm struck dumb for a moment, until I snap out of it. It's too easy to fall under Ryder's spell, but I'm not a naïve teenager anymore. And I haven't forgotten how he broke my heart by dumping me for someone else.

"Why don't you take a seat in the living room while I pull on something warmer." I point in the direction of the living room.

"Don't feel the need to do that on my account." His eyes glimmer suggestively. "I'm quite happy with the view."

"Wow. Original. I bet you give Garrett a run for his money."

The spark in his eyes dies. "Don't compare me to that douche."

"I thought you were friends and partners in crime?"

"We are, doesn't mean he's not a douche."

I roll my eyes. "Make yourself at home. I'll be back in a minute."

I practically sprint to my bedroom, slamming the door closed and leaning back against it as I take deep breaths in an attempt to calm my overactive libido down.

Just because Ryder is hot as sin doesn't forgive his past behavior.

It seems my body needs reminding of that.

I hate that he still affects me so potently, and I wish he wouldn't. Overindulging in wine hasn't helped either, but I'm not letting him get to me. It's obvious why he's here. He's on a mission to convince me to do this, and while Kayla almost persuaded me earlier, I've given it more thought, and there's no way I can commit to this insanity.

He wounded me. As surely as if he'd taken a knife and sliced up my heart. Smiling, flirting, and professing love can't ever erase that truth. And I need to always remember that. My priority here is protecting my heart from further annihilation and the only way I can do that is to stay away from him.

What happened today has forced me to face some facts. One: I'm still completely and utterly, irrevocably in love with Ryder Stone. Two: I'm still undeniably attracted to him on every conceivable level. Three: My willpower is seriously tested in his presence, and I doubt I'm strong enough to resist his allure if I'm faced with all that gorgeousness on a daily basis. And four: I'm pathetic beyond belief and seriously ashamed of how fucking weak I am when it comes to him.

I pull on a pair of yoga pants and zip a hoodie up over my flimsy tank before making my way out to the living room.

I don't sit, and I don't offer him anything to drink because he's not staying long. "I know why you're here, and you're wasting your time. I'm not doing it."

His leather jacket is draped over the back of my couch, and he's leaning back with one leg crossed over the other, looking like he owns the place. He stares at me for a few seconds before responding, and his focused gaze raises all the tiny hairs on the back of my neck.

"Let's just sit and talk for a bit."

I fold my arms across my chest again. "Let's not."

"Please, Zeta." His voice is soft, and he sits up straighter, leaning his arms on his knees. His biceps roll and flex with the movement, and it takes colossal willpower not to drool. Ryder has some seriously hot arm porn going on, and that thought sends a shot of liquid lust straight to my groin. I mentally slap myself upside the head, reminding myself he's no good for me.

"I know I hurt you, but if I ever meant anything to you, please just give me a few minutes of your time," he beseeches.

His earnest expression matches his sincere tone, and I reluctantly nod, sitting on the other end of the couch, putting as much distance between us as I can.

He clears his throat, and if I didn't know better, I'd say he was nervous. "It was really good to see you today, and it made me realize how much I've missed your company and your friendship." His Adam's apple bobs in his throat. "I've wanted to reach out to you so many times—"

"Why didn't you?" I blurt, cutting across him.

"I was afraid you'd want nothing to do with me, and I wasn't sure I could handle the rejection."

That stings, and I want him to know it. "Afraid I'd give you a taste of your own medicine?"

His yellow-green eyes bore into mine, and they're suffused with guilt and regret. "I deserved that, and for what it's worth, I'm so fucking sorry, Zeta."

"It doesn't matter." I shrug it off, adding another layer to the wall around my heart. "It's in the past, and we were just naïve kids with foolish notions."

"Don't do that." He shakes his head. "Don't dismiss what we shared."

"I wasn't the one who did that. That's all on you, Rock Star."

He sighs, dragging a hand through his dirty-blond hair. "Look, I didn't come here to argue with you."

"Why did you come here?" I fiddle with the bracelet on my wrist, confused and conflicted and wondering why the hell I'm entertaining this conversation with the guy who broke my heart and left me bleeding out through open wounds that have never healed.

"Take the job, Zeta. It's a fantastic career opportunity, and the money's great. I don't want you to turn that down because of me. I give you my word I'll behave myself. I won't lay a finger on you"—his lips kick up at the corners—"unless you ask me to."

"I don't think it's a good idea for us to work together, Ryder. I just don't see how it ends well."

He scrubs a hand over his stubbly chin. "We used to work really well together, remember?" I nod, thinking of how we used to spend most every afternoon writing songs. "And you're passionate about music. You'll be in the thick of the whole creative process, and I know you'll get a kick out of that." His voice is animated, his eyes bright, as he continues. "And you'll love the house. It's right on the beach, and it's completely private, and you can swim or run or walk every day, hell, you can even do your yoga on the beach, and—"

"How do you know I do yoga?" Suspicion underscores my tone.

"I was speaking in general terms." He shrugs casually. "Tons of New Yorkers are into yoga, it wasn't a stretch suggesting it."

He looks like butter wouldn't melt in his mouth, and I have no clue if he's lying to me or not. But in the grand scheme of things, it doesn't matter, so I let it go. "The house sounds amazing, and I'm grateful for the opportunity, but it's not something I can get behind. Sorry." I stand, making it clear this discussion is over.

He rises, staring at me across the coffee table. "Zeta, please just think about it. Sleep on it." His soulful eyes plead with me, and I hate that he's starting to suck me in. "We could renew our friendship. Help heal the mistakes of the past. You may not need that, but I do."

"Don't try and guilt me into this, because that will only have the opposite effect."

"That's not what I'm trying to do." He walks over to me, stopping a few inches from my face. "We were the best of friends before we were anything else, and I've missed that. You were the only friend I had who really understood me. And I know you too. I know you want to do this, but you're purposely holding back."

"You knew the girl I was, but you don't know the woman I've become."

"That may be true, but I'd like to get a chance to know her."

I rub a tense spot between my brows. The intensity of this conversation is giving me a headache. Or it's possible it's the wine. "I'll sleep on it," I say, purely to get rid of him. I'm even more determined I'm not doing it now.

Tentatively, he reaches out, running his fingers through my hair. I feel his touch from the top of my head to the tips of my toes, and the most intense longing infiltrates every nook and cranny of my body. I jerk away from him before I do something I'll regret. "Thank you for dropping by, but it's late, and I've got work tomorrow."

A look of incredible sadness appears on his face, and he nods. Bending over the box on the floor, he opens it, pulling out my jacket, scarf, and the envelope with the written offer. "You left these behind," he says, placing them on the table. Then he removes a gorgeous bouquet of colorful flowers, shyly handing them to me. "And this is an apology for acting like an ass earlier."

No one has ever given me flowers before, and the surge of joy lighting up my insides reminds me I'm on shaky ground. "Thank you. They're beautiful."

Our fingers brush as I take the flowers from him, sending fiery tingles zipping up my arm. Electricity crackles in the space between us and from his subtle intake of breath I'm guessing he still feels it too. I shouldn't be surprised because it's not like I ever fell out of lust or love with him. But he did…

My head is a mess as I walk him to the door, and I know I have to ask this. "Who was the girl?"

"What girl?" He frowns.

"The one you left me for." I hate how pitifully sad I sound and how my throat tightens, my heart pounds, and my stomach twists into painful knots. Even after all this time, knowing I wasn't enough for him and that I couldn't hold onto him still hurts.

He takes his time answering me, rubbing his palms down the front of his jeans and shuffling nervously on his feet. In a quiet voice he says. "There wasn't any girl, Zeta. I lied about that. There's only ever been you."

I step back as if slapped, my jaw slackening with shock. Peering into his eyes, I see the truth shining back at me, and I'm staggered.

I've always had tons of unanswered questions because of the way we broke up, but I never doubted there was someone else, because I was hardly the catch of the century and he was so amazing and gorgeous and attentive, and I knew girls must've been throwing themselves at him while I was still in juvie. I also knew he was a virgin back then, and horny as fuck, so I guessed some girl had tempted him with her magical vajayjay and that's why he'd left. That knowledge, and the accompanying pain, crushed me for years, and it took me a long time to move on.

His statement has thrown everything upside down, and I don't know how to think, how to feel. I don't know if this changes anything or not.

The world spins, and I sway a little. He reaches out, holding onto my elbow, keeping me upright, as concern, remorse, and regret flare in his eyes.

"Why then? Why did you do it?"

He stares straight at me, holding nothing back, and so much passes between us in the moment it almost undoes me. His eyes radiate with pain when he answers. "I was scared, and I believed you were better off without me."

Tears prick my eyes, and I can hardly speak over the emotion wedged in my throat. "You cut me out of the decision, and you didn't even have the guts to break up with me in person. You were just gone."

"Because I knew one look at your face would shatter my resolve and I wouldn't go through with it. I also knew you'd come looking for me, so that's why I lied about the girl, but there was no one. I swear."

He takes hold of both my hands, his eyes welling up. "The truth is, I intentionally hurt both of us because I believed I was doing the right thing for you. I loved you enough to walk away even though it killed me, and if I had to do it all over again, I'd still make the same call, because I couldn't take care of you back then. But I can now, and all I'm asking for is a chance to get to know you again. No strings or expectations. Let's just do this and see where it leads."

He rubs his thumb across the back of my hand in soothing circular motions, like he used to always do, and the feel of his callused skin against mine sends memories scurrying to the forefront of my mind.

"You hurt me so much, Ryder, and I don't know that I can ever forgive you. I don't know if this makes any difference," I truthfully reply.

For a split second, I think he might actually cry, but he composes himself. "Everything I said earlier still stands. Don't refuse this opportunity because of me. I promise I won't do anything to make you uncomfortable, and maybe this will help both of us to forget about the past, because I think you need that as much as me."

RYDER

My heart is heavy as I exit the building where Zeta lives. Pulling the collar of my jacket up and keeping my head down low, I run across the street to where Mike has the SUV parked. I climb in the back, and he starts up the engine. "Where to, boss?"

"Home." I stare out the window, not really seeing anything. I was all fired up on my way over to speak to her, but now I'm definitely feeling the blues.

She's going to turn it down.

She's built a cage around her heart, and she's determined to keep me out.

The fact she still loves me is of no consequence if I can't get through to her. I remove the flask from my inside jacket pocket and gulp back a few mouthfuls of vodka.

"You doing okay, Ryder?" Mike asks, glancing briefly at me through the mirror.

"She'll never forgive me," I murmur, keeping my eyes locked on the window as we navigate our way out of Queens.

"What's the deal with this woman anyway?" Mike must have guessed by now she's important to me, but he's never asked me about her before.

I meet his gaze in the mirror. "She's my one and only, Mike. She means the world to me."

He nods. "I thought as much."

We don't talk about Zeta anymore, and that's one of the reasons why Mike is so damned good at his job. He's discreet, and he knows when to put a sock in it.

My inclination is to drown my sorrows in the usual way, and it'd be easy to block all my feelings out, but I can't get despondent at the first hurdle. Nothing worth fighting for in life comes easy, and I've got to stop feeling sorry for myself and finally fucking do something to take back control of my life.

I pull out my cell and call up my financial guy. I don't care that it's almost midnight. I pay him enough to take my fucking call no matter what time of the day or night it is. He answers on the fifth ring. "Mr. Stone. What can I do you for?"

"Two things. That financial transaction I asked you to take care of a few months back, that was done, right?"

"I handled it. The debt has been cleared, and the monthly mortgage payment is being redirected into an interest-bearing account."

"Good. There's something I need you to do for me now, and it can't wait."

"Whatever you need, consider it done."

"I need you to purchase *RockOut* magazine."

𝄞 ♫

"You've lost it, dude. You've seriously fucking lost it." Gar looks at me like I've grown ten heads overnight. "Are you shitting me right now, or you actually fucking did it?"

I shrug, refilling my coffee cup. "I did it. I'm now the proud owner of *RockOut* magazine."

"You really love this girl?" Scott inquires, looking

genuinely interested as he leans his elbows on the counter in my kitchen.

"She's the only girl I've ever loved. The only one I ever will."

"So why are we only hearing about her now?" Micah asks, crossing his legs at the ankles.

"It's complicated." I wonder how much to say. I'm not sure how much Zeta tells people about her past, but if she's going to live with us for the next few months, I doubt it's something either one of us can keep hidden, so I figure I might as well set the scene. "We actually met in juvie."

"Fuck. Me." Gar runs a hand through his hair, shaking his head and sulking.

"What now?" I regard him warily.

"She's sexy, fiery, smart, and a badass, and she just has to be the one woman I have zero chance of nailing."

I slam my mug down, coffee spilling onto the counter. "You're a fucking asshole, you know that."

"Man, you've got to put a lid on that crap," Scott interjects. "You can't speak like that around her or about her. Show some respect."

Gar shoves up his middle finger. "I don't need another lecture. I already got one from the pussy over there." He points at me. "And contrary to popular belief, I'm not an asshole. I'd never hit on any of your women, so give me a fucking break, and get off my back."

I'm not sure how much I believe that statement, but I'll give him the benefit of the doubt. "Okay, relax, we're cool. I've told Rod to make arrangements for next weekend, so you've all got this week to sort your shit out."

"And Zeta's really on board with this?" Scott asks with a hint of disbelief.

I smirk. "She didn't have much of a choice. I seriously thought she was going to punch me in the nuts when she found out."

Micah chuckles. "I would've loved to have been a fly on the wall for that meeting."

Because I wasn't taking any chances, I offered double the market value for the magazine, and the owner didn't hesitate to accept. The paperwork was pushed through fast, and that's how I found myself at *RockOut*'s offices this morning addressing a group of my new employees. Most were shocked and excited. A few were nervous until I explained it was business as usual and there would be no changes. I have zero desire to run a magazine. It was purely a means to an end, so Harrison Meadows will continue in his role as CEO, and he'll report to Rod and my financial guy. They'll look after my investment.

Zeta was fuming, and she threw a hissy fit, screaming and shouting and flinging obscenities at me. It was seriously hot, and I don't know how I resisted body slamming her into the wall and fucking her senseless, but I did. Even the thought of being inside her makes me painfully hard.

I don't blame her for her reaction.

It was a serious asshole move on my part, but I can't lose her again, and I'm taking no chances. Once I win her back, I'll transfer ownership of the magazine into her name or I'll sell it. Whatever she wants. But I'm not sorry I've done this if it means I get a second chance with her. That's worth every temper tantrum she wants to direct my way.

I'M at the twenty-four-hour bar around the corner from our usual meeting point, sipping a beer and trying to quell the rage burning me from the inside out.

It's the same every few months when I have to make the drop-off.

This is the one aspect of my life no one knows about, so I have no choice but to handle this myself even if I truly hate it.

I despise seeing his face up close and personal.

And I loathe handing over the cash.

But he has me by the balls, and we both know it.

So here I am. Eight years later. Still beholden to my past. Still being blackmailed with no end in sight, and it's playing havoc with my emotions. The nightmares are always more frequent after one of the drop-offs, and it's why I usually drown myself in drink, drugs, and pussy for days after I've faced him, because I just can't handle thinking about it anymore.

The guilt is never ending.

Guilt for the boy who didn't get to live his life.

Guilt over abandoning Zeta like that.

Guilt over what I did to Luc.

I'm a bad person.

A selfish asshole, because I should be pushing Zeta away again not trying to reel her back in.

But I need her.

Fuck, do I ever need her.

Since we met again, things have been that little bit more bearable, and I know letting her back into my life will help ease my suffering. That last year in juvie was one of the most stable periods in my life—because of her.

She turned my world from dark to light.

She gave me hope and fostered self-belief.

I always felt like I could do anything when she was by my side.

Her love literally lifted me to new heights.

She made me feel worthy for the first time ever.

I've never felt the same connection with any other woman. They are just nameless, faceless fucks who help me get out of my head for a while, but I've never felt anything when I'm with them, never allowed anyone to get close enough to try.

Not like with her. Zeta only has to step into a room, and I'm drawn to her in a way I can't explain or describe.

"Looking for some company tonight, sexy?" The bartender cuts through my thoughts, leaning forward on the counter, deliberately flashing me her tits.

"Not tonight, Rita." I only ever come to this bar when I'm meeting *him*. A couple times, I've been so traumatized after the drop-off I've come back inside and practically drank the bar dry.

The last time I was here, I fucked Rita in the lane out back, but I was so smashed I didn't even wait for her to come. I was rough, and I came fucking hard, then pulled up my pants, and walked off without a word. I felt bad about that the next day. I always try to ensure the girl gets off, but I was a selfish jackass that night. If I was a normal guy, I doubt she'd be asking for seconds, but most girls have an agenda when it comes to rock stars.

I generally stick to groupies, because most encounters take place when we're on tour, and the chance of bumping into them again is slim.

Fucking women who hang out in the places I frequent in New York is a recipe for disaster, because they always come back for more even when I explain it's only a one-time thing. I've messed up a few times, and it's always come back to bite me in the ass.

I throw a few bills on the counter, slide off the stool, and walk out of the bar.

It's three a.m., but there are still people milling about. I pull my hoodie up over my head and keep my chin down.

One of the things I like most about living in New York is how blasé most people are about the celebrities living in their midst. Greenwich Village is home to plenty of famous people because no one usually bothers us here. I can walk about without being deluged. Sure, you get tourists stopping and asking for autographs, but most locals just stare and drool. I regularly run the streets in the early hours of the morning when I can't sleep, and I love the sense of freedom I feel as I pound the sidewalks.

Tonight, though, I don't want anyone to recognize me for obvious reasons.

I slip into the narrow alleyway and head toward the over-flowing dumpster. He steps out of the shadows, and a red mist ghosts over my eyes like always. Looking at him sickens me every time. He thinks he looks legit because he wears an expensive suit and watch, both bought on my dime, but one look into those cold, hard eyes reveals the truth.

"You're late," he snaps, reaching an arm out for me.

I clamp my hand on his muscular arm, stopping him from going for my throat. I haven't let him touch me like that in years, and I'm not about to let him now. "Take your fucking hands off me, or this'll be the last time you see me."

He chuckles. "You always were a stupid little punk."

I thrust the brown envelope at his chest and turn to leave, but he grabs hold of my elbow, stopping me. "I can ruin your life."

You already have.

"Don't ever forget that." The look he gives me is one I'm well accustomed to, and it never fails to send fear coursing down my spine. "I can snap her neck like a twig." He clicks his fingers. "Just like that, and then your precious Zeta will be no more." I hate how he continues to use her to push my buttons, and I wish I wasn't so transparent when it came to her, but no matter how discreet I am, he always seems to know.

"And what would all your adoring fans think if they knew what you did?"

The thought of the public uncovering the truth scares me. It honestly does. But not as much as Zeta paying the price for my mistakes. If it came down to it, I'd throw my career under the bus without a minute's hesitation if it meant keeping her safe.

I shove his hand off my elbow. "You got what you came for, so just leave me the fuck alone."

"You owe me, boy. You'll never stop owing me."

Frustration gets the better of me, and I round on him, pushing him back into the wall. "You didn't even do time! You're the only one who got away without punishment." I found that out a few years back when I did some digging, and it disgusted me. "I don't owe you shit."

He shoves me away, and I stumble a little. "The hell you don't. It's your fault. It's your fault everyone was sent down, and you'll never stop paying for that." He slams his shoulder into mine as he pushes past me. "I'll see you in three months. Be a good boy, *Ryder*, or you know what'll happen." He walks backward down the alley, pinning me with his evil eye. "I've got eyes on you." He points his fingers at me. "Always. Never forget that."

I spend the next three days permanently high and drunk as I do everything to banish him and my past from my conscious mind. But it doesn't work, because it's indelibly imprinted on my brain, and the internal scars will never heal.

Dark thoughts invade my mind, smothering me, pressing down on my chest, securing a tight grip around my heart, and I just want it to stop. I need it to end. I can't go on existing like this, and someway or somehow, it's going to come to a conclusion, but I don't know if I'll be left standing at the end.

I stagger toward my bedroom, clutching a bottle of Jack to my chest. After draining the contents, I flop back on the bed, my entire body shaking and trembling, and slowly, the tears come, gradually increasing in volume until I'm curled into a ball, screaming and crying into the void, begging someone to end my suffering.

23

ZETA

"You look like shit," I say the instant I open the door to him.

"You can't still be pissed?" Ryder replies, yawning as he pushes his designer shades on top of his head.

"I'll be eternally pissed after the stunt you pulled," I hiss, lugging my case out into the hall and pulling the door to my condo shut behind me. All the rest of my stuff was moved to the Hamptons earlier in the week, so this is the only piece of luggage I'm bringing with me today.

"You're sexy as fuck when you're pissed, so be mad for as long as you like. All it'll do is turn me on." He winks, licking his lips and rolling his hips.

I glare at him. "Are you for real right now? I thought you weren't going to do anything to make me uncomfortable?"

"I lied."

My nostrils flare, and I want to punch something. Preferably him, but seeing as he's my official employer now, in more ways than one, that wouldn't be smart. I start counting to ten in my head as he leans in close, pressing his mouth to my ear. "Besides, you're not uncomfortable. You're turned the fuck on."

"No, I'm fucking not." I brush past him, heading toward Mrs. Peabody's apartment.

"Liar." He grabs hold of me, pulling me into his chest. His breath fans my face, and the fumes are pungent enough to knock an elephant on his back.

"And you're drunk." I wriggle out of his hold, taking a proper look at him. Dark shadows linger under his bloodshot eyes, his lips are cracked and dry, and his skin looks a little gray behind the few days' worth of stubble on his chin and cheeks. I thought he'd cleaned up after his stint in rehab a couple years back, but looking at him now, it's clear he's fallen into old habits again.

A large chunk of my anger dissipates, and an unfamiliar nurturing instinct takes its place. I have an unhealthy craving to bundle him in my arms, run my hands through his hair, whisper soothing assurances, and make his pain go away.

"What's it to you?" he asks in a belligerent tone, and the instinct passes.

"Nothing. It has nothing to do with me. Drown yourself in booze for all I care."

His jaw tightens, and he yanks my case up. "Let's go." He starts walking toward the elevator.

"I'll meet you outside," I call out, heading toward my elderly neighbor's place without looking back at him.

I rap three times on her door, so she knows it's me.

"What're you doing?" Ryder asks, appearing at my side. "The exit's this way." He points down the hallway.

"I'm well aware of where the exit is in my own apartment building." I roll my eyes. "I just have to do something before we go."

The door swings open slowly, and I smile at the glamorous gray-haired lady staring up at me. Louise is away with the fairies most of the time, but she's never anything but immaculately turned out. Years of having to look her best, at all times, has clearly been ingrained in her. Today, she's wearing a light white cardigan over a summery lilac dress, and her long flowing gray locks are held back with two diamante clips. Flat silver bejeweled sandals adorn her feet. "Hello, lovely." She clutches onto my hand with her frail grip. "Are you leaving now?"

I nod, leaning in to kiss her cheek. "I am, but I just wanted to give you some contact numbers before I go." I help her back inside, acutely aware of Ryder's presence trailing behind me.

Once she's seated on her comfy couch, I rummage in my bag for the envelope I prepared earlier.

"Oh my. You're a handsome devil," Louise says, suddenly noticing my companion. I jerk my head up, and she's pressing a hand to her chest as she looks over my shoulder. "I could just look at your face all day and die happy," she purrs in a dreamy tone of voice, and I smother my snort of laughter. Staring pointedly at me, she adds, "Please tell me you're tapping that."

My mouth hangs open in shock as Ryder's low chuckle does funny things to my insides. Reaching down, he takes her hand, planting a gentle kiss on her wrinkled skin. "I'm hers for the taking, but she won't have me," he replies, giving her way more information than I'd like.

"What the hell's wrong with you? Are you rocking a fever?" she asks me. "Or you're just plain crazy?"

"I could ask you the same thing," I mumble, shaking my head as I find the envelope, extracting it from my bag. "Have you taken your meds today?"

Her bottom lip juts out and she pouts. "That bossy bitch made me take them earlier."

"That *bossy bitch* is being paid to ensure you take them, and I'm glad to hear she's doing her job."

"You fuss too much, lovely. I'm perfectly capable of remembering to take my pills." She rolls her eyes at Ryder, as if I'm the overly dramatic one.

"Uh-huh." I narrow my eyes at her. "So, it wasn't you I

had to take to the ER last month to have your stomach pumped because you forgot you'd taken your pills and you took a double dose?"

She flaps her hands at me. "That was an accident, and you overreacted."

"Sure, I did." I shake my head, before sitting beside her and running through the list of numbers. "Kayla will drop by once a week, and she's your second point of contact after Shirley if there's any emergency."

"Shirley's a bitch. I don't like her."

"You said that, and you need to give her a chance. Besides, it's not for long. I'll be back before you know it."

I get up, forcing my gaze to Ryder. He's been on his best behavior, just hanging back and watching our interactions with an amused grin. "Can you keep her company for a second. I just need to check a few things."

Louise squeals, patting the seat beside her, and a flash of concern darts across Ryder's face.

"Watch out for her grabby hands," I whisper as I brush past him, unable to resist teasing him.

I move into the kitchen, checking to ensure Shirley left Louise's lunch and dinner prepared and that the refrigerator and pantry are well stocked. I check the faucets in the sink and then in the bathroom to ensure they're all off. Louise can be very forgetful at times, and she's flooded the place on more than one occasion. All is in order, so I head back to the living room, biting my lip to hold my laughter in as I see her flirting up a storm with Ryder.

We say our goodbyes, and as she's leaning in to kiss Ryder on the cheek, she diverts her lips at the last minute, planting one on him. I manage to contain my laughter until we're out in the hallway and the door is closed, and then I double over, laughing hysterically, with tears pumping out of my eyes.

"Are you done yet?" he deadpans.

"That was the funniest thing I've seen in ages." I keep pace with him as we walk toward the elevator.

"I don't know whether to feel flattered or insulted," he admits. "I'm used to women throwing themselves at me, but that was something else. I have no words."

His reference to other women has the desired effect on my good humor, and my laughter dries up. An awkward silence filters between us, only broken by the ping of the elevator when it arrives.

We step inside with Ryder carrying my case. We stand side by side as the elevator descends, both staring straight ahead. "Does my lifestyle bother you?" he asks, twisting his head to look sideways at me.

"It's none of my business," I reply, refusing to make eye contact with him.

I startle when he cups my cheek, forcing my gaze to his. "None of those women meant anything to me, and the only one I've ever been in a relationship with is you."

"If that's really what we had," I blurt.

He drops his hand, his jaw clenching. "Why would you say something like that? You know what we had, and continuously trying to deny it is just pissing me off."

"We were so young, Ryder. What the hell did we know?"

"I know I loved you!" he shouts, as the elevator doors open. "You can fucking lie to yourself all you like, but I know what we had was the real deal."

"Not real enough to warrant holding on to," I snap back, as I stomp out of the elevator, annoyed that he's bringing this up. If this is how he plans to act, it's going to be a very long couple months in the Hamptons.

Following me, he slams to a halt and pushes me up against the wall in the lobby. His body is pressed against the length of mine as he pins my wrists together up over my head. "Is this how it's going to be? You're going to continue to punish me for trying to do the right thing? Continue to deny what I see in your eyes every time you look at me."

I snort, glaring at him, as I attempt to wriggle out of his hold. "You're so full of shit. The only thing you see in my eyes is resentment for forcing me into this. If you think any of this will earn you a place in my bed or a spot in my heart, you're crazy."

He leans in close, his lips a hairbreadth from mine. "I'm not the one who's full of shit. You want me so bad, but you're too chicken to admit it."

I make another attempt to push him away, but he's too strong, and every time I try to wriggle out of his grip, I'm conscious of the fact he's pressed intimately against me, and my body is responding to that. I need to get away from him before I do something stupid.

Like kiss him.

"Your ego is showing, Rock Star. I'm not one of your groupies, and I won't drop to my knees or open my legs just because you demand it."

His response is to rock his hips against mine, pushing his erection into my lower belly. "Told you your smart mouth turns me on, so keep going, baby. I can do this all day long." He thrusts his pelvis into mine again, and a little whimper flies out of my mouth.

He lifts off me instantly, pinning me with a smug expression as he steps back. "Like I said. You want me."

His arrogant smile infuriates me, and I push off the wall, urging my out-of-control hormones to quiet down. "I wanted the old Ryder. The boy who was sweet and caring and considerate. That boy would never have railroaded me like this or disregarded my feelings."

His shoulders slump, and he sighs, kicking the side of my case with his foot. After a few seconds, he lifts his head up and pins me with an earnest look. "I'm sorry if I'm going about this all wrong. I just want you back in my life. Is that so hard to believe?"

A piercing pain glides across my chest. "I just … look, can we not do this? Can we just try and keep this professional, because I honestly can't do it if you're going to push me at every opportunity."

"Is there someone else?" he quietly asks. "Is that it?"

I shake my head. "There isn't anyone else. I just want this to be about the work, and all the other stuff is going to get in the way. You have an album to record, and I'm tasked with documenting the whole process. And there are other people to consider. The last thing I want to do is to disrupt things with the band, and if we keep doing this, that's exactly what'll happen."

He nods. "You're right, and I'm being an ass again. Forgive me?" He offers me his hand.

"That remains to be seen," I say, refusing his hand and walking toward the front door.

🎼♫

"Do you always travel like this?" I ask, once I'm situated in the back of the limo with a glass of champagne in my hand.

"Sometimes," Ryder acknowledges. He's sitting across from me with Garrett, and Micah is sitting beside me. They'd already explained that Scott is making his way there separately as he's bringing his wife and baby along.

"Our boy's going all out to impress you," Garrett elaborates with a suggestive wink.

"Shut up." Ryder sends him a warning glare, which he surprisingly obeys.

There's a moment of tense silence before Ryder breaks it, filling the guys in on his encounter with my flirty neighbor, including how she kissed him and tried to grab his cock.

"You're kidding. No way." I shake my head, giggling at that revelation, silently high-fiving Mrs. Peabody. The guys tease him mercilessly, and it helps lift the tension in the air.

"I'm not lying. That woman scared me."

"That's priceless, but I shouldn't be surprised. Some of the stuff that woman's done would even make you blush, Rock Star."

"How long have you known her?" Ryder leans back, stabbing me with that intense focus of his, and I subtly squeeze my thighs together, absorbing his heated look as physically as if it was a caress.

"I met her shortly after I moved into the building. She'd locked herself out of her apartment, and she was sobbing in the hallway because she'd left her cell inside, and she couldn't remember her daughter's number. I called the super, and we got the door unlocked. She was still upset so I helped her inside. The place was a mess, and I was concerned." I take a sip of my champagne, recalling our first meeting. "I called her daughter and discovered she was in the hospital with stage four lung cancer. Long story short, her daughter passed away a few weeks later, and I just started checking in on Louise to make sure she was okay, and we became friends."

I hold out my glass to Micah for a top up. "She's had an interesting but tragic life. She was an actress before she met her husband and they moved overseas. When he was killed in a car accident, she moved back to the States with her daughter. She doesn't have any other family, and her health is declining, so I check in on her every day."

"That's why you hired Shirley and asked Kayla to check in on her," Ryder surmises, his knee bouncing up and down.

"Yeah. I didn't want to put her into a nursing home, and it was either that or hire a caregiver."

"Send Rod the details, and I'll cover the cost."

"That's not necessary."

"It kind of is." Ryder leans forward. "If you weren't coming to work for us, you'd be there to take care of her."

"I appreciate the offer, but I got it covered. Thanks."

"Do you have to be so fucking stubborn?" Ryder looks pissed again.

Our little truce didn't last long, and his erratic mood swings are seriously giving me whiplash.

"Do you have to be so fucking controlling?" I retort.

He blows air out of his mouth as he looks up at the ceiling, shaking his head. "Fine. I'll get it added to the terms of your contract."

"You can't do that," I splutter, enraged.

"I think you'll find I can, and I will." He shoots me a tight smile.

"You're being an ass again."

"It's his middle name, he can't help it," Garrett pipes up.

"I'm beginning to think you're right," I say, even though I hate agreeing with anything that jackass has to say.

"For fuck's sake, Zeta. It's just money."

"And now you're proving my earlier point. The boy I knew respected the value of money."

Steam practically billows out of his ears. "Offering to cover the costs of a caregiver for an elderly, ill woman is a worthy use of my money. And I don't disrespect money. Not at all. I've worked hard for my success, but the truth is, I've got far more money than I know what to do with, and you're the one making a big deal out of *nothing*." He roars the last word at me, removing a silver flask from inside his jacket pocket and pouring the contents straight down his throat.

"Yeah, just pour some more booze down your throat. That'll fix everything," I snap.

"You're driving me to it," he yells. "You're driving me fucking insane."

"Well, you're the one who wanted me here. You can always change your mind and hire someone else."

"Don't fucking tempt me," he grits out, burying his head in his hands. "Why do you have to make everything so difficult? I told you I'm fucking sorry. What more do you want me to do?"

"I think you should just fuck each other's brains out and be done with it," Garrett unhelpfully supplies.

"Don't fucking start, Gar. I'm not in the mood for your shit."

No one speaks after that, and I feel awful. I don't know why I'm being so antagonistic. Or, well, I do, I suppose.

It's all my hurt rising to the surface.

Since Ryder reappeared in my world, he's upset the carefully controlled nature of my life, and I'm floundering. I'm feeling so many things I thought I'd buried, and I'm angry with him for that. I'm also terrified of what these next few months will bring and scared I won't be able to resist him and that I'll get my heart hurt again. All of this is driving my behavior, but it's not how I want to act, either around Ryder or the other members of Torment.

I'm a professional music journalist, yet I'm acting like a whiny teenager, and it's clear I'm driving Ryder to drink, which is not something I want to encourage. I make a mental note to ask Rod on the QT about Ryder's stint in rehab and whether he's supposed to be drinking this much.

When we pull up in front of imposing wooden gates an hour later, I smell the fresh, clean air and the salty scent of the sea through the open sunroof, and it brings a smile to my face. I lower the window as the limo glides up the impressively long driveway toward Ryder's house; although calling it a house is a bit of an understatement.

My eyes pop wide as I take in the impressive two-story modern build. It's constructed mainly of wood and glass and it fronts a large, manicured lawn. A humongous garage rests off to one side, and another smaller property resides on the right.

Mike opens the door, offering me his hand and helping me outside. "Thank you." I pull my shades out of my bag and put them on, shielding my eyes from the glare of the midday sun. The rolling sound of the ocean greets my ears, and a gentle breeze blows strands of hair around my face. Closing my eyes, I inhale the peace and quiet and the familiar smells and sounds, instantly feeling more relaxed.

"What do you think?" Ryder quietly asks, speaking to me for the first time since our little blow up in the car.

I open my eyes and turn my face up to the sun, relishing the warmth on my skin. "I think I'm going to love it here," I truthfully admit, noticing how his whole face lights up at my words. "But we need to talk, and I think we should do it sooner rather than later."

24

RYDER

The guys head to their bedrooms to unpack while I lead Zeta through the living area and out onto the upper deck. The architect designed this house with all the living spaces on the second level and the bedrooms, gym, and movie theater on the lower level.

"Wow, this place is magnificent." Zeta leans over the railing taking in the vast infinity pool, surrounding patio, gardens, and basketball and tennis courts. A wooden bridge leads off the far side of the garden, down to a set of narrow steps and directly onto the private sandy beach. "And the views are spectacular. Now, I see why you used so much glass in the design of the house."

"That was the architect's idea," I explain, leaning against the railing alongside her. "I told him I wanted something modern but homey and practical, and then I gave him free rein."

"Well, he did a great job." She points her finger at the wooden structure off to the side of the tennis courts. "What's that building?"

"That's the recording studio."

She turns to face me, and the sun casts her in glorious

225

technicolor highlighting the smattering of freckles across her nose and the subtle reddish undertones in her hair. She's not wearing much makeup and her black knee-length sundress is understated, but she's so gorgeous she almost brings me to my knees. As so often happens in her company, I spew out my thoughts without stopping to apply a filter. "I've imagined you here so many times, Zeta. I'm really glad you're here now."

A delicate smile pulls up the corners of her plump mouth. "Me too," she softly admits. Her eyes penetrate mine and my heart starts going crazy. This girl does things to me I don't understand. "You've done really well for yourself, Ryder, and I'm proud of you."

"You are? I thought you hated me?" This time, I'm not joking around, because I need to know how she's feeling and if there's any possibility of an us again. I can't get my hopes up only to have them dashed.

"I could never hate you." She looks sheepish but sincere. "I tried to. When you left me heartbroken, I wanted to hate you so bad, but I loved you too much to follow through."

"I hate that I hurt you. I hate that so much." I hang my head, wondering how she's even entertaining speaking to me.

"Ryder." My name is a husky whisper on her tongue, and my dick twitches. I haven't had sex in over two weeks, which is a new record for me. It's not for lack of offers, but from the minute she reappeared in my life, I've only had eyes for her. The thought of screwing some other woman makes me feel ill.

Garrett and Micah would piss their pants if they heard my thoughts right now.

I look up when her fingers trail the stubble on my jawline, and a shiver works its way through me. Her touch ignites my blood and kindles my desire, and it's not long before my cock is straining against the zipper of my shorts. "Can we sit down over there?" she asks in that hypnotic tone of hers, pointing at the cozy seated area, and I can only nod.

I take her hand, threading my fingers in hers as I lead us

over to the couch. I always loved holding her hand, and that was probably the only good thing about juvie. Because we couldn't have sex or indulge in any hot make-out sessions, the smaller intimate moments between us were so special and came to mean so much to me. I've never had that intimacy with anyone else, and I've never wanted to hold someone's hand or just hug them and smell their hair the way I do with Zeta.

"Can I get you something to drink?" I ask, opening the lid of the cooler.

"A water would be good, thanks."

I remove two bottles and hand one to her. Then I sit down beside her on the wicker couch, kicking off my Vans and planting my bare feet up on the footstool.

She angles her body so she's turned toward me with her legs tucked up. "I owe you an apology. I've been behaving like an insolent little brat, which is embarrassing to admit, but it's the truth."

"It's okay. I've been acting like a total jerk, so I'd say we're even." I unscrew the cap on my bottle and take a swig. The icy-cold liquid is like a balm to my dry throat and I drain it in one go, reaching over to the cooler for another.

"I'd like to start over," she says, and I nod, silently encouraging her to go on. "I've just been very confused these last few days."

She worries her lower lip between her teeth, and I'm reaching out, gently releasing her lip before I've realized I'm doing it. "You'll hurt yourself," I mumble, feeling my cheeks heat a little.

"Can we be honest with one another?"

"Absolutely. I never want to be anything but honest with you."

Hypocrite.

I push my inner voice and the accompanying guilt away.

"There's a lot I want to tell you. Some of it may hurt, but

I'm not saying it to be cruel," she continues. "I want you to understand where I'm coming from, because if we don't discuss this openly, I'm afraid we'll continue snapping at one another, and it's going to make the tension unbearable around here."

"I can handle it, and I'd rather know what's going on in that pretty head of yours."

She wets her lips in a nervous tell. "When you left me, I was devastated. I didn't realize that when people spoke about having a broken heart it was physically true. I mean, I'm not saying that my heart literally broke apart, but the pain I felt in my chest every day was as close to it as one can possibly get without dying. Your loss was a physical wrench I felt in every part of my body, and it took me a long time to find a way of living without you."

I've never hated myself more than I do in this moment, and that's saying a lot, because I hate myself pretty much all the time. "I'm so sorry," I croak. "And if it's any consolation, my heart was equally broken."

She laces her fingers in mine, looking at me through glassy eyes. "I don't know if it is. I've spent eight years believing you walked away because you'd fallen in love with someone else. I blamed myself for not being good enough for you."

"No, no, no, baby." I scoot in closer to her, linking both our hands. "That couldn't be further from the truth. You were always way too good for me."

"When you told me the truth the other night, you rewrote our history in a way I never contemplated, and I don't know how to process all these new feelings. Knowing you were hurting as much as me only makes me sadder. Knowing you walked away because you thought I was better off without you makes me so fucking mad I could scream. And that's just the tip of the iceberg."

She peers deep into my eyes. "My head's a hot mess right

now, and I'm lashing out at you because deep down I blame you for creating this mess."

She gulps, and a single tear trickles down her face. I brush it away, gently kissing the damp spot on her cheek. Her chest heaves, and a breathy little whimper escapes her gorgeous mouth.

I want to kiss her so badly it feels like I'll die if I can't taste her lips. But I rein my hormones in, because she wants to talk, and I feel like we might finally be getting somewhere. Kissing her could make her fly off the handle again, so I give my dick a silent pep talk, warning it to calm the fuck down. "You should blame me. It *is* my fault."

"I don't want to play the blame game, Ryder. What's done is done, and we can't change it. That's the issue." She looks away, staring at the ocean in the near distance, and I rub little circles on the back of her hand while she gathers her thoughts. Strands of her dark hair lift, swirling around her face, and I can't believe I'm jealous because I want to be the one caressing her silky-smooth skin. When she looks back at me, I'm blindsided by the wealth of emotion glistening in her eyes.

"I closed myself off, Ryder. I threw barriers up around my heart, and I never let myself feel, because I didn't want to go through that kind of pain again." A steely glint appears in her eye, almost like she's waiting for me to challenge her. She juts her chin up and fixes me with a confident look. "I'm sexually promiscuous, because I need it to release all this pent-up emotion I bury inside, but it's only ever sex. It's only ever a physical act. One I usually instigate and control. I rarely go back for seconds, because I don't want to risk growing attached, not that it'd be a problem because I've never felt a connection with anyone the way I feel with you."

My brain scrambles to process all that. I've suspected she might be like me, using sex to bury her feelings, but to have her confirm it has scattered my emotions to the wind. I'm not being hypocritical when I say I hate that she's like that, because I'm not judging her for her lifestyle. I just never wanted that for her. I've always wanted more for her, and I've battled with my feelings over the years when I realized what she was doing, torn between rejoicing at the fact she hadn't fallen in love with anyone else and hating the thought of her feeling as alone as I was.

She's looking at me expectedly, waiting for my response. I cup her cheek. "I've never felt a connection with anyone but you. I've never shared intimacy with anyone but you. And, fuck it, baby, I've lived my life exactly like you. Placing my feelings on lockdown and using sex as a way of feeling in control, but the thought of you being as fucking lonely as I've been hurts my heart so bad, because I didn't wish for that. Leaving you was supposed to make your life better, not harder."

"Ryder," she sobs, tears rolling down her face unbidden. "I've been so lonely, but no one else could ever match up to you."

I throw caution to the wind and yank her into my arms. "I know, baby. I know." I hold her tight, sighing contentedly when her arms go around my waist and her head comes to rest on my chest. Closing my eyes, I nuzzle my face into her hair and inhale deeply. Her hair smells different now, like peaches and vanilla, but she still smells like home.

Like my only place of peace and happiness.

I've missed this close human contact, this intimacy with her, and if it was up to me, we'd be a couple already, but I can't be dismissive of her feelings. Of how *I've* made her feel. I run my hand up and down her back as she sobs intermittently. "I love you, Zeta," I whisper in her ear. I press a tender kiss to her temple. "I still love you so much."

She goes rigidly still in my arms, and I wonder if I've pushed too hard, if I've lost her again. Sniffling, she eases back, looking up at me through tear-stained eyes. "I still love you too, but—"

I don't let her complete that sentence, muting her words by pressing my lips against hers. I kiss her softly, and her mouth instantly responds, moving against mine effortlessly. I sweep my tongue along the seam of her lips, and she opens for me willingly. I pull her into my lap and lean back against the couch, holding her firmly by the waist as I kiss the shit out of her.

My heart is drowning in sensation, my body's on fire, and my head? My head is finally at peace as I just focus on the euphoria of having her back in my arms, of tasting her sweet sexiness on my lips.

Jerking my hips up, I thrust my hard-on into her pelvis, letting her know what she does to me. She rips her mouth from mine, scooting out of my lap and promptly falling on her butt on the floor. "Zeta." My heart is pounding in fear as I stand, helping her up.

"We shouldn't have done that," she says, shaking her head, looking completely flustered, and trying to back away from me.

"Please don't do this. Don't tell me you didn't want that because I know you did!" I drag my hands through my hair as a heavy weight settles on my chest.

"Ryder." She sighs, pulling herself together. Taking a step toward me, she removes my hands from where they're fisting my hair, circles her arms around my neck, and hugs me.

A golf-ball-sized lump of emotion clogs my throat. My blood pressure recalibrates, and my stress levels reduce as I lean into her embrace.

"I want it. I want you. I do," she reassures me, before slipping out of our embrace. She pins me with sorrowful eyes. "But I can't overcome eight years of anguish overnight. I know now you were trying to do the right thing, but I still feel so much hurt, so much pain, all of it unnecessary. I spent years feeling betrayed. Thinking you had cheated on me, thinking everything we'd shared had been a lie, and it cut deep. It's not something I can just toss aside like it didn't matter." She shakes her head, and a veil of sadness shrouds her pretty features. "If you had only waited and talked to me."

She rubs a hand across her chest, and I wish I could tell her the full truth. Scrap that. I know I *need* to tell her the full truth, but the timing has to be right, and we're not there yet. Plus, I need to work up the courage to admit it because I'm not strong enough yet to deal with rejection. If she leaves me for good after she finds out, I don't think I'll survive losing her again. We've only just reconnected, and I've already hit her with so much of the heavy stuff. I need to let her process that first before I drop a loaded bomb. "So, what are you saying?" I ask, needing to know where we stand.

"I'm saying I need a little time and space."

"I can give you that." I reach out, winding my hands through her hair. "But I want to make one thing clear. I want you back, Zeta. You're my girl, and you belong with me."

Tears shimmer at the back of her eyes, and she gingerly smiles. "Can we agree to put the past behind us and start over as friends?"

I press a kiss to her forehead, breathing deeply. "I can agree to that once you agree not to close your mind to more. I hear you, and I'll give you time and space, I promise. But don't shut me out, please."

"I won't." She rests her head on my chest. "I promise."

25

ZETA

Ryder is outside grilling steaks while he chats over a beer with Micah and Garrett. Scott, Linda, and their little boy aren't coming now until tomorrow morning, so it's only the four of us for dinner tonight. I've prepared a green salad, fresh slaw, sweet potato fries, mashed potatoes, and a cheesecake for dessert. Ryder came inside every so often to check if I needed anything, but I shooed him away, telling him to enjoy the sunshine with his buddies.

I feel lighter after our talk, and it's definitely helped to clear the air. I'm not yet in the place where I can hope for more with him, but the layers around my heart are already melting. It felt so natural to kiss him, to be back in his arms, and I was sorely tempted to let it go all the way, but thankfully, I came to my senses before things escalated.

If I'd had sex with him today, it would be no different than any other encounter, and I don't want to do that to us. The past I share with Ryder is unique to him and me, and *if* we find ourselves back in that space again, then I'll happily let him take me to bed, but I want him to make love to me. We've both been using sex as some kind of crutch, and if I'd let him fuck me today, how different would it really have been?

I know he was disappointed, but I believe we need to step back and take things slow. I can't go charging headfirst into a relationship with him, until I know it's what I want, and I'm still so messed up over everything. Professing my love is already a big step forward for me, and maybe it wasn't the smartest decision, but I meant it when I said I wanted to be honest.

We've admitted we both still have feelings for one another, but that doesn't mean anything's changed or that we'll end up back together. I know Ryder wants to go there, but one of us has to be level-headed about it, and I guess that task falls to me. For now, I'm happy to have him back in my life as a friend. We're both different. Older and supposedly wiser. And we have a lot to catch one another up on. The most I can hope for right now is renewing our friendship, and that's what I'm going to concentrate on.

I call Garrett and Micah inside, asking them to help me carry the food and dinnerware to the seated area outside. We're eating on the ground level at the beautiful patio area, which overlooks the pool and gardens.

When the table is set, Ryder plates the steaks, and we sit down to eat. A soft, balmy breeze wafts around us, and I take a minute to enjoy the view. Ryder's house is stunning, and the height of luxury, but I've been surprised at how homey and comfortable it is. I was expecting a typical bachelor pad with minimal décor, leather furniture, and few personal possessions not comfy couches, brightly colored walls, a beautiful Shaker-style kitchen, and little personal touches everywhere from the hand-designed cushions and throws, to the musical inspired paintings and framed photos on the wall.

Most of the photos are with the guys from the band, some of them are with Rod and his family, and the rest are casual pics taken with other rock stars who are clearly friends. I'd pointed out a picture of Ryder and Garrett with the members from BAD. I'm a massive fan of their stuff, and seeing that photo, with all that combined hotness on display, gave me a little thrill. Ryder explained that Sawyer Weston is a good friend of his, and I'm happy he has good people in his life.

The one glaring absence is personal family photos, but that requires no explanation. It makes my heart ache for him though. I'm lucky Jill welcomed me into her family, or that would be me too.

Over the years, I've hated the fact that I had no photos of Ryder and me together. I'm not sure whether it would've brought me some comfort or added to my grief, but not having any record of our relationship, except for the permanent scars on my heart, made me unbelievably sad.

"Fuck, this is good," Garrett mumbles, his mouth full of food.

Micah slaps him across the back of his head. "Have you no manners, you brute?" I smile, taking a sip of my beer. "But he's right for once in his life. This is fantastic. Where'd you learn to cook like that?"

"I taught myself to cook at an early age because it was either learn how to feed myself or starve," I truthfully reply.

"Shit. That sounds rough." Micah's features soften as he looks across the table at me. "Ryder mentioned he met you in juvie, but he didn't explain the circumstances."

Ryder's fork clangs to the table. "For fuck's sake, man. I told you that so you wouldn't ask her anything to make her uncomfortable."

I place my hand over his, smiling. "It's okay, honestly." I turn and face the other two guys. "I'm going to be prying into every aspect of your lives while I'm writing this bio, so it's only fair you should know whatever you want to know about me."

"What bra size are you?" Garrett quips, earning him a contemptable look from Ryder.

"Do not answer that," Ryder says through gritted teeth.

"Relax." I pat his hand. "He's only trying to wind you

up." I poke my fork in Garrett's direction. "Questions of a sexual nature are off-limits."

"Along with flirting, touching, speaking to or breathing the same air as Zeta," Ryder adds.

I shake my head, fighting a smile, wondering what it says about me that I love his jealous possessiveness. "Let's not over-react. I meant what I said earlier."

Ryder visibly relaxes, and I only realize our fingers are entwined when I spot Micah staring at our linked hands. It's uncanny how being back in his presence seems so natural. How we reach out for one another without even thinking about it.

With a smile, I remove my hand from Ryder's and pick up my beer. "While we're being frank, I just want to let you know that Ryder and I have talked things through, and whatever issues we are dealing with won't affect the recording of the album. And I'm sorry for all that shit in the limo earlier. It won't happen again."

"You don't need to apologize to us," Micah says, helping himself to another serving of slaw. "And Ryder already explained. We know you two have special history, and we don't want to get in the way of that."

I nod, popping a piece of steak into my mouth.

"Why were you in juvie?" Garrett asks, and for once, there's no joking quality to his tone.

I'm expecting Ryder to jump in and criticize him, but he doesn't interfere, and I appreciate that he's letting me decide what I want to share. It's not something that usually pops up in conversation, but I have no issue telling the truth. I've worked hard to rise above my background, and years of therapy have helped me accept that I did nothing wrong and I have nothing to be ashamed of.

I have their undivided attention as I explain about my mom, my stepdad, and the circumstances which led to my conviction and subsequent release. They tell me a little bit about their pasts, regaling me with stories of their first meeting, after Rod had auditioned for band members to support Ryder, and some censored accounts of their early days on the road.

After we've finished eating, Micah and Garrett clean up while Ryder and I take a walk on the beach. Daylight is starting to fade, and the sky is a beautiful dusky pink color as we walk barefoot side by side along the sandy shore.

"You guys seem to have a strong bond," I say. "Has it always been like that?"

Ryder nods, shoving his hands in his pockets. "After Rod discovered me busking, he whisked me to New York to meet with some top record producers, and I spent a few weeks recording some of my own stuff. When Rod sent the demo out, we got a lot of interest, but the message was clear—the labels wanted to sign a band, not a solo artist, so Rod talked to me about it, and he organized auditions. I handpicked the guys, and it was as much for their personalities as it was for their musical ability. I knew we'd be living in each other's pockets, and it was important we all got on."

"But you didn't choose Scott from the outset." I'm aware of the band's history as it's been well documented, and even though I've steered clear of media accounts of Ryder's personal life—because looking at him with a succession of beautiful women tore strips off my heart—I've avidly followed the band's career, and I've listened to every album they've released.

"Yeah, Marwen couldn't hack life on the road, so he quit after six months and the label sent Scott to us as a temporary solution. I was worried he wouldn't fit in at first because the rest of us were single and enjoying the, ah, perks of the job"—he runs a hand over the back of his head, looking a little sheepish—"whereas Scott was a few years older, and he was already engaged to Linda, but he's an easy guy to get along with, and it actually helped that he was more mature. He's managed to talk us down from some crazy shit over the years." A knowing grin appears on his face as he pulls me back from the ocean's edge when water rolls in. "We gelled, and we offered him a permanent place in the band, and here we are." He shrugs, smiling at me.

"I'm glad you got to live your dream, and no matter how things ended with us, I was always so proud of you."

Air whooshes out of his mouth as he walks us back a few meters. Plopping down on the sand, he pats the space beside him, and I sit. We both pull our knees up to our chests, staring out at the receding sunlight flickering across the gently lapping waves. "It isn't all it's cracked up to be," he says. "Although, I'm not complaining, because it's an incredible life, but it's not all rainbows and unicorns."

My lips twitch at his words. "In what way?"

"Touring is hard. I love playing live, love the roar of the audience, love hearing them sing our songs back to us, but it's exhausting, and everyone wants a piece of you. This part here is what I truly love best. Writing and recording new material. Having a permanent base for a while." He hooks his pinky finger in mine. "I'm not overly materialistic, and a lot of times I feel guilty about the money, but I indulged with this place because I wanted someplace special to call home, and I love coming here. I love the privacy and the solitude, and it just speaks to my soul. If I could live here year-round I would, but it's not practical or possible."

"Why do you feel guilty about the money? You've worked hard for it. And I know you donate a lot to charity."

His chest inflates and deflates, and his jaw flexes, as he stares out at the ocean. Ryder and I were always comfortable with silence, and I know he'll talk when he's ready, so I patiently wait him out.

"It feels wrong," he says in a low tone a few minutes later. "It feels wrong to have so much when I was responsible for someone losing their life prematurely."

Pain is etched across his face, and I just want to erase it. I thread my fingers through his and he clasps my hand firmly. "You were only a kid, it was an accident, and you weren't the only one involved."

"None of that matters though." He turns to me with tears in his eyes. "I still relive it all the time, and the guilt never goes away. I don't think it ever will."

My eyes search his and I can't bear to see him hurting, so I fling my arms around him, without any hesitation, holding him tight.

Friends hug friends, right?

He leans his head on my shoulder, and I wrap my arms tighter around him. "Some days, I think all the guilt I'm carrying will eat me alive. Some days, it's a struggle to get out of bed. After I lost you, music became my only salvation. I honestly don't know if I'd still be here if I wasn't a musician."

"Don't say that." I hug him closer. "I can't bear to think of a world without you in it."

"I can say the same of you, and I don't ever want you to leave, Zeta, but I'm a selfish prick like that."

"I'm here now." I press a kiss to the top of his head, and he sighs. "Have you ever thought about seeing a therapist?"

"I've seen tons of them over the years. I make some inroads, and then I have to go on tour, and all the progress is undone."

"A good therapist will give you tools to use when things get too much. And even having them at the end of a phone can help. Maybe you just haven't found the right one. I can give you my therapist's details if you like?"

He lifts his head. "You still see a therapist?"

I nod, running my fingers through the soft hairs at the base of his neck. "I go every month, and I think I most likely always will."

"Because of me?" His features are pinched, his mouth turned down.

"We have discussed you," I admit, "but it's mainly my fucked-up childhood and issues with my mom that are my main problems."

"What about your stepdad?"

"He's still locked up, thank fuck, and hopefully, they've thrown away the key."

He closes his eyes for a moment. "That feels nice," he murmurs as I thread my fingers through his hair.

"Lie down," I suggest, and he repositions himself so his head is in my lap. He's staring up at me, and I weave my fingers through his hair as we talk. "I mourned your long hair when you cut it, but it suits you short like this too."

He frowns. "I almost cried the day I had it cut off, but I had no choice. Some bitch decided it'd be fun to give me a DIY haircut when I was passed out drunk. I woke up looking like something from a horror movie. My hair was all different lengths and hacked to bits at the sides. Gar laughed so hard he pissed himself."

"That's what you get for screwing groupies. She probably wanted your hair as a souvenir, or she sold it to the highest bidder on eBay."

"Oh my fucking God. I never thought of that!"

I continue winding my fingers through his hair as the gentle ebb and flow of the sea echoes in the background. It's dark now, and we're the only people on the beach.

"Is my history with women going to be an issue for you?" he asks, tracing the tip of one finger up my arm.

"I won't lie. Seeing you with so many women has hurt me in the past. And let's not even get started on the sex tapes." A look of abject horror appears on his face, and I know why. "I haven't watched them," I blurt, shuddering at the thought. "But just knowing they existed was enough to destroy me."

"I'm sorry, and I wish I could take it back, but by your own admission, you haven't been a saint either."

"I know, and I'm not being judgmental. You were single

and free to fuck who you wanted, but I hate the groupies that hang around the music scene, because they all have an agenda. They're trying to trap a rock star with a baby, or they want bragging rights or photo or video footage they can sell to a tabloid. They're manipulative and taking advantage, and I despise those kind of girls, but I admire girls who take control of their sexuality and aren't afraid to embrace it," I add, just so he understands the point I'm trying to make.

"If I said I didn't disagree, would that make me repulsive in your eyes?"

I shake my head. "You could never be repulsive to me. Never." A flash of pain flickers in his eyes. "What?"

"Nothing." He forces a smile, trailing his finger over the ink on my arm. "Do they mean anything in particular?" he asks, pointing to the images painted on my skin.

"They are ancient Chinese graphical depictions meaning strength, wisdom, and courage."

"And the script on your thigh?"

My eyes pop wide. "When did you notice that?"

"You were wearing those minuscule shorts the day I dropped by your apartment, and I saw the ink."

I think he saw a lot more than that, but I'm not encouraging the direction this conversation appears to be going in. "They're song lyrics."

"Yours?" he asks, and I nod. He sits up, his face all excited. "Can I see?"

"I'll show you sometime," I say, standing. "But it's late, and I'd like to get an early start with work in the morning." I offer him my hand and help him to his feet.

"Nice deflection," he says without a trace of sarcasm. "But I'm curious about one thing." We start walking back toward the house. "How did you end up studying journalism when you had your heart set on songwriting?"

I knew he was going to ask me this at some point, and I've promised him honesty, but this will only add to the considerable guilt he carries around with him, so I'm deliberately vague on purpose, hoping he'll drop it. "I was accepted into the program at USC, but I transferred to the journalism course majoring in music my first week on campus."

He frowns. "Why? You're so fucking talented, and I know it's what you wanted to do."

I look over at his beautiful face, hating what I have to say next. "Songwriting had become something we did together, and I couldn't disassociate it from you."

He stops walking, hurt flashing across his face. "You switched courses because of me?"

I nod, kicking at the sand under my foot. "I didn't write any songs for years. I couldn't. I had the worst case of writer's block."

He scrubs a hand over his chin, starting to walk again. "Man, I really fucked everything up, didn't I?"

"We're not doing this, remember?"

He shoves his hands in his pockets, looking deeply unhappy.

"I started writing again two years ago, and lately, I've been thinking about doing something about it. I love my job, but maybe I could sell some songs on the side." I shrug, feeling a little foolish telling one of the US's best songwriters my silly little plans.

"I'd love to see some of your stuff," he says, finally picking his head up. "No one knows this yet, because we've gone to great lengths to keep it a secret, but the band is setting up our own label. We're out of contract next year, and we want to have full control over our careers. None of us are getting any younger, and we're fed up spending so much time on the road, so we came up with the idea, and Rod has helped us set it up. We've signed a couple of upcoming bands, and we'll be signing more. We're definitely going to need songwriters, so maybe there's a way you could work with our label in the future?"

"Are you serious?" I slam to a halt, my heart doing somersaults in my chest.

"As a heart attack," he quips, and I slap his arm.

"Don't joke about shit like that."

He snakes his arm around my shoulder when I shiver, and I siphon some of his body warmth as we keep walking, nearing the entry path to his house. "You're talented, Zeta, and I hate to see talent go to waste." He grins at me, and my knees turn to Jell-O as I get ensnared in his hypnotic gaze. "I think this opportunity just got a whole lot more interesting for both of us."

26

RYDER

"**M**an, that's hot," Gar says, coming up alongside me as I watch Zeta, through the window, practicing her yoga moves down on the beach. "Bet all that flexibility makes for some interesting times in the bedroom." He smirks.

"I wouldn't know."

"Get the fuck out." His brows climb to his hairline. "You're still not doing the funky monkey with her?"

"Dude, are you, like, five?" I roll my eyes.

"I didn't think you'd like it if I asked why you weren't banging her fucking brains out. You're the one who asked me to be more respectful."

I slap him on the back. "You've reined it in, and I appreciate that, and to answer your question, no, we're still stuck firmly in the friend zone, and I have the blue balls to show for it."

Zeta's been here two weeks, and it's as if she's never been out of my life. We've settled into a nice routine, and I'm happier than I've been in years. I haven't had one single anxiety attack, flashback, or nightmare since we relocated to the Hamptons, and apart from a couple of beers each night, I haven't had to rely on alcohol or drugs either.

I watch Zeta and Linda, Scott's wife, roll up their mats with a big smile on my face. They're laughing and chatting as they make their way back to the house. They've struck up a good friendship, and I love seeing Zeta looking so carefree.

Some mornings, she joins me for a run on the beach, and on other occasions, she does yoga with her new bestie. Then we all eat breakfast together before we head to the studio to work. Linda usually lounges by the pool with the baby, and she has dinner on the table when we finally make our way out of the studio each evening.

Nights are filled with watching movies, jamming casually with the guys, or just laughing and joking around. We haven't stepped foot off the property, and I love it. It's like we're in our own little cocoon, and if I had my way, I'd stay here for eternity.

"With all the PDAs going on, I was sure you'd taken things to the next level," Gar says, following me away from the window as I make my way into the kitchen.

We *are* touchy-feely, but it's purely PG-rated, consisting mainly of hand-holding and hugging, and she lets me spoon her while we lie on the couch in the movie room sometimes. I cherish every touch, every look, and every opportunity she gives me to get close, but I don't want to push the boundaries until she tells me she's ready.

"She needs time, man," I tell him, switching the Keurig on. "I hurt her pretty badly, and she has got lots of stuff to work through."

He leans his elbows on the island unit, looking thoughtful, which is a scary concept for Gar. "The way she looks at you, man." A strange expression crosses his face. "She loves you. Like really loves you."

My heart soars at his words. "I love her so fucking much, Gar, and she makes everything better. Having her here is … more than I ever dared dream."

"I'm pleased for you, dude. You deserve it. You've spent a long time being unhappy, and I know she's the reason you've got this big kickass smile on your face every day and why you're knocking out some fan-fucking-tastic lyrics. She's good for you, and I hope it works out."

"Well, fuck me," Scott exclaims, stepping into the kitchen with his little son in his arms, overhearing the tail end of our conversation. "Was legendary manwhore Garrett Jones really saying that, or have I walked into an alternate universe?"

"Screw you, man." Gar flips him the bird. "I'm all for monogamy if you find the right girl, and someday, I hope to find someone who looks at me the way Zeta looks at this punk." He jabs his finger in my direction.

Scott grins, sliding onto a stool and sitting little Mattie up on the counter. I tweak the cute little kid's nose, and he gurgles and chuckles right on cue.

"Things seem to be going well with you and Zeta," Scott says, smiling. "I'm pleased for you. She's a great girl, and Linda's really fond of her."

"We're still just friends, but I'm hoping it'll be more. I'm just not sure how to move things to the next level when she's asked me to give her space."

"You gotta woo her, man." Scott tickles his son as he talks, and Mattie wriggles and chuckles.

"Talk about alternate realm," Gar mumbles. "What fucking century did you come from?"

Scott grins. "We can learn a lot from our forefathers about the way to win a woman's heart."

"What do you suggest?" I ask, sipping my coffee. Gar subtly leans forward, pretending like he's not invested in his answer.

"Do stuff for her that she likes. Little things that show you understand her and that you care."

"Like what?" I scratch the back of my head, frowning.

"Bring her breakfast in bed, or give her feet or shoulders a rub at the end of the day, run her a bath." He shrugs, continuing to tickle his son as the sound of chatter and approaching footfall reaches our ears. "Women love little gestures like that." He winks at me, lifting his son up into his arms. "You've been writing love songs for that woman for years, so I'm sure you'll figure it out."

I'm still thinking about Scott's words of wisdom later on when we're in the studio, trying to come up with ideas that will prove to Zeta how much I care. Gar and I have been messing about with some melodies while Scott has gone to check on Linda, and Zeta's been interviewing Micah for the biography she's writing. My cell rings just as Zeta and Micah walk into the room, and my heart flips cartwheels as my eyes lock on her pretty brown ones. The smile she gives me almost knocks me off my feet, and I'm in such a trance that it's up to Gar to answer my phone.

"Yeah, hang on. I'll put him on now." The smile drops off my face as I spot Gar's worried expression. He holds the phone out to me. "It's Lucas's sister."

My belly does another flip, but it's not pleasant this time. My heart is lodged in the back of my throat as I take the phone, forcing my vocal cords to work. "What's wrong?" I croak, my mouth as dry as the Gobi Desert.

"He's tried it again," she sobs, and a piercing pain spears me straight through the heart.

"Fuck, no. Is he … is he?" I can't articulate the thought. A dead weight settles on my chest, pressing and constricting, as my heart starts pumping like crazy.

Zeta drops to her knees in front of me, clutching my free hand with tears in her eyes.

"He's alive," Kat manages to say through her cries. "But they've had to have him committed again."

Blood thrums in my ears, and my heartbeat accelerates, my heart pounding and pounding behind my rib cage, like someone's turning a key, propelling it to beat faster and faster. "I'll be there as soon as I can," I say before hanging up.

My chest heaves and I can't breathe. Pulling my hand from Zeta's, I get up, staggering as my legs threaten to go out from under me. The room spins, and I can hear my heartbeat in my ears, pounding and pounding, crashing and careening, and my lungs seize up. I'm gasping loudly, arms flailing, eyes darting wildly about the place.

Micah grabs hold of my shoulders. "Deep breaths, man. In and out. Nice and slow. Bring it back down." He breathes with me, and I watch his chest rising and falling, steadying my own breaths, allowing a rush of oxygen to fill up my lungs.

"Put your hands on your knees," Gar says, rubbing his hand up and down my spine as I bend over, still breathing heavily, waiting for the intense fluttering in my chest to level off.

"I'm okay now." I straighten up, a couple minutes later, accepting the glass of water from Scott and taking a few sips. My eyes search for Zeta, and she's crying, holding her arms around her waist as she stares at me. "He's okay," I reassure her, realizing she has no clue what's gone down.

Standing, she comes toward me, throwing her arms around my neck, and I pull her body into mine, closing my eyes and letting the last vestiges of my panic attack go. Her warmth and her smell wrap around me, settling my nerves, reminding me I'm not alone.

"Not that I'm not concerned for Luc, but it's you I'm worried about," she sobs, clutching me even tighter. The guys slip out of the room to give us some privacy. She leans back, cupping my face. "Does that happen a lot?"

I grip her waist, keeping her flush against me. "Certain things push me over the edge, but I haven't had an anxiety attack in months." She peppers my face with soft, tiny kisses, and tears fill my eyes. "Don't ever leave me, Zeta. Please don't ever go." I'm aware how pitiful I sound, but I couldn't give two shits right now.

I need her.

I need her so much, and if that makes me a pussy, so be it.

She presses a brief, tender kiss to my lips, before resting her forehead against mine. "Wild horses couldn't drag me away from you now. I love you, Ryder, and I'm here for you." She circles her arms around my neck again, nuzzling into my cheek.

"I can't ever be without you, and I love you so, so much." I press a kiss to the top of her hair, finally back to normal. Slipping out of our embrace, I take her hand and lead her over to the couch. Sinking into it, I haul her into my lap. She curls herself around me, resting her head on my chest. "When's the last time you spoke to Luc?" I'm pretty sure I know when it was, but I don't know if he's reached out to her since the accident because I've deliberately taken a back seat in Luc's life the last couple years.

"I haven't spoken to him in five years," she admits, and I hear remorse in her tone.

I lift her head up. "I have a lot to fill you in on, but I need to go see him. Would you like to come with?"

She nods without hesitation. "I only kept my distance from him because I knew he was working with you. I didn't want him to feel like he was stuck in the middle of us, so I stopped answering his calls, and eventually, he gave up trying."

I tuck her hair behind her ears. "He's in a bad way, baby. He tried to take his own life, and it's not the first time."

"No! Oh, God, no." Tears spill down her cheeks again, and I'm struggling to contain my own emotions too.

"He's not going to be the Luc you knew and loved. You sure you're up for that?"

She swipes at the moisture under her eyes. "I'm not leaving you to deal with this alone, and I feel terrible that I cut him out of my life. I'm a horrible friend."

"No blame game, remember?" I rub my thumb under her eyes. "Let's be there for him now."

The guys had called Rod while we were talking, and he's already organized the private jet. Mike drives us to East Hampton Airport, and we board the plane, settling in for the long flight.

My stomach sours when I realize Sarah is our attendant for the duration of the flight. I stupidly fucked her the last time she flew with us, and judging by the not-too-subtle eye-fuck she's just given me, I'm guessing she figures she's in for a repeat performance. I was high as a fucking kite the last time we screwed, and I barely even remember it. I've done a lot of soul-searching since Zeta came back into my life, and I've made some really shitty decisions since I entered the music industry, especially where it concerns women.

"Sit here," I tell Zeta, taking her hand and positioning her beside me. I drape my arm over her shoulder and whisper in her ear. "I need you close."

"Because you want me close or you want to send a message to your fuck buddy that you're not interested this time?" Her tone is curt, and I detect the hurt hiding behind it.

I tilt her face to mine. "I love you. Only you, and I want you close. Always." I keep my eyes on hers as I lower my mouth, brushing my lips softly across hers as I test the waters. I haven't tried to kiss her again since that first day when we made out on the terrace, because I'm trying to respect her wishes. But fuck it. I want to reassure her. And it can't hurt to drill the message home to Sarah either—I'm off the market. Permanently, if I get my way.

When she doesn't push me away, and her eyes flutter shut, I kiss her more deeply, winding my hand around the back of her neck, drawing her closer. Every part of me craves every part of her, and I wish we were alone so I could worship her body in the way she deserves.

"We're about to take off," Sarah barks in my ear. "And the

pilot has asked that everyone buckle up." I pull away from Zeta, noting the hostile vibes Sarah's sending her way.

Out of the corner of my eye, I spot Mike laughing, but there's nothing funny about this situation. Eight hours is a long-ass fucking time to be stuck with a moody broad with her nose out of joint.

We buckle our seats as Sarah stomps to the back of the small plane, strapping herself into her seat. "I'm sorry about this," I whisper to Zeta, rubbing a tense spot between my brows.

"If she so much as lifts a finger to touch you, I will rip the bitch a new one," she hisses, lacing her fingers in mine.

I can't help grinning at her possessive reaction, and my dick approves too, hardening to the point of pain. Taking her hand, I place it lightly over my crotch. "Look what you've just done to me." Her lips curve into a small smile. "No one gets to touch me but you." Her shoulders relax a little as she looks out the window, watching the plane start to move down the runway.

Once we're up in the air, Sarah hands me a whiskey, her thumb deliberately brushing against the back of my hand as she gives it to me. I shove it back at her, drilling her with a dark look. "I didn't order that."

"It's what you usually have." She flutters her eyelashes, wetting her lips with her tongue. "And we have everything you normally order on the menu today." She's about as subtle as a brick.

Zeta laughs dryly, and the look Sarah gives her is almost comical. "Are you seriously hitting on him with me sitting right here?" Zeta narrows her eyes and sharpens her claws. "Because trust me, that won't end well for you."

I pull Zeta into my side, glaring at Sarah. "I've made quite a few changes in my life," I tell her pointedly. "I'll have a soda, and my girlfriend would like a sparkling water." Okay, so I'm stretching the truth a little, but Zeta *is* going to be my girlfriend again, and she doesn't look displeased that I've put it out there.

"She's your girlfriend?" Sarah rakes her gaze up and down Zeta, zooming in on the ink on her arms, her lips pursing in disgust, and all it does is annoy the fuck out of me. "We'd like our drinks now!" I snap, and she jumps, clamping a hand to her chest.

Wearing a frustrated look, she storms off. Mike chuckles, and I flip him the bird. "Your choice in women leaves a lot to be desired, Ryder," Zeta deadpans, scowling and digging her nails into her thigh.

"Tell me about it," I sigh, fearing this eight-hour flight is going to feel more like eighty years.

"Can we forget about the bitch and talk about Luc." She twists around to face me, easing out of my arm.

"Sure." I wipe my sweaty hands down the front of my jeans, attempting to steady my nerves, because this story is not going to be easy to tell. "After Young was released from juvie, he went to live with his sister, her husband, and their two kids, but he couldn't find work, none of his old friends wanted anything to do with him, and he was depressed. His sister reached out to me, and I got him a position with the crew on my tour. It was our first tour as the headline act, and things were pretty crazy." I lean my head back, sighing. "I should never have brought him into that lifestyle."

She squeezes my hand. "What happened?"

"We partied hard, and Luc enjoyed all the perks of the job. Drink, drugs, women. He was right there by my side. I loved having him around because it made me feel closer to you, and he was always like the brother I'd never had. But I was fighting my own demons, and I didn't see what was in front of my eyes."

Sarah returns at that moment with our drinks. When she's handing the glass of water to Zeta, she purposely lets it slip from her fingers, and the contents spill all over Zeta's jeans and shirt. Zeta eyeballs her with barely concealed anger as she pulls at her sodden clothes. "You're pathetic. I'd expect this kind of behavior from a sulky teenager, not a grown woman. Can't you at least try to act professional?"

Sarah pouts, and I stand. "I want a word in private." I point toward the back of the plane before turning to Zeta. "There's a bedroom up there you can use if you want to get changed."

She nods, getting up wordlessly, her jaw tense and her expression ferocious. I pull her small overnight bag out of the overhead cabinet and hand it to her before walking to where Sarah is waiting.

"I knew you'd come to your senses," she says, grinning, as she reaches out for me.

I clasp her wrist gently before she can touch me, dropping her arm back to her side. "I'm only going to say this once, so listen carefully. You either act in a professional capacity, like you're being paid to do, or this is the last time you'll work on any flight for me or Torment. Pull any more stunts like that and you're done."

"But, Ryder, we were so good together." She reaches for me again, and I step back.

"You were a mistake. A drunken fuck I don't even remember. That woman you just threw a drink over is the love of my life, and there isn't anything I won't do for her. Getting a whore masquerading as a flight attendant sacked wouldn't even register on the list of things I'd do for my girl, so get the fuck out of my face unless we need food or drink. You understand me?" I'm being unfairly harsh, but screw this shit. I'm fucking worried about Luc, and Zeta and I finally seem to be getting somewhere, so I'm fucked if some clinger is going to step in and ruin stuff between us.

"You're a total prick."

"I am. And you'd do well to remember it."

I return to my seat, take out my cell, and ping a text to

Rod. I have zero faith that Sarah's going to toe the line, and I'm not putting up with her shit for the duration of the flight.

Zeta returns a few minutes later, wearing a jean skirt and a figure-hugging black top that accentuates her stunning cleavage. It drapes on one side, showcasing her gorgeous shoulder and olive-toned skin. She looks sexy as fuck, and I'm instantly hard again. It takes colossal effort not to drag her into the bedroom and beg her to let me have my wicked way with her.

"I had a word with Sarah, and she knows she's fired if she steps out of line again," I tell Zeta as she brushes past me into her seat. Unable to resist, I run my hand up her bare leg, and she shrieks.

"Ryder, behave. As much as I'd like to stick it to the bitch, I am not getting down and dirty with you on this plane."

"Can't blame a guy for trying," I joke, waggling my brows.

She rolls her eyes, but she's smiling. Reaching out, she runs her fingers through the scruff on my jawline. "I keep imagining what this will feel like rubbing against my thighs," she purrs, lowering her voice so only I can hear.

My dick throbs, and I groan. "Not helping, babe."

"I know. I want to stop thinking about it because it's turning me the fuck on, but it appears I have a one-track mind when it comes to you."

I hope I'm reading this right, because it seems like we might finally be on the same page. Before she has a chance to overthink things, I grab her face and crush my lips to hers, licking the inside of her mouth, pretending it's her pretty pussy I'm licking instead. She doesn't let me down, kissing me back with the same urgency, and I'm mentally fist pumping the air. We're clutching one another, kissing frantically as if our lives depend on it, and I want nothing more than to take her back to the bedroom and bury myself so far inside her we forget anything and everything but the two of us and how right we are for each other.

That thought forces me to pull back, because I know she

doesn't want to have sex on this plane, and I don't want to go there until there's nothing between us.

No secrets.

No lies.

No past mistakes.

Just honesty and love.

ZETA

When we stop at Denver to refuel, another flight attendant replaces Sarah, much to her fury and disgust. Ryder explained he had texted Rod when we were in the air to have her replaced, and I'm touched that he went to so much trouble to put me at ease. I'm not going to lie. I wanted to cut the bitch a new one, but I would've survived. It's not like this is the last time I'm going to run into one of Ryder's conquests, and I'll just have to grow thicker skin and learn to deal with it. I hate the thought of him being with other girls, especially those nasty groupies, but I can't criticize him for having a life when we were apart. He's made it clear none of them were anything more than meaningless sex, so I'm trying not to get all worked up over it. Not when I know what we have is something special.

When he told the bitch I was his girlfriend, it made me silently jump for joy. I know I told him I wanted to take things slow, but I can't hold back anymore.

I want him.

I want him so fucking badly, and the things that were upsetting me a couple weeks ago aren't bothering me as much anymore.

While my hormones would happily approve of any plan which involved jumping Ryder's bones, I still want to hold back on that front. I know when we make love nothing will ever be the same again, and I want to ensure there is no obstacle between us when we do.

Right now, I've got to focus on the important stuff, like finding out the rest of the story with Luc. I managed to fall asleep for a few hours on the plane, so we never got to finish our conversation. Mike is currently driving us to the hospital where Luc is, so Ryder is filling me in on the rest.

"It was two years ago, and we were playing a gig at the Staples Center," he says. "It got really messy at the after-party, and Luc was trashed, but I still left him alone to go back to my hotel room. I hate being back in California. It reminds me of so many troubled memories, and it always brings everything to the surface. My past, leaving you, my fucked-up childhood. All of it."

Unbuckling my belt, I scoot over beside him. He wraps his arm around my shoulder, unbuckling his belt and refastening it over both of us. I snuggle into his side, loving how protective he is of me. Ryder's the only one who's ever made me feel so safe, so protected, so loved.

"What happened to Luc?"

He closes his eyes, and his entire body tenses up beside me. I run my hand up and down his arm, pressing my face into his chest, soaking up his warmth and his delicious smell and wanting to absorb the pain I feel oozing from his every pore. Whatever the truth is, I can tell this is something else Ryder feels guilty about. Something else he blames himself for.

"He nearly died, Zeta. I nearly killed one of my best friends." He whispers it so quietly I'm not sure I heard him correctly.

"What?" I gulp over the painful lump in my throat.

He opens his eyes, and the pain reflected in his gaze guts me. Ryder's pain cuts even deeper than mine, I realize in this moment, as he sits beside me, naked and vulnerable, not shielding anything from me.

"He took a concoction of drugs, and he was completely trashed. He launched himself off the roof of the hotel because he thought he was Superman and he was convinced he could fly." His Adam's apple bobs in his throat and tears pool in his eyes. "He flatlined three times on the way to the hospital in the ambulance, and I thought I'd lost him. The doctors managed to save him, but he's paralyzed from the waist down, and he's in a wheelchair now."

I clamp a hand over my mouth as my own tears make a reappearance. Horror and shame engulf me. I've thought of Luc a lot over the years. Picked up the phone countless times to call him. But I never followed through because of the Ryder connection.

"I called you," Ryder whispers, effectively pulling me out of my mind. "I was pacing the hallways in the hospital while I waited for his sister to arrive, and the only person I was thinking of was you. I wanted you there. Needed you. And I knew you'd want to know, even if you hadn't had any contact with him for years."

"That was you!" I exclaim, clearly remembering the night I got a strange call, and a weird sensation had crept over me. "I heard all this noise in the background. Sirens blaring. People shouting. The sound of footsteps," I say, recalling it vividly. "I kept saying hello, and no one answered."

"I wanted to talk, but I couldn't make myself speak," he says, holding me tighter. "I was standing in the middle of the hallway in the hospital as chaos reigned around me, with tears streaming down my face, listening to your voice and missing you so fucking much I wished I was the one in the operating room, not Luc, because the pain crashing through me was more than I could bear."

"Oh, Ryder."

"You stayed on the line for ages," he whispers, peering down at me.

I stare deep into his eyes. "I couldn't explain it then, and I can't explain it now, but I knew it wasn't a crank call. I think, subconsciously, I knew it was you. All I can tell you is that I was incapable of hanging up, and I stayed on the line until you hung up on me."

"I wanted to speak to you so badly, but then I was ashamed. Ashamed of telling you how I'd let Luc down. How I'd hurt someone else. And that reminded me why I needed to stay away from you."

"Jesus, Ryder. It's not your fault." I grip his face firmly. "You didn't put those drugs in Luc's mouth. You didn't force him up to the roof and push him off. He's a grown man, and he made those choices himself."

"He never would've been there if it wasn't for me!" He looks away but not before I see the sheer agony and torment on his face.

I force his face back to mine. "You gave him an opportunity. If he'd stayed at home in Orange County, who knows what would've happened? He might have ended up in a worse way. You gave him a job and the chance at a different life. The fact he made those choices were his alone. You did the best you could by him."

"But did I?" he yells, and Mike locks concerned eyes with me through the mirror. "I was supposed to be his friend, and I didn't look after him properly."

I grab hold of his cheeks firmly. "You listen to me, and you listen to me good. The only reason Luc Young survived juvie was because of you. You couldn't have done any more than you did for that boy. And when he was released and he needed you, you were there for him. You gave him a job and a purpose, and the fact you weren't watching him twenty-four seven is not a failing on your part. You were crazy busy with your music career, and it wasn't your job to babysit him. This isn't your fault."

Mike clears his throat. "Sorry to interrupt, but we're here."

I nod, keeping my gaze trained on Ryder. "Please don't do this to yourself. You shoulder enough guilt and blame, and I may not know Luc as well as I once did, but I know he wouldn't want you blaming yourself for something he did."

He kisses me softly, keeping his arms wrapped firmly around me. Then he rests his chin on top of my head, just hugging me, and it's a profound moment.

I don't know what awaits me inside the walls of this hospital, only that it won't be pleasant. However, I'm determined to be strong for Ryder, because I can't bear to see him torturing himself like this, and if I can help ease some of the burden, even if just a little bit of it, then I want to be that for him.

Mike and I stand off to one side as Ryder chats with the doctor outside Luc's hospital room. Ryder asked Rod to arrange to transfer Luc to a private room, and it was taken care of while we were in the air.

"You were really good with him back there," Mike says, crossing his arms and never taking his eyes off Ryder. "We've told him that, time and time again, but it never sinks in. I'm glad you're back in his life, and maybe he'll listen to you, because you have no idea the lengths that man goes to in order to torture himself. It's painful to watch."

"You care about him."

"I do. This job is more than just a job to me." He glances briefly at me as Ryder wraps up his conversation with the doctor. "He's a good man, and he does a lot of good things. I know if I ever needed anything he'd be there for me, and there aren't a lot of people who can say that about their employer. I would lay down my life for that guy, and it kills me to see him beat himself up for stuff he couldn't control."

"Me too, and I only wish I'd understood. I could've

reached out to him years ago if I'd known he was suffering too."

He squeezes my hand. "You're here now." He glances up at Ryder striding toward us and lowers his voice. "Be patient with him, and if he fucks up, forgive him. I've never seen Ryder look at any woman the way he looks at you, and I've never known him to be affectionate the way he is with you."

"I know he has a good heart, and I know he feels things deeply. I'm not going anywhere. I'm in this for the long haul." And as the words leave my mouth, I know there's nowhere else I'd rather be than by this man's side.

28

RYDER

I clasp her hand in mine, shooting Mike an inquisitive look. They looked cozy, and I'm wondering what he's said to her. If he's told her anything about the security detail over the years, I'll knock him the fuck out.

"Relax." Mike mouths at me, instantly knowing where my head's gone, his look confirming that he didn't tell her anything. I need to be the one to explain all that. She's probably going to freak when she finds out, but I'll deal with that when the time comes. Right now, I need to prepare her for this.

"Zeta." I turn her around outside Luc's door so she's facing me. "The doctor says Luc is in a very depressive state and he's largely nonresponsive. You need to prepare yourself. He's nothing like the guy you remember."

She nods. "We'll do this. Together."

Together has got to be the sweetest word known to man, and hearing it come out of her gorgeous lips is the icing on the cake.

"Fuck, I love you." I pull her into my arms. I can't seem to stop doing it. Can't seem to stop touching her. Afraid she'll disappear if I can't feel her.

Mike smiles, and I know he's happy I've got her in my life. I know everyone is because I've been calmer and more at peace these last few weeks than I've been in years.

"C'mon." She breaks the embrace first. "Let's see him."

The large room is flooded with light as we step inside. It's painted in cool shades of blue, and there's a seating area with a couch, two chairs, and a wall-mounted TV and an en suite bath with a shower and tub. Luc is lying down on the bed at the top of the room, on his side, staring blankly out the window. A couple tubes are attached to one hand, and a machine beeps quietly in the corner. He doesn't look up as we approach his bed, but I was expecting that.

The last time he tried to kill himself, he was like this. Closed off. Trapped in his own head. The world shut out. It kills me to see him like this. To know he despises his life so much he keeps trying to take it. And I know what that feels like. I've been there more times than I care to count, which only makes this worse, because I understand exactly what he's going through.

Everyone thinks the car accident was just that, but I know the truth. I wanted to end it that night, and I just wanted the misery to stop. She saved me that night, and she doesn't even know it.

I shake myself out of those thoughts because I won't be selfish. We're here for Luc, and I'm going to try and be a friend to him.

He looks like shit, and I can tell by Zeta's horrified expression that she's shocked at his bloated appearance. He's at least double the size he was the last time she saw him. He hasn't cut his hair in so long, and it's hanging in matted strands down his back. His gnarly beard is no better. But it's the vacant, dull look in his eyes and the grayish tone of his skin that's the worst. He looks like the living dead. Like he's got one foot in this world and one in the next.

I'm hit by the usual cocktail of emotions. Despite what

Zeta believes, I *have* failed my friend. I did this to him, and I don't deserve an ounce of the happiness I've been experiencing these last few weeks. I'm a despicable human being, and I deserved to die that night on the I-605.

"Luc." Zeta pulls up a chair beside his bed, lowering her face until she's eye level with him. "Luc, it's me, Zeta. I'm here with Ryder." She takes his hand in hers, squeezing it. He continues to stare vapidly ahead, and it hurts my heart so bad. Zeta looks up at me, agony etched across her face, as she extends her free hand to me.

I walk in slow motion toward her, pulling up another chair and taking her hand in mine. "Hey, buddy. I hate to see you in here again. I wish you'd called me."

Zeta pulls our conjoined hands to her lips, pressing a soft kiss on my knuckles. She keeps a tight grip on Luc with her other hand. We talk to him, but there's no response. No indication that he knows we're here at all. Every so often, Zeta looks over at me with an expression of abject sorrow on her face, and I wish I knew what to do to comfort her.

The door opens, and Luc's sister, Kat, comes inside. I introduce her to Zeta, and she wraps her into a hug. "Luc often talks about you," she tells her. "I know he'd be happy you've come to visit."

"I'm sorry I left it so long. I had no idea."

I pull her into my side, kissing her temple.

"He hasn't been in a good place for a long time," Kat explains. "We try to keep his spirits up, but it's hard when someone's lost the will to survive." Tears roll down her face, and huge wracking sobs heave her chest. I circle my arms around her, running my hand up and down her back, trying to comfort her.

"I should've done more," I say, more to myself than her, but she hears me, and she stops crying.

She shoves at my chest. "You stop that, Ryder Stone. You hear me?! No one could've done more for my brother than you. You've kept him alive all these years. Without you, I honestly don't think he'd still be with us. He had nothing to live for until you gave him that job, and then you bought him a house and a car, and you've made sure none of us want for nothing."

She waves her hands around. "And look at this. You make sure he has the best of care. You couldn't do any more for him." She grabs my chin, and for a small, curvy little woman, she sure has a strong grip. "Stop it. Just stop blaming yourself. That's not how Luc feels, and it's not how I feel, so please just stop."

We leave the hospital an hour later, and I'm mentally and physically drained. Kat insisted there's no point in us hanging around, and the doctor concurred. The last time Luc slipped into a deep depression, he didn't speak to anyone for two weeks. But I still feel guilty and restless as we board the private jet for the return journey.

Zeta yawns, and I tell her to take the bedroom. Mike is already reclining in a chair with a heavy blanket over him, and I intend to do the same.

Her only reply is to take my hand and pull me to the bedroom with her. Her gaze bounces between the bed and me. "I know it's not exactly the biggest bed in the world, but we'll both fit." She caresses my cheek. "I don't want to be alone, and I don't think you should be either."

"You won't hear me complaining." I kiss her forehead.

"Just to sleep though, Ryder," she adds, and I nod, not expecting anything more. Just getting to sleep beside her is more than enough.

She goes to the bathroom to get changed, and I toe off my Vans and shuck out of my jeans and shirt, climbing under the covers in just my boxers.

"I've been thinking," Zeta says as she slips under the covers in her silk pajama top and shorts. I try hard not to lower my gaze to her impressive rack, but it's challenging.

"What's on your mind?" I pull her back into my chest, draping my arms around her waist.

She rests her arms on mine, and a deep sense of contentment settles over me. I nuzzle my nose into her hair, soaking her all in.

"A change of scenery might be good for Luc. Maybe he needs a break away from Orange County. He could come and stay with me for a while."

"With us, you mean." I prop up on one elbow, leaning over so I'm looking her squarely in the face.

"His sister said he's likely to be in the psychiatric facility for a few months, at the very least, so ..."

I can't decide if her uncertainty is cute or delusional or if she's already having doubts. "So, you'll be with me, and he can come and live with us. The U.S. tour doesn't kick off until next year, and while there'll be some promo stuff with the new album release in November, it won't take me away for more than the odd night or two."

She turns around so we're facing one another. "I don't know if I can stay out in the Hamptons that long. I've got work and—"

"And I'm your boss's boss. He'll do what I tell him."

She scowls. "You can't do that!"

"Why the hell not?"

"It's nepotism, and it's wrong. I can't be treated any differently than any other employee."

I kiss the tip of her nose. "Babe, there has to be some benefits to dating the owner."

She quirks a brow. "Is that what we're doing?"

I frown. "It's actually much more than that, but I know you want to take it slow, so dating works for me."

She traces patterns on my chest with her finger. "I think we've moved way beyond that."

My heart stutters, and panic is waiting in the wings. "Please don't tell me you've changed your mind."

"No!" She circles her arms around my neck, and I pull her hot body against mine. "It's far too late for me to protect my heart. We're both way too invested."

I capture her lips in mine, pulling her flush against me, my erection hardening to the point of pain as her taut nipples press into my chest. But I keep my hands loosely on her spine and resist the urge to thrust my hips up into her pelvis, kissing her slowly and passionately, pouring everything I'm feeling into every brush of our lips, every sweep of our tongues. When I reach the point of no return, I gently break the kiss, wrapping my arms around her shoulder and holding her face to my chest. "I love you."

"I love you, too," she whispers, pressing a delicate kiss to my left pec.

The bed sways ever so gently as the plane accelerates, taking off into the sky.

"Sleep, baby. We'll talk more about it when we get home, and we can call Kat and see what she thinks. If moving Luc in with us will help his recovery, then I'm all for it. But only with you by my side."

"Together," she murmurs in a sleepy tone, and I drift off to sleep rocking her gently in my arms, committing my new favorite word to memory.

29

ZETA

I bolt upright, awoken by shouting and movement in the bed. Ryder is thrashing about, legs entangled in the sheets, screaming and whimpering, in obvious distress. "It's my fault! It's all my fault! I'm so sorry." Tears pour out of his eyes, and the most agonizing cry punches through the air, as if it's been birthed straight from his soul.

"Ryder." I gently shake his shoulders, not wanting to alarm him but needing him to wake up. "Wake up, Ryder. You're having a nightmare. It's not real." I caress his face, continuously murmuring the same sentence, until his eyes blink open. He frantically gasps, as if he's just surfaced for air, and I whisper assurances as I stroke my hands lightly up and down his arms, over his face, and across his chest.

The sheet underneath us is stuck to his back, and beads of sweat cling to his forehead, dampening the edges of his hair. "Sit up," I urge, helping him lean back against the headboard, before swinging my legs out the side of the bed. I continue to hold him, watching as his breathing recalibrates to more normal levels. When I feel it's safe to leave him for a quick minute, I press a kiss to his forehead and stand. "I'll be right back."

I head out of the bedroom and hunt down the flight atten-dant, asking her for supplies. "You need any help?" Mike asks, straightening his chair up as he looks at me through troubled eyes.

I shake my head. "Go back to sleep. I've got this."

I take the bottles of water and spare bed linen from the attendant, thanking her before returning to Ryder. His legs are bent at the knees, and he's hunched over his body, softly crying. My heart bleeds for him. Placing the fresh covers down, I sit beside him, wrapping my arms around his trem-bling body. "It's okay, baby. Let it all out." I hold him as he sobs, my heart breaking for him.

When his tears dry, I give him the bottle of water, urging him to drink it all. He stumbles to the bathroom, and I change the bed linen, tossing the sweaty covers in a ball over in the corner of the room.

"I'm sorry you had to see that," he whispers, crawling back up onto the bed, looking at me with bloodshot eyes.

"Don't be. We're together. That means we're there for each other through the bad times as well as the good." I brush damp strands of hair back off his forehead. "And I under-stand better than most how past memories can haunt your sleep."

"It happens to you?"

I nod. "Not as frequently as it used to, but, yeah, I some-times wake up having had a vivid dream of my mom." My voice comes out as a whisper. "I see her bleeding out. Clutching her fingers to her chest, trying to quell the blood flow." I squeeze my eyes shut.

He kisses my lips, softly, a few times until my shoulders relax.

"I tried to kill myself a month after Luc jumped off the roof," he quietly says, and I instantly tense up again. My heart aches as I take his hands, entwining our fingers. "My life was already a mess, and that happening to him was my breaking point. I got fucked up on drugs and booze and took my car out on the highway in the middle of the night. I put my foot to the floor, pushing the car to its limits, knowing I'd spin out of control and welcoming it."

I fight back tears, not wanting to make this about me. He needs to get this off his chest.

The media reported details of his car accident for days, and I've wanted to ask him about that night, but I didn't want to pressure him into telling me. I knew he'd tell me in his own time. What he says next surprises the heck out of me.

"You saved me, Zeta." My eyes pop wide. He clasps my face in his big hands. "I lost control of the car, and I was spinning toward the barrier, head-on, when your face popped up in my mind's eye, as clearly as if you were right there, and I knew in that instant that I couldn't leave you. I managed to jerk the wheel around so the passenger side of the car took the brunt of the impact. If I'd plowed headfirst into the barrier, I would've been dead instantly. As it was, every part of my body was shattered from hitting it at such high speed. I had so many broken bones, and I was in a coma for a couple days."

"I remember." I hold onto his upper arms. "I collapsed when I saw the TV coverage. When I saw how mangled your car was, I couldn't stop crying." I wet my dry lips. "I went to the hospital. I tried to see you. I just needed to know that you were alive, but of course, they wouldn't let me in."

I let my mind wander back to that night. "I joined the fans who were camped outside the hospital, and I didn't leave for three days. My God, Ryder there were so many of them. The police had to put up barricades to control the crowd as thousands of people arrived to be near you. They lit candles, held up banners, played Torment's music, and prayed. As long as I live, I will never forget those few days. The camaraderie and support were like nothing I've ever experienced. It helped to know you were so loved. To know so many people were praying for you to come out of it alive. When a spokesperson came out and told us you'd woken up and were going to be okay, there was a colossal outpouring of relief. We were all hugging and crying, and it was the first time in days I had properly breathed."

"I felt you there," he says, shocking me again.

"What?"

"When I woke up, the first thought I had was of you. I could almost feel your arms around me, almost see your smile, almost smell the strawberry scent of your hair. The feeling was intense, but I dismissed it afterward, blamed it on my wishful thinking and the cocktail of drugs they had me hooked up to. But it was real." He crashes his mouth to mine, kissing me fiercely. "You were there. It was real, and I felt the connection. Do you get what we have, Zeta? Do you truly understand it?" His voice is almost frenzied.

"We're soul mates, Ryder. It's what my subconscious has always believed."

He nods agreeably, and his lips kick up. "I think I've eradicated all evidence of my man card." He tugs me with him as he lies back down under the covers. "Because that word makes my heart sing."

I giggle. "Trust me, I think you're good. The new-age man card allows you to embrace your feelings and still hold onto your masculinity." I press a kiss to his bare chest, inhaling the musky scent of his skin. "You're all man, baby."

"Our bond saved my life that night," he adds, the conversation turning more serious again. "And it forced me to face some harsh facts about my life. Rod had been bitching at me for ages to tackle my drug and alcohol dependence, so I voluntarily checked myself into rehab after I was released from the hospital. Spent ninety days getting clean, trying to come to terms with my past.

"And did you?" I snuggle in under the crook of his arm.

"Not really. I felt more in control, and the psychologist I saw in rehab gave me some strategies for dealing with my panic attacks and nightmares, but they didn't go away, and I don't think they ever will."

"And what about the other stuff?"

He kisses the top of my head. "I can admit to myself now that I was falling into a dark hole again. Recently, I'd been partying too hard, and slipping back into my old ways, but I told myself I had it under control. These last few weeks have helped enormously. Being back in the Hamptons house has always been my salvation. I keep to myself, bury myself in the music, and avoid all other temptations. I never invite people back to my house. It's my only sanctuary. My only privacy. And having you back in my life has given me purpose. Given me a reason to clean up my act." He tilts my face up to his. "Because I want to be the kind of man you deserve."

"You already are." I stretch up and kiss his lips.

"I'm broken, babe, and a part of me always will be." He looks so unbearably sad, and I want to erase all trace of sorrow from his face.

"I'm broken too, Ryder. Maybe that's why it works between us."

He's pensive for a few minutes. Then he looks at me, and a wealth of emotion flickers in his eyes. "Before we get home, I need to know you're mine. I need to know you're in this for the long haul, because there's more stuff I need to tell you, and I can't do this if you're still having doubts. I need to know you're willing to work with me on this. To build something together. Something we should've had all these years but were denied."

I prop up on one elbow, threading my fingers through his beautiful, thick hair. "I'm committed to you. To us. One hundred percent. I know we've still got stuff to work through, and I know it won't be all smooth sailing, but I'm going nowhere. I'm yours, Ryder. I've always been yours, and I always will be."

THINGS SETTLE BACK DOWN over the next few days even though Ryder has horrific nightmares every night, waking up in a cold sweat. Seeing Luc has brought it all back for him. I've moved into his room, into his bed, so I can comfort him through it, and helping Ryder deal with his demons is keeping my own at bay. I'm feeling huge guilt for cutting Luc out of my life, and while I can't change it, I'm determined to be here for him now.

Ryder and I still haven't had sex. Still haven't moved beyond heavy kissing and petting, but neither of us is in a huge rush even though we've both admitted to being horny as teenagers. But this feels normal. Like we're doing things the way they would've been done if we'd stayed together after juvie.

I continue to have weekly Skype calls with Harrison, updating him on progress with the biography and sending him my regular report for the magazine, and the articles are being well received. Sharing little snippets of lyrics from some of the new album has the fans going gaga for more, and it's helping to build buzz for the album and the bio.

Being in the studio with the guys and watching their creative process play out in front of me has been one of the highlights so far. Ryder is their main songwriter, and while he usually comes up with the lyrics, the melody is something they all work on together. It amazes me how Ryder will come up with a loose melody, strumming it on his guitar, and then Gar will come in with the bassline, Micah will effortlessly pick up the rhythm on his guitar, and Scott will start pounding the drums in sync with the beat.

I've been so lost in the music, that half the time I forget to record stuff I should. But it's all good. I've been taking photos and videos, and I plan to link them in the e-book edition of the biography to give fans a real intimate view of the process involved in writing and producing an album. I also spend dedicated one-on-one time with each band member on a weekly basis, asking them questions about their personal lives, and I'm getting to know all of them better.

They're a great group of guys; although I'm still struggling to warm up to Gar, because he has a predilection for speaking before thinking and a mind that's firmly fixed in the gutter. Just yesterday, he told me he's jerking off so much right now he thinks he has repetitive strain injury. I rolled my eyes so hard it's a wonder they didn't roll right out of my eye sockets. From the sordid stories he keeps insisting on sharing with me, it's clear life in the Hamptons is a world away from their usual routine in the city, where they work hard and party hard in equal measure. I worry about Gar's influence on Ryder once we return to New York, and it's something that keeps me up at night.

Ryder spoke to Kat, proposing the plan for Luc to come and live with us when he's up to it, and she was enthusiastic about the idea, suggesting a change of scenery would do wonders for her brother. Ultimately, it'll be Luc's decision, and he's not of sound mind yet to make that call, but I'm really hoping he will come here with us for a bit, hoping to get the opportunity to renew our friendship and support him like I should've been doing all these years.

It's Friday morning, and I'm in the kitchen making eggs and bacon for breakfast with the boys grouped around the counter behind me. Poor little Mattie is sick at the moment, so Linda and Scott have been holed up in the guesthouse looking after the little guy. Louise is on loud speaker, currently flirting up a storm with Ryder, Micah, and Garrett. I've been calling her a couple times a week to check in, and she's on first-name terms with all the guys now.

"Garrett, darling," she purrs, as I plate up our food. "I need another favor."

"Another one?" Gar teases. "You're a dirty, dirty girl, Louise."

Three sets of eyes instantly dart to Garrett.

"What kind of favor are we talking about?" I say, pausing what I'm doing.

"Now, now, lovely," Louise says. "Don't you go spoiling my fun. I may be old but I'm not dead yet. When else am I going to get an opportunity to drool over hot, young men? My darling Garrett understands, so he sent me a dick pic, but I accidentally deleted it when I was trying to enlarge it, and now, I have nothing to get my rocks off to."

Micah spits his coffee all over the island unit while I stand staring at Gar in shock, and Ryder is doubled over, laughing and clutching his stomach like he's in pain.

"You sent her a dick pic?" I screech, rounding the unit. "Are you fucking insane? You'll give her a coronary!" I don't know whether to laugh or cry.

"Chill out. I'm just doing my civic duty." He waggles his brows, smothering a smile. "Helping the elderly is a noble use of my time."

I shake my head repeatedly. "Do *not* send her another one. Next time she's trying to enlarge it, she'll probably accidentally post it online."

"I can hear you, and I'm not a child," Louise pipes up, but we all ignore her.

"The public at large is well accustomed to my dick," Gar says with a gloating smile. He turns to Ryder. "Remember that video the bunny boiler posted? There were closeups of both our cocks on full display in that one, and I have it on good authority that our cocks have their own Twitter and IG accounts." He puffs out his chest as if it's something to be proud of.

"Thanks. That's something I really needed to know," I deadpan, placing the burnt bits of bacon I was going to throw out on Gar's plate and giving his original serving to Micah instead.

I hand out plates as Ryder thumps Gar in the arm while he's promising Louise to send her a replacement pic. We say goodbye, and tension is thick in the air as we eat. Ryder rubs my thigh under the table, but I shove his hand away. I know I'm being irrational, but I hate the thought of intimate pictures and videos of my boyfriend doing the rounds. I know it's in the past, and it means nothing, but I can't help how I feel, and right now, I'm jealous and angry, and I just want to slink away and lick my wounds.

Leaving the guys to clean up after breakfast, I take a long, hot shower, trying to de-stress and let it go. When I emerge from the bathroom, dressed in only a towel, Ryder is sitting on the bed waiting for me. He's in his workout clothes, his ink on full display in the muscle top

"C'mere, sexy." He pats his lap, and I shake my head.

"I need to get dressed, Ryder, and I'd like some privacy." I don't want to be all pissy with him, but I can't help it.

He sighs, clawing a hand through his hair and walking toward me. "Baby, if I could erase my past, you know I would. If I could get those videos removed, I would, but it's impossible once they go viral. We spent hundreds of thousands of dollars on legal fees when the first few videos came out, and we might as well have flushed the money down the toilet. It's impossible to catch these people and hold them accountable, but if you want me to get my attorney on the case again, I will."

I lean my head on his chest and his arms automatically go around me. "No, you don't need to do that." I gulp over the messy ball of emotion in my throat. "Just tell me about the bunny boiler."

"She's no one, baby."

"Ryder." My tone is caustic, and it brokers no argument.

He sighs. "After that happened to Luc, I completely fell off the rails. Was either high, stoned, drunk, or a combination, pretty much twenty-four seven. Ashley had recently joined the label, and she made her interest clear. We fucked a few times, and Gar joined us one time. Then I ended up in rehab, and when I came out, she started pressuring me to put a label on our relationship. I told her we'd never been more than fuck buddies and I wasn't interested. She didn't handle it well. Got clingy as fuck and started showing up at my place uninvited. I warned her I'd report her to the label if she didn't back off. She threatened to leak video footage of our threesome to the media. I thought she was bluffing. Thought the threat of losing her job would be enough, but it wasn't. She sold the video, made a ton of money, and didn't care she was fired. I haven't spoken to her since. The end."

"What a bitch."

"Yep. And I hate that she's still trying to fuck with my life." He holds my face in his hands. "Please don't get upset. Honestly, she's not worth it."

I nod. "I'll try, but it's hard hearing constant reminders of your past. I'm just extra emotional 'cause my period is due soon. Don't mind me. It'll pass."

He holds me tighter, and I close my eyes, leaning against his chest again, enjoying how cherished I feel bundled up in his arms. "Don't apologize for how you feel, and I always want to know what's going through your mind even if it makes me feel like the biggest shithead."

I slide my hand up his chest. "I knew what I was signing up for when I agreed to be together. And I can handle it, most of the time."

"I completely understand if you don't. The thought of there being shit like that about you in the public domain makes me so jealous I could scream. I know I wouldn't handle it well, and I try not to think about those guys you've been with."

I peek up at him. "I've never made a sex tape, so you can dispel that fear."

He kisses me softly. "Let me make it up to you?" His eyes darken, and I feel him hardening against my stomach. He kneads the corded muscles in my shoulders. "You're tense. Let me help you relax."

Butterflies scatter in my chest, and my core floods with heat. "What did you have in mind, Rock Star?" I murmur in my most seductive voice, looking at him through hooded eyes.

"Lose the towel, get on the bed, and let me show you."

30

RYDER

I lock the bedroom door, kicking off my sneakers as I turn around to face her. She fixes her eyes on mine, her pupils burning with anticipation, holding my gaze confidently while licking her lips and moving her hand to the knot on her towel. My cock hardens, and desire rushes through me. Very slowly, she loosens the towel, and it drops to the floor, leaving her standing before me completely naked.

I suck in a breath as my eyes drink her in, sweeping down over her voluptuous tits, her nipples rosy, large, and taut, her skin prickling as my gaze wanders lower to her flat stomach, along the gentle curve of her hip, and on to the neatly trimmed patch of hair over her pussy before gliding down those long, long, shapely legs. She's perfection, and I can't wait to get my first taste of her.

I stride toward her with purpose, lightly placing my hands on her shoulders. "You are so fucking beautiful it hurts." I kiss her mouth before moving along her cheek, to her jawline, and down to that sensitive spot just under her ear. I nip at her earlobe, and she whimpers, her legs buckling. I wrap my arm around her waist, pulling her in close, wishing we were skin to skin, but we can't go there yet. Not until she knows the full truth.

And that's not what this is about.

This is about making her feel good. Cherished. Loved. So she knows she's the only one. So all those doubts and jealousies in her head disappear.

Taking her hand, I lead her to the bed and tenderly push her down on the pillows. She lies flat on her back as I yank my top up over my head, crawling over her in just my running shorts. I hover over her body, enjoying the view, loving how her tits sway as her chest heaves up and down. Her eyes burn with lust, and I capture her mouth in a searing-hot kiss, my tongue plundering her mouth, moaning at the back of my throat as I lick inside her.

I continue my exploration, grazing my teeth along the column of her neck, brushing my lips across her collarbone as I trail a finger down the gap between her breasts. I play with her tits, kneading her flesh and rolling her hard nipples between my thumb and index finger. The sounds coming out of her mouth are almost enough to make me come in my pants like my horny teenage self. I lower my mouth to one tit while I fondle the other. I suck and bite, tugging at her nipple until she's crying out, her back curving off the bed.

"Ryder, please." She props up on her elbows, watching me lap at her tits. "I need your cock inside me."

I crawl back up her body, kissing her passionately. "Not yet, honey. But soon. I promise."

A sigh of frustration leaves her swollen lips, and I devour her mouth again. "I know how to take care of you, I promise."

"Well, show me what you've got then, Rock Star, before I spontaneously combust."

Tell me about it. My dick's so hard it could pound metal.

I move back down her body, my hands, mouth, and tongue exploring every inch of her soft, golden skin. When I arrive at the jagged scar on her lower belly, I press a reverential kiss along the puckered skin, remembering how scared I was the day Valeria stabbed her in the yard, terrified I'd lost her. I look up, locking eyes with Zeta as my lips brush along the permanent reminder of that day.

"I know," she whispers, understanding straightaway the thoughts rotating through my brain. She runs her fingers through my hair. "I love you."

"I love you too." I rest my head on her stomach. "So fucking much." I stay like that for a couple minutes until I've brushed the cobwebs aside. With a sly grin, I bury my tongue in her belly button, and she squirms, squealing as a warm smile spreads across my mouth. She screams, cursing me out, when I bypass the promised land, licking my way down her leg instead. I chuckle, looking up at the furious expression on her face. "Patience, baby."

She flips me the bird before flopping down on her back, moaning in frustration. I pick up her foot, moving my lips back up her leg, slowly, torturously, enjoying every flick of my tongue, drowning in her smell and taste, never getting enough. When I reach the ink on her upper thigh, I trace my fingers along the small lines of script, reading the words she imprinted on her skin with a lump in my throat.

Love is a place where hope and desperation lives
Because even though you're gone
You're still part of me
And I'll always want you back

"Zeta." I choke on the word, tears welling in my eyes.

She sits up, reaching down to caress my cheek. "It's always been you, Ryder, and it always will be. Only ever you."

I press my lips to hers in a fierce, needy kiss, grinding my hips against hers, wanting desperately to be at one with her but knowing I need to hold back. "I love you." I lift my head up, staring into her beautiful eyes, eyes swimming in emotion like my own. "And I need you to understand that every song I've written, every word I've put to paper, has always been about you." I point to the ink trailing from my left arm over my upper chest, tracing a finger behind the images painted on my skin until her eyes pop wide in recognition. "I wanted your name over my heart, but I wanted it private, just for me, so I buried it behind these images." I pull her hand to my chest, placing it over her name. "Every time I felt lost, every time I felt alone, I pressed my hand over my heart, and it helped me find my way back."

"Ryder." Now, it's her turn to choke up, and she presses her lips to the ink, kissing it reverently.

We kiss for a long time, pouring all our emotions into it, until it turns heated again, and my cock strains against my shorts. She's making these little guttural noises as she squirms underneath me, and I need to take care of my girl.

Sliding my hand down between us, I push two fingers inside her warm, wet pussy, and she groans into my mouth, almost making me come. "Lie back, baby. It's time to make good on my promise." She sinks into the mattress with a sigh as I glide down her body, still pumping my fingers slowly in and out of her. Pushing her legs wide, I kneel at the apex of her thighs, parting her with my thumbs, my cock throbbing painfully at the sight of her glistening and ready. I swipe my finger along her slit, and her hips buck up. Lowering my mouth, I lick up and down her slit, while she moans and cries out, writhing on the bed like she can't control herself.

She tastes so sweet, and addictive, and her alluring scent has me diving my tongue inside her channel as my finger rubs circles on her taut clit. I continue to stroke her with my tongue before moving my mouth to that sensitive bundle of nerves, sliding my index and middle fingers into her pussy the same time I push my pinky into her ass.

She explodes instantly, hips thrusting, back arching, as she screams out my name. I stay with her, riding her climax out, pumping my fingers and sucking her clit until she collapses on the bed, fully sated. I crawl up beside her, pulling her into my arms, peppering her gorgeous face with kisses.

Shoving her messy hair back off her face, she leans up, pressing her arms on my chest. "That was fucking incredible." She traces her name on my chest with her finger, smiling, her face flushed in a rosy afterglow. "You've got skills, Rock Star, and I can't wait to see what else you've got for me."

"Oh, baby. That was only the entrée." I cup her face, staring into her eyes. "When I make love to you, you'll forget there was ever anyone else but me."

"You're already all I see," she whispers, her eyes trekking down my body.

She slides her hand down toward my shorts, but I clasp her wrist, stopping her. "You don't have to. This was about you. Not me."

She sinks to her knees on the floor, pulling my legs down over the edge of the bed. "I'm not leaving you with a raging boner, and you're not the only one who wants a taste."

My cock jumps in my boxers, and she smiles, tugging my shorts down my legs. Flinging them aside, she rubs her hand back and forth over my boxers, against my straining cock, wetting her lips with her tongue. "Fuck, Rock Star. You hiding a snake in there?" Her lips quirk in amusement.

"Take them off and find out."

Grabbing the end of my boxers, she yanks them down, and my cock springs forth, hard and already leaking precum. I'm so aroused I'll probably come the instant her hot mouth takes me in.

"Shit. I was only joking. Didn't realize you actually were hiding a snake."

I smirk. I'm well hung, what can I say?

She lifts a brow, grinning as her tongue darts out, lapping up the cum seeping from the tip of my cock. I groan, my cock throbbing with need. She licks up and down my shaft while fisting her hand around the base and stroking me slowly. Stars burst behind my eyes, and a familiar tingle starts building at the base of my spine. "I'm not gonna last long, baby."

Opening her mouth wide, she draws me inside, gliding her lips up and down my length while continuing to pump me at the base. I jerk my hips forward, grabbing the back of her head as I fuck her mouth, my balls tightening, spine tingling as my release builds. "Now, baby." I attempt to pull out, but she suctions on, working her mouth and her hand harder and faster, and I detonate, shooting hot streams of cum down her throat. She doesn't let go, milking my climax until she's swallowed every last drop.

"Fucking hell." I haul her up into my lap, circling my arms around her as I kiss her glistening lips. That was the best damn blowjob of my life. Tasting my essence on her tongue has my cock hardening underneath her ass again. "I'm never going to get enough of you, baby. I'm already insatiable, and I haven't even fucked you yet."

"We could rectify that now," she says, moving her hips and repositioning herself so my cock is at the right angle to sink deep inside her. And it's tempting. So fucking tempting. But I can't make love to her until she knows the truth. Until she knows who I really am. The irony is I have enough courage in this moment to tell her everything, but we can't have this conversation now, not with the surprise I've got lined up for her later, so, reluctantly, I slide her off my lap, seating her beside me.

"When we fuck for the first time, I intend to be inside you all night," I say, pulling her hand to my lips for a kiss. "We don't have time now, but soon, baby. I promise."

🎵

"Oʜ ᴍʏ Gᴏᴅ!" Zeta shrieks when I return to the house from the airport later that night with my surprise in tow. Kayla and her fiancé, Gage, trot in after me, eyes bugging as they take in my place. Kayla races toward her friend, and they fling their arms around one another, hugging it out, screaming and crying.

"I think I just lost hearing in my eardrums," Gage deadpans, holding his sleepy son, Lennon, in his arms.

I chuckle. "I'm glad Zeta has a friend like Kayla and that I could do this for them."

"Yeah, and thanks, man. Kayla was so excited all week. She's really missed her."

The doorbell chimes, and I leave Gage with Micah and Gar while I go to grab the takeout I ordered.

After we've eaten, I take Kayla and Gage over to the guesthouse, introducing them to Scott and Linda. I was happy for them to stay in the main house, but Linda has all kinds of baby paraphernalia here, which makes it a better choice. Gage stays behind to get Lennon settled into his crib while Kayla comes back to the house with Zeta and me. Gar and Micah have cracked open a few beers, and we sit outside chatting until the early hours.

When we finally depart to bed, Zeta and I waste no time undressing one another, and we spend hours getting properly acquainted with each other's bodies. Sex is still not in the cards, but we find plenty of inventive ways to make each other come, and I drift off to sleep feeling happy and sated.

"Does he really have to come with?" Zeta pouts the following morning, with her hands on her hips. "I mean no offense, Mike," she rushes to assure my bodyguard, "but I don't think we need protecting. We're only bringing the baby for a walk, and we'll do a little window shopping, maybe grab some ice cream. I doubt we'll be in any danger."

"There's no point taking any chances," Mike politely replies. "And I'll be discreet. You won't even know I'm there."

"Baby." I pull Zeta into my arms, peering into her eyes. "This is nonnegotiable. This is my life, and you're a part of it now. You can't go out alone anymore. There are plenty of crazies out there, and I won't risk your safety."

"No one even knows who I am to you, Ryder. And this is the Hamptons. It's hardly the crime capital of the world."

"Please, Zeta. I don't want to fight with you about this. You only have the weekend with Kayla, and I want you to enjoy it. I won't be able to relax if you go out unprotected."

Her features immediately soften. "Fine. I don't want you to worry." She kisses me quickly, but I latch on, grabbing the back of her head and deepening the kiss, worshiping her mouth with my lips and my tongue, needing her to understand how much she means to me.

"My ovaries just exploded watching that," Kayla voluntarily supplies. "If I can't have any more babies, I'm totally blaming you." She prods her finger in my chest, but she's grinning.

"I think you're good, Kayla. Gage's super spunk won't let you down," Zeta says, winking.

My face contorts at my girl mentioning another guy's jizz, but she just laughs. "See ya later, Rock Star. Try not to miss me too much!" She swats my butt, and they both laugh as they exit the kitchen with baby Lennon in his stroller and Mike faithfully holding up the rear.

I hang by the pool with Gage, Micah, and Gar. Scott and Linda have gone down to the beach with Mattie. I pop the lid on a couple beers, handing one to Gage. Micah and Gar help themselves. "Zeta has been gushing about your band," I tell Gage. "And we wouldn't mind hearing you some time." I nod at my boys. I'd already mentioned it to them this morning. "It's not common knowledge yet, but we're setting up our own label and we're looking for new talent to sign."

The big guy's eyes light up. "For real?"

"Hell, yeah." Gar chinks his bottle against Gage's before

retrieving his Fender. "Why don't you play us one of your songs. Zeta says your original stuff rocks."

Without breaking a sweat, Gage slides the guitar over his shoulder, tests a few strings, and starts playing. He closes his eyes as he sings, and there's a raw, husky quality to his voice and a rustic sound to the melody as he performs for us. We grin, nodding and slapping him on the back when he's finished, and the dude's grin is so wide it threatens to split his face.

"You got any gigs lined up next weekend?" I ask.

He nods. "We play a regular gig every Friday night in Queens."

"We're coming up to the city for the VMAs that night, but we can drop by and catch your show after."

The girls come back shortly after that, joining us by the pool. Gage goes off to call his brother and the other members of their band to tell them about Friday night, and seeing the look of pure excitement on his face makes me feel good. I remember the buzz when things first started happening for me and how it was the only thing that distracted me from missing my girl. My eyes automatically search her out, and my cock instantly perks up.

Zeta looks completely fuckable in a black and gold bikini that leaves very little to the imagination. She's splashing about in the pool with Kayla and Lennon, and I can't keep my eyes off her. Gar flops down on the lounger beside me, sipping his beer while he does zilch to mask the fact he's ogling my girl with the same intensity.

I thump him in the arm. "Fuck off staring at her."

He rubs his arm, turning to face me. "Sorry, dude. Can't help it. She draws the eye, you know."

"Unfortunately, I do." I sip my soda with a grimace, my jealousy flaring at the thought of any guy eye-fucking my woman.

"Dude, that's the least of your worries. She kinda flipped

out yesterday morning when I mentioned the bunny boiler, so how's she gonna handle the women once we get back to the city?"

"She'd handle it a whole lot better if some asshat stopped rambling about past shit that should be long dead and buried."

"She's gonna find out, Stone. You can't stop that from happening. It's not like you've been a fucking saint or anything close to it."

"She's a music journalist, Gar. She knows how the industry works, and she's handling it fine so far."

He shoves his sunglasses on top of his head. "So, she's okay with you signing tits and asses? With you doing semi-naked photo shoots with supermodels? With you simulating sex with naked women in our videos? With girls throwing themselves at you even if she's on your arm? With how the media will twist innocent situations into betrayals?"

Even though he's telling it as it is, it pisses me off more than I can explain. "She trusts me, and I won't let her down," I say through gritted teeth.

He holds up his palms in a conciliatory gesture. "I'm just looking out for you, man. There will always be bitches looking to land you in trouble, always be paps looking to hang you out to dry. I'm just trying to forewarn you, so no need to get your panties in a bunch."

I flip him the bird just as Kayla and Zeta emerge from the pool, walking our way. With her curvy figure, long legs, sun-kissed skin, and sexy tats, she's like a walking dream. Water drips down her shoulders, trickling down the gap between her glorious tits, running over her perky nipples, and my cock is at full mast in my swim shorts.

"Fuck. Me," Gar exclaims, eyes superglued to her chest, and I slap the back of his head. "I couldn't hate you any more right now if I tried."

"I will knock you the fuck out," I growl. "I'm serious."

"Do we have a problem, boys?" Kayla asks with a smirk, perching her baby son on one hip while she fights a smile. She so knows what's going on.

"The only problem is this pussy here." Gar nudges me in the ribs. "He's worse than any girl on her period."

I flip him the bird again. "Fuck off and find your own girl to drool over." I open my arms for Zeta. "My girl's taken." She crawls into my lap, straddling my hips, and leans down to kiss me. I don't care that she's dripping water all over me. The way she's claiming me is turning me the fuck on, but I know we have an audience, and I'm not giving Gar a show. Reluctantly, I break our kiss, grabbing her waist. "Love you, baby," I say, nipping at her earlobe as I reposition her so she's hiding the monster erection in my pants. She squirms on my lap, the little tease, grinning as she lays back against me.

"Fuck. You two are so hot together," Kayla says, smiling in approval as she carefully places her son in his stroller, pulling up the cover to shield him from the sun.

"Don't encourage that shit, Kayla. I've the worst case of blue balls this side of the Atlantic, and a live porn show will not help," Gar grumbles.

"That's what we get for living like monks since we moved out here," Micah agrees, plonking himself down on the lounger the other side of Kayla. "I think it's time we did something about that." I'm guessing that means he's just broken up with his latest girlfriend. I'd been wondering why Bella hadn't come out to see him.

Gar reaches around, high-fiving him, and I roll my eyes when they both pointedly look at me.

"Just leave me and mine out of your plans, and you can do what the fuck you like."

Zeta and I take a shower together later that evening in preparation for our dinner plans with Gage and Kayla. Scott and Linda kindly offered to babysit for them so the four of us could go out. Micah and Gar declined, saying they have more exciting plans, and I didn't ask for details. I don't miss that lifestyle, and I have no regrets that I've turned my back on it.

I move Zeta's heavy, wet hair to one shoulder so I can suck on her neck, and I know I'm exactly where I want to be. Although, it's getting harder and harder to stay celibate when all I want is to thrust my cock inside her and rock her into blissful oblivion.

I need to talk to her, and soon. I'm scared shitless that telling her the truth is going to result in me losing her forever. But keeping it secret, and having her find out at some later stage, is a sure-fire guarantee of losing her, so I need to be brave, and I need to have faith in her and just get it over and done with.

Monday, I silently promise, as my soapy hands roam her tempting body.

I'll tell her everything I've been holding back on Monday.

ZETA

"Things seem to be moving fast with Ryder," Kayla says from across the table. Ryder has brought us to some top-end restaurant, sparing no expense for my friends. We're seated at a cozy table in the far back, by the window, with magnificent views of the shoreline.

"They are," I admit, taking a sip of my champagne, as I glance at the gorgeous charm bracelet on my wrist. Ryder gave it to me earlier, and I was all choked up as I examined each carefully chosen charm that represents our life together up to this point. "Do you think I should've made him work harder?" I ask.

She shakes her head. "What's the point in playing games? You're a grown woman, and you know your own heart and mind. You've spent long enough apart. Why prolong the agony? You love him. He loves you, and you both want to make it work."

"Just because we both want it doesn't mean it'll work out, and we all know love isn't always enough."

"You're not having second thoughts, are you?" she whispers, peeking over at the guys, but they're deep in conversation and paying us no attention.

"Definitely not, but I overheard something Gar was saying to Ryder earlier, and I'm worried about when we return to the city. Being out here is a bit like being in Narnia." I bite down on my lip. "I'm worried the fantasy won't last once we return to the real world."

"We both know what the industry is like, and we've seen girlfriends and wives eaten alive by fans and in the media, but you know what to expect, and you have thick skin. You'll get through it."

She casts a quick glance at Ryder. "He's crazy about you, Zeta. I've never seen this side of him before, and he's really happy. You both are. It's so easy to spot." She reaches across, squeezing my hand. "I'm thrilled for you, and I have every faith you guys will make it work."

We take a stroll by the promenade after dinner, hand in hand. Gage and Kayla are ahead of us, arms wrapped around one another as they walk. I lean over and peck Ryder on the lips. "Thanks so much for flying them out here. It was the best surprise."

He smiles, pulling me into his side and slinging his arm around my shoulders. "I knew you missed her, and I want you to be happy."

"I am happy. Deliriously happy." I grin at him like the lovesick fool I am.

"Nice dress, by the way," he adds, deliberately staring down the front of the red dress I bought when I was out shopping today.

I was completely taken aback, and a little uncomfortable, when he handed me a platinum credit card in my name and told me to spend whatever I wanted. "I'm glad you like it considering you paid for it," I half-joke.

He stops walking, spinning me to face him. "Babe, please don't let money come between us. You're my girl, and I want to take care of you. Is that so wrong?"

I chew on the inside of my mouth. "No, I guess not, but

I'm not used to it, and I don't want you to think I'm with you for your money." I shrug, my earlier conversation with Kayla coming back to me. "It'd probably seem more normal if I'd been in a relationship before."

He tucks me back into his side, and we hurry to keep up with our friends. "I'm glad neither of us have had other relationships. This way we get to navigate the choppy waters together." He winks, and it's hard to stay mad at him for long.

"And thanks for agreeing to watch Gage's band. You have no idea how excited he is," I add.

"No problem. I can't promise anything, but if the way he played this afternoon is any indication, it could end up working out great for both of us." He tweaks my nose. "Thanks for the suggestion. See, we're already a great team."

I've still got a lopsided, sappy grin on my face as Mike drives us back to the house a short while later.

"What the actual fuck?" Ryder snaps, glaring out the window at the line of cars parked along his driveway. Thumping music and garish lights hit us as Mike pulls the car around the front of the house. "I am going to fucking kill Gar and Micah."

"Oh no," Kayla says. "I hope Lennon hasn't woken up."

"You can take the side entrance to the guesthouse," Ryder says, not looking at either Kayla or Gage because he's distracted by the noise coming from inside the house. Three topless girls wander around the side of the property from the pool area, smoking cigarettes and swirling beer as they giggle, swaying on their feet.

I kiss Kayla and Gage on the cheek. "I'll talk to you in the morning." We wave them off, and then Ryder takes my hand, following Mike into the house.

Half-empty bottles and cans litter the hallway as we walk toward the main living area. Music is blaring throughout the house, and the sights and sounds accosting my ears are making me ill. Sweat coasts down my spine and in the gap between my breasts, and my head spins. I clutch onto Ryder's hand harder as we round the bend, almost barreling headfirst into a couple fucking against the wall.

"Get the fuck out of my house!" Ryder roars, grabbing the guy by the shoulders and yanking him off the girl. She starts mouthing off until she sees who ruined her fun and her facial expression changes so fast it's comical. She reaches for Ryder, but Mike intervenes, stepping in front of Ryder and blocking him from view.

"Get your clothes and leave," Mike tells them before shouting into his earpiece.

"Where the fuck are Danny and Marc?" Ryder demands, rounding on Mike. "You're supposed to be in charge of security, and those assholes should never have let this happen." While Mike is Ryder's personal bodyguard, Danny and Marc also came with us from New York, and they fill in where needed as well as taking turns patrolling the house and the grounds at night. I'm not sure why it's necessary because Ryder has a state-of-the-art security system installed with alarms, panic buttons, a panic room, and cameras all over the exterior of the property.

"Agreed, and I'll deal with it."

"I want them gone," Ryder snaps. "Radio for replacements asap."

Keeping hold of my hand, Ryder brings me through to the main living area, and it's almost like stepping back in time. A cloud of noxious smoke hovers on top of the room, and my nostrils twitch at the scent of marijuana in the air. The room is littered with people, most of them in various states of undress. Bodies are draped over all the available surfaces, indulging in a variety of sexual acts. Booze, cigarettes, and mirrors with lines of coke cover the tabletops.

"Ryder!" A skinny redhead with mammoth fake tits waves her hands in the air at my boyfriend. "We came in from the city to surprise you!" She acts as if it's completely normal to speak to him while she's currently grinding on top of Gar's cock. "You can take my ass again if you want." She makes an obscene gesture with her hand and her tongue, and bile swims up my throat.

After a beautiful romantic night out, the last thing I wanted is such a visual reminder of Ryder's old lifestyle and a flashback to my past. I send her a murderous look, wanting to bitch slap her so bad I could scream.

"Hey, Zeta." Gar waggles his brows at me, licking his lips as his gaze roams my body in my tight-fitting red minidress. His eyes are rolling back in his head, and he can't maintain eye focus. "You look fucking hot. Come sit on my face, baby, and I'll show you a good time."

My stomach churns sourly, and any warmth I was starting to feel toward him evaporates on the spot. He's a fucking tool and the last person I want around Ryder. Ryder's entire body exudes anger like it's visibly seeping out of his pores. I grip his hand tight, flattening myself to his back, keeping him with me.

Micah winks at me as he pounds into a buxom blonde he has bent over the arm of the couch. She's eating out a brunette who's being ass-fucked reverse cowgirl style by some guy with dreads and nipple piercings.

My eyes scan the room, taking in all the debauchery, and I'm transported back in time. The sounds, sights, and surroundings are replaced, and I'm back in that ramshackle house in Garden Grove, being forced to watch as my mother is fucked every which way from Sunday. Ryder lets go of my hand, and I'm vaguely conscious of shouting. Memories assault me, and I stumble on my heels, falling to the floor, scurrying backward until my spine hits the wall. I pull my knees into my chest, shaking all over as fear and disgust swirl around me.

I can smell him—my stepfather—breathing on me with his whiskey fumes, eyeing me up with dollar signs in his eyes, and I feel numerous eyes leering over me and men brushing past and copping a sneaky feel when Bob isn't watching.

"Don't touch me!" I mumble, wrapping my arms around my legs in a feeble attempt to ward off my shivers.

Shouting and screaming pierces my eardrums, and I close my eyes, covering my ears with my hands, trying to drown it out.

Glass shatters, and there's more yelling. Loud thuds startle me, and I'm sobbing, desperately trying to hold myself together, my arms squeezing my torso, my nails digging into skin. A sharp pain stabs me in the foot, but I barely feel it. I'm shivering all over, praying to God to get me out of here, as tears silently cascade down my face.

The commotion seems to last forever. Then someone is crouched over me, and I scream, cowering back. "Don't touch me! Don't touch me!" Someone brushes their hand across my cheek, and I swat their hands away, screaming and shaking. "Leave me alone! Don't touch me! Don't touch me."

"What's wrong with her?" I distantly hear someone ask.

"She's having a flashback, you selfish motherfuckers! This is all your fault! Didn't you listen to a word she told you about her past?!"

"Ryder?" I gulp, my senses slowly returning. "Ryder!" I scream, panic racing through my veins.

"Shush, baby. It's me. I'm here." Ryder's warm breath fans my face. "Can you open your eyes for me, baby?"

I force my eyes open, blinking profusely before my gaze focuses on his concerned face. "Ryder!" I sob, throwing myself into his arms in grateful relief. He scoops me up, cradling me gently against his chest. "It's okay, honey. I've got you. You're safe."

"Zeta, I'm really sorry, I—"

"Shut your fucking mouth, Micah. I don't want to hear it," Ryder snaps, interrupting him.

I glance over Ryder's shoulder and gasp at the state of the

living room. The people are gone, and the music is off, but the room is trashed. Furniture is strewn around the place, glass bottles are smashed and broken all over the beautiful hardwood floors, and cushions, throws, ornaments and picture frames are littered all over the space. "What happened?" I whisper.

"Your boyfriend went fucking psycho," Gar snarls, struggling to stay upright.

I scrutinize his face with little remorse. His left eye is swollen, blood gushes out of his nose, and he has a split lip.

"You're lucky I'm holding Zeta right now," Ryder grits out in a clipped voice, his tone menacing and low. "Or I'd finish what I started."

"Ryder, go take care of Zeta." Mike's authoritative voice booms from behind me. "I've sent Marc and Danny packing. Replacements are on the way. I've cleared the interior and exterior, and I've called a cleaning crew. They'll be here shortly. By morning, it'll be like the party never happened."

"Don't try to fucking pacify me, Mike." Ryder holds me tighter before addressing his bandmates. "I don't want to see either of your faces in the morning. How dare you treat my house like this. This is my sanctuary, and you know how I felt about having strangers here. Plus, you gave no consideration to Zeta's feelings, so get the fuck on a plane back to New York."

"Ryder, I know you're pissed, but the album—"

"Pissed!" Ryder roars, and I flinch. He runs his hand up and down my back. "Sorry, baby." He makes a deliberate effort to soften his voice. "Just get the fuck out of my face, Micah. I can't stand to look at either of you right now." With those parting words lingering in the air, he walks away.

Back in his bedroom, he helps me out of my clothes and then wipes the makeup off my face. My eyes lower to his bruised knuckles, and I dip my head, brushing my lips across his damaged skin. Stripping off his own clothes, he pulls me into the shower with him, holding me upright as the warm water cascades over my frozen limbs. Steam swirls around us, but I'm still so cold. When we get out, he wraps me in a fluffy towel and carries me back into the bedroom. I perch on the edge of the bed, mentally and physically exhausted, barely holding myself together as he dries my body, helping me into my silk nightie before blow-drying my hair. He holds a mug to my lips while I take sips of hot sweet tea, and then he holds me in his arms as I sob. I'm in too much pain to speak, but he doesn't ask anything of me; he just rocks me in his arms until I eventually drift off to sleep.

I go through the motions the next week, but I'm not really present. Kayla called my therapist before she left Sunday afternoon and lined up an appointment for me for Friday morning. Ryder is attentive and loving, and he doesn't push me to speak. It helps that he understands. That he's experienced flashbacks and nightmares, and he knows not to pry, that I'll talk when I'm ready.

It's Friday morning, and we're on the private jet, heading to New York, when I finally feel like I'm human again. Perhaps it's the physical distance that helps, and while I love Ryder's Hamptons house, right now I'm glad to be getting away from it for the weekend. I rest my head against Ryder's chest as the plane takes off. He twirls strands of my hair around his finger while pressing soft kisses to my temple. Tears prick my eyes as I think of all the ways he cared for me this week.

Lifting my head, I kiss him, slowly and passionately, letting my emotions flood through every sweep of my lips. "Thank you for taking care of me and for being so patient. I love you so much."

"It wasn't a chore. I was just worried about you." He cups my cheek. "Are you okay now?"

I nod. "I think so. It'll be good to talk to my therapist, but I'm okay." I peer into his beautiful eyes. They're more green than brown today but no less stunning. "I haven't had a flash-back like that in years, and it was scary. It felt so real. Like I was back there again." A shudder works its way through me. "The mind is a powerful, frightening organ."

"It is. And I've had vivid flashbacks like that too. I know how terrifying they can be."

Ryder drops me off at my therapist and leaves for his rendezvous with Micah and Gar. They've been licking their wounds in the city all week while Scott and Ryder worked on the album at the house. But they need to patch things up if they're to get the album completed by the deadline, so Ryder is meeting up with them to resolve their differences. I've appealed to him to forgive them, explaining I don't want him falling out with his bandmates over me. They were stupid, thoughtless jerks to have a party in Ryder's Hamptons home, but their actions weren't malicious or intentional. They were just bored, horny, and high—a lethal combination for any guy, especially rock stars who are used to acting on impulse without considering the consequences.

When Ryder returns to collect me, both Micah and Gar are with him, and they seem to have patched things up. They apologize to me profusely, and I tell them all is forgiven even if it's only partly true. I have zero to little time for Garrett Jones anymore. He's a rotten egg, and it wouldn't surprise me to hear the orgy had been his idea. But, bearing grudges is the last thing Ryder needs, so I'm letting this go, purely for his sake.

When we make an impromptu visit to Louise, she nearly keels over at the sight of the three, gorgeous, hot, young rock stars at her door, but she recovers fast, ushering them in and fawning over them without any shame. They brought her tons of Torment stuff as well as flowers and chocolates, and I love them for putting such a big smile on her face. The guys are good sports, letting her feel them up and posing for pictures although Garrett draws the line at posing naked for her. I'm glad he has some moral compass, albeit a very flakey one.

We only have thirty minutes to spend with her before we have to leave to attend a charity meeting. I give her a big hug, promising to call next week.

Micah and Gar go their separate ways when we head outside while I hop into the back of the SUV beside Ryder. Mike navigates the rush hour traffic like a pro, determined to get us to the charity's HQ in Manhattan on time. Ryder has had this meeting prearranged for months, and he didn't want to cancel, so he asked me to come with. I was happy to oblige, and I've been drilling him with questions for the last few minutes.

"Tell me about their work?" I ask, while we sit in traffic, wanting to have some background intel before we meet the director.

"They are the nation's leading victim assistance organization, and they've been in operation for over thirty years," he explains, lacing his fingers through mine. "They provide support for victims of crime and abuse, helping children, adults, families, and communities. They have a specialist child advocacy center, a bunch of different counseling centers, and a wide variety of community programs." He glances off into space. "They do wonderful work."

"I think it's great that you support them. That you give so much to charity." I know he donates to other charities too, but this one seems to have a special place in his heart.

He rubs the back of his neck. "I wish I could do more than just donate, but I want to keep my involvement on the down low. If I took more of a public role, the focus would switch to me, and I'd hate that. The work these guys do is what's most important and nothing should take away from that."

The director is waiting for us in the lobby, and she greets Ryder warmly, clasping his hands and kissing both his cheeks.

"This is my girlfriend, Zeta," Ryder says, introducing me, and a heady warmth floods my entire body at hearing those words leave his mouth.

"Lovely to meet you," she says, smiling and shaking my hand enthusiastically. "If you have time, I can give you a brief tour of the facilities after our meeting."

"That would be great. Ryder was telling me a bit about the work you do on the way over here, and I'd love to see it up close and personal."

I'm a silent bystander at the meeting, as Ryder, the director, and the charity's chief financial officer discuss plans and budgets for some forthcoming events Ryder is funding and helping to organize behind the scenes. Ryder kisses me firmly on the lips before leaving with the VP of marketing to sign some stuff while the director gives me a quick tour, explaining the work they do in more detail as we move through the facility. "We wouldn't be able to provide the services we do without the backing of sponsors like Ryder, but his hands-on involvement and dedication is more than most give. It's easy to see he cares. He's a very special young man."

"He is," I readily agree, a surge of pride racing through me. I have no doubt that Ryder's horrific childhood is driving his charitable actions, and I love him so much for trying to give back in a way that will protect other kids from leading the life he led. "And if you're looking for more volunteers, I would love to help out when I'm back in the city."

She smiles warmly at me. "We're always looking for volunteers, and that would be fantastic. If you're sure, we could complete the paperwork now and get the ball rolling."

"Lead the way," I say, returning her smile, happy to be in a position to help and to support Ryder with something that obviously means a lot to him.

32

ZETA

Butterflies are running riot in my tummy, and my legs are shaking so bad I'm wondering if they'll hold me up when we step out of the limo. "Breathe, babe," Ryder whispers in my ear, planting his hand on my thigh.

"Maybe I should just slip in the media entrance," I murmur, as nerves get the better of me.

"And miss the opportunity to show the world how fucking hot you look tonight?" Ryder shakes his head. "Honey, you are drop dead gorgeous, and I want you on my arm when we walk the red carpet. I want everyone to know you're mine."

I look him in the eyes. "Are you sure? What about your fans and—"

Capturing my lips in a pulse-pounding kiss I feel all the way to the tips of my toes, he instantly mutes my nervous babbling. It's easy to forget we're not alone when he kisses me like this because the outside world ceases to exist, and it's only him and I and the multitude of sensations he invokes in my body with his soft touch and his ardent kisses.

When he finally breaks our kiss, he strokes my cheek, staring into my eyes with so much love it almost undoes me. "Better?" I can only nod. "You've got this, babe, and I'm going to make sure you're looked after tonight so you have nothing to worry about. Just relax and enjoy it."

"Here," Gar hands me a glass of champagne as his eyes rake quickly over my body, making me uncomfortable. "Have a few more of these, sexy, and you'll be fine." I open my mouth to call him out on his shameless sleazing but think better of it and clamp my lips shut. I don't want to cause an argument among the guys tonight, so I keep my thoughts and my words to myself.

"You've got this," Micah says, smiling, trying to reassure me.

"Thanks. It's not like I haven't been at this event before, but it's not usually with a spotlight on me." And I know there's going to be a big-ass spotlight on me once I step out on Ryder's arm. He rarely takes dates to award shows or other big industry events, so this is a big deal and the press is going to be all over us like a rash.

"You'll knock 'em, dead, Zeta," Micah adds.

"Linda used to hate coming to these events at the start," Scott supplies, leaning back in the seat as he sips a beer. "But she got used to it. She was actually sad to be missing out on tonight, but she doesn't want to leave Mattie with her folks so soon after he's been ill."

"It would've been nice to have a wingwoman, but I completely understand, and she's right to prioritize your son."

The limo slows down as we approach Radio City Music Hall, joining a line of limos waiting to pull up in front of the venue. I knock back my champagne, taking a deep breath, giving myself a little pep talk. I need to get used to this as it's part of Ryder's life, and I don't want him worrying about me tonight. Torment is up for one of the top awards, and they're also performing midway through the show, and that's all Ryder should be focused on. He seemed a little distracted today, and I wonder if his nerves are at him or if any of them still get anxious before big events.

I quickly reapply a fresh layer of lip gloss, tossing my long hair over my shoulder and smoothing a hand down over my outfit. I feel confident and sexy, and it goes a long way toward settling my frayed nerves.

I'm wearing a fitted red leather jacket over a tight black leather and lace top with a tutu skirt and high-heeled ankle boots. My legs are tanned from weeks in the outdoors, so I didn't bother with pantyhose. Kayla helped me choose the outfit last weekend, and then she came over to Ryder's magnificent penthouse earlier today to help me get ready. I'm wearing heavy makeup with dark eyes, but I kept my lips neutral to balance the look. I wish Kayla was here tonight, but she couldn't get a babysitter, so she's only here with me in spirit.

"Ready, babe?" Ryder asks as the limo stops, and the door is opened from outside. They've set up a short red carpet just for this event, and I can see the entrance doors from this distance, so I tell myself it'll be a cakewalk. I flash him a confident smile, ignoring the jitters in my belly. "Let's do this."

"Love you." He presses a quick kiss to my lips. "I'm really happy you're here with me tonight."

Flashes explode in my face as Ryder helps me out of the car. I clutch onto his arm, smiling and focusing on planting one foot in front of the other rather than directing my attention to the myriad of reporters shouting questions at us. Fans line the short walkway, screaming and crying, some of them holding up Torment posters. Micah, Gar, and Scott stop to take some quick photos, but Ryder doesn't leave my side, just waving, smiling, and blowing kisses at some of his fans.

A couple of reporters know who I am, and they call me by name, hoping I'll stop and give them an exclusive, but I've already agreed that any talking done tonight will be done by Ryder. When we reach the main doors, the guys stop to talk to the reporter from *Entertainment Tonight*, and Ryder confirms my identity, including my status as his girlfriend. The questions leveled our way intensify, but we ignore them, making our way inside the auditorium and taking our seats in the second row.

Before we know it, the MC has taken to the stage, and the ceremony begins. Midway through, the guys leave to get ready for their set. Ryder leans down, kissing me firmly on the lips. "If you need a drink or you need to go to the bathroom, go with Mike or one of the bodyguards. Don't wander off by yourself."

I peck his lips. "I won't, I promise. I'll stick with Mike. Now go do your thing, Rock Star."

The guys appear onstage fifteen minutes later, and my eyes are riveted to Ryder for the whole song. This is the first time I've ever seen them live. I've always known Ryder was hugely talented, but he owns that stage like no other musician of our generation. His charisma and stage presence are off the charts, and it's no wonder the crowd is going crazy. He locks eyes on me frequently, singing some of the words directly to me, and when he points at me, thrusting his hips and gesturing wildly, I feel the concentrated, envious stares from every female in the place.

"What did you think?" he asks when the guys return to their seats after that knockout performance.

"That was incredible. *You* were incredible." I kiss him on the lips. "I'm so fucking proud of you."

His eyes are slightly unfocused as he leans in to return the kiss, and I instantly know he's taken something. Glancing down the row at the guys, I can see Micah and Gar are high too. But I don't say anything, because this is their night, and it's not like I haven't smoked weed or snorted a few lines of coke in the past myself, even if I do worry about Ryder doing shit like that when he's admitted to problems with addiction.

The guys win the award for Best Rock Video, and by the time we're back in the limo en route to the bar to see Gage's band playing, everyone's in party mode. I'm nicely relaxed thanks to a few glasses of champagne and several vodka shots and looking forward to seeing what the guys think of Kayla's man. Ryder drinks whiskey straight from a bottle, guzzling it like its water, before passing it to Gar who then passes it to Micah. Gar produces a tray with neat lines of coke spread across it, and I watch with growing discomfort as all three of them indulge. I decline when they offer me some, and Scott shakes his head, continuing to sip from his beer while watching me with a slight frown. Prickles of apprehension creep up my neck, but I ignore them. The guys are in celebratory mode, and it's nothing unusual. They deserve to let loose and enjoy their win.

There's a bit of excitement at the door to the club when we pull up, but Gage had notified security of Torment's impending arrival, and he'd also reserved a booth at the top of the room near the stage. The band has already started, and heavy beats reverberate around the space as we make our way through the dimly lit room.

Mike creates a path through the heaving crowd, and there are several screams and shouts when people realize they've got rock gods in their midst. Ryder maneuvers me in front of his body, as grabby hands reach out, trying to grab hold of him and the guys, but Mike and the team of three other bodyguards on duty tonight skillfully navigate our way to the booth without any trouble.

An ice bucket is already on the table, filled with a bottle of vodka, mixers, and bottles of beer. Ryder ushers me into the booth, sliding in beside me, wrapping a protective arm around my shoulder while Gar hands out beers.

We settle back, watching the show. Gage gives the guys a shout-out from the stage, and a huge roar echoes through the room. The guys shoot their hands up, waving at the fans, and then Savage Mania begins playing their most well-known song, and the crowd starts rocking out and singing along.

"They're good," Micah says across the table to Ryder, handing him another beer.

"Really fucking good," Gar agrees.

"I think we could be onto a winner here," Ryder agrees, draining half his beer in one go. "And it's all thanks to you," he whispers in my ear before crushing his lips to mine. He devours my mouth as his hand slips under my skirt, sliding up my thigh. His tongue plunders my mouth, and he's kissing me like he wants to gobble me up, holding one cheek firmly in his hand as he attacks my lips with a feverish passion that both excites and frightens me.

When his fingers brush over the crotch of my panties, I swat his hand away. "Behave." I murmur, tugging on his earlobe.

"I'm so fucking hot for you," he growls, yanking me onto his lap and grinding his hard-on into my ass. "I could just slide your panties aside and push up inside you, and no one would know," he says, toying with the tulle layers of my skirt. It's true it would act as an effective shield, but there's no way I'm fucking him for the first time in a booth in a public bar surrounded by the guys from his band.

"Or we could go fuck in the bathroom," I suggest, in compromise.

He repositions me so I'm straddling him, rocking his hips up into mine. "I'm trying to remember why I wanted to wait, and I can't think of any good reason right now," he purrs, sliding his hands under my skirt and squeezing my ass. The band has finished their set, and they're saying their goodbyes to the crowd. "I need inside you, baby," Ryder pants in my ear. "I'm so fucking horny."

Removing Ryder's hands from my ass, I pin him with a cautionary look. "I am not fucking you here in front of everyone, so get that idea out of your head."

He slides his hand around to my ass again, slipping his finger under my panties and pushing it inside me. "You're fucking soaking, baby."

I grab his wrist, pulling his hand out from under my skirt,

as Gage and the guys approach the table. "Ryder," I hiss. "Cut that shit out." He's starting to piss me off now. I try to wriggle out of his lap, but he clamps his hands on my waist, holding me in place.

"I know you want me, baby, so stop playing games."

He buries his head in my chest, and I'm horrified as realization dawns.

He's treating me like one of his groupies.

Like one of those girls who clearly don't give a shit if he manhandles them in public.

A red haze glazes over my eyes, as anger and humiliation wage war inside me. "Ryder, stop." I push at his head, but he continues to nuzzle into my chest, biting and snapping at my flesh through the lacy gaps in my top.

"You okay, Zeta?" a familiar voice asks, concern underscoring Gus's tone.

"She's fine," Ryder snaps, lifting his head from my chest and twisting around to see who asked.

"Hey, Ryder," Gage says, looking a little uncertain, his gaze bouncing between my boyfriend and me. "Good to see you again, man."

"You guys killed it," Ryder says, and air whooshes out of my mouth in grateful relief. I use the opportunity to try and slide off his lap, but he keeps a firm hold of my hips, keeping me in place.

"Ryder," I whisper. "Let me sit down."

"Relax, sweetheart." Ryder squeezes my ass over my skirt, grinning at the guys standing in front of our booth. "It's nothing these guys haven't seen before."

"Ryder, you're making Zeta uncomfortable," Scott intervenes. "Let the girl sit back down."

"Fuck off and mind your own business, White," Ryder barks, and I've reached my tipping point.

"Fucking let me go," I hiss, attempting again to slide off his lap, but the table is at my back, and there isn't much wriggle room, especially with how closely Ryder is holding onto my waist.

"Dude, you need to let her go," Gus says, pushing past his brother and facing Ryder with a thunderous look.

"Gus, don't," I warn, because I don't know how Ryder will react to some strange guy coming to my rescue. He's unpredictable right now and a million miles away from the Ryder I know and love. If this is how he's been living his life, then I'm glad I haven't been around to witness this, because it's breaking my heart.

"You!" Ryder points his finger at Gus, his eyes darkening. Finally sliding me off his lap, he jumps out of the booth, launching himself at Gus and shoving him in the chest. I watch in horror as Ryder brings his arm up, fist clenched, swinging around and aiming straight for Gus's face.

33

ZETA

Gus is a big guy, but Ryder has caught him off guard, so he doesn't react fast enough, and Ryder's left hook glances the side of his jawline, sending him staggering back. Camera flashes go off, and I clamp a hand over my mouth, horrified as Ryder takes another swing at Gus. "You fucking stay the hell away from my girl. I will knock you the fuck out if you touch her!" He swings for Gus again, but Gus has straightened up, and he swings back, punching Ryder square in the nose. Ryder staggers back, falling into Mike, with blood spurting from his nose.

I scamper out of the booth and plant myself in between Ryder and Gus. "Stop! This is getting out of hand."

"You're seriously with this guy?" Gus asks, scowling. "He's a disrespectful asshole, and you deserve better."

"Like you, I suppose," Ryder roars, wiping blood from the end of his nose.

"Too fucking right," Gus retorts, as Gage goes to his brother, pulling him back and whispering in his ear. "I don't fucking care, Gage. I want nothing to do with that fucking douche anyway."

"Can we just get out of here?" I plead with Mike, and he looks to Ryder.

Ryder pulls me to him, kissing me hard on the lips, and I want to knee him in the balls for having the audacity to try and "claim" me to prove some point to Gus. I rip my lips from his, shoving at his chest. "Don't fucking kiss me. Don't even fucking look at me. I'm so mad at you right now."

"Me!" he yells. "What the fuck did I do?"

"C'mon, man," Scott says. "Just leave it. This is gonna be all over social media within the hour."

"Like I give a fuck." Ryder slings his arm around my shoulder. "C'mon, baby. Let's go fuck in the limo."

Gus pushes past his brother, planting himself in front of me. "You don't have to leave with him, Zeta. I'll make sure you get home safely."

Ryder shoves me out of the way, punching Gus in the mouth before he's had time to protect himself. Gus completely loses his balance, making a grab for the table as he falls to the floor. The table wobbles, and the contents slide over the edge, landing on top of him. "Oh my God!" I crouch down over him as glass shatters everywhere. "Gus! Are you okay?"

"We've got this, Zeta," Gage says, lifting me up and over the broken debris. "I think it's best if you just get him out of here."

"I'm so sorry, Gage."

"You have nothing to be apologizing for. Go. I'll get Kayla to call you tomorrow."

Mike has to practically drag Ryder out of the place while Scott escorts me outside. I tuck my chin into my chest, avoiding the cell phones being held aloft as we leave.

I'm beyond livid when we get into the limo, so when Ryder turns and glares at me, I slide down the seat, as far away from him as I can get, sitting on my hands to stop myself from punching him. The car glides out into the traffic, and tension is thick in the air. Micah unscrews the cap on the whiskey, and

Gar lines up some more coke. I shoot daggers at them as Scott lets out a tired sigh.

"Oh my God, Gus! Are you okay?!" Ryder mimics my words and my tone of voice as he whips the bottle of whiskey out of Micah's hands, emptying the contents down his throat.

"Do not even start with me right now, Ryder," I fume, crossing my arms over my chest and glowering at him.

"Me!" Ryder shouts. "You're the one who was fawning all over that asshole."

"Excuse me?" I scream, uncaring we have an audience. "This all started because you were treating me like one of your whores!"

He sends me a scathing look, his eyes roaming my body. "Well, if the cap fits."

Tears stab my eyes, but I force them aside. I will not cry in front of him.

"Screw you, Ryder. You're a horrible drunk, or maybe it's all the drugs in your system fucking with your brain, but if this is what your lifestyle does to you, then I want no part of it."

He swigs out of the bottle, and an ugly sneer twists the corners of his mouth. "No problem, honey. There's a line of girls waiting to ride my cock, and they wouldn't give me this shit."

"Can you stop the car, please." I lock eyes with the driver through the mirror.

"Zeta, don't," Scott interjects. "If you don't want to come to the after-party, I'll stay in the limo with you and see you back safely."

"Let her fucking leave if she wants to," Ryder spews, waving his hands about, whiskey sloshing out of the bottle, over his pants, and down the front of the seat. "Hey, you!" he shouts, leaning forward and pointing at the driver. "Pull the fuck over."

"Ryder, I really don't think you want—"

"You can get the fuck out too, Scott, if you're gonna continue acting like a boring cunt," Ryder snaps.

"Fine by me, dude," Scott clips out.

The car glides to a halt at the sidewalk, and Scott opens the door quickly, not waiting for the driver to come around. He offers me his hand, and I let him help me outside.

"Don't wait up, sweetheart," Ryder calls out before cruelly adding, "I'll be too busy fucking my *whores* to even remember your name."

I slam the door shut with force and step back from the curb. I swallow hard as I watch the limo pull away, my emotions all screwed up. "That's not who he really is," Scott quietly says.

"Don't defend him. Please. I just don't want to hear it."

He slings his arm around my shoulders, squeezing me. "I don't know what demons haunt Ryder, but something must've happened tonight for him to regress. I've never seen him as happy as he's been with you these past few weeks."

"Well, if it did, he didn't tell me. We're supposed to be a couple. He should've talked to me instead of treating me like one of his groupies." I swipe at the hot tears rolling down my face. "I've never been so humiliated."

"He's going to hate himself tomorrow for this."

"It didn't look like he gave two shits," I say, pulling out my cell to call an Uber to come pick us up. Just then, a blacked-out SUV pulls up to the curb, and Mike slides out from behind the driver seat.

"What's happened now?" he asks in a resigned tone.

"Ryder's spiraling," Scott says. "And he was an even bigger asshole in the car. Do you have any idea what's going on?"

He shakes his head, and sighs. "I know I've no place saying this, Zeta, but those things he said and did back there are not the real Ryder. He's going to beat himself up over this when he comes down from his high." He tilts his head to one side. "You remember what I said to you before?" I nod. "I know it's not easy. I know it's asking a lot, but he needs you, he just doesn't realize it."

"Don't lay that guilt trip on Zeta, Mike. That's not fair."

"He's his own worst enemy, and when he realizes what he's done tonight, I fear he's going to go totally off the rails." Swiping his finger across his cell, he silently hands it to me.

I watch the TMZ video report with a pain in my heart. They've just added a feed of the guys arriving at the venue for the after-party. Ryder staggers out of the car, almost face-planting the ground. He's carrying the half-empty bottle of whiskey in his hand, letting loose a string of expletives at the waiting paparazzi. He doesn't even acknowledge his fans as he stumbles his way into the hotel. The reporter suggests Ryder's behavior indicates he's relapsed and questions my absence.

"He needs you," Mike quietly reconfirms.

Scott opens his mouth to interject again, but I hold onto his arm, stalling him. "No, it's okay." I shake my head, sighing. "I can't leave him like that. If anything happens to him, I'll never forgive myself."

I'm pissed and hurt and questioning everything I thought I knew about Ryder and our relationship, but I can't abandon him, not after seeing that. He's his own worst enemy right now, and if the tables were turned, I know he wouldn't leave me.

So that's how I find myself being escorted into the after-party, flanked by Scott and Mike, a half hour later. It's being held at a snazzy Manhattan hotel, and barricades have been set up outside the entrance, keeping the crowd at bay. Reporters are screaming my name and asking questions about Ryder, as we pass, but I ignore them. "It's gone viral about you two," Mike confirms, leading me down the hallway to the elevator. "You can expect more of that in your future."

We arrive at the ballroom, on the third floor, a few minutes later. The room has been constructed around a large circular dance floor. Two long bars reside on either end of the room, fitted into the wall, and massive chandeliers hang from numerous points on the ceiling. Plush velvet-backed booths are arranged in a circle around the dance floor with high tables and stools in a row behind them. The room is packed with partygoers eager to have a good time. The scent of booze, expensive perfume, and illegal substances is pungent in the air. Strobe lights cut across the crowd writhing to beats played by a renowned DJ as I scan the room, trying to locate Ryder.

Mike is a good head taller than me, and he spots Micah over by the side of the dance floor, so we head in that direction. As we approach, I see he's dancing with a well-known actress from one of those popular teen soaps. Although calling it dancing isn't strictly true. Simulating a live porn act would be more akin to describe how they're grinding and pawing at one another.

"Zeta, baby! You're here!" Gar shouts into my ear from behind, and then I'm lifted up and draped over his shoulder before I know what's going on.

"Gar, put me down, you ass!" I pummel my fists into his back, pleading with Mike and Scott to help.

"Oh fuck." Mike glances ahead, closing his eyes and sighing.

"Look who I found," Gar proclaims, plonking his butt down in a booth with me on his lap. His dick's hard as a rock, prodding into my stomach, and I puke a little in my mouth. Before I can get away from him, he grabs hold of my hips, angling me so I'm facing the table.

My stomach drops to my toes and bile floods my mouth as I stare at the girl currently occupying Ryder's lap. "Who the fuck are you?" I snap, shooting daggers at her.

"Everything you'll never be," she proclaims, wrapping her arm around Ryder's neck while sipping champagne from a bottle through a straw.

If Ryder wanted to go out and find my exact opposite, he's certainly achieved it. She's tiny with a nonexistent waist and perky little boobs. Her long white-blonde hair hangs in straight lines down her back, and she's dripping in expensive jewelry. Wearing a strapless cream and gold bejeweled dress, she's as far removed from me as you can get.

And, definitely, no groupie.

Ryder runs his fingers through her hair, and a heavy weight presses down on my chest, restricting my air supply, making breathing difficult. Pain lodges in my throat and stings the backs of my eyes.

"What the fuck is wrong with you two dipshits?" Scott barks at Gar. "How the fuck can either of you let that bitch anywhere near him!"

"Dude, chill. Ashley's cool now." Gar waves his hands about, his eyes rolling around his head. He shifts underneath me, jerking his hips up, his erection now prodding my ass.

"*You're* Ashley?" I blurt.

"I see my reputation proceeds me," she purrs.

"Yeah, I'll bet your mom's proud." I narrow my eyes at her, trying to ignore the fact Ryder is now running his hands up and down her arms.

"Jealousy is very unbecoming, and so common," she says, leaning back against Ryder's chest. She twists her arm around, running her fingers through his hair, and I want to gouge out her eyeballs with my nails and pull every strand of silky hair from her head.

When she starts peppering little kisses along his jawline, and he doesn't stop her, something dies inside me. A sharp pain spears me in the heart, and I feel it rupturing, splitting apart, still too fragile from the last time Ryder annihilated it.

I can't bear witness to this. I can't sit here and watch him ruin everything we've ever shared. I climb out of Gar's lap, grabbing onto Mike's arm to steady myself as I scramble out of the booth. "This was a mistake," I tell him, fighting tears. "I can't do this. I'm done."

I don't look back as I walk away, smothering tears the

entire time. A lump the size of a baseball is jammed in my throat, corking my sobs, but I know it's only temporary. The pain pressing down on my chest is excruciating, and I just want to get home and forget I ever laid eyes on Ryder Stone.

A familiar face steps into my path, his brow furrowing as he notices my distress. "What's wrong?" Brody asks, closely examining my face. I haven't seen him in forever as I haven't stepped foot inside *RockOut*'s offices since the day Ryder announced he'd bought it.

"I'm an idiot. That's what's wrong," I fume, so furious with myself for falling back into Ryder's arms so easily.

"Hey, don't cry." Brody slides his arm around my shoulder, and I lean into him for strength.

"I'm not crying over that jerk," I say, more for my benefit. "I've done enough of that in the past and he's not worth another single tear." I push forward, and Brody keeps pace with me, still holding onto me.

"Zeta, wait." Mike comes up alongside me, casting a wary glance in Brody's direction. I don't bother introducing him to my colleague. "Let me drive you back to the penthouse."

Yeah, as if I'm ever stepping foot in that place again. I open my mouth to protest but think better of it. There's no way Mike's going to drive me back to my place or let me leave here alone or with Brody. Whatever instructions Ryder's given him before tonight clearly prevent him from abandoning me. I quickly concoct a plan of escape. "Okay, thank you."

"Zeta, I—"

I despise the look of pity on his face, so I cut him off. "Please don't say it. I just don't want to hear it."

He nods, his features sad as he walks me outside the room. I say goodbye to Brody in the hallway, assuring him I'm fine with Mike. He kisses me on the cheek, eyeing Mike suspiciously before reluctantly walking away. Mike says nothing as we enter the elevator and descend to the ground level.

I've been in this hotel one other time for a press conference, and I remember the downstairs bathroom backs onto the parking garage, so when I tell him I need to use the restroom before we leave, I've already made up my mind what I'm going to do.

I wait in the bathroom until everyone's gone, and then I lock the door, running to the window and sliding it open. It's a bit of a tight squeeze, but I manage to wriggle my way through. Out in the parking garage, I walk with purpose, as fast as I can in my high-heeled boots, wanting to put as much distance between me and the carnage back there.

I can't believe I was so naïve.

So foolish.

I knew once we withdrew from our little Hamptons bubble that things would be challenging, but I had no idea how fast things would turn to shit or how quickly Ryder would revert to form.

I was stupid to have trusted him so blindly. To have given in so easily.

He's not the same boy I remember because that boy would never have taken a machete to my heart the way that man just did.

I don't belong in this world, and I guess it's better I found out now before I invested even more of my time and my future. It's such a mess, and I'm going to be a laughingstock once the media discovers Ryder's already dumped me for the girl who betrayed him. I'll have to quit the magazine and find a new job. Probably find a rock somewhere to hide under until all the media furor has died down. Maybe I'll go stay with Jill and Liam for a while. I haven't seen them in ages, and a visit is long overdue. And, if anyone understands how easily I shatter when let down by that man, it's my aunt.

I'm distracted, running through options in my head, so I'm not paying attention to my surroundings.

I'm nearing the front of the parking garage when a man in a tailored black suit steps out of the shadows directly in front of me. His face is completely covered with one of those creepy white masks, and it scares the fuck out of me. Startled, I scream on instinct, and he covers my mouth, grabbing me in a chokehold and dragging me over to the wall.

Blood thrums in my ears, and adrenaline courses through my veins as my heart starts pounding wildly in my chest. Although I'm terrified, I raise my leg and stretch my hand back, ready to implement years of self-defense lessons when something cold and sharp presses against my throat.

"I wouldn't do that if I were you." His voice is gruff and deep, his breath foul smelling as he presses his mouth to my ear. "I'd hate for Ryder to find you with that pretty neck slashed wide open and bleeding out all over the ground."

A sting pricks my neck as he presses the knife farther into my flesh. A chill tiptoes up my spine, and raw fear takes hold of me. "What do you want?" I ask, hating how my voice trembles and my knees almost go out from under me, but I'm unable to stop my body's natural reaction to the situation.

"What do I want?" Keeping the knife pressed against my throat, he moves his other hand up along the curve of my hip and higher. "That's an interesting question." His hand continues to wander upward until he cups my right breast. I squeeze my eyes shut, praying that Mike has figured out I've run and that he finds me before it's too late. "Ryder sure has good taste in women," he rasps, sliding the knife lower, making a clean cut straight through the front of my top. Strips of material float to the ground, leaving me standing in my leather jacket and strapless bra. He moves the knife back up to my throat as his other hand slips into my bra and over my bare skin. Tears sneak out of my eyes as I think about how I avoided this for years growing up, despite daily threats of sexual assault, and it was all for nothing, because this guy is going to either rape me or kill me or maybe do both. His fingers tweak my nipple, and a sob rips from my mouth.

He laughs, and it's the most menacing laugh I've ever born

witness to. If this was a movie, you couldn't make it any more cliché. A course of shivers ripples through my body, and my throat seizes up, my lungs stop working, and I'm struggling to breathe, as an intense anxiety attack grips hold of me.

"I'm almost tempted to take you with me," he says, slowly removing his hand from my breast. "But letting you live, for now, serves a greater purpose." His hand glides down over my ass, and he tugs at my skirt, ripping through the layers of tulle to palm the bare cheeks of my ass before grabbing hold of my crotch from behind. He digs his fingers in, rubbing his hard-on against my ass, and I almost puke. Tears roll silently down my cheeks, and I want to die. In this moment, I seriously consider asking him to dig the knife into my flesh and end it all.

He continues to rub against me, pawing at my pussy, and tears streak down my face.

"Tell Ryder the next time he ignores me, you won't be so lucky."

I gasp as a sharp, pulling pain wrenches across my neck. Grabbing hold of my throat, he lifts me up off the ground with my legs dangling in the air. He squeezes hard, and black dots distort my vision. When he lets go of me, I plummet to the ground, my vision blurring as I crash onto the asphalt, a jolt of pain rattling through my skull and zipping up my spine.

I lie on my side, groaning as my hands automatically fly to my neck. Warm liquid coats my fingers, and I tremble, more terrified than I've ever been in my life. Pulling one hand away, I inspect my bloody fingers in shock.

He cut me! The bastard cut me!

That's the last conscious thought I have, and with the sound of his retreating footsteps echoing in the background, I escape into darkness.

34

RYDER

"Get the fuck away from me." I glare at Ashley, grabbing her hand before she reaches my cock. She laughs, throwing her hair over her shoulder, slapping me in the face with it. "I said get off me," I grit out, losing patience fast.

"What the hell's your problem?" She twists around on my lap, and I get up, letting her slide to the ground before she can make any more moves on me.

"You're my fucking problem," I snarl, ignoring the way my head spins as I try to focus on her face. How the hell I ever thought she was pretty is a mystery. She looks like bad judgment and regret, and I've just swallowed a second helping.

My head jerks up in the direction of where Zeta went fleeing, and a horrible pain slices through me as the image of her devastated face flits before my mind's eye. And then some douche appeared out of nowhere to comfort her, and I saw red all over again. I was two seconds away from charging up there when Mike took control of the situation. I know I can trust him to keep her safe, but it should be me.

I should be the one by her side, and the reason I'm not is all on me.

The damage is already done, and I have no one to blame but myself.

What the fuck have I done? I cradle my head in my hands, closing and then rapidly opening my eyes, when the world starts shifting. My veins are buzzing, blood thrumming in my ears, and my limbs are jittery, restless. My mind is whirling in a million different directions, and I can't stabilize it fast enough to form a coherent thought. I start pacing, grabbing handfuls of my hair, craving an outlet for the wired-up mess twisting my insides into knots.

"Ryder, baby." Ashley's hands slide around my waist, and I shove her off instantly.

Turning around, I pin her with my most venomous look. "Do not touch me. Do not talk to me. And, most certainly, do not call me baby."

"But … what was that? I thought—"

"You were a means to an end. One I already regret, so fuck off and manipulate some other sad fucker." I can't believe I just pulled that shit with Zeta. Or that I used Ashley to do it.

I deserve to lose her, because that was the shittiest of shitty moves. But the rage burning through my limbs at the thought of that asshole with his hands on my girl, mixed with the poison swirling through my veins, forced all logical thought out of my brain.

I was hurting. And I wanted to hurt her too.

Well, mission accomplished, jackass.

In a fast move, Ashley grabs a drink off the table, flinging the contents at me. Sticky, amber-colored liquid drips down my face and over my chest. Security for the event approaches our table in a flash. "Mr. Stone. Is there a problem here?"

"Yes," I say, yanking my T-shirt up, using it to wipe the wetness off my face. "Can you get rid of the trash." I jab my finger at Ashley.

"Come with me, miss." He gestures for her to walk ahead

of him, and the serious look on his face shows he means business. "We can do this the easy way or the hard way," he adds, when she doesn't budge.

"Fuck you, Ryder." She shoves me. "And fuck you too!" She lunges for the poor man only doing his job, but he sidesteps her, pulling her hands behind her back and forcing her to move forward. She screams bloody murder, drawing attention, and it takes three security personnel to drag her from the room.

"I hope you're happy now, you stupid prick," Scott says, glaring at me. "I can't believe you just did that. With Ashley of all people. I've known you to act foolishly before but never to be so petty and juvenile."

"Fuck off. We can't all be choir boys like you." How dare he sit there looking all sanctimonious.

"You've royally screwed things up." He shakes his head. "I really don't get you. It's like you have this self-destruct button you can't resist pressing. She's the best thing to ever happen to you, and you just fucked it all up. You'll be lucky if she ever speaks to you again, let alone finishes the biography."

"Who gives a shit about the biography, and I don't need a lecture, *Dad*." The word tastes bitter on my tongue. Maybe if I'd had a dad, or a worthy male figure in my life, I wouldn't be such a screwup.

A waitress appears with a tray laden down with drinks. Scott hands her a wad of cash and sends her on her way. "Drink this, you stupid fucker." He thrusts a bottle of water into my chest. I'm about to pour the contents over his smug face when he adds, "I'm trying to help you here. You need to stop snorting that shit up your nose, sober up, and then go and find your girl before it's too late."

Panic and fear sticks in my throat, and all my fighting instincts fade, as I realize the enormity of what I've just done.

I might have just lost Zeta for good.

Dropping into the seat beside Scott, I knock back three

bottles of water without uttering a word. Gar is passed out on the seat across from us, and Micah has disappeared with that actress. I'm sipping coffee, deliberating how to fix this mess, when Scott decides to impart his next words of wisdom. "Did you do that deliberately to ruin things because you think you don't deserve to be happy?"

I shrug. Truth is, I don't really know. Since I got *his* text earlier today, I've been on a downer. That dose of reality crashed into me, forcing me to question everything I've been promising Zeta, making me realize how selfish I've been. I've risked her life, and I haven't even had the guts to fess up to her yet.

What kind of a bastard does that to the woman he loves?

Did I set out to deliberately hurt her? To say unintentional cruel things to her? To let that fucking bitch crawl all over me because I knew that would be the last straw for Zeta?

No.

I didn't set out to do that.

But I was on edge all evening, and when Gar offered me the solution just before we went on stage, I didn't stop to hesitate.

And that's exactly where I went wrong.

"Boss." Mike materializes in front of me as if from thin air. His face is a little flushed as he leans in, planting his hands on the table. "We have a bit of a problem."

"What kind of a problem?" Goose bumps sprout on my arms as a horrible sense of foreboding creeps over me.

"I've lost Zeta."

I jump up. "What do you mean you've lost her? I told you to stay with her no matter what. That includes me being a fucking asshole. She comes first. Always."

"I know, and I was with her, but I think she ditched me. Or, at least, I hope she did." Frown lines crease his brow.

"You're not making any sense, and my patience is in

limited supply." I rub my aching head. At least the world isn't spinning anymore.

"She locked herself into the bathroom on the ground level. I have Denver waiting downstairs for hotel security to arrive to unlock it."

"Oh fuck." I start running as horrific thoughts begin floating through my mind. If she's done anything to hurt herself because of me, I'll never forgive myself. Never.

I push past people, ignoring their cussing and shouting, slamming into the doors, and out into the hallway. I run five miles most days, and I'm quick on my feet, even in my current fucked-up state, so Mike and Scott don't catch up to me until I'm at the elevator. The door pings open as they arrive, and we pile in. "This is all my fault."

"Yeah, fucktard. It is." Mike doesn't mince his words.

"You don't think she'd do anything to hurt herself, do you?"

"I don't know, boss. She was very upset. Trying not to show it, but I could tell."

I press my forehead to the wall. "I've messed everything up."

Neither of them dignifies that with a response because we all know it's the truth.

Denver, one of the new bodyguards, is waiting for us when we emerge on ground level. "I tried your cell, but the call kept dropping," he explains to Mike. "She's not in the bathroom, sir. It seems she climbed out the window which leads to the parking garage."

The fact she wasn't planning to hurt herself is of little comfort now. Because she's out there somewhere. Alone. And that asshole could know it. I grab hold of Denver's shoulders. "Which way to the garage?"

"Follow me."

We race along the hallway behind Denver, pushing through double doors into the rear lobby, and out through another set of doors which brings us into the garage. I run to my left, following the exit signs, presuming she went this way. When I round the next bend, I almost trip over my own feet as I hear someone screaming for help. All the tiny hairs lift on my arms as I push my limbs harder, running in the direction of the voice.

Fear pummels my body, and I try to force myself to calm down, but my heart is racing crazy fast, and the pressure in my chest is intense. When I round the next bend and find a stranger crouched over Zeta's prone body, I almost lose the contents of my stomach.

She's lying against the wall, on her side, with her hands clutched around her neck. Blood trickles between her fingers, and black mascara streaks have dried on her cheeks.

"I've called an ambulance," the strange woman says, trying to disguise the little gasp of recognition she emitted when I sank to my knees beside her.

I don't even acknowledge her, focusing on Zeta. "Zeta, honey, it's me." I press my lips to her forehead, almost collapsing in relief at the feel of her warm skin against mine.

"Jesus Christ." Scott crouches down beside me, alarm etched across his face. Mike is already on his cell, calling for assistance. "Who did this?" Scott asks the woman.

"I didn't see. I was driving past when I spotted her lying unconscious on the ground. I pulled over and called nine-one-one."

"Thank you," Scott says.

Zeta stirs, and a strangled moan slips out of her mouth.

"Baby," I choke. "Can you hear me?"

"Ryder?" Slowly she blinks her eyes open, and it's the most beautiful view.

The woman and Scott stand, moving over to talk to Mike.

"I'm so sorry, baby," I whisper. "I left you unprotected."

Tears well in her eyes, and she shivers all over. I only then notice her state of undress. All the blood drains from my body, and my stomach lurches violently. Removing my jacket with trembling hands, I cover her up. "What happened?" I whisper.

"He … he …" She bursts out crying, and I'm imagining all kinds of horrors.

I carefully pry one hand off her neck so I can inspect the damage. "Let me look." I tear off the bottom of my shirt, gently cleaning the exposed area of her neck so I can assess the depth of the cut. It's only a surface wound, the blood making it appear so much worse, but it does little to comfort me.

She's not saying anything, just looking straight ahead, tears rolling down her face, as if she doesn't even see me. Wresting her other hand off her neck, I place her trembling hands at her side, kissing her cheek. "It's okay, baby. I'm here now, and I'm gonna take care of you."

Like I should've been doing. Instead of acting like a giant bag of dicks. But I push my guilt and remorse aside to revisit later. Because right now, Zeta needs me. There's nothing more sobering than finding the girl you love bleeding and broken. Especially knowing it's all your fault.

I clean the other side of her neck, staring at the small, thin line sliced across her throat, with barely restrained rage. I want to believe this is a random attack, but I just know it isn't.

I rip another strip off my shirt, wadding it up and pressing it to the wound, as Zeta stares blankly off into space. I quickly scan every inch of her, looking for signs of other visible injuries, but I don't see any.

At least not on the outside.

Nausea swims up my throat at the thought of him touching her in places I can't see.

Mike crouches down on the other side of me. "Is she okay?" he quietly adds, his voice laced with guilt.

"The cut isn't deep." My voice is raw, my throat clogged with heavy emotion.

"I've called the cops and the hotel has a medical team en route. They're also cordoning off the garage, and they'll ensure no one gets through."

I nod, but I don't take my eyes off her. She's still staring straight ahead, saying nothing, and it's really scaring me. I sit down beside her, carefully taking her into my arms, grateful she doesn't resist. She's shivering, and I hold her tighter as turmoil twists and turns in my gut. I press a kiss to the top of her head, almost crying in relief when she leans her head on my shoulder, turning into my body for comfort.

I glance at Mike, gesturing with my eyes, and he nods, walking off to give us some privacy. "I'm sorry," I choke. "I'm so sorry, baby." Tears flow freely down my face as she fists a hand in my shirt, clinging onto me.

"I thought he was going to rape me or kill me," she whispers, and I openly sob.

There are so many things I want to say to her, but this isn't the time. Now, she needs me to support her and take care of her, not listen to my pitiful apologies. So, I force my tears back inside, strengthen my resolve, and wrap my other arm around her front, keeping her real close. "You're safe now, baby. No one is going to hurt you."

I don't get to ask her anything else because the medical team arrives then, and I step aside to let them do their work. I watch as they perform a variety of physical checks, clean the wound on her neck, and apply paper stitches before bandaging it.

When the cops arrive, I walk with my arm around Zeta to an office at the back of the hotel reception area. I keep Mike with us as the two detectives start asking her a bunch of questions. When they ask if she knew the man who attacked her or if he said anything which might reveal his identity, she glances briefly at me before shaking her head.

Everything goes on lockdown mode inside me, and I wipe my sweaty palms along the front of my jeans. That one look has confirmed my suspicions, but I'm trying not to let my mind go there, because I don't want to fucking lose it in front of the cops.

When they pull up the camera feed from the garage and play back the scene, I work hard to contain my emotions. You can't see his face, because it's hidden behind a mask, but I'd know him anywhere. I start shaking, and I probably shouldn't watch, but I can't force my eyes away from the screen. When he shreds her top and shoves his hand into the front of her bra, I projectile vomit all over the floor.

I can't stop shaking even as Mike helps me up, forcing me out of the room and into the adjoining bathroom. I rip my shirt off, twist the faucets on full, and splash cold water over my face and chest, but nothing quells the swirling tornado building inside me.

"Fuck!" I lash out at the wall, kicking it over and over. Then I slam my fist into the mirror, repeatedly, barely feeling the pain as little shards of glass embed in my skin. Mike tries to pull me back, and I swing at him, landing a glancing blow to his jaw. He grabs me into a headlock and ducks my head into the sink, directly under the flow of water, keeping me down until my inner fight has receded.

Yanking me up by my hair, he puts his face all up in mine. "Get yourself together. That girl needs you to be strong."

"He hurt her, and it's my fault!"

"You think I don't fucking hate myself too? But bitching about it now isn't going to change anything, so get your shit together and get back in there and support her." He pushes me away, leaving the room for a couple minutes while I clean my hands and put a leash on my emotions. When he returns, he wraps my hands in bandages and hands me a clean T-shirt with the hotel logo imprinted on it.

Zeta has finished making her statement when we return. The detectives eye me circumspectly before handing me their business card, telling me to get Zeta to call if she remembers anything else.

By the time we're in the SUV on the way back to the penthouse, I've somewhat gotten control of myself. The only way I can do it is to not think about *him*. To cradle my girl in my arms, holding her tight and whispering how much I love her.

We arrive back at my place a little after three a.m. Mike half-carries a semi-conscious Gar into one of the guest bedrooms. Scott kisses Zeta on the cheek before going to bed. Holding Zeta's hand, I take her into the kitchen, helping her up onto a stool. I want to make her a hot drink, and I'm not letting her out of my sight. From now on, she's going to be attached to my hip, and me to hers.

"Who is he, Ryder?" Zeta asks in a much too calm voice.

My spine stiffens, and I place both mugs down, turning to face her. My voice is shaky as I speak. "What did he say?"

"That the next time you ignore him I won't be so lucky."

Everything I've worked hard to contain detonates inside me, and I lose it as frustration and rage consume me. Swiping my hand across the kitchen counter, I knock all the contents to the floor with a loud crash. China smashes. A couple glasses break. Canisters roll, spilling their contents across the floor. The physical aggression sweeping through my veins can't be contained. I race into the living room, tearing through the space, upending furniture, ripping paintings off their hooks, throwing glassware and ornaments at the wall and the wooden floors, watching them shatter and spray shards of glass across the room.

I'm vaguely conscious of Mike trying to pull me back. Of the other bodyguards entering the room. Of Scott shouting at me to stop. Of Zeta's tear-stained shocked face as she watches me self-destruct.

I pick up everything that isn't nailed down, destroying it with my fists or my feet. I even yank the TV off the wall, slamming it to the floor, enjoying the sound as it breaks into a hundred pieces.

Voices argue around me, and then her scent accosts my senses, swirling around me as her arms go around my neck. I try to push her away, but she holds on, pulling me into her body. "Breathe, baby. Just breathe." Her soft voice penetrates soul deep, and I feel some of the anger slipping from my veins. I fall into her, exhaustion overwhelming me, and she wraps her arms around me, holding me up.

My arms snake around her, and I close my eyes, absorbing her scent and the feel of her against me, using it to bat the last vestiges of my rage away. "I let you down, when I promised I'd always protect you. I'm so sorry," I sob, and then the dam breaks, and I'm crying. Huge, wracking sobs that rip from my very core. I cling to her, soaking her neck with my tears, crying and pleading with her for forgiveness. She's crying too and clinging to me just as hard, and I wish I could rewind this night and get a do-over.

I don't even remember going to bed, but the last thing I'm aware of is her curling into my chest and my arms automatically going around her as my eyes shutter.

35

ZETA

Beams of golden sunlight trickle through the blinds in Ryder's bedroom as I sit in a chair watching him toss and turn in the bed. I tried to get some sleep, but it was futile. I couldn't switch my brain off, so I got up, made some chamomile tea and toast, and then returned to his bedroom, taking this chair and trying to make sense of the mess in my head.

Kayla called a couple hours ago, and I went up to the rooftop terrace to fill her in. She wanted to come straight over, but I told her to stay at home with her baby. I'm not good company right now, and while I know she wants to provide moral support, I need to speak with Ryder, and that's something I need to do alone.

I cast a glance at the bed with a heavy heart. He looks so vulnerable and innocent when he sleeps, and my heart aches for him. For me. For us. Even though I'm still pissed, I can't help hurting for him. His pain is palpable. That scary demonstration of rage last night confirms it.

I think I must be in shock or denial because whenever I think about that man from the hotel, I feel a kind of strange numbed acceptance. Whatever is going on, I just know it's something Ryder is dealing with by himself. It's why I didn't tell the cops what that man said or mention anything while the others were around. I know, deep down, I've got new scars and that I'll carry the attack with me for some time. But, in this moment, the only thoughts I'm focusing on, the ones occupying center stage in my brain, are trying to figure out who he is, how he knows Ryder, and what hold he has over my boyfriend.

If that's what Ryder still is. Because the other events of last night haven't been forgotten. I should be more upset over almost being raped or killed, but my brain is seriously fucked, because I'm way more upset over Ryder's actions. The image of that bitch touching and kissing him is seared into my brain, poking little daggers into my heart every time I think of it.

Ryder stirs, crying out a little, and I wonder if I should wake him. I need answers, and he's going to give them to me today whether he likes it or not. I lean my head back, closing my tired eyes, feeling emotionally and physically exhausted.

"Zeta." I slowly bring my head up, opening my eyes, watching Ryder scoot up in the bed, yawning and rubbing his eyes. "How long have you been awake?"

"I never went to sleep," I admit, tucking my knees into my chest under the blanket.

"How are you feeling?" He scrubs a hand over his stubbly jawline, pinning me with sad, remorseful eyes. "Are you okay?"

Air oozes out of my mouth in noisy spurts as I contemplate how to answer his question. My throat is dry when I finally speak. "Numb. Upset. Confused. Sad." I shrug, because that only scratches the surface. "How are you feeling?"

"I'm fine." He attempts to bat my concern away.

"Don't pretend you're fine. That outburst of aggression last night is not the actions of someone who is fine. I've never seen you lose it like that."

"I'm sorry if I scared you." He looks instantly remorseful.

"I was only scared because I'm worried about you. What caused you to react like that? And don't say it's because I was randomly attacked, when we both know it's way more than that."

He nods slowly, pain embedded into his features. "I know I have some explaining to do, and I am going to tell you everything, but first, I owe you an apology." He crawls across the bed, coming to kneel on the ground before me. His hair is sticking up adorably, and he's naked except for his boxers, but I'm too drained to do more than acknowledge that fact. He takes my hands in his, and I let him. Tears glisten in his eyes as he stares up at me. "As long as I live, I will never forgive myself for treating you like that last night. I'm so ashamed."

"You humiliated me." Tears well in my eyes, spilling down over my cheeks. "And it hurt so much."

"I messed up. Got shitfaced and lost sight of reality. Even as I was saying that shit, as I was pushing you away, I was screaming inside." He rubs circles on the back of my hand. "But there are no excuses that make it in any way acceptable, and there's nothing I can do to take it back. All I can do is promise it won't happen again and show you how serious I am through my words and my actions. I'm not even asking you to forgive me, because I don't deserve it. But I am asking that you don't give up. I know I don't deserve another chance, but please give me one. Please don't leave because I love you, and I need you, and I want to prove I can take better care of you than I did last night."

"What about her?" I spit out. "How could you let her sit there and touch you and say those things to me?" My voice breaks and a trapped sob breaks free. "Did you fuck her?"

"No! I was doing it to make you jealous, but I got rid of her the minute you left."

"Well, I guess that makes it okay then," I sneer, sarcasm lacing my tone.

He looks completely ashamed, and I'm glad to see it. "It was immature and cruel and completely stupid. I'm so sorry, baby." His eyes plead with me. "I hate myself for using her to upset you like that. I'm a shitty boyfriend, but I swear to you I'll do better. I'll do whatever you want me to do to show you that that asshole you met last night is not who I really am. I know I need to do better to demonstrate I'm worthy of you, and I promise I'll do whatever it takes to prove it to you. Last night will never happen again."

I swallow over the burning lump in my throat. "I put my trust in you, and you let me down. That's not something I can get over just because you promise it won't happen again. You have a habit of promising me things and then letting me down."

"That's completely fair, and I can't defend myself. I know I have no right to ask you to give me another chance, but you already know I'm a selfish prick, so this shouldn't come as a surprise."

I could tell him it *is* a surprise because his behavior last night seemed to confirm his love of partying took precedence over me. And while it's nice to hear him say these things, they're only words. Words are meaningless if they're not true. If you can't back them up with your actions. But I don't articulate these thoughts because there's a bigger picture here, one I need to understand, so any discussions about our relationship will have to take a back seat. For now.

"Who was that man, Ryder, and what is your involvement with him?"

Removing his hands from mine, he sits up on the edge of the bed and buries his head in his hands. I wait him out. Watching his chest heave and his body tense up, I still love every part of him with every part of me even though he crushed me last night.

When he lifts his head up and stares me straight in the face, he looks like a scared little boy. More vulnerable than I've ever seen him. The urge to comfort him is riding me hard, but I don't move a muscle, because I need him to be honest with me.

"I was always planning on telling you this. I'd plucked up the courage to admit it on Monday, but you were still upset over the party, so I put it off." He shakes his head. "I should've told you at the start, but I was scared, because there's a very real risk you'll want nothing more to do with me after you know."

"Just spit it out, Ryder. Tell me everything. Hold nothing back."

He nods slowly. "I lied to you." His Adam's apple bobs in his throat, and my stomach contorts sourly. "I've been lying to everyone pretty much my entire life." He rubs a hand across the back of his neck, breathing deeply. "When I told you the reason why I was in juvie, I didn't tell you the full truth." He looks me directly in the eyes, and I see so many conflicting emotions there. "Do you ever remember hearing about Cory Barnes?"

The name rings a bell, but I frown as I search my memory for more intel. "Vaguely, but I can't recall any of the details."

"I was ten, so you would've only been nine when the story broke." He clamps a hand down on his thigh to halt the jerking of his leg. He never loses eye contact as he starts telling me how it all went down. "Everything I told you about my mom was true, and how I roamed the streets rather than go home to that fucked-up shit. I mentioned I started hanging around with the wrong crowd, but I didn't elaborate for a reason. Gangs were rampant in our neighborhood growing up, and everyone wanted to be in the Z-Crew, but they were close-knit, and they rarely let anyone in. To this day, I don't know why Ren approached me in the first place. He was their self-appointed leader, and most of the boys in the hood were scared shitless of him. I never was. I was tall for my age, handy with my fists, and I had a reckless disregard for my own life."

He pauses for a minute, looking pensive. "Maybe that was it, or he saw something in me that reminded me of him." He shrugs. "He asked me to join, and I didn't even consider turning him down. At first, I loved it. You had to be fourteen to join Z-Crew, so I thought I was the shit being inducted at such an early age. I looked up to him initially. He was seventeen, and he loved bragging about all the stuff he'd done. After a few months, I began to see a side to him I didn't like, but I was trapped then, so I sucked it up and got on with it."

His shudders, briefly closing his eyes. "Cory Barnes lived a few blocks away from me. His mom was a hooker too, under the control of the same pimp as my mom. There was six years separating me and Cory, but that didn't stop his mom from leaving him with me for hours on end when she was working. It started when he was a baby. I was only a fucking kid, and I had no clue how to look after a newborn, but I did my best."

He worries his lower lip between his teeth, and I can tell how difficult this is for him, so I let him talk uninterrupted. "They moved away for a while, but when they returned, his mom started putting him out of the house when she wanted to entertain johns. He was only four, so I took him under my wing as best I could. It wasn't a problem until I joined Z-Crew. He was always trying to follow me around, but I couldn't have him messed up in the shit we were doing. I tried everything to get him to stop clinging to me, including bribing a few of the local girls into minding him, but he always found a way of sneaking off."

His lower lip wobbles, and he draws several sharp breaths before continuing. "The day it all went down, I was with my crew when we robbed a local grocery store. Ren was walking away from the checkout with a bagful of cash when one of the cashiers pulled a gun out from under the register. His second in command, Johnny, saw what was happening, and he wrestled the female cashier to the ground and grabbed the gun. Ren was a crazy fucker, so he didn't hesitate. He pumped three bullets into her. I can still remember how paralyzed with fear I was. The other guys were laughing, everyone except Vincent and me. Vincent was the second youngest in the gang at fourteen, and he was the closest I had to a friend."

He rubs a hand over his chest, and I'm barely breathing at this stage, my insides all twisted up, fearing where this story is going. "The sound of sobbing muted everyone's laughter. Then Cory rushed forward from his hiding place inside the front door, hugging my leg and crying for his mommy."

A single tear rolls down his face, and it's hard not to grab him into my arms and comfort him, but I hold back, needing to hear the rest.

"Ren was furious. He grabbed Cory by the scruff of his neck and punched him in the face. He passed out straight-away, and I was so scared he was dead." He looks down at his hands. "It would've been better for him if he had've gone like that."

I press a hand over my mouth, preparing myself for what-ever he's going to say next.

Swiping another tear away, he looks up at me as he contin-ues. "Ren took him with us to our base, which was this big ole warehouse at an abandoned airstrip. I tried pleading with him in the truck on the way, telling him Cory was only four and he didn't really understand what he'd seen. I assured him I would convince him to say nothing, but he told me to shut up. I couldn't keep quiet though. I had to keep trying, because I cared about that little boy like he was my baby brother, so I kept talking and pleading until Ren lost his patience and attacked me. The others watched as he punched me repeat-edly, and eventually, I realized there was nothing I could do or say to stop it, so I gave up trying. I was sick to my stomach, Zeta," he whispers, rubbing a hand back and forth across his belly. "Cory woke up shortly after we got to the base, and the guys started in on him. Kicking and punching him. The harder he cried, the harder they beat him."

He squeezes his eyes shut, his body shuddering, and I can't stay away any longer. I sit beside him, sliding my arm around his back, but he pushes me away, scooting farther up the bed until his spine hits the headboard. "Don't do that. Don't console me, because I don't deserve it."

"I remember who he was now," I quietly admit. "I remember watching all the reports on TV and crying."

Silent tears leak out of his eyes. "I tried to stop it again. I begged Ren to let Cory go, but he pinned me to the wall, made it clear what would happen to me if I wasn't on board with it, so I shut up after that."

A strangled sound rips from the back of his throat, and tears are silently falling down my cheeks now too. "I watched them beat him to death. Watched his tiny little chest inflate with his last breath. Watched as his life force was extinguished." He fixes me with a look of sheer torment, and I feel his pain as acutely as if it's my own. "I stood by like a coward. I did nothing as they beat that innocent little boy to death."

He leans his head back, looking up at the ceiling, breathing heavily. When he resumes speaking, he sounds different, lost and like he's no longer here. "Ren warned us not to tell anyone, but I couldn't live with it. Not when Cory's mom started looking for him. She didn't give a flying fuck about him when he was alive but when he went missing, she involved the police and gave interviews to reporters like she was some kind of celebrity." He shakes his head in disgust. "I woke up screaming every night for a week after he died. Every time I closed my eyes, I saw Cory's face, and I knew it wasn't right, so I went to the local cop station and told them everything. They rounded up all the boys, and that's when the story went viral. The whole world was in shock. Disgusted at the murder of an innocent little boy at the hands of other kids."

He looks sideways at me, but he may as well be looking

straight through me. "I wanted them to kill me, because I didn't want to live with what I'd done. Instead, they gave us all new identities, to protect us, because we were still minors, and they sent us to different juvies. The older boys got longer sentences, and some of them are still in adult prisons, but, because I was the youngest, I played no part in the actual murder, and I voluntarily went to the authorities, I was given a shorter sentence and released at eighteen. Vincent was let out then too, although I haven't spoken to him. Part of our release conditions are to have no further contact with one another. We aren't to ever disclose our true identities, and I have to visit a probation officer every couple years to check in."

He stops talking, and silence engulfs us. I'm in complete shock, and I don't know how I feel, or what to say. We don't speak, but neither one of us moves either. So many thoughts flit through my mind, and I want to reach out to him, but I don't know where to start.

"Do you hate me now?" he quietly asks after what feels like an eternity of silence.

I immediately shake my head, turning to look at him. "I could never hate you, Ryder. And while I won't pretend this hasn't shocked and upset me, it doesn't change who you are. If anything, it helps me understand you a bit better."

"I killed a little boy, Zeta! How can you even stand to look at me?"

"*You* didn't kill him, and you were only a little boy, too. Neglected and deprived of love. You tried to look out for him. And you did the right thing by confessing to the authorities."

"I stood by and did nothing!" he shouts, his voice cracking at the end. "And he was only there in the first place because of me."

"That doesn't mean you're responsible, and you've served your time. You're continuing to serve time," I add, because now it all makes sense. The nightmares, pushing me away, the anger that seems to flare up for no reason, his addiction to drink and drugs as an attempt to blot out reality. "What's your real name?" I softly ask.

Strain is etched across his face as he utters the words. "Jack Hill, but that's not who I am anymore. I'm Ryder Stone. I never want to be Jack Hill again."

"He's a part of you, and he always will be, especially if you continue to hate yourself for the role you played in Cory's death."

"It's never going to end, Zeta. I will always remember who Jack Hill was." He sighs heavily. "Ren will make sure of it."

"Ren was the man in the garage. The guy who attacked me," I surmise, and he nods. "Why isn't he in jail?"

"I discovered after I was released that the others had all colluded to spare him. They told the cops he wasn't there that day, and Johnny took the fall for him. He confessed to shooting the cashier too." He shakes his head repeatedly. "Ren hasn't served any time, and that makes me sick."

"And now he's blackmailing you?" I guess.

He nods again. "He's the reason I left you," he admits, and I urge him to continue with my eyes. "He was waiting for me outside juvie that last time I came to visit you. He told me I had a debt to pay because I was the reason everyone was sent down. He had pictures of you, and he made it clear he'd seek revenge through you if I didn't start giving him cash. I was terrified he'd hurt you, and I had nothing to offer you back then. No way to protect you, so I thought if I left, if I put distance between us and cut all ties, that he'd see I didn't care about you and leave you alone. And it worked, until you reappeared in my life, and I was too weak to send you away. I convinced myself that it'd be different now. That I had the resources to protect you. That it'd be safer for you to be with me than not with me. I foolishly thought the fact I've paid him millions in hush money to keep my identity a secret from my fans would be enough. But I was wrong."

He buries his head in his hands, and his shoulders heave

painfully. I can't watch him beat himself up any longer, so I crawl up the bed and wrap my arms around him, just holding him, resting my cheek on his back, in a kind of numbed-dazed state.

After a while, he lifts his head up, peering into my eyes. "I love you, Zeta, even if I've done a piss-poor job of showing you how much. I don't have the words to describe how sorry I am for dragging you into all this." Gently, he brushes his fingers against the bandage on my neck. "He hurt you because of me, and I'll never forgive myself." Closing his eyes, he presses a fierce kiss to my forehead. "I know I've most likely lost you, and I won't fight you if that's what you want, but I'm promising you now, that no matter what happens between us, your safety is my number one priority. I'm going to ensure he doesn't get near you again, and that is one promise I'm not breaking for anything or anyone."

36

ZETA

We return to the Hamptons that evening, and the atmosphere is subdued on the plane and in the SUV. I sit beside Ryder, but we don't talk, and we don't touch. He told me nothing happened with Ashley, and I believe him, but it doesn't eradicate the hurt or the sense of betrayal. He also concealed his past from me, putting me in danger by not revealing the truth. While a part of me understands why he did it, and I can't deny he took measures to try and keep me safe, I'm still upset that he didn't confide in me. I've told him I need space to sort out my feelings, and he's agreed to give me as much time as I need. I think he expected me to leave as soon as I heard the truth, but I'm not going to run away without thinking everything through.

Things are tense between the guys too, and by Tuesday, I can't bear the uncomfortable mood in the studio, so I excuse myself for the rest of the week, choosing to work on the biography out on the upper level terrace instead. Writing helps keep me distracted, and I sorely need that right now.

Every morning, a delivery of fresh flowers arrives for me with a different romantic note from Ryder. My bedroom smells like a florist shop, and they never fail to bring a smile to my face, but it's going to take more than flowers to convince me I should completely forgive him and give things a go again.

Social media goes crazy when Ryder releases a statement publicly apologizing for letting me down. He ended it with a heartfelt declaration of undying love for me, which has his fans swooning over him even more. While I'm grateful he set the record straight, it hasn't changed anything.

On Thursday, Ryder ups the ante, surprising me with a romantic dinner on the beach. The guys helped him build a little makeshift gazebo, and he cooked the dinner from scratch himself. After we eat, he plays a new song he wrote for me, explaining how, in juvie, he used to daydream about serenading me on a beach.

I cry myself to sleep that night, my heart torn and so conflicted. A part of me wants to cave. To say fuck it. That he deserves another chance.

But the part of me that spent years hardening my heart isn't as forgiving.

I swore I would never let another man shatter my heart in the way Ryder Stone had. Now, finding myself in a similar position, thanks to the very same man, makes me feel weak and lacking in resolve. Then I think of the intense connection we share, the strength of the love that exists between us, how sorry he is for the mistakes he's made, all the ways he's shown me that he cares, and I feel foolish for turning my back on the love of a lifetime.

Round and round it goes. Churning and churning. Without any resolution.

I've returned to the guest bedroom, because sleeping beside Ryder when our relationship is in flux doesn't feel right, but I'm lonelier than ever.

Ryder has nightmares, most every night, and I go to him, holding him until he falls back asleep, and then I return to my room. I'm existing on minimal sleep, because I can't switch off with everything going through my mind.

Every night, like clockwork, I bolt awake at four a.m. as terrifying visions of Ren's assault inflict my mind. I stay up after that, usually reading, sometimes writing, or occasionally baking, because these things help ease my mind.

"Fuck, these are gorgeous," Gar declares, stuffing another blueberry muffin in his face. I only took them out of the oven twenty minutes ago, so they're still all fluffy and warm. "If you break up with Stone, you can come live with me, on condition you bake these muffins every morning."

Even though he can't see me from this angle, I roll my eyes at the suggestion. I can barely tolerate being in the same room as Gar these days. If he keeps talking shit, I'm likely to ram that muffin down his throat until he chokes. I glance at Ryder, but his head is still bent over his cell. The drumming of his fingers off the tabletop is the only indication Gar's comment has gotten to him.

If this was before, Ryder would've ripped Gar's head off, but he's been quite withdrawn and sullen this week. I suspect he thought his romantic gesture on the beach last night would send me falling back into his arms, and he's dejected because it didn't happen. I want to tell him it's okay, that we can get past this, but I won't lie to him, and I don't know that yet.

However, I'm hoping the fact I'm still here tells him I haven't given up on us. That I'm still processing everything. Despite what he thinks, I know he's not a bad guy.

I'm shocked over what happened with Cory, but anyone looking at Ryder can see the overwhelming guilt and remorse he struggles with daily. He's being punished every single day, and I don't hold that over him. It's more his failure to disclose the full picture and his destructive, hurtful behavior the night of the awards that has me unsure of our future.

"Boss." Mike strolls into the kitchen with three strange men following him. From their builds and stoic expressions, I can tell they are part of the new security detail. Ryder has gone into uber protective mode since last weekend, doubling the size of the bodyguard team, installing new cameras in the living areas and hallways of the house, insisting I have two bodyguards whenever I step foot off the property, putting monitoring devices on my cell and laptop, and checking the locator app on his cell incessantly when he thinks I'm not looking. I understand it, and I'm not going to criticize him, especially as it helps me feel more secure.

"I want to introduce you to the new faces on the team," Mike adds.

A frown puckers my brow as I stare at the familiar guy with the strawberry-blond hair. "I know you."

Alarm sweeps across Ryder's face as Mike cusses under his breath.

I round the island unit, my gaze bouncing between the new guy, Mike, and Ryder. "You were the one who came to my aid the night that guy was chasing me," I supply, remembering the incident from three years ago as clearly as if it was yesterday.

After what transpired that night, I stopped jogging through the park near my home after dark. I'd been running my usual route when this guy appeared from behind me, instantly giving me a mad case of the heebie-jeebies. Keen to outrun him, I'd stepped up my pace, but so did he, and soon, it became obvious he was chasing me.

The man currently standing in front of me—looking scared shitless I might add—had materialized at my side, quickly telling me he meant me no harm, advising he'd deal with the guy following me, and to run home. I hadn't needed any further encouragement, and I'd barely paused for a breath the whole way back to my condo. I'd thought of my savior often in the weeks that followed, but then I forgot all about it.

Until now.

"What's going on?" I spin around, facing Ryder, who

appears to be having some sort of silent conversation with Mike.

"I'd like to know that too," Ryder says, glaring at Mike and the new guy. "Why is this the first I'm hearing about this?"

Mike levels a direct look at Ryder. "I'm sorry, boss. Lar reported the incident to me at the time, but I thought it best to hold that information back. Zeta was safe, and you would've just freaked out like you did when…"

Ryder silences him with a loaded look.

"Will someone please tell me what's going on?" I cross my arms over my chest, beginning to form a picture.

Ryder extends his hand toward me. "Let's go for a walk."

He doesn't want to talk in front of the others and neither do I, so I take his hand and we walk in complete silence out of the house and down to the beach.

It's a beautiful summer's morning, and the sun heats my bare shoulders as we tread a path through the soft, warm sand. Ryder shares this private strip of beach with a few of his neighbors, and I can make out a few kids playing up ahead as we walk.

"I may have left you behind, Zeta, but I never forgot about you," he begins explaining, lacing his fingers more firmly in mine. "Once the band made it, and the money started rolling in, I had the resources to keep an eye on you." He stops in front of me, linking both my hands in his. "You're probably gonna freak the fuck out when I tell you this, but please believe me when I say everything I did was done to keep you protected."

"What did you do, Ryder?"

"I've kept tabs on you over the years. I wanted to know you were happy. And that you were safe. When you moved to New York, I panicked, because I knew Ren showed up every three months to collect money from me, and there was a good chance he was living in the city. So, I hired bodyguards to follow you."

"Bodyguards? As in plural?" My eyes almost bug out of their sockets.

He nods. "One to watch over you during the day and one to protect you at night."

"I … that's … how did I never notice?" I finally exclaim.

"Because these guys are good at their jobs, and they're paid to blend into the shadows."

I slip my hands out of his, dragging them through my hair as I contemplate exactly what this means. "And they, what, like reported to you about me?"

He nods, at least having the decency to look ashamed. "Mike got weekly reports, which he shared with me."

Planting my hands on my hips, I glare at him. "What was in these reports, Ryder? And don't even attempt to lie to me."

He cringes a little. "Summaries of your daily routines, places you visited, people you hung out with…" He trails off, shoving his hands in the pockets of his shorts, waiting for me to erupt.

"Oh my God! You got reports on the men I was having sex with?"

"I needed to know you were safe. He'd threatened you, and I wouldn't put it past him to try and hook up with you," he murmurs.

I prod my finger in his chest. "Don't give me that crock of shit. If you were that worried about Ren, I'm sure all the bodyguards at least had a description of him."

"They did," he freely admits, "although none of them knew who he was or why he was a threat. Mike included. No one knows about Ren but you."

A thought lands in my mind, and my jaw hangs open as realization dawns. My eyes pop wide and my fists ball up at my sides. "That's why you went apeshit on Gus the other night! You knew who he was! You knew I'd slept with him!"

"Don't fucking remind me." He scowls. "But yes, that's why I went for him. The thought of any guy putting his hands on you infuriates me."

"You're a damn hypocrite!" I roar. "The notches on my bedpost fail miserably in comparison to yours, and I've had to watch media reports of your conquests for years! You even flaunted that fucking whore in front of me at the after-party, and I didn't go after her in the way you went after Gus."

He doesn't need to know I thought about it.

"I'm sorry, Zeta. Attacking Gus was completely out of line. But I'm not going to apologize for wanting to keep you safe."

"It's a huge invasion of my privacy!" I fling my arms into the air, completely conflicted. One part of me loves that he's just proven his words. That I know, categorically, how much he's cared for me during the period of our separation. That he's gone to so much trouble and expense to keep me protected speaks volumes. But there's another part of me that sees this as borderline stalking, and I'm not comfortable with it.

"I don't see it like that. I just wanted to know you were okay, and it helped me feel closer to you. I liked knowing about your life."

"This is so fucked up." I sigh, scrunching my hands in my hair again. "Please tell me this is it. That there are no more secrets you're hiding from me."

He shuffles nervously on his feet, and ice replaces the blood flowing through my veins. "What else, Ryder? What else don't I know?" I wrap my arms around my torso, instinctively protecting myself.

"I paid off your mortgage. The monthly payment you deposit goes into a savings account. And I'm an investor in your aunt's business."

My jaw drops to the floor. Before I can respond, he adds, "Oh, and I paid off Louise's debts last month, bought you a new car, which I was going to give to you as a surprise, and I, ah, put ownership of *RockOut* into your name."

"You did what?" I shriek.

"What the hell do I want with a magazine?" He shrugs, like it's no biggie. "You're the writer, not me. And I was going to tell you all this when the time was right."

I pinch the bridge of my nose. "Please tell me you had nothing to do with me getting my job at *RockOut*, because, I swear to God, if you've manipulated my career, I'm out of here."

He vehemently shakes his head. "I had absolutely nothing to do with that. You won that job on your own merits. I would never interfere like that. I just tried to ease the burden on you, that's all."

I flop down on the sand, propping my chin on my bent knees, staring out at the water, utterly flabbergasted. He sits down beside me, staring at my face as I look straight ahead.

"Say something," he pleads.

"I don't know what to say," I truthfully reply, turning my head toward him. "My brain is overloaded with all this stuff, and I don't think I can take much more."

"All I've ever wanted to do is to make you happy, yet I've ended up doing the opposite. I know it's a shitty way of saying I love you, but I do love you."

Sighing, I link my pinky in his. "I know you do," I softly say, "and I love you too. I'm not going to deny that, but I just don't know if it's enough, and I can't make sense of the mess in my head." An idea floats in my mind and I don't know why I didn't think of it before. "I'm going to visit Jill for a while. I think we could both use a little distance right now."

"Don't leave. Please." Agony repaints his features, and I hate that I've put it there, but I won't lie to him.

"I need to. I need headspace if I'm going to figure out what this all means."

I stand, and he climbs to his feet, his eyes wild and frantic as he cups my face. "Don't leave me, Zeta. Please don't leave me."

The vulnerability is back, and it's hard to deny him anything, but one of us needs to be strong. I kiss him briefly on the lips, pulling back before he can return it. "I'm coming back. Okay?" I thread my fingers through his hair. "I just need time alone, but I will come back." I wouldn't lie to his face, and I mean what I say. He's panicked at the thought of losing me, and the last thing I want is him sitting here worrying that I've disappeared on him.

"You promise?"

The agony in his tone and his face is killing me, but I must remain strong. "I promise, Ryder. I promise I'll be back."

JILL, Liam, and the kids are delighted to see me, and I feel guilty I haven't visited in so long. I take Kendall and Kyle to the beach for a few hours, grabbing some takeout burgers and fries on the way home. After they're fed, I help bath them and then take turns reading them bedtime stories. Jill and I finally get a chance to speak once they are both fast asleep.

"Have fun, ladies," Liam says, placing an ice bucket with a chilled bottle of sauvignon blanc on the table along with two wine glasses. He leans in to kiss his wife. "I won't be too late," he promises before leaving to rendezvous with his buddies at a local bar.

"You two make it look so easy," I say, pouring wine into both our glasses.

"We work at it," she says, chinking my glass. "And anyone who tells you relationships are easy is a damn liar."

I kick off my shoes, tucking my bare feet under my legs, as I bring the glass to my lips. My aunt pats my knee. "Tell me what's going on with you and Ryder. I thought things were good?"

I've been updating her during our weekly phone calls, but I hadn't mentioned what went down at the awards ceremony or the fact I was attacked after the after-party. Once I've dealt with her concern, I tell her as much as I can about what's going on. I don't tell her Ryder knows the guy who attacked me or that it was a form of revenge, because that's not my secret to tell, so I skirt around it, giving her enough to form a good picture of how messed up I am. When I get to the part about the protection-slash-stalking, she tenses up a little.

"You knew," I say, stating the obvious.

"Not at first." She puts her glass down. "I know you're probably pissed but hear me out." I nod, taking a big glug of my wine. "When Liam and I left our jobs to set up our own company, we knew our savings wouldn't be enough to develop the system the way we had planned, so we hired a financial guy to seek out suitable venture capitalists who would be interested in investing in a start-up tech company. He secured three investors for us. Two of them we met in person, as they had questions they wanted us to answer face to face. The third investor wanted to remain anonymous, and while it's unusual, it didn't trigger any alarm bells. We were thrilled to have outsiders believe in our idea enough to put their money behind us."

She purposely clears her throat. "Two years ago, we discovered the anonymous investor was Ryder. I was stunned, to be honest." She clasps her hands in her lap. "I reached out to him, and we arranged to meet in New York the next time I was in the city visiting you." I knock back my wine, stunned at what I'm hearing. "I wanted to tell you. I wanted to tell you so badly, but he explained that he'd had to leave you because his past had come back to haunt him, and it potentially placed you in harm's way."

Wow. I'm shocked Ryder even admitted that much, knowing how risky it is to divulge anything.

"He told me he had assigned bodyguards to watch over

you, and he assured me he would keep you safe. I had no reason to doubt him because the look on his face when he talked about you said everything." She grabs my free hand. "He loves you, Zeta. Like soul mate, one true pairing, crazy kind of love. I tried to persuade him to contact you, but he'd convinced himself he wasn't worthy of you, that you deserved better, and it kinda broke my heart."

Her smile is sad. "I spoke to Liam about it when I came home, and we talked it over for hours, wondering if we should intervene, but, in the end, I decided not to, because I had a strong feeling you two would find your way back to one another." She squeezes my hand. "I knew you weren't over him. I knew your reluctance to date was down to how you still felt about him. I knew those lyrics on your thigh were written for him."

"I love him, Jill. He's the only man I've ever loved but there is so much hurt and pain between us, and we're both broken in different ways, and I don't know if we can ever overcome it." I suddenly need to tell her everything, because I need her to help me figure out my feelings and she can't do that with half the facts. So, I tap out a quick text to Ryder, asking permission to reveal the truth, which he readily gives.

I fill Jill in on the rest of the story, and she listens with her hand over her mouth, much like I did when Ryder was telling me.

"Oh, dear Lord." She knocks back her wine when I've finished explaining, moving to refill both our glasses. "I remember that case so well. I was twenty-one and getting ready to leave for Australia when the news broke." Her eyes fill with tears. "Cory Barnes was Kyle's age when he was murdered. The thought of anyone hurting my little boy…" Her voice trails off, a sob breaking free, and I wonder if I've been selfish telling her this.

"That was one of the first thoughts I had when Ryder told me too," I admit.

"I can still see Cory's little face. It's never left me. That blond hair, those gorgeous hazel eyes, those cute dimples." She flops back against the arm of the couch. "Jesus, Zeta."

I lean back, sighing. "Ryder's blamed himself his whole life, Jill. I see it in his behavior. In all the things he's done. And he's tried to give back. He does amazing work for charity, and he's donated millions, mainly to help kids or anyone suffering from abuse or the effects of violent crime."

She lifts her head up. "He's a good man, Zeta. Hearing this doesn't change my opinion of him."

"I agree."

"So, what's the problem?"

"How can I trust him when he's kept so much from me? When he does things driven by this pent-up rage and frustration he's carried with him for years?"

"You help him deal with it, Zeta."

"I don't know how."

She sits up, scooting in closer to me. "You love him, and you support him through it, that's how." She leans in, kissing my cheek. "I know you love him deeply. And I know he feels the same. He's spent years proving that to you. You just didn't know it. Now, it's your turn to be that for him."

I nod. "I want to be there for him. I'm just scared. Scared of me hurting him and him hurting me."

"That's only natural, but there is nothing between you now. All the cards are on the table, and it's up to you how you manage the hand you've been dealt. True love is messy and complicated, and it hurts. Sometimes, it's necessary to feel that pain to remind us why we should fight for love, especially if it's been hard won, like you and Ryder."

Tears pool in my eyes. "I should just ditch my shrink and have you on speed dial instead," I tease, sniffling.

She wipes my tears aside. "Sweetheart, I'm always here for you. You can call me as many times as you like because I love hearing your voice. The day you came back into my life was one of the happiest days I've ever experienced. I know we missed out on the first eighteen years together, but to me, in every way, you are my daughter more than my niece, and your happiness matters to me."

Wracking sobs burst free of my chest, and she pulls me into her arms. "Ryder is a good man trapped in a bad situation. He hasn't been able to figure his way out of this because he hasn't had you in his life for the past eight years, but he needs you now, sweetheart. He needs you to help him fight."

"I'm not going anywhere," I sniffle. "I always knew that."

"Good." She brushes my hair back off my face. "Because true love is being there for your significant other through the bad stuff as well as the good times. It's caring for your partner when they're incapable of caring for themselves. It's being their strength in times of need. But, above all, it's about forgiveness. And, maybe, just maybe, if you can forgive him, he can start to forgive himself."

37

RYDER

The bed dips, and a warm body curls around my back, rousing me from slumber. "Go back to sleep," Zeta murmurs. "I didn't mean to wake you."

I twist around until I'm facing her, rubbing my eyes and wrapping my arms around her waist to ensure I'm not dreaming.

"How are you here?" Mike didn't tell me they were coming back early, and I wasn't expecting her for a few days yet. Not that I'm in any way complaining.

"I missed you too much," she says, pressing her hot body in closer. She throws her leg over mine, and my dick starts hardening.

"I missed you too." She has no idea the hell I've been through these past five days, torturing myself over thoughts I'd lost her. Having her back in my arms is more than I dared to hope for.

"I'm sorry I put you through hell," she says, as if she has a direct line to my inner thoughts. "But I didn't want to say anything or promise anything until I processed everything."

"And you have now?"

She nods, smiling expansively. "I love you, Ryder Stone.

And I love Jack Hill, the boy I didn't know, the boy who grew up to become the man I love."

My eyes penetrate hers, wondering if she means it, because how can she say she loves the real me when she knows what I did. "You can't mean that."

She places her hand on my chest, staring deep into my eyes. "I love every part of you, and I know who you are. You are a good person. A good man who was caught in an ugly situation, but it doesn't change what I know is in your heart." She traces her finger around the tattoo of her name on my chest. "You loved Cory Barnes. You took care of him as best you could. You tried to save him, and when you couldn't, you ensured he got justice. You made sure people the world over knew who that special little boy was, and you have done so many good deeds in his name. If there is a heaven, then Cory Barnes is there, and he's looking down at you, telling you to forgive yourself." I don't even realize I'm crying until she wipes my tears away. "And if you're not ready to forgive yourself yet, that's okay, because I'm going to help you get there."

"I don't deserve you," I whisper.

"You deserve all the love in the world, and I'm going to give it to you." She presses her lips to mine. "I love you, and I'm not going anywhere. All I ask is that you never disrespect me or our love because I won't tolerate being treated the way you treated me at that party. That's a deal breaker for me."

"That will never happen again." I wind my fingers through her hair. "While you were away, I contacted your therapist, and she put me in touch with a local outpatient rehab program. I've been seeing a therapist daily, and I'm committed to staying away from drugs. They make me do shit I don't ever want to do again, so I'm cutting them out. I can tolerate a few beers, but I won't be drinking to excess either."

"You're serious about this?" Hope sparks in her eyes.

"One hundred percent. I'm doing this for me, for us,

because I want to be a better man, the kind of man you deserve, but I'll need your support, because it won't be easy."

"You've got it. Whatever you need. I'm there for you."

A giant layer of stress lifts off my shoulders as we grin at one another. "You're really back? To stay for good?"

She props up on one elbow. "I'm in this for the long haul. I'm yours. And I won't flake on you again." She runs her fingers around my face. "From now on, we're a team, and nothing is going to break us apart."

"Together," I say.

"Together." She leans in and kisses me deeply, probing my mouth with her tongue. My cock strains against my boxers, and I pull her in flush to me, needing to feel her body against mine. She thrusts her hips forward, moaning as my erection presses against her belly. "Ryder?" She's breathless as she pulls back, inspecting my face. "All the secrets are laid bare now, and I want there to be nothing else between us." Sitting up, she pulls her silk nightie up over her head. She isn't wearing any underwear, and my dick pulses with need. "Make love to me?"

I push her gently back down on the bed, crawling over her. "It would be my absolute pleasure." I've never made love to a woman before. I've fucked. Hard and fast. A purely physical release without any emotion, but as I worship Zeta's body, licking, sucking, and kissing her from head to toe, I know, without a shadow of a doubt, that this experience is going to be different.

I climb out of the bed, pulling the top drawer of my bedside table open as I kick my boxers off.

"I'm on the pill," Zeta confirms. "And I'm clean. If you are too, I want to do this without a condom. I want to feel all of you, Ryder."

Precum leaks out of my cock at her words. "I'm clean too. Are you sure?" I crawl back into the bed.

She nods, curling her hand around the back of my neck

and pulling me down on top of her. "I've never been surer of anything. And I've never done this with anyone else."

"I haven't either."

The biggest smile spreads across her face as she hooks her legs around my waist. "We didn't get to experience a lot of firsts together, but I'm glad we get to share this one."

"Me too, baby." I crash my mouth down on hers, kissing the shit out of her lips as we rock against one another. I trail a line of kisses down her neck and along her collarbone, stopping to worship her gorgeous tits. She almost bucks off the bed when I tug at her nipples, biting and then lapping the sting away. My mouth explores every inch of her soft flesh as I move down her body, positioning myself in between her legs.

I lick her slit from top to bottom, burying my nose in her pussy and soaking in her essence. She smells divine. Tastes divine. And I'm too worked up to wait. I devour her pussy with my tongue and my fingers, and when I slide my pinky into her ass, she goes wild, screaming and writhing as she comes all over my face. Without leaving her time to recover, I slide inside her in one fast thrust. We both groan, and I don't move, holding perfectly still, just enjoying the feeling of being inside her for the first time with no barrier between us.

"Ryder," she cries, tears leaking down her face as she's overcome with emotion. I know, because I'm feeling it too. Leaning down, I kiss her tears away, fighting my own emotions. "I love the feel of you inside me," she adds, fisting her hands in my hair. "But I need you to move, baby. I want to feel you moving inside me."

Holding her hands above her head, I thread my fingers in hers as I start to slowly move inside her for the first time. Our eyes are locked on one another's, and everything I'm feeling is radiating back at me from her adoring gaze. We move gently against one another, in a way I've never experienced, and my mind is blown, my heart so full of love for this woman, the only woman who has ever meant anything to me. "You complete me," I whisper against her mouth, capturing her lips in mine. "You are the other half of my heart and soul, and I want this with you forever."

Her hands move up and down my spine, and she emits the most delicious little noises as we rock against one another. "No one else has ever made me feel the way you do," she tells me. "I will love you every day for the rest of my life."

We don't speak after that, but no words are needed. I make love to her, softly and slowly, drowning in the emotions filtering between us, enjoying every thrust, every caress, feeling our bond intensifying as we stare at one another with nothing but love between us. And when we both reach a peak, crashing together, I know tonight has changed me, rebuilt something inside me that's long been broken, and that I'll never be the same again.

WAKING up with Zeta wrapped around me, all naked and warm, is the best feeling in the world. "Morning, beautiful," I whisper when she finally stirs a half hour later. I'm dying for a piss, but I didn't want to wake her. Didn't want to tear myself from her arms. If she knew I'd just been staring at her incessantly, like the lovesick fool I am, she'd definitely start reassessing her stalker theories.

We both freshen up and then retreat to bed again. My cock is already rock hard, and when I push my fingers inside her, she's every bit as aroused as me. Crawling into my lap, she slowly lowers onto my dick, and I see stars. She starts off slow, softly moving up and down, her tits bouncing, nipples in stiff peaks, and I thrust up inside her, moaning as she rocks my world.

When she picks up her pace, grinding down on me, I grab hold of her hips, thrusting into her more aggressively before sitting up and pounding into her as she digs her fingers into my shoulders, riding me roughly. Our kissing is frenzied, and our hands frantically explore one another as we fuck, the crescendo building inside me until a familiar tingling in my spine signals I'm close. We're both sweating and panting when we explode together, moaning and clutching onto one another as waves of ecstasy wash over us.

After, I spoon her from behind and we start making plans for the future, talking for hours about everything we want to see and do together, and when we finally wander out of the bedroom, late in the afternoon, I'm like a different man.

The weeks that follow are nothing short of blissful. Getting to spend my days and nights with the woman of my dreams is something I never thought I'd get to enjoy. We've missed out on a lot, and I take none of it for granted.

But we can't avoid reality forever. The guys pack up and leave for the city once the album is a wrap. We've decided to stay here for the moment, neither one of us in any hurry to return to the city. Zeta is busy writing the biography, and that gives me plenty of time to think about where I go from here, but I'm struggling to draw any conclusions.

I've never missed a drop-off with Ren before, but I didn't show last time. There's no way I'm giving that monster any more of my hard-earned cash, and after what he did to Zeta, I don't trust myself with him. Don't trust I won't kill the bastard with my bare hands. He's furious, sending copious texts to the burner cell he gave me all those years ago. I'm tempted to dump it in the ocean, but I won't, because it's evidence. Evidence I'm hoping, one day, to be in a position to use against him.

"You look a million miles away," Zeta says, circling her arms around me from behind as I put the finishing touches to our dinner.

Turning the heat off at the stove, I turn around, reeling her in for a long kiss. As usual, my dick gets excited, and I can't help pressing my semi against her.

"You're insatiable," she says, nipping at my lower lip.

I grab her ass, giving it a firm squeeze. "Sex with you is incredible, and I can't get enough." I'm having more sex than I've ever had in my life, and we can't keep our hands off one another. I've never had this level of intimacy before, and I'm addicted to this woman.

She pecks my lips. "Ditto, babe. I could happily spend every waking hour in bed with you." Pulling back, she eyeballs me seriously. "But no deflecting. What's on your mind?"

I begin plating our dinner, and she leans back against the counter, eyeing me with concern. "I'm trying to decide what to do about Ren." I don't hesitate to tell her the truth because being completely honest with one another is one of our new rules.

"It's been on my mind a lot too." She opens the refrigerator, removing a bottle of sparkling water and grabbing two glasses from the overhead cupboard. "Let's discuss our options after dinner."

We walk out to the patio area to eat. "Dinner's up," I tell Mike as I pass, knowing full well he will reheat his pasta later, rather than leaving Zeta and I unprotected out here. He's a good leader, always taking care of his team before attending to his own needs.

"You can eat with us," Zeta says, like she does every day, knowing he'll turn her down.

"Thanks for the offer, but I'll eat after you're finished."

Zeta leans in to kiss his cheek, and I swear the big guy blushes. I send him an amused smirk, and once Zeta's back is turned, he flips me the bird. I'm still laughing as I sit down. "What's so funny?" she asks.

"You made the big guy blush, and he hates that I noticed."

She swats my arm. "Play nice."

"I'm always nice." I nip her earlobe. "Especially with you."

"You were especially nice to me this morning," she agrees

with a twinkle in her eye. She purposely drags her lower lip between her teeth, knowing it turns me on.

And now I'm thinking about a repeat of this morning's performance.

"I was." I shove my tongue in her ear, and she squeals. "And I'll be nice to you again. After we eat." I swirl a forkful of pasta and lift it to her lips, and she dutifully opens for me, making my cock throb in my pants. "Fuck, you even make eating sexy."

She snakes her arms around my neck. "That's just cause we're hot for one another all the time."

"Damn straight, baby." I kiss the tip of her nose. "But I didn't spend an hour slaving over a hot stove for us to ditch the food in favor of bed, no matter how tempting you are, so eat."

We make quick work of our pasta and then wander down to the beach for a walk like we always do after dinner. Mike hangs back at a discreet distance allowing us privacy to talk. "I've been thinking about the situation," she says, "and I think you're right. Ren's not going to go away. He's going to constantly hold the threat of disclosure over your head unless you take back control."

"I agree, and that's why I've decided I'm going to make a public statement. I'm going to tell the world who I really am."

She stops walking, examining my face to see if I'm serious. Taking my hand, she pulls me down onto the sand. She's quiet as she considers it. "If you reveal your true identity, you're breaking the terms of your release agreement. They could send you back to jail."

I swallow over the lump of emotion clogging the base of my throat. "I know, but it's a risk I think I should take. If I do this, I remove the threat he's been holding over my head for years, and he can't blackmail me anymore. It also means I can report him to the cops, and that's the best way to keep him away from you, to keep you safe. I have evidence of the blackmail, and I can tell them he's the one who's really responsible for the death of that cashier and Cory's death."

She doesn't take her eyes from mine as she offers another suggestion. "Or you could hire a hitman and put a bullet between his eyes." I examine her face to see if she's joking, but she's deadly serious.

"I have thought of that over the years," I admit. "But the one thing that always held me back is the fact that would make me a murderer, just like him, and I'm nothing like that asshole."

"You're not. There is no comparison." We both stare out at sea, and I wrap my arm around her shoulder as she leans into me. "You think I'm crazy for suggesting it?"

"No. Like I said, the thought has reared its head on more than one occasion, but it's not a viable option. Fessing up is the only solution that makes sense, even if I do get sent down for it." Naturally, I don't want that to happen, but I'm tired of living a lie. This is the best way to protect the woman I love, and that's all that matters. Worrying about Ren's retaliation is keeping me awake at night, and I'll feel safer knowing the authorities are aware of all the facts.

"Your fans would be up in arms if they did that," Zeta says, thinking it through. "I'm confident that won't happen although, if we are going to do it, we'd need to get some legal advice. I think the fact you're handing over the real culprit will negate any potential fallout for you."

"The fans might turn on me. On us." I've given this a lot of thought, and it's a very real concern.

She straightens up, tilting my face to hers. "I honestly think they'd stick by you. They love you. And if you explain it the way you explained it to me, they'll understand."

"Maybe, but it'll bring a lot of heat at a time when we're due to release our next album, go on tour, and announce our own label. If this just impacted me, I'd do it right now, but I can't ruin everything for the guys. I'll have to walk away from

Torment, but if it means I get to keep you safe, then it's worth it."

She shakes her head. "I'm not letting you do that, and I don't think the guys would either. You need to talk to them. Tell them everything. Even if we don't go ahead and do this, I think they should know. I think you'll feel lighter once all the people who love you know the truth."

I love how everything is "we," and having her in this with me means more than I can say. "What if they hate me? What if they turn their back on me?"

"Then they aren't really your friends. And if they do, screw them. We don't need them." She throws her arms around me. "We only need each other."

"Together," we both say at the same time and I'm smiling as I lean in to kiss her.

WE TAKE a few days to discuss it at length, debating all the pros and cons, until I finally decide it's the right course of action. It's the only way to get Ren out of our lives. Before I broach the subject with Rod and the guys, we visit my attorney in the city to get some legal advice. Once he has all the facts, he believes there is minimal risk of me being prosecuted, but he can't guarantee that there won't be some form of punishment.

We stay at the penthouse that night, talking it through, and we both agree it's worth the risk. The next day, I call Rod and the guys over, and I tell them everything with Mike in the room, because he deserves to know the truth too.

The guys are visibly shocked, but I'm surprised at the reason for it. They're all upset that I've carried this burden on my own for so long. And they're a bit pissed that I didn't share it with them sooner. Rod, of course, knew most of this, but he wasn't aware of the blackmail, and he's livid with me for not involving him from the outset.

Zeta leaves us to help Maggie with dinner, and we talk it through, particularly the potential ramifications for the band if I go ahead with my plan. The guys are unanimously behind me, and I'm a bit of an emotional mess, if truth be told. These guys are like the brothers I never had, and their unflinching loyalty means the world to me.

It's after midnight when we call it a night, and I'm pretty drained from reliving the most traumatic parts of my life, but I also feel freer, like a giant weight has been lifted from my shoulders.

That night, after a marathon sex session that left both of us sweating and exhausted, I sleep more soundly than I have in years, and I can't help wondering how different things might've been if I'd spoken up sooner.

I wake ahead of Zeta for a change, and I sit in the chair by my bed, smiling at my sleeping beauty, so grateful she came back into my life. Without a shadow of a doubt, I know she's the only one I want by my side for eternity.

I should wait.

Plan this properly.

Make it romantic and something she can talk about to our kids.

But I'm done holding back on my life. Now that I've decided I'm revealing the truth to the world, and Rod's setting the wheels in motion today, I want her with me at the press conference, standing by my side as my wife.

I flip open the little black box I've had in my safe for years, grinning as I gaze at the custom fit engagement ring I had created especially for her. I'd done it on a whim, never truly believing I'd be in any position to give it to her. This moment is a moment I've wanted for years, and I'm silently begging my sleeping girlfriend to wake the fuck up, because I can't wait a minute longer to propose. I can't wait to call her my fiancée.

38

ZETA

"Hey, baby." I lift my head, surveying Ryder through blurry eyes. Peeling back the covers, I pat the empty space beside me. "Come back to bed, and let me demonstrate how much I love you."

Morning sex is a relatively new concept for both of us, and I know he's come to love our morning quickies as much as I have. I've never had any of this before—a proper relationship, living with someone twenty-four seven, amazing sex on tap. But I'm loving it, and it's as natural as breathing for us. With the exception of the Ren stuff hanging over our heads, I've never been this happy before.

"As tempting as that is, I thought we might do something else today," he says, getting up and rounding my side of the bed. His eyes shine with emotion as he leans down to kiss me.

I pull back as his tongue seeks permission. "I don't want to inflict my morning breath on you. Let me brush my teeth real quick." I fling the covers off, and his eyes follow a path up my bare legs and over my very naked body.

"Fuck, you're beautiful, and I don't give a shit about morning breath. I love kissing you anytime." Ignoring my wishes, he leans down and kisses me again, lapping at the

375

seam of my lips until I open for him. He sits down on the floor, pulling me into his lap, and we kiss deeply and passionately while his hands roam up and down my back. "I could kiss you forever, but then I'll want to do more, and my plans for today will be forgotten," he says, when he finally breaks the kiss.

I circle my arms around his neck, curling my fingers into the hair at the nape of his neck. He's letting it grow out again, and I can't wait until it's longer so I can fist my hands in his hair when he's fucking me. "What plans?" I ask while he practically purrs at my touch.

My fingers stall as he looks at me with emotion brimming in his eyes. Butterflies scatter in my chest as I wait for him to speak. "Let's fly to Vegas and get married."

I blink profusely, sure I must have heard him wrong. "What?" I splutter.

Holding onto my hips, he slides me off his lap, positioning me on the edge of the bed as he drops to one knee. My hand is shaking as I raise it to my mouth. He flips open a little black box, and tears pump out of my eyes as I stare at the exquisite ruby and diamond ring. "From the instant I laid eyes on you, that first day back in juvie, I just knew you were the one. I know it sounds crazy, but it was like being struck by lightning, and I was never surer of anything than we were meant to belong together. We share an intense connection, and it's only grown stronger over the years. Nothing in my life has ever felt right unless you're in it. I love you so fucking much."

His voice cracks a little, and the smile he gives me is tinged with nerves. "You're the only woman for me, and I know I will love you every day for the rest of my life. We lost years, and I don't want to waste any more time. I want to wake up beside you every morning and go to sleep with you at night. I want to navigate all the highs and lows with you by my side. I want to watch my babies growing in your belly, and I want a family, something I never thought I could aspire to, but with you, everything is possible, and I want the world for us."

He takes the ring out of the box, holding it out to me. "I want you to be my wife. I want you to call me your husband. And I don't want to wait another minute longer. So, please, will you fly with me to Vegas today and marry me?"

"Yes. Yes. A million times yes." I'm sobbing. Huge, big, fat monster tears roll down my face, but I've never been happier.

He pulls me down onto his lap, cradling me in his arms, and I nuzzle my face in his neck, crying and laughing and just living. "Thank fuck. For a minute there, I was terrified you'd say no."

"Haven't you noticed I have an issue saying no to you about anything?" I laugh through my tears. "Because I only ever want to say yes. I only ever want to make you happy."

"Give me your hand, baby." I hold my left hand out, grinning the biggest grin as he slides the ring on my finger. "I hope you like it," he says, as we both share an awestruck expression staring at the glittering ring on my hand. It's perfect. It's not too big, not too small, and the teardrop-shaped ruby surrounded by a line of fine diamonds is different from the traditional engagement rings but most definitely to my taste.

"I love it. And you couldn't have found a more perfect ring for me."

"I had it designed for you," he admits, tucking errant strands of my hair behind my ears. "Four years ago."

My jaw slackens. "You did?"

He nods. "I didn't know how I could make it happen, but I always hoped I'd propose to you one day, and I wanted to be prepared."

I slam my mouth down on his, kissing his lips and then dotting little kisses all over his face. He chuckles, clearly delighted at my enthusiasm. "You know," he says, looking a little more serious. "If you don't want to elope, if you want the big white wedding, we can wait. I don't want to force this on you today if it's not what you want. I guess I can try and summon patience from somewhere," he adds with a teasing grin.

"Ugh, no." I scrunch my nose. "A big white wedding has never been in the cards for me." I peck his lips. "I want to elope to Vegas with you today. I love that it's just us. And maybe we can organize a small celebration here when we come back?"

"That sounds perfect, and you're perfect." He nips at my earlobe, sending a shot of liquid lust straight through me. "I thought as much, but I didn't want to assume."

I jump up, clapping my hands and shrieking. "We're getting married today!!!"

Climbing to his feet, he hauls me into his arms, kissing me with obvious intent. "We have a lot to arrange, but I don't think we should let our engagement pass without celebrating it." His eyes glint wickedly as his hands slide down to my bare ass, and he yanks me hard against his growing erection. I moan into his mouth, sighing contentedly as he takes my hand, leading me into the shower.

I switch the shower on, testing the water with my hand while he makes quick work of his clothes. He steps in behind me, and I tilt my face up to the warm water as his hand creeps around my waist, moving up to cup one of my breasts. He rolls my nipple between his thumb and index finger, and the bud instantly hardens. Pushing my hair to one side, he grazes his mouth along my sensitive skin while he continues to fondle my breast. His hard length pulses against my ass, and I shiver all over. His other hand moves down between my legs, and he thrusts two fingers inside me without warning. I automatically clench around his digits, moaning as I lean back into him, extending my neck and opening my legs a little wider, to give him more access.

"Fuck, I love those little sounds you make," he says,

rocking his erection into me. "And I love the look on your face when I make you come."

I twist around, pushing my tits into him as I greedily claim his mouth. "I love your cock," I murmur over his mouth, moving my hand down to grip him. "Especially when you're rutting into me like a wild animal." I stroke his length in quick strokes, sucking his lower lip into my mouth as my hips buck up.

"That sounds like a challenge." He nips my earlobe, and a pleasurable moan escapes my mouth.

"Fuck me, Rock Star. Fuck me so hard I don't even remember my name."

His eyes turn dark with desire as he grabs both my hands, hoisting them up over my head. He pushes me back against the cool tile wall, dipping his head down to suck on my nipple. I writhe against him, wet and aching for him. "Wrap those gorgeous legs around me," he commands, lifting my left thigh. I do as he says, lining my pussy up perfectly as my legs fit around his waist. In one skillful thrust, he's inside me, and I cry out as he fills me up and holds still, staring deep into my eyes as he holds our bodies in place. "I fucking love you so much."

"I love you too." My eyes close as his mouth descends on mine, and his kiss is tender and sweet until he starts moving his cock in and out of me, and then the tempo amps up.

Capturing my lips in a bruising kiss, he thrusts his hips forward, pushing his cock into me as far as it will go, and I see stars. The beginnings of my orgasm are already building as he picks up his pace, jutting his hips in and out as my legs cling to his waist. My arms drop as he slides his hands to my ass, tilting my hips up at an angle so he can bury himself deeper. I cry out as he grinds into me, both of us groaning in ecstasy.

He fucks me hard and fast under the cascading water until we both fall over the ledge, literally seconds apart. He stays inside me for a few minutes, kissing me softly as I run my fingers through his wet hair. Then he eases out slowly, carefully setting my legs down, keeping an arm around my waist until I'm steady. "I love you, soon-to-be Mrs. Stone." He pecks my lips, and I fling my arms around him, not wanting to let him go.

"I can't wait," I truthfully admit, easing back to cup his face. "This is exactly where we are both meant to be."

He takes my hand, placing it over his heart. "This only beats for you."

We take turns washing each other before getting dressed and packing our overnight bags. Ryder's on the phone, making plans, while I fix breakfast. A half hour later, we're in the SUV, with Mike and Lar, en route to the airport, kissing, touching, and laughing as we bask in the euphoria of our special day.

When we land in Vegas, we head straight to a trendy designer store to find something to wear. Ryder called in advance, and the store has been cleared for our private fittings. Neither of us is bothered about tradition, so I choose a figure-hugging black, red, and gold dress with gold-spiked black-velvet stilettos while Ryder picks out gray skinny jeans, a white shirt, and black jacket.

Next, we stop at a jewelry store and select matching wedding bands.

Then it's on to the Marriage License Bureau to pick up the marriage license Ryder registered for online, and then we proceed to the chapel he booked for the actual ceremony. I can't believe he set all this up so fast, but he forgot nothing, and we're really doing this. I'm giddy with excitement, and my heart is so full. I know this day will be a day I'll cherish forever.

We complete the paperwork, hand over our IDs, and Ryder pays the fee. Then I'm walking up the aisle on Mike's arm toward my clearly emotional fiancé.

We hold hands throughout the short ceremony, never

taking our eyes off one another. The only part of it I remember is reciting our vows, exchanging rings, and cementing our marriage with a panty-melting kiss. When the celebrant announces we are man and wife, I cling to Ryder, kissing him again and again, my heart swollen with so much love. Mike takes some photos, and then Ryder whisks me to our suite in The Venetian where a sumptuous dinner and a bottle of expensive champagne awaits us. After gorging ourselves on our wedding feast, we make love in the jacuzzi, and then Ryder takes me to bed where we consummate our marriage until the early hours of the morning.

We stay another day and night in the hotel although we don't step foot outside our suite. Ryder surprises me with a stunning ruby and diamond necklace to match my engagement ring, and I'm raging I didn't think to get him anything in the store when we were there.

While he's asleep, I write him a love song, offering it to him as part one of his wedding gift when he wakes up. The second part of his gift was something I ordered online while he was snoozing. I paid extra for a rush job so his new custom-made, personally engraved Fender should arrive at our Hamptons house within the week, and I can't wait to see his face when he gets it.

I call Jill and Kayla and give them the good news while Ryder updates Rod and the guys. When I get off the phone, I throw myself at my husband, showering him with kisses. "Not that I'm complaining, but what's that for?" he asks, pulling me into his arms.

"Kayla just told me what you did." I kiss him again. "Thank you."

He shrugs. "It was the right thing to do."

When Kayla told me Torment's new label had offered Savage Mania a recording contract, I almost fell off my chair. But when she explained that Ryder had personally called Gus to apologize, I nearly burst into tears. I know that couldn't have been easy, and that he was doing it for me, and I couldn't love him any more than I do. "It was, but it took balls, and I'm proud of you. And I'm so excited for Gage and the rest of the band."

"I think they have a bright future in the industry, and we look forward to working with them." His hands move to the knot on my toweling robe. "Now, enough talk of your ex. I want you underneath me, naked and screaming out my name, Mrs. Stone."

I shimmy the robe off my shoulders, letting it pool at my feet. "I think that can be arranged, Mr. Stone." I drape my arms around him. "Lead the way."

♪

"How DID your meeting go at the charity?" Rod asks as we arrive at the Manhattan hotel where the press conference is being held. We'd stopped at the charity's HQ on the way to meet with the director. Ryder wanted to explain the situation to her before he announced his identity to the world. Considering the nature of the services the charity provides, it's a sensitive situation.

"About as well as expected." Ryder shrugs, trying his best not to look dejected.

"They're naturally shocked, and the director said they need some time to consider the potential impact on their operation," I explain. "They're grateful for all Ryder has done for the charity, and more understanding of why he wanted to keep his involvement on the down low, but they may come under scrutiny because the donations that come from the annual Torment charity concert are a matter of public record. She's not sure how that will be perceived."

I squeeze Ryder's hand, as Rod ushers us into the building via a concealed back door. Judging by the screams and shouts reaching us from the front of the hotel, I think it's safe to say quite the crowd has amassed. When Rod issued an announcement a couple days ago, confirming Ryder Stone was holding a press conference, speculation among the media and his fans was rife. Everyone is wondering what today is about, and interest is high.

"I hope it works out," Rod says, patting Ryder on the back. "I know how much the charity means to you."

"We've actually discussed starting a new charity in Cory's name," I supply.

Rod slams to a halt. "I think that's a wonderful idea, and if you need any help with it, you know where I am."

Ryder slings his arm around my shoulders, smiling at me. "It was my wife's idea, and I couldn't be prouder of her."

I stretch up and kiss his cheek. "You hanging in there?"

He sucks in a sharp breath, and tension lines his jaw. "I just want to get it over and done with."

"It'll be fine, Ryder," Rod says. "And we'll deal with whatever shit comes at us as a team."

When we walk into the side room, at the back of the ballroom where Ryder will make his statement, I'm surprised to find Gar, Micah, Scott, and Linda there along with Jill and Liam and Kayla and Gage.

"What are you all doing here?" Ryder asks, shock splayed across his face.

"You didn't think we were going to let you do this by yourself now, did you?" Micah says, grabbing him into a hug.

"Can't let you hog all the limelight," Gar adds, slapping him on the back.

Scott approaches next, offering him his hand. "We're all proud of you and behind you one hundred percent."

I'm hugely emotional at the outpouring of love for Ryder, knowing how much he needs this because he's been a nervous wreck all day. Jill pulls Ryder into a hug. "You're doing the right thing," she says. "And people will understand once they hear the full story."

"Good luck, Ryder." Liam shakes his hand, smiling at me.

"You have a good heart, Ryder," Kayla says, grabbing him down to her level so she can kiss his cheek. "And everyone will see that."

"Savage Mania supports you," Gage says, hugging him briefly. "And if you need us to do anything, you've only got to ask."

"Thank you," Ryder chokes out. "Thank you all for being here."

When it's time, we walk out into the ballroom where the world's media is congregated. I take my place at Ryder's side as he stands before the curious crowd, holding his free hand. The remaining members of Torment, and Rod, line up behind us with the rest of our crew standing off to the side.

Some reporter notices our wedding bands, asking if we're married. "Yes, we got married recently, and I'm proud to call this beautiful woman my wife," Ryder confirms, shooting an adoring glance my way. "But that's not what today is about. Today is about a little boy named Cory Barnes and a past I have hidden from the world." Hushed whispers echo around the room. "I have a statement prepared, and I won't be accepting questions." I squeeze his hand as he begins to read out his statement, keeping my eyes focused on him and shutting out the room, as he tells the world the truth. His voice breaks in a few places, and I slide my arm around his waist, offering my physical support. Reporters shout out questions while he speaks, but Ryder ignores them, reading the words he'd painstakingly written. I'd helped him with it, but it's still so emotional listening to him reading the words out loud. At the end, he confirms our intent to set up a charity in honor of Cory and promises more details will be forthcoming in due course.

When he's finished, his shoulders collapse, and I can tell he's barely holding it together. His head hangs down, and he won't meet anyone's eye. Pulling him into my arms, I hug him close. "You did good, baby. I'm proud of you."

Rod makes a brief statement on behalf of Torment, confirming the band's support of Ryder, and then we make a fast exit. I try to block out the questions being shouted as we leave but it's hard to blot it all out, and some of it isn't pleasant.

Ryder doesn't speak as we make our way out of the hotel and into the waiting limo. He wants to get out of the city as fast as possible, so we've already said our goodbyes to the others inside. Rod is the only one still with us, and Mr. Jenkins, Ryder's attorney, is waiting in the limo. We head straight to the police station where Ryder makes a formal statement and lodges an official complaint about Ren Winters. Mr. Jenkins has already applied for a restraining order in both our names, and he anticipates it being approved within the next twenty-four hours.

Our last point of order is a conference call with Ryder's probation officer in Orange County. He's not pleased Ryder didn't inform him in advance, and he cautions there may be serious consequences. Already, social media is blowing up, and it's brought a spotlight on Orange County and the case all over again.

We shake hands with Mr. Jenkins and Rod after the call has concluded, and I'm confident both those guys will do everything in their power to ensure Ryder is kept out of jail. Then we head to the airport, and I only feel Ryder start to relax once the plane is taxiing down the runway.

When we get home, we change into comfy clothes, order takeout and snuggle on the couch. Ryder hasn't said much since the press conference, but I don't pressure him to talk. I'm just there for him, hugging and kissing him, letting him know how much I love him. We purposely avoid checking out comments online and head to bed early. Tears stream down his face as he tenderly makes love to me, and I hold him close all night, praying we've done the right thing and that this will finally enable him to move on and leave the past in the past.

"WHAT'S ALL THAT?" I ask a few days later when Mike arrives in the kitchen carrying four massive gray sacks.

"Fan mail sent over from the label."

I frown, wondering if it's wise to show that to Ryder. He's been very melancholy and closed off the last few days. "I think I should check some of it out before Ryder returns from his run. I don't want him upset if there's anything nasty in there."

The story of Ryder's true identity has gone viral, and public debate is divided. His fans have stuck loyally by his side, defending him online, while various expert child psychologists argue about the case in scheduled TV interviews. Some are siding with Ryder, explaining he was a vulnerable child who was preyed on by older boys and he's already served his time, while others argue his youth and his lack of involvement in the actual murder don't negate his culpability. Parent support groups lambast him for being a bad role model for their children, and calls for his resignation from Torment are widespread.

I'm trying to shield him from the media, but he's prone to self-destructive behavior and I've caught him checking out stuff on his cell on countless occasions. I've beseeched him to not look at it, but I can't force him to ignore it, and I know it's easier said than done, especially when you know the whole world is talking about you and casting judgment.

I'm trying to keep things as normal as possible at home, and keeping conversation away from those tough subjects, but it's challenging. Mr. Jenkins confirmed the restraining orders are operational, but Ren is in the wind. The police say there is no official record of Ren Winters after age seventeen, and he's clearly using a false identity.

They have taken fresh statements from some of the other members of Z-Crew, and they've confirmed the truth. It appears languishing in a jail cell for eight years has relinquished their supposed loyalty to their old gang leader. Vincent, Ryder's only friend back then, and the only other member who is currently free, has also corroborated Ryder's account of events. All the statements are classified, in order to protect the identities of those involved and to keep the media from blowing this up into an even bigger shitstorm.

"Good idea," Mike says, propping the first bag up on the island unit and pulling out a stool. "I'll help."

I have a healthy pile of letters and gifts open in front of me by the time Ryder arrives back from his run. Tears are streaming down my face as I read every heartfelt message.

"What's going on?" Ryder asks, using the bottom of his tank to rub the sweat from his forehead.

I jump up and throw my arms around him. "I've been reading your fan mail. You should too. You need to see how loved you are. How much your fans support you."

Ryder extricates himself from our embrace. "I'm all sweaty and gross, babe."

I circle my arms around his neck again, pulling him back into me. "I happen to love you all sweaty." I wiggle my brows suggestively.

Mike coughs loudly. "I do not need to hear that shit. It's bad enough listening to the moans and screams coming out of your bedroom at night."

"You need to get laid," Ryder quips.

"Don't I fucking know it," Mike laments with a pitiful sigh, as he touches his fingers to his earpiece, tuning us out.

Ryder looks over at the bags on the floor. "That's a lot of fan mail."

"I can go through it for you if you like, but I really think you should read it. I think it'll help. They're all on your side."

"Honestly, babe," he says, going to the refrigerator and removing a bottle of water. "The only two things that'll help is knowing that shithead is behind bars and finding out if they're going to prosecute me for anything." I know he's on edge waiting to discover if they plan to charge him with anything. Mr. Jenkins is in daily contact with the authorities in Orange County trying to smooth things over.

"Eh, boss." Mike rubs the back of his neck, standing. "We have a bit of a situation out at the front gate."

"What kind of situation?" I ask before Ryder can.

"There's an unknown man asking to be let in."

"Just tell him to fuck off," Ryder says. "He's probably just paparazzi." We've had reporters and TV crews camped outside the front gate since the story broke. A well-known network even sent drones overhead trying to capture footage. They have no sense of decency. No moral compass whatsoever.

Mike steps up to Ryder, eyeballing him with evident concern. "He's claiming he's your father."

39

RYDER

I stumble back, staring at Mike in shock. "He's lying," I blurt. "I've never known my father. I'm not sure my mother even knew who he was."

"He says he has photos and paperwork that prove he's your dad."

I shake my head. "I … no. It's got to be a ruse. Some creative paparazzo trying to worm his way into the house."

"Den was at the gate when he arrived, and he's already verified his identity with his police buddy. He's not a journalist or paparazzi. He's actually a doctor. An ex-US-Army doctor. His credentials are stellar. I don't think he's lying."

My mouth hangs open, and a thousand thoughts are racing through my mind.

"Babe." Zeta cups my face. "Look at me, Ryder." I stare into her eyes and some of my stress evaporates. Her touch and her belief in me gives me strength every day. "Why don't I go down to the gate with Mike and talk to the man. We'll determine his agenda and call you then."

I find myself nodding. "Yeah, okay." I look over at Mike. "Den's sure he's not Ren." I wouldn't put it past that asshole to show up here. It's one of the reasons I've increased the security detail again. I doubt even the president is as well protected as we are. But I'm taking no chances. Ren is out for my blood. I have no doubt about that.

Mike nods. "He used the image software checker on him. He's not Ren. He's too old anyway."

I blow air out of my mouth. "Okay." Pulling my wife into my arms, I say, "Be careful. I'll wait for your call."

Zeta leaves with Mike, and after a quick shower and a change of clothes, I spend an anxious fifteen minutes pacing the length of my living room waiting for her call. I jump on my cell when it rings, answering it immediately.

"Babe, I think you need to sit down," Zeta says.

I slump to the ground on the spot. "It's true?"

"The minute we set eyes on him we knew. You're the spitting image of him, Ryder. It's like looking at an older version of you. In the photos he had of him with your mom, it's like looking at your doppelganger. He has some letters they exchanged, and it seems to be legit." She pauses for a bit. "What do you want to do? Shall I bring him up to the house, or do you need time to process this?"

"What does he want from me?"

"He just wants to talk. He didn't know where you were, Ryder. He's spent years trying to find you. He has a thick file from a P.I. confirming his efforts. I think he just wanted to find his son."

"How can he want to know me after discovering what I've done?"

"From what he's said, he feels bad that you were exposed to such a horrific childhood, and he doesn't blame you."

I drag a hand through my hair, my heart thumping wildly against my ribcage. "I don't know, Zeta. I don't know what to do. What do you think?"

"It's your call, Ryder. But I think you should speak to him. He's been at the gate for over an hour, and those asshole reporters have been sniffing around, like bloodhounds. It's safe to assume they're going to discover who he is and break the story. It might be best to have spoken to the man first, and ... he seems lovely, genuine. I don't think there is any malicious intent."

"Okay. Bring him up to the house." I hang up abruptly, race to the bathroom, and puke my guts up. After rinsing my mouth out with water, I return to the main room, pacing the floor as I wait. My hands are shaking as footsteps approach, and I'm rooted to the floor, my eyes fixated on the entry point to the open-plan living area. Blood thrums in my ears; my heart is beating crazy fast, and my palms are sweaty. I hear Zeta's voice and another deeper one, and I feel like puking again. They come around the corner, stepping into my line of sight, and everything locks up inside me.

Holy shit.

Zeta was right.

It's like looking in a futuristic mirror and seeing an image of myself twenty years down the line.

He's tall like me with dark blond hair worn much shorter than mine and the same hazel eyes. Even the shape of his jawline and high cheekbones is identical to mine. He's wearing khaki pants, a white button-down shirt, and a navy blazer. He's rooted to the spot too, and we're just staring at one another across the room. Zeta has her hand to her mouth, and there are tears in her eyes. Mike has discreetly removed the men standing guard in the room, giving us privacy.

My heart is thudding painfully, my breathing ragged, as I'm grappling to deal with this. So many different emotions are racing through me, and I'm overwhelmed, unsure how to handle this. My eyes must display my panic because Zeta is across the room in a flash, hands on my face, forcing my gaze to hers. "Breathe, honey. Nice and deep. In and out." She draws breaths with me, keeping her eyes on mine, until my anxiety dampens down.

"Ryder. Are you okay?" The man—my father—asks.

"I don't know," I croak, my throat dry.

"I didn't come here to cause you any pain, and I can come back another time if this is too much now."

I'm struck dumb as I stare at him. When I was little, I used to imagine what my dad looked like. I used to wish he'd show up and whisk me away. But he never did. "Why didn't you care about me?" I blurt. "You never came."

"I didn't know you were mine until it was too late." His eyes turn glassy. "If I had known, I would never have left you with Brenda."

"Why don't you sit down, and I'll make us some coffee," Zeta suggests, pulling me over to the couch and gesturing for him to follow. She pushes me down onto the couch, kissing me on the lips. "Ryder, you need to hear what Noel has to say. Trust me. You want to hear this."

She leaves us to get drinks, and I scrub a hand across my jaw. "Okay. Let's hear it."

"I grew up around the corner from your mom. Had a massive crush on her when I got older and started noticing girls."

"I guess there's no accounting for taste." My scathing tone reveals my bitterness.

He shifts a little on the end of the couch, looking forlorn. "She wasn't always like that. Brenda was actually really sweet when I first knew her. We dated for a few years, and things were good between us until she changed. She became secretive and started blowing me off a lot. I discovered she'd been using drugs the same time I found out she was cheating on me. It broke my heart to break up with her, but she wasn't the girl I'd fallen in love with. Turns out, the guy she left me for was a pimp, and soon, she was … well, I think you know."

"Opening her legs for any asshole. Yeah, I know that part." A sour taste floods my mouth.

"I found out she was pregnant a few months after we split up," he continues. "I went to her. Asked her outright if the baby was mine, and she laughed in my face and told me no. She'd been having sex with this older, rich man. Someone her pimp had lined up, and she told me he was the baby's father. I had no reason to doubt her, and I was heartbroken at learning the extent of her betrayal."

He clasps his hands in his lap, staring at me with honest eyes. It's hard to look at his face and see my own features reflected back at me. "I joined the army straight after that, and I was overseas for a few years. I did a couple missions abroad before I was promoted and stationed at the military base in Boston."

Zeta comes back into the room, handing coffees out before sinking into the seat beside me. She places her free hand on my thigh, rubbing my leg in a soothing gesture, and I pull her in closer to my side. "Congratulations on your wedding, by the way. I saw the reports online. I'm happy for you." His smile is sincere, but I'm not about to get all buddy-buddy with him until I have all the facts.

"Thank you," Zeta says. "We've waited a long time to be together."

"When did you find out I was your son?" I ask, jumping in before the conversation gets derailed.

"Your mother called me when you were on trial." A muscle ticks in my jaw. "I was shocked at her complete lack of remorse when she admitted she'd lied. She confirmed you were my son. She had used you to blackmail that other man she'd been sleeping with. He'd been handing over child support for a few years before he asked for a paternity test. He cut her off when he discovered you weren't his child. She told me she tried to find me, no doubt to extort money from me too, but she was unsuccessful, until Monica gave her my details."

"Cory's mom?" I frown.

A pained look stretches across his face. "Yeah."

I'm about to ask why the hell she'd have his details, when

he speaks up again, continuing his explanation. "I told Brenda if the paternity test confirmed you were my son that I'd take responsibility for you. She took great pleasure in telling me what'd happened and that you'd most likely be sent to juvie. I hung up on her when she told me that. I was in complete shock. I …" He draws a shuddering breath, his eyes filling up.

"You hated me," I supply. "You were glad you'd had nothing to do with me." Zeta wraps her arm around me, and I put my cold coffee down.

"No, I … well, I was very confused, and it was a hugely upsetting time for me. I was devastated that you were involved. It took me a few months to deal with the … implications, but Clare—she was my fiancée then—she helped me deal with it. You were only a kid, and I knew you'd had no positive guidance in your life. I spoke to Monica, and she told me how you used to babysit Cory, how you looked after him, and that helped me come to terms with it."

"Yet, you still did nothing," I say through gritted teeth. "So, you hadn't really come to terms with it. And, you know what, I get it. Your son was a monster. No one would blame you for wanting to keep your distance." Zeta rubs her hand up and down my arm.

He shakes his head. "That's not how things happened." He places his empty coffee cup down on the table. "Your mom had been sending me threatening messages and calls for months. She told me unless I gave her ten thousand dollars she'd go to the press and reveal I was your father. At that time, I had just set up my medical practice, and Clare and I were due to get married soon. I didn't want the press attention, for me or you, but I also didn't want to abandon you. So, I struck a deal with her. I told her I'd give her the money provided she got me your DNA for a paternity test."

"That's why she visited me." I shake my head. "She only came that one time, and I never understood why she swabbed my mouth." My eyes burn with renewed anger. "She was only doing it because there was something in it for her."

"I'm sorry, Ryder. I'm sorry you had to grow up like that. If I'd known, I would've fought her for custody. That's what my plan was when she eventually told me the truth, but I wanted proof you were mine first because I didn't trust a word out of her mouth by then."

"So, what happened?" Zeta asks.

"Brenda overdosed the day after I got the results confirming you were my son. You were already in the system, and your identity had been changed, and I didn't know how to find you. She hadn't completed any of the paperwork before she died, so I hired a lawyer to help me, but we kept hitting red tape and a brick wall. Your identity was sealed, and I was told that information could not be disclosed. The only thing the authorities would agree to was that you would be notified and given my contact details upon your release."

"No one told me anything."

"Zeta just mentioned that, and I'm furious. I received confirmation that you had been notified, and I'll be sending a strongly worded communication via my attorney demanding the truth. All these years, I've believed you knew who I was but didn't want to have anything to do with me. I thought perhaps you were afraid that I wouldn't be able to love you after what happened to him, but that's not the case. I've spent thousands of dollars hiring various private investigators to try and find you, because I wanted to speak to you face to face, to tell you I love you and I forgive you. That it doesn't mean we can't have a relationship because of what happened with your brother. My sons were watching your press conference, and they called me in to the room. I couldn't believe it was you although there was no denying the resemblance. Wilder and Wes were so excited, because they've known how long I've tried to find you. I came here as soon as I located your whereabouts because I would really like an opportunity to get to know you. Clare and the boys would too. In fact, they can't believe Ryder Stone from Torment is their big brother."

I'm stunned at the news I have half-brothers, but I'm more concerned with something else he said. "What did you mean by what happened with my brother?" He's not making much sense.

He draws a long breath, dragging his hand through his hair in a gesture that is freakily similar to mine. "It's okay, Ryder. I don't blame you. Not anymore. After talking with Monica, I drew some comfort from the fact you loved him while he was alive, and I know you did your best to stop it from happening that day. I've made plenty of mistakes in my life, and it was those mistakes that led to your brother dying that day. I accept the part I played in the whole horrible mess."

A shiver works its way through me, and I'm chilled to the bone, my brain refusing to go there. "I don't understand." Zeta bolts upright, her eyes wide with alarm. Bile travels up my throat, and ice has replaced the blood flowing through my veins.

"You're not saying …" Zeta's voice is laced with shock and concern, and she holds onto me tight.

Noel's brows climb to his hairline and his eyes pop wide. "Oh my God. You don't know?" He stands and starts pacing the living room. Horror washes over his face.

I'm immobile. I can't move. All my muscles have tensed up.

This can't be happening.

It's not real. It's not real. It's not real.

I wipe my sweaty palms down the front of my jeans, and my heart is beating so fast it feels like I'm on the verge of a coronary.

Noel bends down in front of me. "Ryder, I thought you knew, but they never told you, did they?"

"No! No! Get out!!" Zeta takes hold of Noel's arm, yelling

for Mike. "You can't come in here and drop a bomb like that! You can't do that to him!"

Somehow, I find the strength to look him in the eye. I'm shaking all over, screaming inside my head, but I can't deny the truth anymore. His words all slot into place. "Cory was your son too, wasn't he?"

He nods with tears streaming down his face.

Oh, fuck no.

My heart is pounding, and blood rushes to my brain, leaving me light-headed. The room spins, blurring out. Cory's sweet little face flashes before my eyes, and I squeeze them shut, willing him to go away. When I reopen them, he's gone, but so is everyone else. I exist in a void, and nothing or no one else is here for me. I'm alone with this. Drowning. Suffocating. Grasping for air.

Wrapping my arms around my waist, I start rocking back and forth as the magnitude of Noel's revelation sinks in. "I killed him. I killed him. I killed my own brother."

40

ZETA

Ryder has completely checked out. He's staring blankly into space, rocking back and forth, with his arms clutched around himself, murmuring "I killed him" over and over. Every few seconds, he shivers profusely, but he doesn't stop the rocking motion, and it's destroying me seeing him like this. Noel is sobbing, and I'm still in complete shock as Mike bounds into the room, quickly surveying the scene. "Fuck. What's happened?"

"I need you to escort Noel out." I'm amazed at how polite I sound when I'm screaming and crying on the inside.

"Zeta, I'm so sorry. All these years, I assumed he knew," Noel's voice is laced with anguish. "Monica never said he didn't, and I presumed that's why Ryder kept his distance from me all these years. That he thought I hated him because he was involved in my other son's murder. When he spoke out at the press conference, I thought he'd come to terms with it all. That I'd finally get a chance to connect with my son. I would never have come here like this if I'd known."

"Noel, I don't know what to believe, and I'm not being rude, but my primary concern right now is Ryder."

We both look at my husband, and my heart aches looking

at him holding onto himself, staring blankly off into space. His jerky rocking movements attest to his fragile state of mind.

"Try talking to him," Noel says, swiping his eyes and standing. He hands a set of keys to Mike. "I know you want to throttle me right now, but I promise I mean him no harm. He's my son, and I want to help. Can you get someone to grab my medical bag from the trunk of my car? I fear he's having a dissociative break, and I can assist in getting him the care he needs."

"Zeta." Mike looks to me for guidance.

I glance at Noel as I kneel down in front of Ryder. There is nothing but genuine remorse and concern on Noel's face, and I have no fucking clue how to help Ryder, so I need him to stay. "Get the bag."

"Ryder, honey." I gently place my hands on his face, and his skin feels cold. "Baby, I'm here. What do you need me to do?" He's still rocking, looking straight through me, as if I don't exist. "Ryder, can you hear me?" I press a kiss to his forehead. "I love you." He keeps rocking, staring vacantly into thin air, as if he's no longer aware of his surroundings.

"What do I do?" I beseech Noel.

"Exactly what you're doing. Just stay with him and let him know you're here for him. Let him know you love him. I'll check his vitals, and we can wait a bit to see if he comes out of it."

"And if he doesn't?"

"Then we'll need to call in a specialist to help."

I rub a tense spot between my brows as I take Ryder's hands in mine, working hard to keep calm. I want to scream at Noel. To shout this is all your fault. To rewind time and never suggest we let him in to the house. But I don't want to do any of that for fear it may startle Ryder.

The longer he sits there in a catatonic daze, just rocking back and forth, uncommunicative and unfocused, the more worried I become. He's been dealing with so much for so long, and he was already stressed out enough over his recent admission without this adding to the pile. I'm seriously concerned for his mental state.

When Mike returns with Noel's bag, we share worrisome expressions while Noel performs a few quick tests. "Ryder, honey. I'm right with you. Can you let me know if you hear me?" I implore, waiting patiently for some kind of sign, but there's nothing. Mike squeezes my shoulder in solidarity while Noel taps away on his cell.

"Zeta." I look across at Noel. "I think we should consider referring Ryder to this place."

I walk to his side, accepting the cell and swiping through images of a private psychiatric hospital about an hour away. "Do you really think it's necessary?" I hate the thought of sending him someplace like that.

"Look at him."

As Noel says that, Ryder jumps up screaming, and he starts pacing the room, grabbing fistfuls of his hair. "No! No! No!" He slams his fist into the wall repeatedly, and my heart is breaking. "Leave him alone. Just leave him alone!" When he swings around to us, his face is pale, beads of sweat dot his brow, and his eyes are manically searching for something we can't see. "I said leave him alone!" he roars, running across the room and slamming into the glass wall before any of us can stop him. Falling to the ground, he curls into a fetal position, moaning and crying, and I rush to his side with tears pouring down my face. Blood trickles out of his nose, and a slight lump is swelling on his forehead. He holds onto himself, curled into a ball, rocking on the floor.

"Make the call, Noel," I say as Mike drops to his knees beside me, barely holding back tears. He wraps his arm around my shoulder, comforting me as I watch helplessly while my husband falls to pieces in front of my eyes.

Several hours later, Ryder has been admitted for assessment at the psychiatric hospital on the south shore. Because he wasn't lucid enough to sign himself in, I had to do it. It's one of the hardest things I've ever had to do, but I don't see that I have any choice. Ryder has spent the last few hours alternating between manic and catatonic episodes, and I'm at a loss how to help him, because he's not in the real world right now. His mind is clearly crashing, and I've got to trust he's in the best place to help him.

Over the course of the next seventy-two hours, I only leave the hospital to go home and grab a quick shower and some clean clothes, and then I'm back by my husband's side.

They sedated him the first twenty-four hours, for his own safety, and since then, he's seen a succession of different doctors and psychologists, who have all confirmed he's in the middle of a mental breakdown. He's going to need long-term intervention to deal with the symptoms and the causal effects and to help restore his mental health.

Although he's a shell of his former self, his behavior has stabilized, and he's aware of his surroundings now. But he's crying all the time and clinging to me, and I hate to see him like this. Mike and I are the only ones who have been with him. Noel voluntarily went back to Boston, understanding that seeing his son now might trigger another episode. I took his contact details, and I promised to call him soon.

My own therapist has been a lifesaver. She flew down to meet me, and we've discussed the options for Ryder's recovery. She helped me to identify a fantastic facility in Florida offering holistic and experimental residential treatment in serene surroundings especially tailored for patients in need of post-traumatic stress disorder recovery. They focus on the under-lying issues, getting to the root of the matter, and help patients work through them via a variety of different programs. It's set on an extensive estate with outdoor cabins, and there are a lot of physical activities and different therapy options on offer, which I think will suit Ryder.

I'm loath to leave him in a hospital like this where the

approach is a combination of drugs and therapy. While that may work for some patients, with Ryder's drug abuse background, I want to try an alternative method. The Florida facility seems perfect. The difficult part is the fact we'll be separated while he's receiving treatment, but I can't be selfish. I just want him to get the help he needs. I feel guilty that I didn't see he was seriously struggling and recommend something like this before he had a break, but all that matters is getting him the appropriate help now and supporting him in whatever way I can.

Ryder is hugely reluctant to agree, at first, but he eventually approves it, because he knows he needs the help, and I'm glad that he wants to get better rather than falling back into his usual addictive behaviors.

The day I drop him off is a horrible day. We're clinging to one another. He's crying, and I'm trying my fucking hardest not to. I feel like my jaw might break from forcing myself to smile so much. I won't see him for six weeks, and I already miss him.

The instant Mike drives away from the center, I burst out crying, and I can't stop. Everything I've been holding in the last few days is let loose, and anguished howls rip from the back of my throat. Mike pulls over to the side of the road, wrapping his arms around me. "You're doing the right thing, and Ryder knows that too. He would never have agreed otherwise. This is the best way to help him."

"I love him so much," I sob. "And I feel so useless."

"Just be there waiting for him, Zeta. That's the best way you can help him. And make sure to look after yourself too."

As we fly back to the Hamptons, I think of Mike's words while I flip through the educational material the kind woman in the center gave me to read before I left. It outlines the four-day family week I'll be allowed to share with Ryder once he's gotten the first six weeks behind him. There are special educational sessions for family members to provide tools to enable us to support our loved ones when they return home. There are also group therapy sessions and various other activities we can do together to aid his recovery. The brochures discuss how looking after my own mental health and wellbeing is just as important, and I vow to do everything I can to ensure I'm strong enough to help Ryder through this.

One of the first things I do is organize Luc to come stay. Ryder had been making plans with his sister Kat before he had his breakdown. She travels with him on the private jet Rod organized, staying for a couple of days to help him get settled.

I love having Luc around, and it helps me feel closer to Ryder. I don't feel as alone with him here, and he provides much-needed comfort. I never forget that Ren is still out there somewhere, and while this place is like Fort Knox, and I can't imagine anyone getting in, I'd be lying if I said I didn't wake up constantly during the night, feeling lonely and afraid.

Luc also offers me invaluable encouragement because he's only just come out of a mental health treatment program, and he understands, to a point, what Ryder is going through. We spend hours trawling the grounds of Ryder's vast estate, and I push his wheelchair along the promenade in town while we talk and catch up.

"I'm so happy you're here, Luc. I think I'd be going out of my mind without your company," I admit, as we sit outside on the terrace one evening. We're both covered under a thick plaid blanket, sipping drinks as we watch the waves crash onto the shore in the near distance. Now that we're into October, the weather has cooled down, and it's no longer shorts and T-shirt season. The crowds have significantly died down around the town and a lot of the stores and restaurants have switched to off-peak hours. From what Ryder's told me, he would usually be back in the city this time of year, only venturing down here on weekends when he had free time. But I don't mind it like this. I love this house, and I feel very settled here.

"Glad to be of service, ma'am," Luc jokes, chinking his glass against mine. "This is helping me too. It's exactly what I needed, and it's been great to catch up. I missed you."

I lean in and kiss his cheek. "I missed you too, and I'm sorry I wasn't there for you when you needed me."

He swats my concern away. "Stop apologizing. There's no need, and we've already discussed this. I've spent a lot of time in therapy trying to move past my regrets. It's a negative emotion and one that has the potential to drag me down, so I'm trying to live more in the moment."

"And you're feeling good now?" I don't want to pry or pressure him into talking if he doesn't want to.

He nods, smiling slowly. "For the first time in ages, I'm actually focusing on the future. On all the things I can still do instead of fixating on all the things I can't." He squeezes my hand. "Please don't worry about me because I'm good. Ryder should be your only concern. I'm here to ease your burden, not add to it."

I kiss his cheek again. "You could never be a burden. Never. I love that you're here with me."

"You might regret saying that when it's time for me to leave and I don't want to go," he semi-jokes, taking a quick slurp of his soda.

I sit up straighter, looking him directly in the eyes. "There's no ticking clock here, Luc. You can stay with us for as long as you like. Forever if you want." I nudge my head in the direction of the guesthouse. "We have plenty of room, and I know Ryder would love you to stay, so please don't worry about that. You are free to come and go as you please."

"Thank you." He turns to me with tears in his eyes. "I didn't realize how much I needed you guys back in my life."

"I know the feeling well." I curl my feet underneath me, resting my head on his shoulder. "I'm missing him really badly today."

"I know you are, sweetheart." He presses a kiss to the top

of my head. "But it's only two weeks until you'll see him again."

"I can't wait—even if I know he might not be himself. I don't care. I just want to hold him and tell him I love him."

"I'm so happy you guys got married. I always knew it would happen, and you're good for him, Zeta. You were the only one who ever put a smile on his face."

"I hope he's happy with the work we've done on the charity."

"Of course, he will be. He'll be proud of how well you're coping. It's not easy dealing with the fans and the media, writing Torment's biography, helping me set up the charity, and running a magazine from here."

I take a sip of my wine. "I'm not the one running a magazine. Harrison Meadows is." When I called the CEO a few weeks ago to advise him to hire someone new in my position, I could tell his nose was out of joint at the fact Ryder transferred ownership of *RockOut* to me. I did my best to reassure him, confirming I had no plans to return at this time or to interfere in his competent management of the business, and as long as he updates me weekly, I'm good with that for now. I'm not sure whether I'll want a more hands-on role once Ryder is back, but my priority is helping him readjust, and I just want to be here for him.

I've made great progress on the biography these last few weeks, and I'll have my first draft for the editor ahead of schedule, which takes some pressure off me. I want to be able to give Ryder my undivided attention once he's back home and I'm going to do whatever is needed during our separation to pave the way for that.

AFTER WHAT FEELS LIKE ETERNITY, but is actually three months in reality, Ryder is finally coming back home. As I stand on the asphalt of the private runway, watching Ryder's jet crawl to a standstill, I'm bursting with excitement and happiness at the thought of having my husband home. I look down at Luc, and he raises his hand for a high-five, just like he used to do when we were in juvie. I throw back my head, laughing as our palms connect.

I'm watching the plane like a hawk, desperate to see my husband's beautiful face. Although I got to visit him twice, for two four-day family stays, I have missed that man more than I ever thought it was possible to miss a person. In some ways, it reminded me of what it was like when he left me after juvie, and I hated the old feelings it resurrected. But I got through it because I could see how much it was helping Ryder. The facility worked wonders for him, and he's in a much better place even if there's still a lot more he needs to process. It's why he will continue with a treatment program locally with my full backing and support.

My pulse spikes when the door to the jet opens, and I hold my breath as I wait for a glimpse of my love. The instant his booted foot lands on the top step, I take off running, my heart pounding, adrenaline coursing through my body. He's running toward me too, and we meet halfway, crashing into one another.

Cupping my face, he smashes his lips to mine as my arms curl around his neck. Our kissing is ravenous, hungry, needy, and we cling to one another, afraid to break apart in case it's not real. The gentle whirring sound of Luc's approaching wheelchair reminds me we're not alone, and I break our kiss, keeping my arms wrapped around my husband as I turn us to face our friend.

"Young." Ryder grins, reaching down to do the whole man hug thing. "Great to see you. Thanks for looking after my girl again. I owe you."

"It's my pleasure, but let's not aim for a third time, right?"

He presses a fierce kiss to my temple, hugging me closer. "I'm never leaving her again."

Ryder rolls down the window on the SUV as we leave the airport, waving to the legion of fans lining the road.

Although we tried to keep details of his treatment from the media, someone leaked the news, and I felt the need to address it. After consulting with Rod and Ryder, I took over Ryder's social media accounts and posted regular updates. I didn't disclose anything private, but I let his fans know he was doing well and asking for them. The outpouring of love bolstered me on bad days, and I know Ryder will be blown away by all the messages and posts and the mountains of fan mail and gifts he's received.

"It's fucking great to be home," Ryder says once we're back at the house. "I've missed you so much," he adds, pulling me into his arms. "And we have so much lost time to make up for." He discreetly nudges his hard-on into my belly, and my core pulses with need.

"That we do, dear husband." I can't contain my glowing smile as I think of the happy news I have to tell him. I called his therapist at the center before he left, because I was concerned the timing was all wrong, but he believes this is exactly what Ryder needs to focus forward and look to the future instead of remaining trapped in the past.

After we demolish the pot roast I made, Luc retreats to his room, knowing we need some alone time. Ryder all but sprints to the bedroom, and I'm laughing as he pulls me inside, shuts the door, and pins me up against the wall. "I know we have lots to talk about, but I need to be inside you, baby, because you've never looked more beautiful than you do today." He cradles my face. "I cannot begin to explain how much I've ached without you. I might as well have chopped off a limb. Being away from you was the worst kind of physical and emotional wrench, and I'm determined to avoid that again at all costs."

His hand slowly slides up my thigh and under my dress, but I clasp his wrist, gently nudging him aside. Taking his hand, I walk us over to the bed, sitting down on the edge and patting the space beside me. He frowns, looking a little hurt, and I can't help but smile. "Don't worry, I'll be naked and moaning underneath you soon enough. I just have something I need to tell you first."

"Okay."

The frown is still in place, and I rub my thumbs across his furrowed brow, smiling as tears burn the back of my throat. "This is a good thing, honey." Or at least, I hope it is. We've spoken about starting a family before, and I know he has some concerns, but he never said he didn't want kids. I kiss his gorgeous mouth, and when I pull back, a sneaky tear has crept out of the corner of my eye. "I'm pregnant, Ryder. We're going to have a baby."

41

RYDER

I blink rapidly as I stare at my wife. My eyes lower to her belly, and I notice the tiny little bump there. At least now I know why she's positively glowing and why I haven't been able to keep my eyes or hands off her since I exited that plane.

"Say something."

I jerk my head up at the hesitation in her voice. "My baby's really growing inside you?" I ask, my tone incredulous, as my hands slide over her belly. "This is really happening?"

"Yes," she whispers. "Are you happy?" I hear the uncertainty again, and I snap out of my head. I never want to cause my wife another moment's pain, and I'm already fucking this up.

I pull her into my lap, circling my arms around her waist. "I'm deliriously happy. How could I not be? A little piece of you and a little piece of me is growing inside you." I kiss her lips tenderly. "Wanting a family with you has been my dream for so long, but I'm a little scared too. What the hell do I know about being a dad?"

"About as much as I know about being a mom," she admits. "But I believe that makes us ideal parent material because we know exactly how not to be." Her hands drift to her belly, and she smiles. "You are going to be the most loved little baby on the planet," she croons, and fuck, if that doesn't shoot my emotions into overdrive.

"Damn fucking straight." I rest my hands over hers, and her smile is blinding when she lifts her head to look at me. "I love you, Mrs. Stone, and you've made me unbelievably happy."

Pushing me down on the bed, she straddles me with a naughty look in her eye. "Well, today's your lucky day, Rock Star," she says, popping the button on my jeans. "Because I'm about to make you even happier."

We tear our clothes off in record time, and I'm pushing inside her warm heat a minute later, reveling in the feel and touch of our bodies as we rock against one another. It feels like I've waited a lifetime to make love to my wife again, and while I want to take it slow, my greedy cock has other ideas. "I'm not hurting you or the baby, am I?" I yank her legs up over my shoulders, tilting her hips up and jerking my cock all the way up inside her as I feverishly fuck her, thrusting in and out, my orgasm already building.

"Not possible," she pants. "I asked my Ob-gyn, and she said sex as normal was fine. You're good, baby. Fuck me hard."

And who am I to deny my wife anything?

We spend hours alternating between making love and talking, and having my wife back in my arms seems almost too good to be true. "I think we should move back to the penthouse," I say after we've been discussing our plans. "It's safer and less isolated in the winter. You'll be close to the magazine, and I need to be in the city for the promotion of the new album and getting our label up and running." The guys put everything on hold for me, and I can't ask them to wait any longer.

"I love it here, and I hate the thoughts of going back to

the city, but you're right, it makes the most sense. But can we move in January as I'd really like to do Christmas here?"

"Me too." I nuzzle my nose into her neck. "I was thinking you could ask Jill, Liam, and the kids, and maybe Luc could invite Kat and her family, if they want to come and celebrate Christmas with us? And maybe the guys and Kayla and Gage could come out a few days later, and we could have that wedding party we didn't get around to?"

She twists around in my arms, grinning. "I would love that. We could make it a joint wedding party and baby shower?"

I tweak her nose, my eyes fliting to her little baby bump again. "Have I told you how much I love you?" I murmur, raking my lips up and down her neck.

"You might have mentioned that one time or twenty." She teases, twisting around to kiss my lips. "But you could tell me a thousand times, and it'd never grow old."

"I plan on telling you gazillions of times because the way I feel about you will never grow old."

Christmas and New Year's comes and goes, and soon we're all packed up and moved to the city. I know Zeta's not a big fan of my penthouse, and I suspect I know the reason why, so I've hired a realtor to find us someplace new. "You don't have to do that, Rock Star," she tells me, handing me a plate with eggs and bacon on it. Maggie only comes in every second morning now because Zeta likes to do most of the cooking herself and she still has an issue with anyone picking up after her. "I know you've got a lot to do with the album and label release. We can house hunt after the baby arrives."

Getting up, I wrap my arms around her from behind, rubbing my hands over her noticeable bump. She's eighteen weeks along now, and the world knows I'm due to become a father.

Of course, that unleashed another round of debate with many claiming I'm unfit to be a father, but I invoked my new strategies to avoid reading anything that could set me back. My weekly therapy sessions are helping keep me on track, but there are certain things that I'm careful to avoid in case they trigger a relapse.

My father is one.

Ren Winters is another.

I'm still on edge because I know he's out there somewhere, plotting his revenge, and now I have a wife and child to protect.

Zeta never complains.

Not even when I smother her with my overprotectiveness. Three bodyguards go with her everywhere, and I have had locator chips installed on all her technical devices and the brand-new bulletproof SUV I bought her for Christmas. I'm taking no chances when it comes to that asshole.

"It's not any trouble, babe." I brush her hair to one side, kissing her shoulder. She shivers, and I smile into her skin, loving how responsive her body is to my touch. "I want you to be happy, and I know you're uncomfortable in my bachelor pad."

She spins around in my arms. "I'm sorry if I've made you feel like that. It's fine."

I drill her a look, as her cell pings on the counter behind her. "Babe. Honesty, remember?"

She grabs her cell, sighing. "I know it's only a house and I'm being silly, but sometimes, the thought of all the parties and girls gets to me. I hate sleeping in our bed imagining all the things you've done with other women in it."

I tuck her hair behind her ears. "And that's why we need to move. I don't ever want you feeling like that. That's another lifetime and a different me. You're the only woman who's ever captured my heart. The only woman who's ever known the real me."

"I know, babe." She frowns as she reads her new text.

"What's wrong?" I tip her chin up with one finger, forcing

her to look at me. She bites the inside of her cheek in an obvious tell, and I can almost hear her brain churning. "Just tell me."

"I've wanted to mention it, but you didn't bring him up, and I don't want to upset you."

My shoulders instantly stiffen, understanding who she's referring to. "You're texting with Noel?" I have trouble referring to him as my dad.

"I kept him updated when you were in the treatment center. I didn't want to keep that from you, but your therapist feared talking about him might set you back. He told me to wait until you brought it up, but you never mention him, so I wasn't sure what to do."

"I don't mention him because that's still the one thing I'm really struggling with," I admit, because I owe her this honesty. We spoke a little about this during our family therapy sessions at the center, but I haven't discussed it since I came home for a reason.

It hurts too much to think about it.

Taking her plate, I pull her over to the table, helping her into a chair and putting a fork in her hand. "You need to eat, babe." I kiss the top of her head and take a seat across from her. We're both quiet for a few minutes. "What kind of a man fathers kids with two different women, women who were friends, and then abandons them both?" I ask, shaking my head.

"It wasn't like that. He's spoken to me about it."

"You've talked with him?" I can't hide my surprise.

She nods, slowly chewing as she contemplates how to tell me this. "Luc and I went to see him in Boston. It was after I'd spoken to your therapist. Noel was calling me almost daily, and I just needed to know the full picture before I could trust him with details of your recovery."

My fork clangs to the table. "You've been to his house? Did you meet his wife and—" I'm unable to say it, because it's all tied to my guilt. My half-brothers are innocent, and in shutting Noel out, I'm shutting them out too, and that doesn't sit right with me. But I don't know how to have a relationship with them if I don't have one with our father. And do they even want one with me assuming they know what happened with Cory?

"I've met Clare and your brothers." She offers me a shaky smile. "They look like you too. Wilder is fifteen, and he—" She stops, obviously noticing my expression. "I don't have to tell you if you'd rather not know."

"I'd like to know," I whisper.

She reaches across the table and my hand meets hers half way. We link fingers and that small contact, that skin to skin touch, reminds me I'm not alone in this anymore. "Wilder reminds me of you so much. Not just physically, but he's crazy about music and computers, and he plays the guitar and writes songs. He's a typical teenager though," she laughs. "I swear he pouts better than any girl I've ever met. Wes is a little sweetheart. He's twelve, and he adores his big brother. He's also very excited to meet you. He plays football and basket-ball, and he's a really happy well-rounded kid. Clare was very warm and welcoming, and she was concerned about you."

Her smile fades when she spots the pain in my eyes. She comes and sits beside me, squeezing both my hands. "Are you mad at me for not telling you? Because, I swear, I wanted to, but the center advised me not to pressure you to talk about anything, to take your lead, and to try and get things back to normal. I swear I'm not keeping anything else from you, and I was just trying—"

I shut her down with a kiss, reeling her into my arms and pouring all my emotions into our lip-lock. "Babe. I'm not mad at you. Not at all. No one has done more for me than you, and I could live a thousand lifetimes and never get to thank you enough." I clasp her beautiful face in my hands. "You're my rock, Zeta. You've kept everything going in my absence. My fans adore you. The band adores you. Luc adores you." I rub a hand across her belly. "Our baby adores you. I adore you. So, no, I'm not mad at you. I'm just feeling ... conflicted. I want to meet my brothers, but Noel …"

"Hang on a sec," she says, getting up. "I have something that might help."

She leaves the room, returning a few minutes later with something clutched in her hands. Reclaiming her seat, she hands the items to me. "They are from your brothers. They asked me to give them to you."

I swallow over the lump in my throat as I open the hand-made card from Wes, tearing up at his childish handwriting and the innocent sentiment behind his words. I look up at Zeta as I open the second page. "Wilder wrote you a song," she softly explains, and tears roll down my face as I read over it.

"It's good. Kid's got talent," I rasp, my lips breaking into a smile.

"It's in his DNA." She caresses my face. "I could arrange a meeting with them if you want. You don't have to meet Noel. I can explain, and he'll understand. I think he's a good man, Ryder. He just wants to get to know you, and he understands it might take time, but I think it would be a mistake shutting him out of your life permanently."

"Why does he want to know me? How can he forgive me for the things I've done?" That's the crux of the issue for me. "How can I face him knowing I played a part in Cory's death?"

"I don't have all the answers, Ryder. You need to ask him that yourself. All I can tell you is he has accepted it, and he has forgiven you. I get a sense he blames himself too. For not being there for either of you."

"Tell me what he told you. About Cory's mom."

She swivels in her chair until she's facing me. "Are you

sure you're up to hearing it?" I nod, and she pecks my lips. "I love you, Rock Star."

I kiss her back. "I love you too."

Drawing a large breath, she starts to explain. "He told me that after he joined the army, he struggled to forget your mom even after everything she'd done to him. I think he really loved her at one time."

She looks sad, and I kiss her forehead. Even after everything she's seen and been through in her life, my wife is a firm believer in true love, and it saddens her that not everyone gets their happy ever after like us.

"Anyway," she continues, "it had been over five years since he'd seen her, but she still occupied his thoughts, so he decided to pay her a visit. He'd just come off a particularly difficult mission, seen a lot of horrific things, and he wasn't in a good place. Your mom wasn't at home, but Monica spotted him leaving the house and cornered him. The gist of it was he was vulnerable and she was manipulative. They ended up having sex, and he walked away more disgusted with himself."

"It seems I'm not the only one prone to moments of absolute stupidity," I admit.

"It's fucked up all right. Like history repeating itself. Monica wrote to him via the army, but he was overseas on a tour, and he only received her letter when he returned. She told him she'd had a baby boy and she needed help. He called her and arranged for her to come up to Boston. Once he confirmed that Cory was his, he set her up in an apartment and looked after them. He wasn't with her, as he'd already met Clare by then, but he told her he'd support them both until Cory was eighteen."

"That's where they disappeared to," I say, remembering the period when Cory was gone.

She nods. "Noel had to go away for a few weeks, and when he returned, Monica was gone. He guessed she'd returned to the old neighborhood, and he was disgusted to find she'd returned to her old lifestyle. He was in the process of seeking full custody of Cory when he … when he died," she quietly adds.

"Fuck." I rest my head on her shoulder, and she runs her fingers through my hair. Pain slices through me as I think about how close Cory came to getting out of there. To having a normal life.

"Noel now thinks Monica lied to your mom about who Cory's father was and that she only handed over his contact details while you were on trial to stick the knife in further."

"What a bitch."

"Yep. Although, it's possible that Brenda hadn't told Monica the truth about your father either and it all only came out later." Zeta shrugs, smoothing a hand up and down my back, and we don't talk for ages.

When I lift my head, her face is bursting with concern. I kiss her cheek. "I'm okay. I mean, I don't know what to do about Noel or my brothers, but I suppose it helps that he didn't deliberately abandon Cory either."

"He didn't willingly abandon either of you, and I know enough about him to believe he would've taken both of you out of that situation if he'd been aware in time."

"That does change things, but I still can't believe he can find it in his heart to forgive me enough to want to have a relationship with me. I'm ashamed, and I don't know if I can face him, face any of them."

"You don't need to make a decision on it now. Think about it. Let me know if you want to talk more about it or discuss it with your therapist. No one is rushing you. They will still be there waiting, whether it's one month or one year from now." She cradles my face in her hands. "And I'll be with you, every step of the way, supporting your decision, no matter what you decide."

42

ZETA

"Are you nervous?" I ask Ryder, turning around and sweeping my hair up into a messy pile on top of my head.

"Fucking terrified," he admits, pulling the zipper up on my maternity dress. He plants a soft kiss to the nape of my neck, and I tingle all over.

I spin around, draping my hands on his shoulders as my hair tumbles down my back. I move as close as I can get before landing one on him. I'm twenty-eight weeks pregnant now, and my belly's ginormous. But I can't complain because this pregnancy has been a dream. And Ryder's joy every step of the way has only made me love him even more. He hasn't missed a single appointment, and he treats me like a princess. My heightened sex drive and bigger boobs have only added to his enthusiasm, and our sex life is off the charts. We still can't get enough of one another, and I love it. I hope the fire that burns bright between us never fades.

"Your fans are going to love it, and I know you'll be amazing." This is Ryder's first time on stage since the VMAs, and after the last eight months we've had, he's understandably nervous.

He's also officially unveiling the Cory Barnes Foundation for Neglected Children tonight. Luc has worked tirelessly to set it up with the support of a small administrative team, and Ryder and I have been very hands on too. Ryder appointed Luc as CEO, and he's going to take charge of the charity because Ryder is busy with the label and the band is still promoting Torment's new album. The guys all agreed to postpone the tour, and now that they're not beholden to any record label, they can make that call and not have someone screaming in their ear. Linda, Scott's wife, is pregnant with their second child, and neither Ryder nor Scott wanted to be away touring when both babies are so small.

Luc moved into his own apartment in Greenwich Village the same time we moved into our new brownstone. He's only a few blocks away, which means we still see a lot of each other. He's been quietly dating one of the girls working for Torment's label for the last few weeks, and every time I see him, he has the biggest smile on his face. It warms my heart to know everyone is in such a good place.

Ryder's doing great, but he hasn't resolved anything with Noel or met his brothers yet although he did write back to them, and they are sharing regular messages and emails now. The Ren issue is still a noose around our neck, too, but I refuse to think any negative thoughts tonight, because this is a time to celebrate.

The band booked a small, exclusive venue for the show tonight. There were only one thousand tickets available, and they raffled two hundred tickets that were given out to members of their fan club. The other tickets sold at premium value with all proceeds going to the charity. The Cory Barnes Foundation will now be the sole beneficiary of the funds raised from the annual Torment charity concert too.

Fans line all roads leading to the venue, and a couple of press helicopters hovers in the skies overhead when we arrive. My eardrums protest loudly when Ryder helps me out of the limo to deafening roars and excited screams and shouts. The band members wave to their fans and pose for a few quick pictures before they're ushered inside.

I make my way to the private area secured for family and friends with Linda, Kayla, Mike, and a couple of other bodyguards. Savage Mania is playing a few numbers before Torment headlines, and it's their first official gig since they signed with the label. The guys pull off an incredible opener, and the enthusiastic crowd gives them a standing ovation when they finish.

My heart almost bursts with pride when they play the song I wrote for them, and it's definitely a moment I will cherish for the rest of my life. I'm working with them and another new sign-up on another couple of songs.

It seems Ryder's determined to make all my dreams come true.

As if I needed additional reasons to love my husband.

The audience almost lifts the roof off when Torment appears, and I'm screaming and shouting along with them. Watching Ryder on stage is hypnotizing. It's so easy to tell he's in his happy place when he's up there, serenading the crowd with his sultry voice, heartfelt lyrics, and flawless guitar playing. The songs from the new album are a big hit, and I especially love "Rewrite Our History," the song he wrote and dedicated to me. They play a pared-down acoustic version of it tonight with Ryder on guitar and Scott on the drums, and there isn't a dry eye in the house.

After the show is finished, I rush backstage to congratulate my husband. He swings me up into his arms—no easy feat with the extra weight I'm carrying—kissing me all over my face. His joy is contagious, and I'm grinning ear to ear when he finally puts me back down. They crack open a few bottles of bubbly, sharing the celebration with Savage Mania. I nudge Ryder in the ribs when I spot him glaring at Gus. "Stop that!"

"Don't worry, baby," he purrs, wrapping his arms around

my belly from behind and whispering in my ear. "I love winding him up any chance I get."

"You're terrible." I roll my eyes, but I'm grinning. Gus raises his glass to me from the other side of the room, waiting until Ryder looks up before blowing me a kiss. I crack up laughing. "I think you might have met your match with Gus."

Ryder chuckles. "He's actually a good guy, and we're good. Don't worry, baby."

We head out of the venue via the front entrance because the guys want to spend a little time thanking the fans outside. It's dark out, but the lights of the venue illuminate the substantial crowd outside.

I hang back with Linda and Kayla, surrounded by body-guards, as we watch our men working the crowd. I'm not even mad at the women who make blatant grabs for my husband or the ones who try to pull his head around for a kiss. Ryder effortlessly deflects their advances, and I know their love for him helped both of us through the rougher times. It's helped put things in perspective.

The groupies, now, are a completely different matter, but until they go on tour, I don't have to worry about that threat yet. And I trust my husband one thousand percent to stay faithful to me so I'm not losing sleep over it.

I'm smiling as I scan the crowd when a little flash captures my attention. A flickering light draws my eyes to a man standing in the middle of the crowd, staring at me. All the blood drains from my face as I instantly recognize him from the sneaky photograph Ryder took one time at a drop-off. His lips are curved into a sneer as he waves at me, intentionally ensuring I see him. But it's the raised gun in Ren's hand that scares me the most because he's aiming it directly at Ryder.

"Ryder!" I act on instinct, pushing past Mike and racing toward Ryder, trying to keep my eyes trained on Ren as I run. I'm screaming Ryder's name as he looks up, his eyes popping wide when he sees the alarm on my face. "Ren!" I yell. Ryder jerks his head around in the direction of my pointed finger as Mike barks out orders to the crowd. People start screaming and running in all directions, and it's complete chaos. I'm only a few feet away from Ryder when Ren twists around, angling the gun in my direction.

Intense pain explodes in my chest, rippling through my body as I fall backward. My hands instinctively cover my belly as my body impacts something hard. A blanket of darkness sweeps across my eyes right before I lose consciousness.

43

RYDER

I whip my head around when Zeta screams Ren's name, horror engulfing me as I lock eyes with my nemesis. I'm turning to run toward my wife when Ren switches his focus, directing the gun at Zeta. "No!" I roar, shoving Gar and Micah aside to get to my wife.

A shot rings out, as if in isolation, because I hear it so clearly despite the panicked cries of the crowd. My heart slows down as I watch the bullet enter my wife's body. Watch her glazed eyes flicker in and out as she tumbles to the ground. Mike reaches her before me, catching her head in his lap before it impacts the ground. I barely hear the gunshots being traded behind me, and I've no concern for my own safety. I have single-minded focus: Get to my wife and baby.

I drop to my knees when I reach them. Mike is cradling Zeta's head in his lap, his fingers pressed to the pulse point in her neck as he screams down the phone.

"Zeta, baby, can you hear me?" I'm trembling as I take hold of my wife's hand. Her skin feels cold, and I'm terrified. Blood oozes out of the wound in her chest, and I press my hands over it in a feeble attempt to stop the flow.

"Let me through! I'm a doctor!!" I lift my head up at the sound of his voice.

"Mike!" I nod in Noel's direction. "Get him over here now."

He nods, signaling to his guy to let my father through. "Ambulance is on its way."

Noel sinks to his knees beside me, looking into my face. "Don't look at me!!" I yell. "Look at her! Help her!" Blood continues to leak from her chest, coating my fingers.

He takes Zeta's pulse and leans his ear down over her mouth. "Her pulse is weak, but she's still breathing." Removing a bunch of gauze out of his medical bag, he hands it to me. "Put this over the wound and keep pressure on it." I place the wadded-up bandages over her chest, pressing down hard as instructed. "Someone get me a blanket!" Noel hollers, looking in the direction of the small group of staff who has gathered at the entrance to the venue.

I touch her cheek with a bloody finger. "Zeta, please hold on. Please don't leave me. I need you. Our baby needs you." Sirens blare, getting closer, and I pray to a God I long stopped believing in, begging him not to take my wife and my baby.

A young girl rushes over with a thin blue blanket. Noel thanks her before covering Zeta with it while I continue to put pressure on the wound. "Can you check the baby?" I plead.

He pulls a stethoscope out of his bag, shielding Zeta with his body as he gently rolls her dress up, placing the instrument on her bare belly. He listens for a few minutes, his brow furrowing, and I will the ambulance to hurry the fuck up. His eyes dart to mine, and a lump the size of a rock forms at the back of my throat. I can't even form words.

"The heartbeat is elevated. The baby could be in distress."

"But he's alive?" Mike asks, and I've never been more grateful because I couldn't force the words out.

Noel nods. "Yes, but we need to get her to hospital asap."

A flurry of activity at the other end of the venue draws my

eye, and I almost collapse at the sight of the EMS medics running toward us. Behind them, I spot several police cars pulling up to the scene.

I step aside, feeling utterly useless and completely destroyed, as the medical personnel converse with Noel, and they get Zeta onto a stretcher. "Go." Mike pushes me forward. "I'll talk to the police and handle whatever needs to be handled, and I'll meet you at the hospital."

"Ren?" I croak.

"Dead. Denver shot him."

I can't even feel any relief because I feel dead inside myself, but I force myself to snap out of it, locking my emotions up because my wife and child need me to be strong.

Zeta doesn't regain consciousness in the ambulance, and as I hold her hand, looking at her pale skin, the blood covering her immobile body, and the tubes and wires she's hooked up to, I pray like I've never prayed before.

At the hospital, they whisk her away from me, and I'm left pacing the hallway, alone with my fears until Rod and the guys arrive. Rod takes charge, getting us moved to a private waiting room, away from prying bystanders. I'm going out of my mind with worry, and no one will tell me a fucking thing.

When Noel arrives with a tall boy I'm guessing is Wilder, I rush toward him. "They won't tell me anything. I don't know what's going on!" My voice is cracked, my emotions veering all over the place as my mind wanders to places I don't want it to go to.

Tentatively, he places his hand on my shoulder. "I'll see what I can find out. I know it's hard, but try to keep calm." He looks at the boy at his side. "I know this isn't the time or place, but your brother wanted to come. This is Wilder. Wes has gone back to the hotel with my wife."

I swallow hard, looking at my brother for the first time, urging Noel to leave with a flash of my eyes.

"I'm sorry about what happened, and I hope Zeta's okay," he says in a surprisingly deep voice.

"Thanks. I'm sorry we had to meet under these circumstances." I scrub a hand across my chin. "What were you all doing there?"

"We came to watch the show." His eyes light up. "Man, you were fucking awesome. My mom started crying when you sang that song for Zeta."

"I'm glad you came," I say, surprised at the honesty of my response. "Next time, you let me know, and I'll get you VIP tickets and backstage passes."

"For real?" Boy looks like he might collapse with excitement.

"Of course. What good is it having a brother in a band if you don't get special treatment?"

A strangled sound alerts me to Noel's presence. He has tears in his eyes as he looks at both of us.

"Did you find anything out?"

He quickly composes himself. "She's in surgery, and while she's in critical condition, she's stable. The doctor will come speak to you when he can."

"And the baby?" I whisper.

His face softens. "The baby was in distress, from Zeta's body going into shock, so they had to deliver him."

"What? She's only twenty-eight weeks along! Is—"

He clamps a hand on my shoulder. "Your son is a fighter, Ryder. He's in ICU, but he's doing as well as can be expected. You can see him now if you like."

I burst out crying. My shoulders heave as sobs wrack my body. Noel pulls me into his arms, and I let him hug me, sobbing into his shoulder as pain and relief wash through me.

"Ryder, what's happened?" Scott asks, and I look up into the troubled faces of my bandmates and best friends.

"I have a son. Want to come see him with me?"

Noel leads us outside where a nurse escorts us up to the

baby unit in the ICU ward. Gar, Micah, Scott, Noel, and Wilder surround me as I take a first look at my son. We're not allowed into the room because they are still performing some checks, but we get to watch my little boy through the glass as he sleeps in an incubator. I press my nose to the window, taking in every little perfectly formed part of him. He is so small and so fragile looking, but as I watch the tiny rise and fall of his chest, I know he's a fighter, a survivor, and that he'll pull through. I'm overwhelmed with a love that's so powerful it's like being hit with ten thousand volts. The only other time I've felt such intense love, such an immediate bond, is the moment I laid eyes on his mother. I wish Zeta was here to share this experience with me, and I hate that that bastard robbed her of this moment.

Forcing all thoughts of Ren from my mind, because that asshole isn't going to take up anymore of my headspace, I refocus on my son. While I hate seeing his tiny body hooked up to so many tubes and wires and it's not the way I wanted our first born to come into the world, I'm so grateful he's alive, and my heart is swollen with love for him.

Three hours later, the doctor finally appears in the waiting room, and I hold my breath, bracing myself for what I might be about to hear. Kayla hooks her arm through mine, her lower lip wobbling as she fights to hold her emotions at bay. I cling to her arm, needing to lean on her for strength.

"Your wife is out of surgery and in a stable condition," he says, and a sliver of hope flares inside me. "We've removed the bullet, drained her chest, and we're treating her with intravenous antibiotics to ward off infection. She's going to make a full recovery." He smiles. "She's extremely lucky. It's almost miraculous. Someone up there was looking out for her."

Grateful tears leak out of my eyes. "Thank you, Doctor. Thanks so much. When can I see her?"

"She's in recovery right now, but when we've moved her to her private suite, I'll get one of the nurses to come for you."

The nurse pops her head in the door forty minutes later, and I follow her lead like an excitable puppy. Before we enter the room, I take hold of her elbow, stalling her. "Can our son be brought here in his incubator? I know my wife will want to see him."

"I doubt that will be possible, Mr. Stone, but I'll ask."

"Or else can you arrange for my wife to be brought to him. She needs to see her baby."

"Leave it to me. I'll see what I can do."

I push into the room and head straight toward the bed. Zeta's eyes are closed, and the only sound in the room is the intermittent beeping of a machine. Taking a seat by her bed, I wrap my hand around hers, grateful to feel the warmth of her skin. I lean over and kiss her forehead, content to just be with her until she wakes up.

"Ryder?" She blinks her eyes open slowly a few minutes later.

"I'm here, baby." I squeeze her hand. "I'm right here."

She turns her head, a frown marring her beautiful face as she takes in her surroundings. The beeping of the machine elevates as her eyes pop wide and her hand slides down to her belly. "No! Our baby!"

"He's fine," I rush to reassure her, standing up and leaning over her. "Our son is fine. They had to deliver him because he was in distress, but he's okay."

"Really? You wouldn't lie to me?"

I shake my head. "I would never lie about something like that. He's okay, honey. I've seen him. He's tiny and so fragile looking, but he's a fighter." I lean in and kiss his forehead. "Just like his mom."

"What happened?" she asks. "I just remember seeing Ren and running toward you."

"He shot you, baby." I lose the tenuous hold on my emotions, breaking down and sobbing, but I quickly compose myself, wanting to be strong for her. "Sorry. I was just so worried. I thought I'd lost you. Lost our baby."

She reaches out, stroking her thumb along my cheek. "You can't get rid of me that easy, Rock Star," she teases.

Unable to resist, I lower my mouth, placing a soft kiss on her lips. "I love you, Zeta. So, so much."

"Love you too, babe," she says, stifling a yawn, fighting a battle with her heavy eyelids.

"Go back to sleep. I promise I'm going nowhere, and I'll be right here when you wake."

She shakes her head. "I want to see our son."

"Rest, babe. I'll take care of it while you sleep."

Zeta sleeps for another few hours, and when she wakes, I help the nurse lift her into a wheelchair, and I wheel my wife over to the ICU unit our son is currently calling home.

This time, we're allowed in, and we're both in a flood of tears as we sit by his incubator, marveling at his tiny little hands and feet and his small but perfectly formed features.

As I wheel my sleepy wife back to her room a little while later, I wonder if the doctor is right.

If someone up there really was looking out for my family today.

And I can't help wondering if that someone was my brother Cory.

EPILOGUE

Ryder – Five Years Later

"Your brother is as crazy as our son," Zeta says with a laugh, holding onto my hands as we watch Wes race Zander into the sea. It's only mid-May and the water's still chilly, but that doesn't stop the two clowns from charging through the placid waves like it's sixty degrees.

Our five-year-old is a crazy little dude with a larger-than-life personality and an even bigger zest for life. Maybe it's because of the crazy way he entered this world, but our boy is as mischievous as they come and always getting into trouble. But I wouldn't have him any other way. He's a free spirit. Always happy and laughing, and I hope his life always stays so care free.

I rest my chin on Zeta's shoulder, rubbing our conjoined hands across her growing stomach. "Wes is great with him."

"He is." Zeta turns around to face me, wrapping her arms around my neck. "Did you ever think we'd have all this?" She gestures behind me, and I turn us around to survey the madness that is Etta's third birthday party.

My little princess is currently squealing as Gar chases her around the bounce house. Scott and Linda's two join Jill and Liam's two plus Gage and Kayla's son and Micah's daughter on the bounce house, and they're all enjoying themselves, taking turns jumping on Uncle Gar's back when they think he's not watching.

"I dreamed of all this," I say, holding my wife closer. "But the reality is so much more."

My stepmom, Clare, approaches with a big smile, offering a bottle of water to Zeta and a cold beer to me. "Thought you might be thirsty."

Noel stepping up to help Zeta the night she got shot ended up being a turning point in our relationship. His quick thinking helped save my wife. But it was Zander who really put everything in perspective. The love I felt for my son was instantaneous and all-consuming, and in the days that followed, I understood a parent's capacity for love. No matter what happens, I will always be there for my children, and there isn't anything I can't forgive or overcome in the name of love.

It was a defining moment for me, and it enabled me to open my heart, and my life, to my father, his wife, and my two half-brothers. My life is infinitely richer having them in it.

"Thank you." Zeta leaves my arms to hug my father's wife. "And for agreeing to babysit tonight so we can go out with the others."

"No problem." Clare pats Zeta's bump. "That's what family is for." She smiles at me. "You doing okay, Ryder?"

"I'm perfect." I kiss her cheek. "I'm just taking a moment to appreciate all this. I never thought I'd have this, and I don't ever want to take it for granted."

"If I wasn't already happily married, I'd run away with this one," she jokes with Zeta. "He's a keeper."

"Back off, woman. He's mine." My wife grins, sliding her arm around my back and down lower, giving my ass a cheeky squeeze.

"What'd I miss?" Noel asks, slinging his arm around his wife's shoulders as he comes up behind her.

"Same ole. Same ole." I waggle my brows. "Control your woman, Dad."

He rolls his eyes. "She hitting on you again, son?"

"Damn straight. It's just embarrassing at this stage."

We all laugh at the familiar banter. "Thanks for coming out. We're glad you could make it," I say in all seriousness.

"I wouldn't miss my granddaughter's birthday for the world," he says. "And we don't get to see enough of you."

It's true. Life is pretty hectic these days. Between two kids and another one on the way, overseeing the great work Luc is doing with the charity, running the label, and a new Torment album to promote, there is little downtime. Zeta is as busy as me too. While we share the child-rearing duties, she's the one who is with the kids most days. She still oversees the magazine although her input is minimal now Kayla is CEO. Mostly, her time is taken up writing and producing songs.

There are lots of reasons why I am proud of my wife, but one of my proudest moments was when she won a Grammy for Song of the Year for a song she wrote for Savage Mania. The song spent twenty weeks on the Billboard Top Ten and it was a multi-platinum selling single in more than forty countries around the world. The guys have scaled heights even Torment hasn't achieved and are the label's biggest success story.

"It's a pity Wilder couldn't be here today," I say, missing the little punk ass.

Clare clutches her chest as Noel says, "Don't mention the war, Ryder. Clare's missing him terribly."

"Don't get me wrong," Clare interjects. "I'm so proud of

him and the band, but I miss him dreadfully, and I worry about him with all those drugs and groupies hanging around."

"It's part of the business, Clare," I say, refusing to lie to her. "But I've made sure he's surrounded by good people who have his best interests at heart. They'll look out for him."

My brother Wilder plays guitar for Ruminate, another one of our signings. Although they're a relatively new acquisition to the label, they're already making waves as one of the support acts on Savage Mania's current world tour. I predict big things for his future.

"And Ryder talks to him at least a couple times a week," Zeta reassures her. "He'll help keep him on the straight and narrow."

I'm not so sure I can or that I should. He's twenty-one and living the rock and roll dream. Even if I could stop him from overindulging, I don't think it's my place to tell him what to do. When he asks for my advice, which he regularly does, I tell it to him straight, but it's up to him to make his own decisions. And making mistakes is part of growing up. Everyone knows I've made my fair share, and things haven't worked out too badly for me.

After I nearly lost Zeta, I did a lot of extra soul-searching, and something shifted inside me. Maybe it was the fact Ren was no longer a threat and the authorities had confirmed I would face no further prosecution, but whatever it was, something altered for me that day and I haven't looked back since.

"He's a good kid," I say, circling my arms around my wife. "And he'll find his own way."

As I look around at my family and friends, I know that I've finally found mine. I've learned to leave the past in the past and focus on the present and plan for the future. My dad, my wife, and my kids have taught me a huge lesson about love. They've shown me how much capacity the heart has to love and that nothing is insurmountable—even obstacles that seemed impossible to climb.

I'll never forget Cory, and I'll carry a part of him with me every day that I live.

I've come to accept that the best honor I can bestow on my brother is to live the best life that I can. To embrace all my blessings and live my life to the fullest.

And this woman in my arms has made it all possible. Without Zeta's love, I don't know that I'd be where I am today. She saved me in every way possible. She's given me a life I didn't dare to hope for. And, as I look back to that first day we met, to that fire that sparked the instant we locked eyes on one another, I know I caught a glimpse into my future that day.

And as surely as I knew that truth back then, as I look into her eyes right now, I know I'm looking into the eyes of the only woman I'll ever love. The woman who will be by my side until my dying breath.

It's only ever been her.

If you would like to read more emotional, angsty, stand-alone new adult romance I can recommend *When Forever Changes*, *Inseparable*, *Incognito*, *Surviving Amber Springs* or my *All of Me Duet*.

If you need to talk to someone regarding suicide, please call the American Foundation for Suicide Prevention in the US at 1-888-333-AFSP (2377) or via email: info@afsp.org

If you need to talk to someone regarding sexual assault, please call the National Sexual Assault Hotline in the US at 800-656-4673

If you need to talk to someone regarding any mental health related illness, please call the National Alliance on Mental Illness in the US at 1-800-950-NAMI (6264) or info@nami.org

If you require support dealing with PTSD, please contact PTSD United: http://www.ptsdunited.org/contact/

The Childhelp National Child Abuse Hotline in the US is available 24/7 at 1-800-4224453 https://www.childhelp.org/hotline/

If you've lost a child due to violence, you can seek support from POMC at (513) 721-5683 or via email to: natlpomc@pomc.org

The Compassionate Friends provides support to families after the death of a child. You can contact them at: (877) 969-0010 https://www.compassionatefriends.org/

If you live outside the United States of America, please call your local support services.

ACKNOWLEDGMENTS

Thank you so much for reading *Still Falling for You*, and I hope you enjoyed it. If you have read some of my other books, you will know I tend to gravitate toward controversial or sensitive topics. I don't always know why that is. Sometimes, it's because I feel strongly about a topic and I want to explore a different side to it. Other times, an idea just pops into my head out of nowhere. With this book, it was the latter, but as I was writing it, I couldn't help but remember James Bulger. I was twenty when he was murdered, and I shed plenty of tears for that poor little boy and his parents. My intention with this book was not to draw parallels, to cause any offense or upset, or to in any way excuse or condone what happened to James, or to cast any aspersion or make any judgments about his killers.

In my fictional story, I wanted to explore child abuse/neglect in different forms and to examine how far-reaching and devastating the consequences can be. But I also wanted to focus on a topic that I believe is often overlooked in our society, and that is mental health illness specifically as it impacts males. Why is there still such a stigma attached to it? Why is it not acceptable for our fathers, husbands, brothers, sons, and boyfriends to say they are depressed or suffering from anxiety? And when men do speak up, why is there a perception that it's weak or they are somehow less manly because they have a mental illness? Yes, I understand there is still stigma attached to mental illness in general, but it's more pronounced with males, and I believe it's wrong. Men should be able to openly discuss any mental health issues and seek out support without judgment. Failure to do that leads to men bottling up these issues which can have detrimental consequences.

In this story, both main characters have experienced trauma in childhood. Both have been significantly impacted by it. They helped each other heal, but Zeta was in a better place than Ryder, and she was able to support him in his recovery. That was important for me to showcase, because in a lot of novels, it's often the opposite. Ryder is, undoubtedly, my most tortured hero to date, and it was difficult to write some of those scenes, but I didn't want to hold back. I wanted to show how broken he was. How vulnerable he was. How he hid behind his addictions. How fragile he was when he reached his breaking point. And how Zeta's love gave him the strength to survive. To take control of his life. To fight for the future he dreamed of. His weakness was also the source of his strength, and for that reason, in my opinion, he is one of the most swoon-worthy leading men I've written. I hope I've shown that men can be traumatized and damaged but still strong, supportive, sexy, and desirable.

Lots of people have helped me on this project, and I'd like to thank Kelly Hartigan, Robin Harper, Sara Eirew, Ciara Turley, Susan Alexander, Christina Santos, Jennifer Gibson, my beta team, my proof team, my ARC team, Sarah Ferguson of Social Butterfly PR, and all the bloggers who helped spread the word about this book. Thanks to the members of Siobhan's Squad on Facebook for always being my happy place.

Massive thanks to you, dear lovely reader, for picking up this book. Your support is everything to me. Thank you for all your wonderful reviews, comments, posts, and emails which warm my heart and keeping me going on tough days.

A special shout out to the super-talented and very lovely Dee Kelly. Thanks so much for allowing me to feature Sawyer Weston—one of my favorite book boyfriends—in this book. It was so much fun writing that scene! Readers - if you haven't yet read Dee's Illusion Series you are missing out and I strongly advise you to check it out now! It's one of my all-time favorite series and I can't recommend it more highly.

Thank you to my husband, Trevor, and my sons, Cian and Callum. They are my biggest supporters, and they sacrifice a lot so I can pursue my dream. Love you to infinity and beyond.

I hope I haven't forgotten anyone, but if I have, please forgive my oversight and know it doesn't diminish my gratitude (It's only testament to my shitty memory.)

I love to hear from my readers, so feel free to email me anytime—siobhan@siobhandavis.com; however, please bear with me if it takes me a few days (or more) to reply.

I'm head over heels in love with my best friend. Although, I can't pinpoint exactly when Reeve Lancaster became my entire world. Was it when we were little kids, practically brought up together, after Reeve's mom died during childbirth and his dad subsequently fell apart? Or when I doodled his name in my school journal at age ten? Maybe it was when we became boyfriend and girlfriend at fourteen or when we shed our virginity at sixteen, pledging our forever?

I was there as his star ascended—like I'd always known it would—and there wasn't a prouder person on the planet. As the only child of Hollywood's golden couple, I've lived my life in the spotlight enough to know it wasn't what I wanted for my future. But I sacrificed my own desires, because Reeve's happiness meant everything to me.

Until he crushed my heart into itty-bitty pieces, forcing me to fly halfway around the world just to escape the gut-wrenching pain.

The opportunity to study at Trinity College Dublin came at the perfect moment, and I jumped at the chance without hesitation. If I'd known fate was meddling in my life, perhaps I would have chosen differently, but my future was cemented the instant I laid eyes on *him*.

Dillon O'Donoghue was Reeve's polar opposite in every way, and perhaps, that's why I felt drawn to him. He was the dark to my light. The thorn in my side, irritating me with his cold disdain, wild recklessness, and a burning rage hidden deep inside him that spoke to a silent part within me. Yet Dillon showed me what it was like to truly live, opening my eyes to endless possibilities.

What happened next was inevitable, and I only have myself to blame. He warned me, and I knew my reprieve was temporary, because there is only so far I can run.

Especially when fate hasn't finished messing with me yet.

The **All of Me** series is available now in ebook, paperback, and audiobook format. Check your local Amazon/Audible store.

any more pain. Until Jared rocks up to the art gallery where I work, with his fiancée in tow, and I'm drowning again.

Seeing him brings everything to the surface, so I flee. Placing distance between us again, I'm determined to put him behind me once and for all.

Then he reappears at my door, begging me for another chance.

I know I should turn him away.

Try telling that to my heart.

This angsty, new adult romance is a FREE full-length ebook, exclusively available to newsletter subscribers.

Type this link into your browser to claim your free copy: https://bit.ly/TITMHFBB

OR

Scan this code to claim your free copy:

ABOUT THE AUTHOR

Siobhan Davis is a *USA Today, Wall Street Journal,* and Amazon Top 5 bestselling romance author. **Siobhan** writes emotionally intense stories with swoon-worthy romance, complex characters, and tons of unexpected plot twists and turns that will have you flipping the pages beyond bedtime! She has sold over 2 million books, and her titles are translated into several languages.

Prior to becoming a full-time writer, Siobhan forged a successful corporate career in human resource management.

She lives in the Garden County of Ireland with her husband and two sons.

You can connect with Siobhan in the following ways:

Website: www.siobhandavis.com
Facebook: AuthorSiobhanDavis
Instagram: @siobhandavisauthor
Tiktok: @siobhandavisauthor
Email: siobhan@siobhandavis.com

BOOKS BY SIOBHAN DAVIS

NEW ADULT ROMANCE SERIES

Kennedy Boys Series
Rydeville Elite Series
All of Me Series
Forever Love Duet

NEW ADULT ROMANCE STAND-ALONES

Inseparable
Incognito
Still Falling for You
Holding on to Forever
Always Meant to Be
Tell It to My Heart
The One I Want

REVERSE HAREM

Sainthood Series
Dirty Crazy Bad Duet
Surviving Amber Springs (stand-alone)

DARK MAFIA ROMANCE

Mazzone Mafia Series
Vengeance of a Mafia Queen (stand-alone)
*The Accardi Twins**